HELL OF DEATH

VINCE KRAMER

ERASERHEAD PRESS
PORTLAND, OREGON

ERASERHEAD PRESS
P.O. BOX 10065
PORTLAND, OR 97296

www.eraserheadpress.com
facebook/eraserheadpress

ISBN: 978-1-62105-284-5
Copyright © 2020 by Vince Kramer
Cover design copyright © 2020 by Hauke Vagt

Printed in the USA.

AUTHOR'S NOTE

Hell of Death was written in October of 2016. Donald Trump had not yet been elected President and a lot of people (myself included) thought that Hillary Clinton was going to win. And more importantly, *Star Wars: The Last Jedi* wasn't going to be released in theaters for another year. Some at-the-time current references and jokes in this book may be quite outdated by now.

I wrote this book in a dark cabin on the Oregon Coast, during a week of violent storms which pelted rain at the shack-like building. I wrote in the upstairs loft, surrounded by various beach spiders the likes of which I had never seen before. Sometimes they would fall from the ceiling onto my laptop, having just died. My friend joked that a particular spider was throwing the bodies at me as an offering, so that I might not kill it.

My friend stayed outside the whole week to write his own book. He likes to smoke while he writes, so he set up various umbrellas tied up with duct tape to shield him from the rain. His laptop died at one point. It had finally succumbed to being full of water. He was also attacked by raccoons the whole time, which was probably my fault.

All of that really happened.

This is my fourth and final book. Enjoy!

—Vince Kramer, 11/16/2019,
3:39 PM, Happy Valley, Oregon

PROLOGUE TO HELL

Helldate: October 66ᵗʰ, 2016, in a suburb of Philadelphia, Pennsylvania.

"*IT'S A GOOD TIME FOR THE GREAT TASTE OF DEATH!*" said the disgruntled McDonald's employee as he fired his assault rifle into a group of girls at the Bensalem Township High School. A super-gothy girl's head exploded and blood, bone and gray matter spattered the group of screaming students. *Death tastes terrible* one of them thought, spitting out a mouthful of splattered brains.

The gunman was suddenly in her face and her face was being held at gunpoint. "Do you like McDonald's?!" the shooter asked murderously.

"What?" she said, spitting out her friend's brains.

"DO YOU LIKE MCDONALD'S?!" he shouted, pressing the barrel of his gun against her face.

She teared up and closed her eyes and confessed: "I KNOW I'M NOT SUPPOSED TO, BUT I LOVE MCDONALD'S! THE FRENCH FRIES ARE *SOOO GOOD!"* she sobbed.

Keeping the gun pointed at her, the gunman removed the weapon from her face, still ready to shoot at any time. He could sense she was telling the truth.

"Are you loving it?" he asked, pressing the gun to her face again.

"What?" she asked, black mascara running down her cheeks.

"ARE YOU LOVING IT?!" he shouted.

She held her hands up and screamed, *"I'M LOVING IT!"* she sobbed. *"OH MY GOD, I LOVE MCDONALD'S! I LOVE IT SO MUCH."*

The gunman smiled, lowered his weapon, and said, "Thank you."

And then he left, stalking down the hall after the retreating group of students. He shouted after them, "WHERE ARE YOU GOING? THERE'S A MCDONALD'S FOR EVERYONE!"

The students screamed.

The blood-covered girl looked down at her friend's headless body. Tissue, bone, and sinew were reforming like death in reverse.

"What the fuck?" the girl said, picking brain out of her hair.

The decapitated goth girl was apparently growing a new head.

"Virginia?" the girl gasped, shocked in disbelief.

"LOOK FOR THE GOLDEN ARCHES!" the shooter commanded, catching a group of kids coming out of the cafeteria off guard. They all looked in different directions for golden arches as if they were just suddenly challenged to a new game in the hallway. They noticed the gunman all too late. A pretty blonde girl let out a blood-curdling scream when she saw him and dropped her lunch tray on the ground. There was salad everywhere.

The gunman looked at all of the students' lunches. ALL salads. VEGANS!

"VEGANS!" he accused.

He pointed his gun at the blonde,

"YOU DESERVE A *BULLET* TODAY!"

He fired.

At the last split second, the student to her left, an average-looking, brown-haired boy, pushed her out of the way with an almost inhuman strength. She went skidding down the hall and crashed against some lockers. You could hear her bones crack as she slammed against the metal, leaving a big dent where she hit.

Her shriek of pain distracted the shooter enough for the student to make a move. With incredible speed, he threw his Philadelphia Avengers Trapper Keeper at the middle-aged, Mickey D's lovin' madman. It hit him on the bridge of his nose. The shooter grabbed his face and yelled as blood started pouring out. He stumbled around, but did not drop his gun. Instead, he fired off a bunch of rounds as he staggered, trying to get his footing.

This gave the leaf-eating students a chance to scatter. Off they went in different directions. But not the average-looking, brown-haired boy. He was already at the blonde's side, offering his aid.

"LUCY!" he shouted, turning her over and cradling her in his arms.

"Jasin…" she cringed through the pain of her broken arm and ribs, and dislocated shoulder.

"How did you…" she cried. "Oh Jasin, it hurts so much!"

His eyes welled with tears.

"Oh Lucy, I'm so sorry! There's so much I want to tell you."

He rubbed the tears from his eyes.

She looked up at him slightly confused.

"OK, first off. I'm not a vegan. I was just pretending to be because I really like you. I second, I haven't told anyone yet, but I have an even bigger secret…"

And then Jasin was shot through the chest, his

heart bursting all over his crush's face.

"TAKE THAT YOU MILLENNIAL PIECE OF SHIT!"

The killer smiled, smoking gun slung over his shoulder.

Lucy let out an ear-piercing girl-scream and pushed Jasin's lifeless corpse away from her. It flopped onto its back.

The killer grabbed a piece of heart and held it out to the terrified girl, and with a deranged look on his face, said, "Things that make you go, *mmmmmm!*"

He shoved the heart into her mouth, muffling the screams she desperately tried to let escape her throat.

"We do it all for you!" he shouted.

She noticed his employee nametag with the big yellow "M". It read Marvin McMelvin.

"WE DO IT ALL FOR YOU!"

Lucy passed out.

The killer left, stepping over Jasin's dead body. He cocked his head at the corpse, noticing bright green spandex beneath the boy's shirt around the gunshot hole, shredded and neon, soaking with blood.

Hmmmm, Marvin McMelvin thought, before he went back down the hall to enter the double doors to the cafeteria, where he was likely to shout another McDonald's slogan before opening fire on more of the teenage students of the Bensalem Township High School.

Marvin McMelvin kicked open the doors and entered dramatically with his weapon drawn. He looked around at the mostly empty cafeteria until he spotted a group of students huddled together behind a big, round lunch table.

"Holy shit!" one of them said out loud. "Isn't that the guy from the McDonald's down the street?!"

The rest of the students gasped at their location being revealed, as if the shooter couldn't see them anyway.

"Did somebody say *McDonald's?*" the killer asked, crooking a smile.

He fired a round into the air. A young, sheepish-looking girl with glasses put her fingers in her ears and cowered.

"Fuck this!" another student yelled, and then took off, sprinting away from the group towards the exit.

The killer just trudged forward and let another shot off into the air, and said, "Two all-beef patties..."

He shot the ceiling again. Another student took that as his chance to get away and ran for the exit as well.

"Special sauce..."

He shot skyward again. The nerdy girl cringed and crouched lower to the floor, like she thought it would make her disappear.

"Lettuce, cheese..." he continued.

He shot at the ceiling again, this time blowing out a light. It sparked and rained shattered glass onto the lunch table. Another student ran for their life.

"Pickles, onions…"

He shot his gun up in the air one last time. Another student made it to the exit, leaving only the terrified young girl with the glasses, fingers still in her ears and tears pouring down her face. He was right in front of her now, having walked around the table to where she was unsuccessfully hiding.

He pointed the gun at her and she looked up at the killer, Marvin McMelvin, who had a gold star after his name on his nametag, which probably meant he was a great employee.

He grinned down at his victim, and said, "*…on a sesame bun.*"

"NO!" she screamed.

And then he blew her away.

Marvin searched through the empty halls for more students to pump his bullets into. But there were none—the halls were empty. And he hadn't even thought to check the classrooms for students yet. They were quite possibly hiding behind desks. It seemed like a no-brainer, but perhaps Marvin had become a little shortsighted, gripped by the insanity.

He eventually reached the front doors of the high school, and looked out the window. There were no police cars in the parking lot. No flashing red and blue lights. No cops with guns drawn, pointing at the entrance. No one on a megaphone, shouting "This is the police. McDonald's isn't even food. Come out with your hands up!"

This was all to be expected. Marvin had a plan for this.

But since the parking lot was still empty, Marvin realized he had more time and suddenly had an idea.

I'll go back and check the classrooms! he thought, finally giving us a peek into the sick mind of a mentally deranged, mass-murdering serial killer.

But then he heard a noise. It was the static sound of a walking talkie. He recognized the sound immediately. He and his friend used to play with walkie-talkies way back in the '80s, the era when he was a kid. They played cops and robbers. He preferred this game much more than truth or dare—because he always ended up getting his friend's dick in his mouth somehow. But he never wanted to look like a chicken, so he sucked it every time.

Anyway, the sound was coming from the principal's office. Marvin creeped toward the closed door, gun drawn. He heard a whispering voice coming from inside.

"This is Officer Lucas Kapowski, we have shots fired at the Bensalem Township High School. I need backup immediately, over."

"Negative, Officer Kapowski," a voice replied over the speaker. "We have a shooter at the McDonald's on Sixteenth Street and Franklin. Looks like one of these liberal vegan tree-huggers has finally lost their mind and gone postal. They have hostages and are making demands, over."

"You can't send any of the force at all? Over." Officer Lucas Kapowski queried.

"No, the police force is totally occupied, sir. Over."

"But it's a school!" Officer Kapowski pleaded. "It's full of kids! Over."

"Who cares, it's just a bunch of Millennials," the officer on the other end laughed. "Over."

"Goddamnit!" Officer Lucas Kapowski shouted, slamming his walkie-talkie down on the desk. He totally forgot to be quiet.

Oh shit, he thought.

And as if on cue, the killer kicked the door open, gun pointed at the cop in the principal's office. The cop immediately raised his arms in surrender.

"Trying to use *the Force*, Luke?!" the killer teased.

"Marvin?" Officer Lucas Kapowski asked, noticing his old friend. "Is that you?"

Marvin looked up and down at his grown-up friend, who he was totally imagining would be in a police officer's uniform. Instead, Luke was wearing the trendiest and latest Millennial fashions, which you could only describe if you were a Millennial yourself. The "costume" was topped off by a black wig that resembled some kind of faggy emo haircut. The thirty-five-year-old was obviously trying to impersonate a high school student.

Marvin almost laughed. He asked his old friend,

"What, are you an undercover cop now? Trying to blend in as a…" Marvin stifled another laugh, "high school student?"

"Yeah," Luke smiled, hands still in the air. "Just like in *21 Jump Street*."

"The old one, not the new one, right?" Marvin asked.

"Exactly," Luke nodded. "The one that matters."

Marvin smiled back for a second, lowering his gun. Luke noticed this and started to lower his hands. Then Marvin's expression changed to anger and he raised his weapon again. Luke's hands shot straight back into the air.

"*Have you ever seen the new one?!*" Marvin snarled.

"*No! I swear! I would never watch something like that!*" Luke pleaded, being totally honest.

"*IT'S THE WORST THING EVER!*" Marvin yelled.

"*IT'S THE WORST THING EVER!*" Luke agreed.

Marvin relaxed a little, sure his old friend was telling the truth. Marvin hated remakes. They destroyed his childhood.

"So," Marvin asked, gun still pointed at the undercover, middle-aged, Generation X-er. "What exactly are you doing here?"

"I'm investigating a string of murders, where the

victims have been exsanguinated. I'm pretty sure it's a goth girl. You know they like to pretend to be vampires and shit like that. I'm trying to be as emo as possible to gain their trust."

"Ah," Marvin nodded. "I killed one of them earlier. Hopefully that was the head vampire. If that's the case, then all of the other goth girls shouldn't be goth anymore."

"But..." Luke interjected, "if the girl was really a vampire, then you can't kill her by shooting her."

"I blew her fucking head off," Marvin countered. "That should be enough."

"But that wouldn't matter. Their head will just grow back. You have to use a wooden stake through the heart."

Luke knew that the girl couldn't possibly be a real vampire, but found himself arguing with his old friend about the dynamics of fictional supernatural beings just like they used to when they were kids.

"That could be true..." Marvin pondered, slightly lowering his gun again.

Luke started lowering his hands again.

"WHAT ELSE?!"

They shot up in the air once more as Marvin turned angry again and raised his weapon.

"I'm also investigating a vigilante! They call him The Frogger!"

"Is he one of those Philadelphia Avenger freaks?" Marvin scoffed, disgustedly.

"No," Luke said. "We think he's just some young kid. We heard he goes to school here. So, I'm trying to find out who he is. If one of the kids here is a new superhero they have to be registered and transferred to the Young Powers Academy in…"

"Upstate New York," Marvin grimaced at the very thought of the place.

"Yeah," Luke agreed, and then scowled. "Fuckin' New York."

They both shook their heads at the very idea of that city. It was such a retarded place compared to Philly.

"So…" Officer Lucas Kapowski addressed his old friend, for the last time.

"Why are you doing this? What happened to you, Marvin?"

Marvin's demeanor changed.

"YOU WANT TO KNOW WHAT HAPPENED TO ME?!" he offered.

Officer Lucas Kapowski, undercover and possibly popular police officer at Bensalem Township High School, shook his head in terror, somehow knowing that this was it. It was all over. And he hadn't even seen the new *Star Wars* movie yet!

"SINCE WHEN DID *YOU* CARE?!"

He charged at his friend with his weapon, "GO TO HELL!" he commanded, and shot him six times in the chest.

As Lucas Kapowski died, his last thoughts were of what Luke Skywalker was going to say to Rey in Episode VIII.

Probably something really nice… Luke smiled at that thought, and died.

Marvin McMelvin actually chose to shoot up this school because they recently had an anti-McDonald's protest. There was a big demonstration on the school's front lawn. It made the national news. They handed out flyers that said things such as "MEAT isn't MURDER—MCDONALD'S IS!" and "I'm lovin' it—*HEART DISEASE!*"

Marvin was sick of hearing anti-McDonald's propaganda and these teens were obviously being indoctrinated at a young age by their health-nut parents. There's actually nothing wrong with eating McDonald's. Sure, if you ate it all the time it would be unhealthy, but you'd be a big fat ass in the first place so you'd be unhealthy anyway. It's not even in the top ten list of America's unhealthiest fast food restaurants. But you never hear about an anti-Wendy's protest. And you should, because Wendy's fucking sucks.

Marvin's worked at McDonald's since high school. He didn't have to. He was attending college but didn't really think anything would be a good fit for him down the line. So, he dropped out, and devoted himself to McDonald's—in his opinion, the best restaurant in the WORLD. And now someone was shooting up the particular McDonald's he worked at. He was going to have to do something about it. Most of the kids had fled the high school anyway, the cops still hadn't shown up, and his car was still parked in the back so he could make an escape.

Then he heard a whimpering sound coming from the girl's lavatory in the hallway as he walked by it. Apparently it was another survivor. He stomped up to the door to the restroom. Normally he would never enter the girls' bathroom, but this was just to kill someone, so it was totally fine.

He opened the door. There was blood everywhere. But no one was to be found. The bathroom stall doors were wide open but there appeared to be no one inside.

What the fuck? Marvin thought, confused. He was sure he had heard the sound of a girl crying.

Then he heard an ungodly shriek and a heavy weight hit his back as a girl fell on top of him, apparently from the ceiling. She held onto his face, scratching it up with her long Hot Topic nails, as he swung around shooting blindly in each direction. He struggled and struggled to shake her off. She screamed and clawed, and he just couldn't get her off.

Finally, he was able to hit her head with the butt of

his gun by swinging it back over his shoulder. She eased her grip enough for him to grab her and throw her off his back. Over his shoulders she flew, crashing into the bathroom stalls, splintering the wood and sending it flying everywhere. Marvin shielded his eyes.

When he looked, the girl was standing in the rubble, her black dress clung tightly to her body, soaked in blood. It was the goth girl whose head he blew off! She must be the head vampiress of the Bensalem Township High School!

She shrieked an ungodly shriek, and levitated off the ground several feet. She brandished her razor-sharp Hot Topic nails and flashed her silvery fangs, and then flew straight at him. Marvin jumped forward, ducking underneath her fearsome goth attack and ending up in the destroyed stalls. She spun around. Marvin could see her glowering cat-eyes sparkle like she was a demon from Hell.

"Oh, burger!" Marvin said, grabbing for something to defend himself with.

She flew back towards him, wailing like a banshee.

He brought up a long sharp piece of wood from the shattered bathroom stall and impaled her with it, right through the heart.

She stopped screaming and grabbed the wooden stake, like she was going to try to pull it out. She looked extremely worried. Scared, even. She looked like an innocent little girl for a second, but then she started burning up. Her veins glowed like streams of lava, getting ready to burst through the skin, which was quickly flaking into black ash.

Marvin smiled and got in her face,

"AW!" he taunted. "Looks like someone's about to have a *BIG MAC ATTACK!*"

He kicked the stake, sending it further into her chest. The vampire girl exploded in flames, sending cinders flying in every direction as dark soot filled the room. Toilet paper rolls and paper towels caught fire and smoke filled the room. Marvin coughed through it, got on his hands and knees, found his gun, and retreated through the bathroom door.

This is why you should never go in the girls' room. Not ever.

Marvin hastily retreated through the back door. That is, after returning to the girls' room with the fire extinguisher. He put out the fire growing in there that would most definitely have consumed the school in flames. He just wanted to kill children, not burn the school down. He wasn't an arsonist or anything. He was just a child murderer.

After putting out the fire, he went to check out the front to see if the police were there yet (the police were still not there yet), see if there were any donuts in the employee breakroom (there was a Boston cream left, his favorite.), and went to the bathroom to take a leak. He thoroughly washed his hands in the sink, fixed his hair in the mirror, and then got a drink from the water fountain in the hall nearby.

And THEN he walked out the school's back door. He immediately noticed the sound of heavy metal music blaring on a stereo. But it sounded like that nu-metal/metalcore garbage that kids listened to these days. He went down the case of concrete steps and turned the corner. There was a group of teens jamming to the music and smoking. They had been completely oblivious to the school shooting, not hearing one gunshot at all.

Marvin snarled when he saw one of the kids was wearing a Cattle Decapitation t-shirt. Cattle Decapitation was an annoying, vegan deathcore band with a clear anti-McDonald's agenda. Marvin shot the stereo. It only partially exploded and clattered to the ground, the tape still playing, but at a slowed-down crawl. It sounded like Enya.

"Hey man, that was the new Atreyu!" one of the teens protested.

Marvin cocked his gun, and shot the stereo again. This time it exploded everywhere. A piece of shrapnel hit one of the boys in the face, grazing his nose. He held his hand against his face as blood streamed down, screamed *"MOMMY!"* and ran off.

Marvin aimed his gun at the fleeing boy.

"NO! WAIT!" one of the other boys protested.

Marvin swung his gun back at the group. They all had their hands held up in surrender. One of the boys stepped forward.

"Let him go. Please, let them all go. Take me instead."

"Steve, no!!!!" one of them protested.

"*SHUT UP SHUT UP,*" Steve said through gritted teeth. "I know what I'm doing."

Marvin looked up and down at the kid. He looked like the biggest poser ever. Everything about him clashed and didn't make sense. He wore a Black Dahlia Murder t-shirt depicting a vampiric goth girl with upside-down crosses for fangs. He wore a pentagram necklace on a silver chain, as well as the heart logo for the band HIM on a black leather rope string. On top of that, around his neck and draping down off of his shoulders—was a Harry Potter scarf, with the class colors of The Harry Potter School, which is the school that Harry Potter attended.

The teen wore black skinny jeans with a Misfits-skulls belt, and had a pair of red Doc Martins with *Nightmare Before Christmas* laces. His fingernails were painted black, and he had a Green Lantern ring on his finger, but it was painted black as well. His hair was shoulder length, and dyed jet black. His blond roots were exposed. Marvin noticed the books stacked nearby his book bags. There was a copy of *Harry Potter and the Invincible Wizards* beneath Anton LaVey's *Satanic Bible*, and on top of that lay another Harry Potter book—*Harry Potter and the Invisible Shadows*. The kid's backpack was nothing but a big yellow plush Pikachu, lightning-tail zipper and all.

Marvin almost laughed, strangely intrigued.

He motioned his gun to the side a few times, signaling the other kids that they could leave.

They grabbed their things and ran off. Steve walked slowly toward the shooter, lowering his hands. Marvin cocked his gun up at him.

"It's just you and me now," the boy said.

Is this kid a little faggot or something? the shooter wondered, still curiously confused at his audacity.

Steve slowly lowered his hands until they were flat together in prayer. He knelt his head and closed his eyes, and uttered, *"De Nomine Dei Nostri Satanas Luciferi Excelsi."*

The boy smiled, raised his head, and opened his eyes.

Marvin started laughing his ass off at him. Steve frowned.

"What the fuck was that, you little poseur?" Marvin laughed. "A satanic spell or something?"

Marvin continued laughing, having lowered his gun completely.

"Where'd you learn that, one of those Harry Potter books?"

Steve was totally dismayed, and a little hurt. It was

totally a satanic spell, he thought. And he didn't read it in a Harry Potter book. That was insulting. They don't put real satanic spells in those books because they don't want people to hurt themselves. Then Steve had another idea. He flashed devil horns at the shooter, with both hands, shooting them back and forth like he was Spider-Man.

Marvin laughed even harder. The boy was apparently trying to stop him with devil magic.

"And what the hell is that?" Marvin laughed.

"It's the sign of the Devil!" Steve shouted, still shooting devil horns at the man.

Marvin laughed, wiping a tear from his eye he was laughing so hard. Then he cocked his gun back up at the boy. Steve threw his hands in the air, still making devil horns and looking just like he was at a metal concert.

Marvin aimed his gun at the young "satanic" "metalhead", who closed his eyes tightly.

"And this is the sign of *DEATH!*" the Bensalem School Shooter said cockily, and pulled the trigger. The bullet hit young Steve between the eyes and pierced his brain, killing him instantly.

When Steve opened his eyes, he was surprised he wasn't dead. And not only that, the killer was gone. And he was in a very dark room.

I must be in my room at home! Steve thought, happily.

And then he felt a sharp prick in his calf muscle.

He yowled at the sudden pain.

Steve looked down. There was a tiny brown goblin staring up at him with bright red eyes, so bright that they illuminated the whole creature. It held a tiny pitchfork in one hand, dripping with blood. It opened its mouth revealing rows of jagged pointy little teeth, and spoke.

"JIBBA JABBA JUBBA!" it said.

Steve screamed his head off.

CHAPTER 666
PART ONE – WELCOME TO HELL

The dark room became illuminated as more goblins opened their eyes and jumped out of the darkness. The chamber glowed red. The tiny goblins jumped up and down, shaking their action figure-sized pitchforks.

"This isn't my room!" Steve shouted.

He felt them jabbing the back of his ankles.

"OW!" he cried.

They kept jabbing him, seemingly trying to push him in a certain direction.

They continued their jabbering, "JIBBA JABBA JUBBAH!"

Steve painfully walked across the room as carefully as he could through the group of goblins, as they kept poking him.

"STOP IT! IT HURTS!" he pleaded.

He eventually hit the wall, pressed against it—trapped.

And then it burst open and he fell through to the outside of the goblin chamber. He got up from the rubble, painfully feeling his feet, and dusted himself off.

His mouth dropped wide open when he saw what he saw before him. And what he saw was this—a massive lake of fire, lava flowing backward up rivers carved into cragged mountains. It looked totally like a CGI George Lucas nightmare. There was no sky. A rocky ceiling covered in stalactites dripped with blood. It was strangely cold there. A howling wind peppered his face with dying cinders. They tasted like cinnamon. Steve hated cinnamon.

"Where the hell am I?!" Steve said aloud to nobody.

Strange whispers broke out around him, mimicking his words. It freaked him out.

"*WHERE THE HELL AM I?!*" Steve screamed the question this time.

He didn't have to wait for an answer.

"Hell, obviously."

Steve turned around to see who it was that answered him.

It was Virginia, the goth girl. He kind of had a thing for her.

"Duh," she said to him, dismissively.

Steve rubbed his eyes. He couldn't believe what he was seeing. When he opened his eyes there she was, holding a golden ticket, and waiting at the end of a line at the top of a cliff.

"Virginia?" he asked, walking over to her. "What are you doing here?"

"I'm dead, dummy. So are you."

"What?! I'm not dead. Am I...?" Steve remembered. The guy with the McDonald's name tag had shot him after his spell hadn't worked.

"Oh my god," he frowned. "He shot me. Right between the eyes."

Steve looked back at Virginia, curiously.

"Did he shoot you too?"

Virginia averted her eyes, and said, "Uh... *sure*."

It was kind of true. She just thought that maybe she would leave out the part where she was staked through the heart and exploded in flames because she was a vampire.

"Me too!" said another voice, all nerdy like.

Steve looked down the line. A dorky-looking girl with glasses was raising her hand. He recognized her, but didn't know her name.

"The shooter got me in the cafeteria."

She retrieved her inhaler from her pocket and took a puff.

"And then I ended up here. I don't know why."

"We'll find out soon enough," an authoritative voice said, from further down the

line. Steve looked to see who it was. It was that cool kid, Luke. Steve really liked him a lot.

"Do you have your golden ticket?" Luke asked.

"What golden ticket?"

And as if on cue, a goblin poked him in the leg. He looked down at the creature, and it was holding up a small white envelope, with a wax seal imprinted with a pentagram.

"JIBBA JABBA!" it offered.

Steve grabbed the envelope from the goblin, broke the seal, and opened it. It was a golden ticket just like the others had. The inscription on it said, *Please give to the jetboat driver as payment for the trip. Your first golden ticket is free. There are more in the gift shop at the end of the river. Enjoy your time in Hell.*

"That doesn't sound so bad!" Steve said, thinking that they're just getting to visit Hell for a short tour before they move on to… wherever they're supposed to go.

"Turn it over," Luke said.

Steve turned it over. The inscription on the back read, *Haha, just kidding. You're in Hell for eternity. This is a one-way ticket. Give it to the oarsman in exchange for passage across the River Styx™. At the end you will be assigned to a circle of Hell, where you will be tortured forever. Welcome to Hell, sinner!*

Steve gasped. He thought it must be a total mistake. He thought that becoming a Satanist would put him on the side of Satan, like he would become part of the team. Steve was sure he could just tell the oarsman when they meet and explain the whole thing. He would probably understand and take him to Satan's house, where he can presumably hang out and do important satanic things with the rest of his time in Hell.

"Yeah, I think it must be a mistake too," said an average-looking kid, apparently hearing Steve's thoughts with his... *frog* ears.

Steve recognized the kid as Jasin Jackson, an unremarkably normal guy he had known since elementary school. Steve thought he was kind of a dork because he played Magic: The Gathering, and Steve was way too cool for that. He played Pokémon like a real man.

"I'm going to have a talk with this boat driver when we get down there. I'm sure I can straighten everything out," Jasin said, assuredly.

Steve joined the group at the end of the line and looked down the cliff. There was a long staircase carved out of the jagged rock that led down to a dock on the lava lake. A long boat was returning to it. It looked like a Venetian gondola. A skeleton man in a hooded cloak was at the rudder. The boat docked, and the gate the group were waiting at buzzed. A light turned red, and the gate opened. Then the fivesome descended the stairs into Hell.

A shadow-clad man emerged from the chamber entrance just in time to see Steve's head disappear into the darkness below. A goblin shouted up at the man, *"JIBBA JABBA JUBBA JIBBA JABBA JUBBA JIBBA JABBA JUBBA!"* and he crushed him beneath his heel.

CHAPTER 666
PART TWO – RIVER OF SATAN, RIVER OF DEATH

"Welcome to the River of Satan," the Oarsman said.

The teens were surprised that he could talk, being a complete skeleton man and all. There was a passing sense of magic to the moment, where it seemed like they were entering a world of wonder instead of a world of suffering.

"Don't you mean the River Styx?" Steve asked, pretty sure that's what it's called. He even checked his golden ticket again.

"No, it's the River of Death," said the Oarsman. "We changed it from River Styx to the River of Death because too many people started getting excited at this point if they were fans of the band Styx. We had to change it around Nineteen Eighty-Six. Too many people started singing Mr. Roboto, which is a really fun song. Not even their best. But anyway, Death sounds better. I forget why it was called Styx in the first place, honestly. But I'm like six hundred and sixty-six million years old or something."

"Is that why you're a skeleton?" Virginia asked, really impressed that The Oarsman was a living skeleton.

"No, no," the Oarsman shook his head. "I have always been like this."

"Were your parents skeletons?" Jasin asked.

"No, I had no parents."

"Aw! That's so sad!" said the girl with the asthma, who then took a puff off of her inhaler so you would know who she was. She hadn't said her name yet.

"But wait," Steve interjected. "You're saying it's the River of Death now, but at first you said it was the River of Satan, even though it's clearly printed on this golden ticket that it's the River Styx."

"Look kid, it's whatever the fuck you want it to be called, alright? Now get in the fucking boat before I shove this oar up your ass. I'll do it, too. It would be but a small taste of the torture you'll be subjected to within the Nine Circles."

The group of teens got in the boat. The Oarsman cranked up the motor and held onto the rudder, steering it away from the dock as it took off. He wasn't using an oar at all. Steve noticed this but was too scared to mention anything again.

"So, nine circles?" Virginia asked, kind of interested. "Like as in the Nine Circles of Hell?"

"Yeah," Steve confirmed. "Just like in the Harry Potter book, Harry Potter and the Big Hole of Darkness."

Luke shook his head at the uneducated teen.

"It's like Dante's *Inferno*, you idiot."

"Dante's *Inferno*?" Jasin asked, confused. "So, Dante's *Inferno* is real?"

"Of course not," the Oarsman interjected. "That's as fictional as your Harry Potter books. I've never even met anyone named Dante in my long life. He's never been down here."

"But why do you have nine circles of Hell too?" Virginia pressed.

"Look, because shut up, all right? It's just a coincidence."

The Oarsman looked annoyed, if a skull could look annoyed, which it did.

"OK, fine." Virginia said, sorry for asking.

"And besides, I'm not a tour guide. I'm normally not even allowed to talk to sinners," the Oarsman said, and questioned himself as to why he was even doing it. It was strange.

He shook off the idea.

"Your demon guide will explain everything to you at the docks. And look!" the Oarsman pointed towards the shore. "There he is now!"

The Oarsman was relieved he soon wouldn't have to be talking to these kids anymore. He had to return to the other side to pick up the five new souls that were in the queue.

The group noticed the demon waiting for them. He had a short, stocky build. A head that looked like a cross between a bulldog and a gargoyle. He held on to the straps of his backpack with his stubby hands with four clawed fingers each. His skin was brown and rough-looking, leathery. He wore khaki shorts, a plain khaki button-up shirt, and brown sandals with white socks.

He looked just like an eager tour guide ready to take a group on a hike.

The group got out of the boat on the dock and gathered in front of him, super curious about the demonic tour guide due to his unthreatening appearance. They were even a little excited perhaps by where they would be going. He actually looked that nice. But there was no way that could be true, right? Some of them figured they should maybe brace themselves a little.

"Don't worry!" the Oarsman said, kicking off the dock so his boat would drift back away from it. "He doesn't bite! Goodbye!"

The group turned to wave. The Oarsman waved back, skeletal arm and all, no ligaments to hold it together. The group was almost again lost in the magic of it all.

"I SO CAN TOO BITE!" the demonic guide shouted after the Oarsman.

"I'D LIKE TO SEE YOU TRY, YOU PUSSY!" The Oarsman shouted back.

"*AAAARGH!*" the guide screamed, and grabbed the asthmatic girl by the arm and chomped into it, biting deep, and then grinding his teeth on the bone.

She let out a long wail followed by an uncontrollable coughing fit.

The Oarsman put his hand over his mouth to hide a chuckle, amused that he actually goaded the demon guide into it. It was the best thing he'd seen all day.

When the demon dropped the girl, the group ran over to her aid, shocked at the serious turn of events. She still whined and screamed and coughed, fumbling for her inhaler. It lay over near the demon, and when she noticed it, it was too late. The demon noticed it too. He stepped on it with his sandal and ground it into dust. The girl screamed,

"My inhaler!"

"Never mind inhaler, stupid girl!" the demon shouted. "Girl is dead! Girl no need drugs no more! Girl has no asthma!"

"You mean, since we're dead..." Virginia asked, suddenly realizing, "Anything wrong with us in life, is now gone?"

"Yes, yes," the demon agreed. "Dead and gone."

"Oh!" Virginia couldn't wait to find a mirror

somewhere so she could see her reflection. She hadn't seen it in almost two years! It would be a huge relief not to be a vampire anymore, if not for just that very reason.

"Now group come here. We need to get started."

Jasin helped up the nerdy girl with the glasses.

"Where are my glasses?" she asked.

"Right here," Jasin said, handing them to her.

"Oh," she said. "Thank you."

She put her glasses on, and then noticed her arm was completely healed. There was no longer a big bloody chunk missing from it. Now it was totally fine. But she still acted like she needed the glasses to see. Jasin also noted that, and thought it was weird.

"My name is Jasin," he said.

She blushed.

"I know," she said, and smiled.

"And what's your name?"

"Sandy!" she exclaimed. "Sandy Hook. Pleased to make your acquaintance, kind sir."

He smiled at her. He had noticed how pretty she looked without her glasses. She looked beautiful. And Jasin knew that even though inner beauty mattered a lot, outer beauty was probably a hell of a lot more important. He was a horny teen, after all.

"C'mon!" Steve shouted. "You two can fuck later! I can't wait to see Hell!"

Sandy blushed again, enthralled at the idea.

"Yes, kids," the demon said. "Fall in line. This no summer camp."

And then he motioned to the packs against the wall.

"Everyone now grab a backpack. I have maps, bug spray, and some trail mix," the demon smiled. "I made myself. You for enjoy."

Everyone grabbed a pack and got them on, ready to go to Hell.

"Now follow me, we go to First Circle of Hell."

"Is that where we'll be staying?" Officer Lucas Kapowksi inquired. "For the rest of eternity?"

"Up to Belial," the demon told him.

Officer Luke shuddered at the thought. He'd heard of demons like that before from reading lyrics to old Morbid Angel albums back in high school. That music was a bit too extreme for him. He didn't want to go to Hell for listening to too much death metal.

But why am I in Hell now? he wondered.

I don't know why I'm in Hell either, Jasin thought back at him, with his frog powers.

Who is that?! Luke thought back.

Uhhhh... Jasin remembered that Luke must've been that undercover cop that was looking for him. *This is a demon from around here! Don't worry about it.*

Luke was worried about it.

The Oarsman returned to the docks at the Gates of Hell to retrieve more passengers. When he arrived, he noticed only a lone figure waiting. The man had a gun, and at his feet lay the bodies of four sinners, bullet-ridden and bloody.

"*BAL-SAGOTH!*" The Oarsman cursed, as if Bal-Sagoth was Hellspeak for *jesus christ*.

"No," the man disagreed, and pointed to his nametag. "*Marvin*. Marvin *McMelvin.*"

"But… you *killed them!*" The Oarsman shouted.

Marvin looked down at them, and back up at The Oarsman.

"They made fun of my name."

"But! *You killed them!*" The Oarsman exclaimed again in disbelief. "That's impossible!"

The disgruntled McDonald's employee smiled at him. It was a cocky smile. A smile that said he had already won.

"Anything is possible…" Marvin disagreed, and pointed his gun at the Oarsman.

The Oarsman shielded his face with his bone arms.

"You just have to believe!"

Marvin pulled the trigger. The Oarsman screamed *NOOOOOOOO!* as the bullet broke through his arms, sending bone splinters in every direction, and then into his face, where his whole head exploded in a cloud of crumbled, white dust, kept mostly contained by the

Oarsman's hood on his cloak.

His lifeless body slumped into his seat on the boat, impossibly lifeless – and dead forever.

The Bensalem School Shooter got in the boat and started the motor. Then he steered himself straight into the depths of Hell.

CHAPTER 666
PART THREE – 1ˢᵀ CIRCLE
BELIAL

Belial heard a knock on his front door. He sighed, fumbling for the television remote control, annoyed at having to put aside the bowl of snacks he was enjoying. But when he found the remote and tried to press pause, it didn't work! He pressed it again, to no avail! He was missing Julia Roberts' dialogue! There was a knock on the front door again. He banged on the side of the remote. Was he going to have to change the batteries? No, all of a sudden the red light at the tip went on. Then he was able to pause his movie.

Errrrrgh, that's so frustrating! he thought angrily, getting up off his sofa to answer the front door.

"This wouldn't happen if Satan were still in office,"

he muttered beneath his breath as he opened the door.

On the doorstep was a local demon guide and five teens. Belial perked up. They looked absolutely delicious. Most sinners he had pass through here were elderly, or their bodies destroyed by drugs or healthy living (he honestly couldn't tell the difference anymore.) He invited them in.

"Come in, come in!" He smiled at them.

"Belial," the demon guide said, "these new sinners—"

"Yeah, yeah," Belial said, cutting him off. "I know the drill."

The demon gave him a slightly wounded bulldog/gargoyle look like he felt his position was being undermined.

Belial noticed this and sighed.

"Look, when six hundred and sixty-six years old you reach, have much time for bullshit you will not."

One of the teens got excited hearing the line.

"Hey!" Jasin said. "That's from Star Wars!"

"I know, I know," Belial said, and smiled. "I watch a lot of movies."

The teens were a little impressed at how cool he seemed.

"Come in and grab a seat," Belial offered.

He checked out Virginia's ass as she walked by. He said, "And you, little girl—want to come have a seat on my lap?"

She scoffed, almost telling him off nastily until she remembered that maybe she shouldn't be rude to one of Hell's official lords.

"*Uh...*" she fumbled for the words. "No thank you, Lord Belial."

"Hmmmph," Belial said, in an impressed way since she addressed him as "Lord".

"Belial, these damned souls..." the demon guide addressed him once more.

"SHHHH!" Belial held up a hand to shush him, and grabbed his remote control. He rewound to the beginning of the part the demon guide interrupted when he knocked on the door.

He pressed play.

"*I'm just a girl... standing in front of a guy... asking him to love her,*" Julia Roberts said, tearfully, in one of her many romantic comedies.

Belial sniffled and wiped a tear from his eye. Then he pressed pause and put down the remote.

"I love this movie," he said, turning to the group.

They were a little confused. They didn't even know which movie it was. It looked like something their parents would watch.

"So, what can I help you all with today?"

"We here to see if they good fit for circle," the demon guide said. "To see if they deserve your punishment."

Belial looked pissed off.

"*Punishment...*" He scowled. "You say punishment, but eternity in my circle of Hell is anything but."

The demon guide rolled his eyes.

"*Uh...*" he said. "Why not you describe to them what your circle like?"

Belial's face lit up.

"Why, of course!" he said, getting exciting. He turned to the teens again.

"We watch movies! Everything, from my entire collection."

"Oh, wow, really?" Steve asked. "I love movies!"

"Yes, I have it all. I have a massive library of Blu-Rays, DVDs, videotapes, laserdisc, and even Beta! I also have everything in my DVR library, and I record everything I can from On Demand or Video on Demand. Sometimes I just rent them online because it takes almost three years for a package to get down here. Two years with Amazon Prime."

"Wait," Virginia asked. "You have the internet down here?"

"Of course we have the internet," Belial confirmed.

The teens wondered why they had never bothered to check their cellphones the whole time. They reached for them, but then suddenly forgot what they were doing.

"Wait," Luke asked. "You said you have everything..."

"Yes?"

"Do you have *Star Wars Episode VIII*?"

Belial almost laughed at him.

"Of course not! It's not even out yet. Hell is on the same time that Earth is, you know. I can't possibly get movies from the future."

Luke frowned.

"But *Rogue One*, on the other hand. I have a decent bootleg copy."

Belial grinned.

"So, wait a minute," Virginia interjected. "Let me get this straight. We stay in your circle of Hell, and we get to stay in your living room and watch movies for the rest of eternity?"

"It's even better than that," Belial smiled, and then his eyes glowed red.

"Now come sit on my lap, baby girl."

Virginia pretty much flew across the room towards him until she was cradled in his arms.

The group gasped.

"Now look at the television," Belial pointed out. The screen was split five ways. It looked like security cam footage of the room they were in, except it was of each of them alone in a room with Belial.

"Look at the one we're in together, honey," Belial pointed to the square with Virginia in it.

He was furiously fingering the girl on his lap while she pounded on his chest in protest.

And then they all noticed their square. Most of them were just sitting on the couch with Belial or somewhere else in the room, snacking, and watching a movie. But Jasin was on his knees giving Belial a blowjob. And Luke on second glance noticed, that even though he was across the room from Belial on an opposite sofa, they both had their dicks out and were masturbating.

Eh, Luke thought. *That doesn't seem that bad.*

How do you know?! That's like, only a minute of time! a voice screamed back in his head.

Luke was caught off guard.

Oh no, he thought. *Maybe I should start listening to the voices in my head.*

Jasin was relieved to hear that thought because he was worried about being found out.

Yeah you should! the young, aspiring superhero thought back to him.

I better try harder not to broadcast my thoughts, Jasin pondered. *If only I had more training...*

What? Virginia thought. *Jasin, is that you?*

Jasin sighed.

Yeah, Virginia. It's me.

You're the Frogger, aren't you? I heard that he was part telepathic.

Yeah, it's part of my frog powers.

Cool! I'm a vampire. But you probably already knew that.

No, I was not aware that you were a vampire.

Oh, maybe it's because vampires are dead and I didn't really have any brainwaves.

But we're both dead now, and besides, if I had known, I would have stopped you.

Uh... gee, good thing I'm not a vampire anymore, I think.

You think so? I still have my powers. So, you're probably still a vampire.

GUYS! PAY ATTENTION! Belial mind shouted at them.

Oh, sorry, Lord Belial, Jasin thought.

I've got this girl on my LAP and she's still paying more attention to you than she is to me.

Sorry, Lord Belial, Virginia apologized. *I forgot you were even there.*

Sigh, kids these days, Belial thought.

You literally say the word 'sigh' in your head when you think it? Jasin asked.

*I—*Belial began to answer, but then there was another knock on the door.

"Everyone hang on a minute!" Belial shouted, mad to be interrupted.

He still hadn't shown the teens the bigger grid view on his television that would reveal the *THOUSANDS* of souls he currently had in a room with him, and what he was doing with them. He also hadn't shown him the list of films that he had planned out for them to watch over the next hundred years. It was mostly romantic comedies starring Julia Roberts, plus a few Renee Zellwegger ones. Not *Jerry Maguire* though. Belial hated *Jerry Maguire*.

The knocking continued.

"Hold your horses! I'm coming," Belial said.

He opened the door. There was a man with a gun. Belial looked at him strangely.

"Now who the hell are—"

Belial's head exploded all over the group as he was shot by the Bensalem School Shooter. The contents of the demon's head rained down on them. His head was apparently full of...

"*Smarties?!*" Steve asked, surprised to see perfectly wrapped portions of the small and tangy candies that you would usually get at Halloween.

"*MARVIN?!*" Luke screamed.

"*What are YOU doing here!?*" Jasin shouted.

"*AAAAAAAAAAH!*" Sandy screamed, terrified.

Virginia grabbed a handful of Smarties, wondering if she could eat them. It might prove whether or not she was a vampire anymore.

"I found you fuckers!" Marvin shouted matter-of-factly, smirking like a nerd-dork.

The demon guide went over to Belial's lifeless body and picked it up in his arms to inspect it.

"Belial dead," he confirmed, looking up at the group of the damned. "You can't kill Belial."

"I can kill whoever I want," Marvin disagreed. "On Earth as in Hell, one by one they fell."

"Don't rhyme at me," the demon guide sneered. He hated rhyming. The shooter smiled, baring his teeth like a deranged maniac. He was totally going to try rhyming more. He didn't like being told what to do.

The guide looked back at the kids, and said, "Kids, get out of here. I have some cleaning up to do." He motioned to the dead body of Belial and then to Marvin, like he was going to fix whatever went wrong.

"But where do we go?!" Sandy asked.

"Door."

Then red light started creeping through the wall behind them, door-shaped, until it was no longer door-shaped light, and just a door instead.

"Go," the demon guide said. "Me meet you in next circle."

Marvin cocked his gun, and said to the group, "I'll see you there too, so you better run, bitches!" and then he took aim at them, pretending he would shoot. He even made the gunshot noise with his mouth.

The teens screamed and ran for the door, fumbling to get it open. When it opened, they fell through it into a pile.

It was a pile of shit.

CHAPTER 666
PART FOUR – 2ᴺᴰ CIRCLE
BEELZEBUB

The teens slid through the bowels of Beelzebub's dominion, a world of shit.

"EW!" Virginia shouted, as they landed at the bottom. "It smells like... *strawberry Pop-Tarts?*"

"Not to me," Steve disagreed, wiping huge handfuls of shit off his arms. "Smells more like... *cinnamon* Pop-Tarts."

"I smell blueberry," Jasin said. "But that doesn't make sense. This shit is just designed to smell like our least favorite Pop-Tart flavors?"

"Oh my god, this is just fucking stupid," Luke said. "Let's get the fuck out of here."

And then they heard buzzing, and then loud buzzing. It got louder and louder, like it was getting closer.

Can we reboot this chapter? The Frogger kid asked the author.

I was hoping someone would say that, Vince Kramer thought back at him. *I haven't interacted with a character in one of my books, while writing the book, in a few books.*

Yeah... Jasin continued. *I think you need some more coffee.*

Agreed! Vince Kramer agreed, and took another sip, deciding to reboot the chapter. He would copy and paste the chapter's name first, though, and begin anew from there—probably deleting this shit later.

Pop-tarts? Really?

CHAPTER 666
PART FOUR – 2ND CIRCLE
BEELZEBUB

"EW!" Virginia shouted, as she slid down a mountain of…

"SHIT!" Luke screamed, right behind her.

They landed at the bottom with a wet squelch. Luke's face ended up in her breasts, which were full of shit. He spit shit out of his mouth at her face, by accident, and she hissed at him.

Luke rubbed the shit out of his eyes and looked around. There were mountains of black shit piled high, though he could barely see through all the darkness. They were in an almost lightless pit, and a red hue glowed in the distance. The others were nowhere to be seen.

Virginia was sitting with her face in her knees, sobbing. Luke consoled her.

"Look, I'm sorry I had my face in your breasts. Trust me, I'm not interested in minors. I'm an officer of the law. Hell, I'm thirty-five years old, if you didn't know."

Virginia wiped the tears from her eyes, still crying.

"I know," she said. "It's not that."

She sobbed some more.

"What is it then?" Luke asked.

"When we were falling, I tried to fly. It used to be so easy for me. But I couldn't. I really am not a vampire anymore at all!"

She wailed.

"Vampire?!" Luke was shocked. "So you're the girl I've been looking for. You're the killer!"

"Yes!" she sobbed. "And now I'm in Hell for it! Are you happy?"

Luke thought about it.

"Yeah. I mean, yeah. Kind of. I just wish I weren't in Hell too. I don't know what I did to deserve this…"—he shook his hand off some more—"*shit.*"

She wailed again and threw her face back into her knees. "YOU HATE ME!"

He went over to console her this time, as if genuinely. He just could not stand to see a child hurt.

"There, there," he said, consoling her by rubbing the back of her shoulders. "It's going to be alright."

Virginia perked up, and smiled.

"Really?"

"Sure," Luke said, and kept rubbing her shoulders.

Virginia hadn't been touched this way by a man since Count Grishnack took her and made her vampire in his upstate sex castle in Centralia.

Virginia wanted the man.

"You know," she said. "I've been a vampire for almost three years now. I'm technically not a fifteen-year-old girl."

"What?" Luke said. "So?"

"So…" she continued, "it wouldn't be illegal to have sex with me. I mean, if you wanted."

"Wait a second," Luke said.

"What?"

"You said, *almost* three years. How long until you would actually be eighteen? Days? Weeks? Months?"

Virginia seemed a little annoyed by the question.

"Does it matter?" she asked.

"Of course it matters! Even if we're ignoring the technicality that you're no longer a fifteen-year-old girl because of the actual passage of time, you're still not eighteen yet. Actually, you're still underage either way, now that I think of it," Luke said, hand on his chin, thinking about it.

She scoffed.

"Let me see your ID," he said, lunging to grab at her pockets for her wallet.

She pounded her fists on his chest.

"OK, FINE! I'M NOT EIGHTEEN! ARE YOU HAPPY!?"

"Yeah, because I couldn't argue in a court of law—"

She interrupted him: "THERE IS NO COURT OF LAW! WE'RE IN HELL!"

"AND WE'RE COVERED IN SHIT!" Luke countered. "I'm not fucking some underage Millennial vampire unless we both take a shower first!"

"ERGH!!!!" Virginia grunted, and huffed off in a huff.

She looked at the red glow beyond the mountains.

"I wonder where the others are," she wondered.

"WHERE ARE WE?" Sandy Hook screamed, as she slid down the mountain of shit into the pit of Hell below.

Jasin was near enough to hear her cry, and leaped to her aid, following her voice. He grabbed her, and shot his tongue out to a nearby rocky surface that came out of nowhere. It stuck, and the twosome flew up there adventurously.

"SAFETY!" Jasin said proudly, sticking the landing.

"The Frogger!" Sandy said in astonishment.

"That's just my superhero name. You may know me better as just your normal, average ordinary high school classmate, Jasin Jackson!"

"That's so cool!" Sandy marveled. "You've been doing a lot of good for the community."

"Thank you! I try my best!" Jasin beamed with pride.

Sandy gasped, with an idea.

"You should join the Philadelphia Avengers!"

"I think I need more experience, but it's my dream to someday be a member."

"You would be *great*," Sandy gushed over the boy wonder, totally forgetting that they were both covered in a little shit, and dead. And in Hell.

"How did you get your powers, anyway?" she asked. "Was it a frog bite? From that time in science class when the frogs weren't completely, uh… *croaked*?"

She giggled a little.

"No," Jasin shook his head, amused by the idea. "That would be ridiculous. My dad is just from New Jersey."

"Oh," Sandy said. That explained everything.

"Now let's see how we're going to get off of this rock and find the others."

Jasin turned to look out off the cliff into the distance. A red hue emanated from far off mountains, but then seemed to be blacked out by sudden darkness. He heard the distant buzzing of a thousand wings.

"Uh-oh," Jasin said.

"What is it?"

He looked at the nerdy girl with glasses, and said, "Trouble."

But the girl was certain that with ordinary, average high school student Jasin Jackson, otherwise known as *The Frogger*, everything was going to be OK.

"Fuck this shit!" Steve shouted, kicking a piece of shit on the ground, like some kind of common country shit-kicker.

The boy was all alone, and lost in Hell. It seemed like the time to finally start becoming fearful. Everything had kind of been exciting and a bit interesting up until this point. He was even looking forward to meeting another demon and figuring out his true place in Hell. He imagined he would get a spot in Satan's mansion as one of his main bros, or security or something. Maybe Satan could teach him some more magic spells, and then Steve could turn him on to some of the cool new metal bands he had stored on his iPhone, which he totally had with him.

But it was dark, and scary. He was also sure the shooter would catch up to him soon, and he would definitely die for good if he got shot again. That would be even shittier than this, so there had to be a way out. Steve decided to start walking towards the distant red light. But then he heard a voice.

"Hey Steve!" it said.

Steve turned to see a figure peering out of an open wooden door in the side of the crevice. The light of candles warmed the inside with their yellow-orange glow.

"Who's there?" Steve asked, and walked closer.

"Why, it's me, Steve," the voice said.

"Who?"

Steve got a good look at the man, if you could call him that. His skin was blood red, and the horns on the top of his head as black as obsidian. He didn't have a black goatee, but had shoulder-length black hair growing beneath the circle of baldness atop his head. He wore a black jean jacket vest, covered in metal band logo patches, the likes of which Steve had never seen before. The devilish man also wore black sweatpants, and... *fluffy puppy slippers?*

"Satan," the man said, confirming his identity as the Prince of Lies, Lord of Darkness, the Anti-Christ, among the many other titles that have been given to him throughout time. And he wore fluffy puppy slippers.

"Satan?" Steve asked. "Is it really you?"

Satan fumbled around, grabbing for his pockets, jokingly.

"Well, I don't have my ID on me currently..."

Steve laughed. It really was Satan. "What are you doing here?"

"I was nearby taking a shit and I heard my name pop up when you were thinking, so I thought I'd pop by really quick and say hello."

"Is this your circle of Hell?"

"My circle of Hell?" Satan laughed. "No, no... this is Beelzebub's. Everybody here just uses his circle as a toilet."

"Beelzebub?" Steve asked.

"Yeah, Beelzebub. You know, Lord of the Flies, King

of the Bugs, etc. etc.," Satan said almost dismissively of the demon lord. "He thinks he's hot shit because he was one of the three angels who fell here from heaven. Like we should all treat him like a Prince or something. Well, fuck that shit. He's kind of a dick."

Steve smiled in awe of him. Satan was cooler than he had ever dreamed.

And then he heard the distant buzzing. It was like the wings of a thousand insects were rubbing together in a cacophony of impending doom.

"Oh, shit," Satan said, looking off into the distance. "And here he comes now. I'm out of here, dude. I owe him a little money."

"Wait!" Steve pleaded. "Take me with you!"

"No can do, Steve-o. You're Beelzebub's now. Don't tell him I was here, alright? Thanks, you're a babe."

And with that, Satan closed the door to wherever he really was and disappeared, the door and all, like it was never there.

"Wait!" Steve yelled.

But it was no use. Satan was gone. Steve fell to his knees in sadness, left alone in his despair. Tears welled up in his eyes.

"Wait..." he muttered, weakly.

The buzzing became louder, closer.

Steve started screaming when the sounds became loud enough to make his ears bleed.

The five teens were on display on a large raised clearing in the center of a massive cavern, surrounded by trillions of zzzzillions of buzzing insects. Crucified on large x-shaped stands, the teens' screams were muffled by the blankets of crawling insects that covered every square inch of their bodies.

"Yes!" they heard a voice say. "Lick them! Lick them, my pretties! Lick them clean!"

The bugs were in a frenzy on the teens' bodies, as if they were picking the flesh from their bones.

But slowly, the bugs started to fly away, more and more joining, leaving the teens' bodies like they had had their fill, until they had completely vacated, to reveal…

Five completely clean teenagers, with not a trace of shit on them. Clothes completely perfect and unstained. Hair well-kempt. Even their fingernails were perfectly filed. They let out a sigh of relief.

"Don't relax yet, guys," Steve said. "I heard this is Beelzebub's circle of Hell, and if this legion of insects is any indication, he's going to be the most terrifying fucking demon of all time."

"Who?" Virginia asked, motioning over to the nearby figure on the clearing. "*That* guy?"

A tall, white man stood there wearing an extravagant costume with purple butterfly wings, red velvet gloves, dark blue spandex tight on his body, a black mask with a protruding mosquito-like proboscis on it, and two orange, fuzzy balls on the end of long springy stalks on his head.

"Buzz buzz buzz," he said, prancing around in a gay manner. "I'm Beelzebub."

Virginia let out a laugh, and Beelzebub sent a horde of flies at her face from the cavern wall, muffling her.

Virginia cursed her own stupidity for laughing at the demon god, and also made a mental note to remind the author that only four of them were teenagers when referring to them as a group, since Luke was an adult.

"Welcome to my circle of Hell, young ones," Beelzebub said, moving his arms around with his hands primed like pincers. "My pretties will get you off of those stands now."

A swarm of termites devoured the wood posts almost instantly.

The group was torn between being terrified and amused with the fancy, bug-suited man.

"Buzz buzz buzz... Beelzebub," he said again, lollygagging towards them. He put his nose up to each of their necks, one by one, and made disconcerting sucking noises. It was apparently meant to be playful, but still felt like being taunted by some kind of deranged serial killer.

"Yesssss..." he buzzed. "You all taste so *niiiice* and *cleeean*."

Beelzebub made a bone-chilling slurping sound by erratically sucking his tongue.

The teens, and also the one adult, were terrified.

"Bring them," Beelzebub said, and five groups of buzzing insects descending from the ceiling, each carrying something.

When they got closer, the group could see that each blurry haze of insects was holding a costume much like Beelzebub's. They dropped one of them on the ground in front of each sinner.

"Put them on," Beelzebub commanded, obviously wanting them to wear the same exact super-gay butterfly costume he was.

"Oh my god, this is so fucked up," Luke whispered to Steve.

"Shhh…" Steve said, *"Just do as he says. He might hear you."*

"I think he's going to rape us, dude. He's going to make us put on these little bug costumes and rape us."

"Calm down!"

"What seeeems to be the problemmmm here, boyzzzzz?" Beelzebub asked.

"Nothing! Nothing sir, we're just really excited about putting on the costumes. They're so awesome!" Steve said.

"Excellent!" Beelzebub said. "How splendid!"

"Oh my god, dude," Luke continued back to Steve. *"I'd rather die than put this on."*

"WHAT WUZZZ THAT?!" Beelzebub asked, totally hearing him this time.

Beelzebub motioned his hand towards Luke and a rush of insects flew straight at him, as if they *were* his hand, and grasped Luke to pull him forth until he was staring right at the moth man's face.

"TELL ME EXACTLY WHAT YOU SAID, OR I WILL SUCK YOU SO HARD THAT THERE WILL BE NOTHING LEFT TO SUCK!"

Beelzebub was furious, and in the full grip of an overblown tissy fit.

Luke looked away from the demon lord's face and shut his eyes tight, and then he cried, *"I'D RATHER DIE THAN PUT ON THE FUZZY PURPLE MOTH COSTUME! I'D RATHER DIE!"*

"That can be arranged," a voice nearby said.

Beelzebub turned around to see a lone man with a gun, in a purple uniform, who obviously didn't belong there.

"Ah, delightful," Beelzebub said. "Another guessssst."

"MARVIN!" Luke screamed. "DON'T!"

Beelzebub turned back to Luke, and asked "Don't? Marvvvin?"

And then Marvin pointed his gun at the Lord of the Flies and shot him in the back of the head. The insects that were holding Luke immediately loosened their grasp, and Luke fell to the ground as they scattered. As he got up and looked at Beelzebub's dead body, he could see a stream of red glitter pouring out of the bullet hole in his head. It was disturbingly bizarre, almost as if Marvin had just murdered a random *Wizard of Oz* character.

"Uh, thank you?" Luke said.

Marvin replied with another blast from his gun. The bullet grazed Luke's shoulder, and hit a wall of crawling insects behind him. They dispersed instantly, flying straight toward the gunman. Luke ducked for cover and they flew straight at the Bensalem School Shooter with such force they knocked him clear off the platform into the abyss below.

Luke looked back for a second, and then went to the team, and said, "RUN!"

And run they did, through an exit door that suddenly appeared in a flash of bright purple neon. The door swallowed them whole and transported them out of Beelzebub's circle of Hell, and into another.

CHAPTER 666
PART FIVE – 3ʳᵈ CIRCLE
BELPHEGOR

Belphegor loved being organized. He shopped at *Satan Max* so often for office supplies that he had a membership card. His office's boardroom had a wall-sized dry erase board, with room enough for him to draw up as many big schemes as he wished. He had every colored marker you could buy, and his erasers were always clean—he only used clean ones, almost obsessively. It was just the nicest way to clean the board, if the erasers were already clean as well.

Belphegor finished collating the papers he just printed out into five stacks and each stack into a clear plastic-covered binder. Then he put each binder on the boardroom table in front of a seat, and then pulled each seat out enough so the occupier would have an easy time sitting down. Belphegor smiled proudly at his work. He was going to make his new recruits quite comfortable. He was one hell of a recruiter. He might have lost his bid for the presidential election this year, but he was still doing what he did best—enlisting Hell's damned into a program where they can make riches beyond their wildest dreams.

It was all quite wonderful.

There was a knock on the office door. Belphegor lit up, excited his guests had arrived! And he finished all of his work just in time. Perfect!

Belphegor opened the door and greeted his guests.

"*HELLOOOO!*" he said grandly. "Come in, come in!"

He ushered each sinner in, shaking each and every one's hand as they entered.

"I'm Belphegor. Nice to meet you!" he said to each one. "Please have a seat. I have a wonderful plan for you all, just wait and see!"

But the last person at the door didn't have a hand.

"Yeah, yeah, Belphegor, we get the point," said a dog-faced, gargoyle-like demon, who was missing his left arm.

"Oh…" Belphegor said irritably. "It's *you.*"

"That's me alright," the group's demon guide said. "Now look, we've seen some shit. Me am still working on it. In meantime, take care of these children. And I try to keep the shit away."

"Well, very good then!" Belphegor smiled. "We wouldn't want anything to get in the way here, now would we?"

"Whatever," the demon guide said, shaking his head. And then he walked toward the entrance of Belphegor's circle of Hell – the 3rd one.

Belphegor shut the door and turned around to see his guests sitting down already, some even thumbing through their guidebooks.

"Splendid!" Belphegor clasped his hands together. "It looks like we're all ready to begin!"

Belphegor walked to the center of the boardroom, standing in front of his large dry erase board and facing the group at their table. He was noticeably well-groomed and well-dressed, his pitch black skin contrasting nicely with his white suit. He looked good. You might even say, *devilishly handsome*.

"This guy is going to die," Luke whispered to Steve. Steve nodded.

"Now let's begin!" Belphegor started.

By the time Belphegor's presentation was over, they had all totally been signed up for a pyramid scheme. After seeing dozens and dozens of slides of the wonderful things they were going to someday acquire with their riches—from yachts to mansions to jet skis—they all had broken down and signed the contracts to become part of The Belphegor Group. And now it was time to start tracking down other sinners to get them to join as well. If they didn't, they would never advance up the pyramid, which would be the worst kind of hell.

Belphegor opened a bottle of champagne to celebrate, and had a couple of low-level demon servants bring out a dish of caviar and fancy crackers. Belphegor reveled in the opulence of his lifestyle, hoping that it was catching on nicely with the group. It kind of was.

"I definitely could get used to this kind of thing," Luke said, looking like he could totally get used to this kind of thing.

Steve slammed his glass of champagne, and said, "Don't get used to it, we're moving on soon. And you know it."

"Excuse me," Jasin spoke up. "Mr. Belphegor, sir? I'm not old enough to drink."

"Yeah, I'm not either," Sandy added.

Virginia rolled her eyes at them.

"You what?" Belphegor asked, as if he didn't hear them right the first time.

"We're not old enough to drink," Jasin said again.

Belphegor sneered.

"You're not *old enough* to drink?! You *dare* deny my gifts to you!? You *dare?!*"

Belphegor rolled up his sleeves and stormed over to the table of nice food and drink that were laid out for them, and flipped it over, end over end. The glasses crashed all over the floor, and everything was ruined.

Everyone gasped, shocked at Belphegor's outrage, and knowing they were in trouble…

"I'm sorry, sir!" Jasin begged. "I didn't mean to-"

"*RAAAAA!*" Belphegor screamed, and rushed at Jasin.

Jasin leapt out of the way instinctively, leaving Sandy open for the demon's attack.

He tore through her like butter, his demon claws sliding through her body like hot knives. She barely had time to scream as she was torn apart.

"HOLY SHIT!" Luke cursed. "Is she going to be OK?"

He looked at Steve, "She's going to be OK, right?"

"Probably," Steve said, unworried.

"Get down from there!" Belphegor yelled at Jasin, who clung to the ceiling, like a cheap Spider-Man rip-off.

"NO!" Jasin screamed.

"Get down from there or I'll make you come down!" Belphegor commanded.

"I'd like to see you try!" Jasin taunted.

"*RAAAAAA!*" Belphegor yelled, and flexed his muscles so hard that his shirt ripped off. Black tendrils vomited forth from the demon's mouth and grabbed Jasin, and pulled him apart in every direction. Like Sandy, the boy had no time to scream either.

Steve and Luke just kept watching while eating caviar on crackers.

Virginia cowered behind a chair.

Belphegor turned back to the group, trying to compose himself.

"Now, where were we?" he asked, and suddenly, as if by magic, the table was back upright with all of the glasses on top unshattered. The kids were fully intact like nothing had happened, and Belphegor's clothes were back to their original perfection.

"Ah," he remembered. "That's it. You two were saying how you aren't old enough to drink."

He looked at the two recently dismembered teens with a smile that said, *c'mon, try me.*

Jasin spoke up quickly.

"What I *meant* to say was, we weren't old enough to drink on Earth, but now that we're here, we can drink as much as we want!"

Jasin gave Sandy a nudging look.

"Right, Sandy?"

"Right!" she said. "Now let's party! Give me some of that champagne. I want to get all the drunk right now!"

Belphegor brought over two new glasses and poured them each champagne.

"Very good," he said.

"Well, now that that's over," Luke said. "Let's get shitfaced!"

"Whooo!" Steve said. "Fuck yeah!"

"Yeah! That's the spirit!" Belphegor said. *"Whoooo!"*

Virginia still cowered behind a boardroom chair. She knew Marvin McMelvin would probably come crashing through the door any minute to kill Belphegor and chase them further into Hell. It was getting repetitive, and totally cutting into the time she needed to unravel the mystery of her possibly-receded vampirism. If only she could find a bathroom so she could see herself in the mirror.

Then there was a knock on the door. Virginia took it as a cue to run off down the hall in search of a bathroom, and perhaps even somewhere to hide from the killer. She hadn't forgotten what happened to her the last time she was in the bathroom. And maybe she wanted revenge.

When Virginia found the office bathroom and entered, she did not see her reflection in the mirror. If she had, she would have seen the massive smile on her face. She was still vampiric! Then she heard gunshots. She turned to lock the door. It was time to think of something.

Belphegor had Steve and Luke duct tape the Bensalem School Shooter to an office chair while Sandy tended to the gunshot wound on the demon lord's arm with a 666th aid kit that he kept in the break room for emergencies. Jasin was at the doorway holding a towel to their demon guide's bloody stump, where his *other* arm used to be, trying desperately to stop the bleeding. Belphegor said he was not allowed inside until it had stopped. He did not want blood all over his clean carpet. It was an expensive imported carpet from Chinese Hell.

Belphegor scowled at the Bensalem School Shooter. He held a cup of hot coffee in one hand, while he held the other up in the air as his wound was bandaged. It was not going to heal up immediately like it normally would have. Something was very wrong here. Plus, his expensive silk shirt was tattered and ruined.

"So, you're the one who's been causing all of this trouble, huh?"

Marvin stared alertly at the demon. He had finally met someone in Hell he was terrified of. Not only was Belphegor completely malevolent, but he always thought the rich suits type were unpredictable and dangerous in society. Not like he wasn't himself, but the elite were beyond him. He felt like he'd been put in his place.

"This is the fucker that MURDERED us!" Steve yelled.

"Is that so?" Belphegor asked, smiling devilishly, in a devilish manner.

"It's true," Sandy said, taping up his bandage—the finishing touch. "He shot up our whole school for no reason. I didn't deserve to die."

"Not only that," Jasin said. "We didn't deserve to go to Hell either."

Belphegor laughed.

"Of course, that's not true, young man."

"Why? I've only tried to do good in the world. I've never been religious, but I don't think I deserved to go to Hell."

Belphegor was amused.

"Your parents must have thought so. They decided to spell your name incorrectly, with an 'I' instead of an 'o'. Having the word 'sin' in your name is more than enough to end up here."

"What?" Jasin asked, saddened by this impossible truth. "Why?"

The boy looked like he was going to cry.

"Why not?" Belphegor asked.

Jasin started crying.

"Look," Belphegor offered. "Ask Leviathan. He's the one in charge around here. He makes the rules, not me."

Belphegor stood up and started unbuttoning his shirt, took it off, and put the fresh one Sandy had brought him over his head, and tucked it into his pants.

"Ever since Leviathan has been in office there's been a lot of changes around here. It might even explain why this foul sinner has been able to kill us. We, the Lords of Hell, are the unkillable. We are forever. We are young. We are invincible. The magic of Hell must be broken."

"That may be my fault," Steve said. "Before he killed me, I cast a spell at him."

"A spell?" Belphegor asked.

Marvin smiled and finally spoke up, "It was just some crap from one of his Harry Potter books!" he laughed.

"No, it wasn't!" Steve said, furious at being teased by his killer. "It was from *The Satanic Bible*!"

"What were the words?" Belphegor pressed.

"It's all in a different language, so you might not be able to understand," Steve said, snobbishly. "But it goes – *In Nomine Dei Nostri Satanas Luciferi Excelsi.*"

Everyone froze, and then looked around to see if something was going to happen.

Marvin started laughing.

Belphegor joined in.

"Kid," he laughed. "That means nothing. He must have been enchanted by some other means."

Belphegor stood up straight and got serious, like it was time to get back to work.

"And we're going to find out. Gather near, my minions."

They flocked to him obediently.

"I am sending you all to the Hell House on an important mission. And yes, if you are assuming that the Hell House is Hell's version of the White House, you are assuming correctly. You are to tell President Leviathan everything about this chain of events. Take these business cards and show them to the demon lords of the next five circles of Hell. They are anointed with the oils from my own personal fragrance line,

Belphegorgeous. This will give you free passage through their realms as you make your way to the Hell House. If you run into Satan on the way, tell him he owes me money. Hell, if he has it on him, maybe try to get it back if you can."

"Does he owe you six hundred and sixty-six dollars?" Luke asked, trying not to laugh.

Belphegor dismissed the question as ludicrous.

"Of course not! That would be ridiculous," he laughed.

"Satan owes me six hundred and sixty-six *thousand* dollars. He's one of the biggest failures in the money pyramid here in my circle. He's just too lazy to get more recruits. It's embarrassing."

Their demon guide came back inside and asked the group, "Ready go?"

"Grab your backpacks, my minions," Belphegor commanded.

"What backpacks?" Jasin asked, and then noticed five nice-looking bags on the boardroom table, all ready for them.

"Oh," he said.

"Inside, there will be everything you need on your journey. I have given you each a surprise particular item that holds a mystical power. It will help you on your quest."

"Cool!" Steve said, excited to see what his magic item would be.

"But wait a second," Sandy asked, reluctant to put on her pack. "Our killer is tied up here and helpless. Could we maybe, *uh*... have a little fun with him first?"

"I was hoping you would ask," Belphegor smiled. And suddenly they each held a sparkling and bejeweled dagger, blades shaped like a serpent's tongue.

"Sandy!" Jasin shouted, disappointed in her.

"Oh, come on, Jasin!" Sandy shouted back at him. "You know you want to."

"Don't worry," Belphegor smiled. "He will completely regenerate. Stab away!"

They all approached their killer, brandishing their daggers threateningly.

"What are you doing?" Marvin asked, terrified.

They closed in on him.

"*What are you doing?! Noooo! Get away!!*"

Marvin screamed in agony as their knives plunged into his flesh, again and again. He suffered each stab without any hope of the quick release of death.

Belphegor smiled.

They all must have forgotten about me, Virginia frowned, still alone in the bathroom waiting, completely right in her suspicions. She was also completely missing out on a good chance for revenge. Maybe if she wasn't such a coward and confusing mess of a character she would have stuck with the group to contribute a little more. But no, she had to run off to "find herself". Or something.

When she turned to look back the mirror, it appeared as though her reflection had returned.

Oh, goddamnit! she thought. *I'm human again! What is happening?!*

But then her reflection held a finger up to its lips and said, "*shhhhhh.*"

She gasped, caught off guard.

"What the fuck is up with *that?*" Virginia asked, walking up to the mirror to see what the fuck was up with that.

Her mirror reflection started to quickly decompose. The eyes sunk back in the head, the skin tightened around muscle tissue and bone, the hair grayed and lengthened. You know, all that fast-forward breaking down of a corpse stuff.

"Ew!" Virginia gagged, disgusted.

And then the corpse shrieked a deathly howl, and reached out and grabbed Virginia by the shoulders. Its head broke through the shimmer of the surface and faced Virginia. She was gripped, paralyzed by terror.

And then the ghoul retreated back into the mirror world with Virginia in a flash. The mirror in Belphegor's bathroom exploded, sending shards of glass flying everywhere. The wall bled where the mirror had been. Blood trickled down to the floor and created sanguinary pools that rushed over the clean white tiles.

Belphegor was going to be pissed.

CHAPTER 666
PART SIX (SIX-SIX?) – 4ᵀᴴ CIRCLE
ASTAROTH

The teens, plus Luke—who was not a teen, but an adult man who had been posing as a teen undercover at their high school—were anxious to open their backpacks and see what kind of magic items Belphegor had given them. Their demon guide stood watch over them like an armless sentry.

Sandy Hook was gifted a magic cloak that rendered her invisible. Luke Kapowski received a sword, which glowed with a cool green fire when he gripped the handle. Jasin Jackson had a large metal shield, black, with a giant red pentagram emblazoned upon it. And finally, Steve Stevenson (yes, his last name is Stevenson if that hasn't been mentioned before) got a signed hardcover copy of Belphegor's autobiography – *Belphegor and Lovin' It!*

"What the fuck?" Steve griped, to no one in particular. But the others were too busy playing with the awesome things they got in their backpacks from Belphegor.

"Hey!" Steve yelled. "That's not fair!"

Luke was swinging his green sword playfully at Jasin's shield, who kept blocking the attack and leaping all over the place. The kid was only wearing his superhero costume now, which was just a head-to-toe green neon spandex suit, with giant white circles for eyes.

Steve saw Sandy about to try on her cloak again.

"Hey Sandy!" he yelled. "Can I try it?"

She smiled and shook her head. And then she pulled the hood over her head and vanished.

"Hey!" Steve yelled. "Come back!"

He felt around for her but to no avail.

"Don't make me cast one of my satanic evil spells! Because I will!" Steve threatened.

Then he saw his book levitate over where he left it on his pack. It opened and Sandy appeared to be flipping through it. And then she gasped, and pulled her hood down, becoming fully visible again.

"Uh, guys…" she said. "You better listen to this."

They gathered around, their curiosity piqued.

She pushed her glasses up the bridge of her nose so they were tight on her face, which was really just a long way to explain that she had nerdy attributes. Then she read out loud from the book.

"The teens, plus Luke—who was not a teen, but an adult man who had been posing as a teen undercover at their high school—were anxious to open their backpacks and see what kind of magic items Belphegor had given them. Their demon guide stood watch over them like an armless sentry."

The demon guide perked up, interested to hear he was still part of the story.

"But…" Jasin said. "That's us."

"It would appear to be," Sandy confirmed.

"But wait," Luke said. "If it's the story of us, does it say what's going to happen?"

"I don't know, let me check," Sandy said, flipping to the last page.

"*NOOOO!*" Steve shouted, and ran over to snatch the book from her clutches.

"Steven!" she protested.

He held the book against his chest, protecting it.

"You *never* skip to the end of the book! *Never!*" he whined.

"Why not?" Jasin asked. "Some stories go on too long, and it would be nice to know what happens to us at the end."

"Maybe it even says what happens in the next *Star Wars* movie," Luke said, walking towards Steve and the book, anxious to check.

"No!" Steve stood his ground. "You can't just spoil what happens. Even if it's *our* story, knowing the ending would ruin the journey! That's the worst thing ever! It's just like killing a dream!"

"He's right," Sandy said, walking up to stand beside Steven. "And these are *our* dreams. *Our* adventures. I don't want to know what happens next—I want to see it for myself!"

"But the book is probably so long!" Luke complained. "Hell, I bet it's six hundred and sixty-six pages!"

Steven thumbed through the book to check, and almost laughed at the revelation.

"Actually," he said. "Every page is number six six six."

"Of course it is!" Luke shouted, fed up with this shit.

"Don't despair, dude," Jasin said, looking at Luke. "You know they're right."

"Fine!" Luke said, picking up his sword and grabbing his pack, ready to move on.

"That's the spirit, Luke!" Jasin smiled, and did the same with his things.

"Guess it's time to get a move on," Steve said, putting his book back in his backpack. Sandy kept her cloak on but stayed visible by keeping the hood down.

"Lead the way," Steve told their demon guide.

He just stood there armless and grunted, annoyed he was unable to point out the way. He finally huffed and stormed off. The group followed.

"Don't worry, dude," Steve said, trying to comfort him. "I'm sure I can learn a spell that will grow your arms back."

The demon guide wasn't holding his breath.

Virginia was having one hell of an experience in the mirror world. But you can't see it because it's in another dimension.

The group took the left-hand path at the fork in the road and eventually came to a wicked large black castle. It was covered with flashy neon signs, the largest of which said "ASTAROTH'S". Various banners said things like, "Free PBR – *forever!*", "PBR – the *only* drink in Hell.", and "SOLD OUT OF PBR." Words scrolled by on an LED sign – *BEST WI-FI IN HELL, EVERY DAY IS TACO TUESDAY, HAIL PRESIDENT LEVIATHAN,* and so on. It was all a lot to see and even a little hard on the eyes.

They approached the bridge over the moat. Sandy looked over the side into the moat below, and it was full of screaming goats drowning in blood. But Sandy was so used to Hell at this point that it wasn't even surprising.

When they got to the other side, they all just stood there and stared at the drawbridge for a little while. They were already *on* a bridge, so the drawbridge seemed a little redundant.

"Uh," the armless demon guide started. "Can someone knock?"

"Sure," Steve said, but then stopped to ask him something that just crossed his mind. "Hey, what's your name, anyway?"

The demon guide grunted.

"I've no name," he said.

"Why not?"

"Him afraid to give one."

"He who?" Steve asked.

The demon guide looked up, as if trying to peer into the heavens.

"The writer."

"What writer?"

"He who lives above."

"Why would he be afraid to give you a name?"

"Because power. There is much power in a name. Him afraid to give me one. Maybe he don't want me to be real."

"But you are real," Sandy said. "This is so sad!"

"Yeah," Steve agreed. "Maybe if this fucker gave you a name, your arms would grow back."

"Could be," the demon guide said, open to the possibility.

They all looked up at the sky for a while.

Nothing.

"Just knock on drawbridge door, Steve," the guide said, looking down at the ground, slightly disappointed.

"OK, OK," he agreed.

As Steve approached the door, he noticed a small sign nailed to it.

"THIS MAN IS BANNED FOR LIFE! NO ENTRY UNDER ANY CIRCUMSTANCES!"

Under the words there was a big picture of Glenn Danzig.

Steve let out a laugh when he saw the warning. It was that Generation X singer that he thought was a total poseur. Maybe this place would be pretty cool, he thought.

Steve went ahead and knocked on the door.

The drawbridge fell on the group with a loud slam, smashing them like bugs.

They found themselves inside completely reformed and all of their things intact.

"That was shocking," Luke said.

"Eh," Sandy disagreed, shrugging.

"Welcome to Astaroth's!" a demon host welcomed them at the entrance.

"Hello," their demon guide addressed him. "They here to see-"

"SILENCE, NAMELESS ONE!"

And then the host snapped his fingers and said, "WAIT OUTSIDE!"

The demon guide vanished.

Steve whispered over to Luke, "Hey, that's what we should call him."

"What?" Luke asked.

"*The Nameless One!*"

"Whatever."

Luke was getting sick of all of this Millennial bullshit. Steve was getting on his nerves. He couldn't believe his Hell would be hanging out with these kids for the rest of eternity. He really wanted to get his hands on that book and see what was going to happen. He wouldn't mind skipping all of this. Meanwhile, Steve was acting like this was some kind of magical Harry Potter adventure. Luke felt like he was the only one who had a clear understanding of what their mission was. Luke was used to missions. He was a police officer. There was nothing he couldn't accomplish with a little help from the force.

"Right this way," the host said, motioning for them to follow him.

They passed through the rather large establishment together, finally getting a glimpse of various denizens of Hell. There was a large assortment of low-level demons, ghouls, goblins, fairies, and familiars. The bar's servants were famous dead celebrities, but none worth mentioning. It appeared that their hell was just going back to doing what they did before they got famous—working as a server. And as for the rest of it, it probably could not be properly described without being labeled as just another *Star Wars* alien cantina rip-off. Even if it were a totally cool *Hell* version of the cantina, it still could never be anywhere near as cool as *Star Wars*'s. Ever.

When they arrived in Astaroth's throne room, they had suddenly come across something so original that it could totally be described without being compared (maybe) to anything out there. And maybe it would even add to the story.

The demon lord Astaroth sat atop a throne of skulls, with a gold plaque on the top that was engraved with the words "Prince of Thrones #1". The group noticed another throne to his left, which hovered several feet off of the ground. It was made of swords. Another throne to his right appeared to be made of glued together Popsicle sticks. Above Astaroth there floated more thrones, made of all different types of things—gold, silver, bones, and even a throne made of thrones.

It appeared as though Astaroth took being the Prince of Thrones seriously.

The lord himself was a pale-skinned ginger wearing a royal gown with a flowing red cape that looked of satin, but Satanic satin, so it was totally *satinic*. A crown encrusted with jewels sat upon the arm of his throne. He looked at the group as if they weren't interesting, and yawned.

"More sinners?" he asked no one in particular. "Great, send them through the back where they can be with the others, forever and forever, wallowing in their own misery and blah blah blah…"

Astaroth rolled his eyes.

"Wait," Luke said, reaching into his pocket. "We're here on official business from Lord Belphegor."

"Is he the lord of gluttony?" Astaroth asked.

"No," Jasin said. "I think he's the lord of sloth."

"Whatever," Astaroth yawned. "I don't care. Bring me what you have there, young man."

Luke approached the Prince of Thrones and handed him the card. Astaroth sniffed it.

"Ah, yes," he said. "*This* guy."

"This gives us free passage through your circle of Hell. We're on a mission."

"Sounds exciting," Lord Astaroth said, sarcastically.

"So, can we be on our way?" Luke asked.

"Sure, but only if you can take care of something for me first."

"What would that entail?"

The demon lord sighed, and got up from his throne.

He headed toward an exit on the far side of the room.

"Follow me, I guess. I'll explain along the way."

They arrived in the main part of Astaroth's circle of Hell—where his sinners were being punished for all eternity.

It was just nothing but coffee shops. They were occupied by what appeared to be hipsters. Millions and millions of hipsters, drinking coffee and talking.

"I give up on these people," Astaroth told the group. "They've turned my Hell into their heaven. They're completely content to sit for eternity and argue about politics, get into heated disagreements with each other, and complain about everything there is. This used to be total hell for some people, but they seem to be thriving."

The dismayed demon lord continued, "I should never have given them the notion that they had a counting vote in the presidential election. That perhaps gave them a little power, *I know, my mistake.* And by then it was too late for me to do anything about it. I tried everything within my power. I offered the correct answers to anyone who had a question about any philosophy. Finding out the disappointing truths to humanity's greatest questions did nothing to placate them enough to stop debating. I offered them fantastical things, like the power of invisibility, and paths to treasures far beyond mortal reach, but they just wanted more coffee. I gave them power over serpents, but they just filed a petition with President Leviathan to give freedom *to* serpents, and the president actually granted it!"

Astaroth scoffed, "They went over *my* head, and told the president of Hell on me? *Fuck these guys.*"

"So," Luke asked. "What do you want us to do?"

Astaroth looked relieved already, he was just getting to that part.

"Take them away from here," he said. "Take them with you into the next circle of Hell and let them be *Sonneillion's* problem. I'm done!"

Astaroth threw his arms up to convey how done with it he was. Which was like, totally.

"OK…" Luke said, looking at the labyrinth of hipster-filled coffee shops. "So how do we get a legion of hipsters to follow us?"

"That's easy," Astaroth offered. "Just tell them that Sonneillion has better Wi-Fi."

Luke laughed mockingly.

"It can't be that easy."

It was.

CHAPTER 666
PART SEVEN – 5ᵀᴴ CIRCLE
SONNEILLION

Sonneillion did *not* have better Wi-Fi, so there was a full-on hipster riot in his circle of Hell.

"Sorry, sir," Officer Lucas Kapowski, better known as Luke, said to the demon lord of the 5th Circle.

Sonneillion handed back the card from Belphegor, and said, "Don't worry about it, I'm the Lord of Hatred. This it totally my wheelhouse. I already have a legion of sinners that hate hipsters. This couldn't have worked out better. I'm looking forward to watching this fight progress. The riot is just the beginning. So, thank you."

"You're welcome!" Luke said, pleased that he could help.

Sonneillion shook everyone's hand and said goodbye as they left through the gate to the next circle.

Meanwhile, in the mirror world, everything was backward. The dimension wasn't very forward thinking at all, and that was why they needed a human being amongst them. But not just any ordinary human being, one that was just a pale reflection of their former self—a vampire.

"So, I'm a vampire again?" Virginia asked.

The voices of a thousand whispers answered.

"In this dimension… you are not in Hell… you are your former self… after your former self."

Virginia seemed a little confused by the answer.

"So does that mean I'm a vampire again?"

"*Uh…*" the voices answered. "Sure."

"Awesome!" Virginia smiled.

"Now what do you desire?" the voices asked.

Virginia didn't have to think about it.

"Revenge! I want to drain every last drop of blood from my killer, the one who followed me and my friends through Hell, I want him to *BLEED!* All in my mouth."

"You cannot harm him in his realm, but we could bring him to you *here* where that would be possible."

"Yes! Do it!"

"We will. If you do something for us first."

"What is it? I'll do anything."

"We want Hell. Fly. Betray your friends. Bring us the head of Leviathan. All shall be yours."

"Not a problem!"

"Take this amulet," the voices offered. It floated down magically in front of Virginia so she could grab it. Its mirrored chain glinted in the darkness of the mirror room. The large red jewel reflected a crimson color onto Virginia's face.

Virginia put the amulet around her neck.

"This amulet will allow you to retain your vampire powers while you are in Hell."

"For how long?" Virginia asked, thinking there was probably going to be a catch.

"For as long as you wear it…" they said, and paused. "We run a pretty tight ship in mirror world. What you see is what you get. No lies. No betrayal. We are not of the real world."

Virginia smiled.

"The real world is overrated anyway."

And off she flew on black wings to Hell.

"Tell me your life story, in nine hundred words or less," Belphegor told the Bensalem School Shooter.

"I will if you loosen these restraints," Marvin smiled devilishly at his captor.

"Sure will!" Belphegor said, and sipped on his fresh cup of coffee. He wore a new tie that he liked that features little prints of roses with bleeding thorns. "*After* you tell me your story."

Marvin McMelvin began his story with the first time his parents took him to McDonald's, and then just focused on his lifelong love of the chain after that. He also got sidetracked by spewing hateful venom towards vegans, Millennials, homosexuals, and even Burger King and their preposterously plastic "King of the Whopper" or whatever the fuck their mascot was called. It didn't have anything to do with his life story and was more of a rant. When he got to the part about the school shooting, he kept it short and sweet.

"I thought of a lifetime of my favorite McDonald's commercials as I killed them. My rage was blissful, and I welcomed the end."

When he finally finished, Belphegor went *hmmm*, and nodded in approval.

He took another sip of coffee, and then said, "That was all very interesting, Marvin."

Marvin smiled, happy that he had won Belphegor's approval.

"But that was nine hundred and ONE words, not exactly the nine hundred words that I asked for, now is it?"

Marvin grimaced.

"Well... *fuck! Fuck you!*" he said.

Belphegor jumped at him from across the boardroom table and bit at his face and tore off his ears. Marvin screamed and bled and then choked. Belphegor made Marvin eat his own ears, shoving them down his throat.

Marvin coughed, and opened his eyes to see

Belphegor smiling lasciviously over him.

"HOW DARE YOU LOOK AT ME!" the demon lord screamed. *"I'LL PUT OUT YOUR EYES FOR THAT!"*

Belphegor reached into Marvin's face and plucked out an eye with his sharp, black-clawed fingers. Belphegor put it in his mouth and bit down on it. Eye juice squirted in Marvin's other eye, and the black demon swallowed the eyeball as he plucked out the other, and fed it to Marvin.

The Bensalem School Shooter screamed and cried like a little bitch the whole time. As he choked, Belphegor covered Marvin's mouth with his hand. He had one last thing to shove in there and he was going to make damn sure the mass murderer swallowed it before he puked it all up. He cut Marvin's nose off with one of his razor-sharp nails, and then shoved that down his throat as well. Marvin choked on his face, trying to breathe, and Belphegor poured his hot coffee in his mouth, and the man finally swallowed.

It took a minute, but Marvin eventually retched up his own facial features. His ears, his eye, his nose, and even parts of his tongue—they all lay on the ground as chunks in the pungent offal. Belphegor picked at the pieces in the puddle of puke and grabbed the eye. It was split down the front and full of vomit. He stuck it into the hole left behind by Marvin's nose. And then he stuck one of his ears in his eye socket, and the tattered piece of his nose in the other. He shoved pieces of his tongue in his ear canal and put his other ear... back on the other side where it belonged.

Belphegor smiled at his grotesque creation, a macabre kind of Mr. Potato Head. Marvin writhed in abject agony.

"Now," Belphegor said. "Tell me how you died."

"*HURPGH GUR-HURR!*" Marvin protested.

"What was that?" Belphegor asked. "I can't hear you."

"*HURPGH GUR-NURR-HURR!*" Marvin whined.

Belphegor sighed,

"Very well."

He snapped his fingers and Marvin became his normal self again, face intact and all. He took a deep breath.

"I went back to my McDonald's to confront the other shooter that was there and I thought maybe I would help the police take him down but I was hit by an ambulance as I was crossing the street and died and *oh my god...*" he cried. "*It hurt so bad!*"

Belphegor smiled as Marvin sobbed. His tears were like crack to him.

"*OH MY GOD!* I forgot all about that until now!" Marvin sniffled, horrified by the memory.

"GOOD!" Belphegor said

Marvin looked up at his dark god, with a face like a question mark.

"But I'm not done with you yet."

Belphegor smiled, for probably the 666th time that day.

CHAPTER 666
PART EIGHT – 6TH CIRCLE
LUCIFER

The Son of the Morning tightened the laces on his running shoes, and then adjusted his sweatband. And then he brought light to the cold darkness of his circle of Hell and took off on his jog. The palm trees on his neighborhood's property unfurled in the heat of his light, but burst into flame as he passed them by. Sinners that he let be his neighbors came out as well, some for a jog and some to walk the dog, and they also exploded into flames as the Lord of Light ran by.

Lucifer smiled. He just had a feeling it was going to be the best day ever.

And then a bunch of kids fell through a green-lit doorway that appeared from out of nowhere, dumping them onto the street in front of Lucifer's feet. He stopped in his tracks. The doorway disappeared as quickly as it had appeared, in like about, five seconds.

Four of the five of them shielded their eyes from the light. (The fifth one didn't because he didn't have any arms.) They screamed as their skin touched the hot asphalt.

"WHAT THE FUCK, DUDE!" Steve screamed. "It's hotter than the lake of fire!"

"Fuck that!" Luke disagreed. "It's hotter than Arizona!"

"You're both wrong," Sandy countered. "It's just the real Hell! It must be the final circle! The one, true Hell!"

"Really?" Jasin asked. "It just reminds me of Los Angeles."

Lucifer smiled at what the green kid said, and helped him up off of the asphalt.

"Thank you! I modeled it after Los Angeles! It's my favorite place on Earth! I used to work up there and I love it, *love it, LOVE IT!*" Lucifer said, giddy with excitement.

"Yeah…" Jasin said. "I went there once on a class trip."

"What class trip?" Steve asked. "I was not aware of a class trip to Los Angeles."

"Maybe if you hadn't been so busy slacking off and tried to focus more on getting good grades…" Luke suggested.

"Wait," Sandy said. "No, he's right. There was never any class trip to Los Angeles."

She put her hand on Jasin's shoulder, gently, and asked, "What were you really doing there, Jasin?"

"Alright, alright. Fine. I was there trying to do a team-up with Los Angeles' biggest superhero—*Numero Uno*."

"That Mexican superhero?" Steve asked.

"Yeah."

"I thought he was just a flying Mexican ninja," Luke said.

"No," Jasin responded. "Numero Uno is the real deal. But anyway, the team-up didn't work so well."

"Aw!" Sandy said, patting him on the back tepidly to console him. She didn't actually care.

"And I lied just because I keep forgetting that having a secret identity is pointless now. You all know who I am. I guess I'm just not used to being dead yet."

Lucifer disagreed with him.

"Having a secret identity is never pointless!" he smiled. "Hell, I used to be Paul Newman. But look at me now! I was Lucifer the *whole time!* And I have a sauce line that will last *forever*. I still rake in the bucks from that!"

"Sounds cool!" Steve said. He had always secretly wanted to go to Hollywood. Start a cool band and write scripts for new Harry Potter movies. It almost seemed like knowing Lucifer would be a good way to start.

"Anyways," Lucifer said. "Nice of you to drop in, but what can I do for you?"

Luke fumbled for Belphegor's card and handed it to the Lord of Light.

"Ah, Belphegor!" Lucifer said, delightedly. "Really a stand up guy, don't you think?"

"Yeah," Sandy said. "He's alright."

Sandy thought it was a little cool that Belphegor was so popular with the other demons. It felt pretty badass to be associated with him. She smirked, though, like it was no big deal.

"*Anywho*," Lucifer continued. "I'll see you through to your mission. Follow me."

Lucifer took off jogging at a brisk pace. The group jogged with him. They worked up a sweat in no time.

"So, Lucifer," Luke asked. "What's it like to work with Tom Cruise?"

"Wonderful!" the demon lord said. "He is the utmost professional on set."

"Really? And is he, *uh…* you know…"

"Gay?"

"Yes, gay."

"Totally!"

"I knew it!" Luke said. Finding out the truth of these little mysteries almost made dying and going to Hell worth it.

Luke wondered what else he could ask.

He quickly thought of something, and caught up to Lucifer's pace again.

"Did OJ kill his wife?"

"Of course he did!" Lucifer said.

"Wow!"

"He had a little help though," Lucifer added, and

then looked over at Luke and gave him a wink.

"And how about Michael Jackson?" Luke asked. "Did he really fuck all those kids?"

"No!" Lucifer said. "God rest his soul, Michael Jackson is up in heaven with the angels. He's one of the best of them."

"Wow," Luke said. "No shit."

"He's even recorded a new record since his death."

They slowed down as they reached the end of the road.

Luke leaned over with his hands on his knees, panting. It was a pretty good run. He was used to getting a lot of exercise on the force. It was one of the reasons he was chosen to pose as a high school student. He was in good shape.

"What's the album called?" Luke asked Lucifer.

Lucifer smiled, and shouted, "The Prince of *Lies!*"

And then Lucifer kicked Luke over the side of the road, into a pitch black hole of oblivion.

"Why'd you do that?!" Sandy yelled, out of breath. If she was really asthmatic still, or had her inhaler, she sure would have taken a big puff right now.

"Where'd he go?" Steve asked.

The group all gathered at the end of the road and peered over the edge into the darkness, trying to see where Luke went. They caught the faintest glimpse of him before he disappeared into the black. They stared harder into the well of nothingness.

"Don't do that!!" Lucifer said.

"Why?" Jasin asked, looking back at the Lord of Light.

"When you stare into the abyss, the abyss stares back at you!"

"Why should we believe anything you say anymore?!" Sandy griped, turning back to face him. But her face was gone. In its place was nothing, like a black oval in a photograph where a face should be.

"You're the Prince of Lies!" she whined.

They all gathered around. Jasin gasped when he saw her.

"Sandy!" he said.

"What?!"

"Your face is missing!"

"My *face* is missing?!" she panicked, feeling for her face where her face used to be.

Lucifer laughed at her. But it was more like a *"ha-ha"* laugh than a hysterically evil one.

"My face!" she screamed. "You took my face!"

"I told you not to look into the abyss that long!"

Steve wondered if his face was gone too. He had only taken a quick glance into the abyss. It probably wasn't enough time for the abyss to look at him until his face melted off.

He felt around for it.

It was all still there.

"YES!" he shouted, pumping his fist victoriously. But then he had a thought,

"So, wait a minute," Steve asked Lucifer. "If you're the Prince of Lies, then is everything you told us not true?"

"Correct."

"Don't listen to him, Steve!" Sandy pleaded. "Everything he says is a lie."

"Well, not everything, young girl," Lucifer said, scratching the back of his head. "That would be ridiculous."

"But anyway," Steve continued. "That would mean OJ really didn't kill his wife!"

"So what?" Jasin said. "That's just like something my dad would care about. We weren't even born yet when it happened. I'm more concerned that Michael Jackson was really a child molester!"

Lucifer looked at him like he was an idiot.

"Oh, *c'mon*," he said. "You didn't really think he was innocent."

"Well, no… I guess." Jasin said.

"Then who killed OJ's wife?" Steve asked.

"That Marilyn Manson freak," Lucifer said.

"Oh my god!" Steve screamed, then smiled. "I *love* Marilyn Manson!"

"You would," Lucifer replied, dismissively.

"But why'd you kick Luke off the edge?" Jasin asked, wondering why they let themselves get so distracted by Lucifer's lies instead of what's important.

Lucifer sighed, and adjusted his wristbands.

"Everyone follow me, I'll explain everything."

And then he took off jogging.

"But I can't see!" Sandy protested.

Jasin jogged up beside her and offered his shoulder for her to hold onto.

"C'mon, Sandy. I got you," he said.

"And so Tom Cruise wasn't even a professional on set?" she asked.

"Probably not, but the real question is whether he's really gay or not," Jasin wondered.

"Who cares who's gay?!" Sandy asked.

"Lots of people."

Luke continued his fall into the abyss. He could totally feel it staring at him from every direction.

"Stop staring at me!" he yelled at the darkness.

The darkness laughed at him, as if that was ridiculous.

After a long time, Luke got used to falling and finally found a way to make himself comfortable. His legs straight and crossed at the ankles, his back straight, and his hands behind his head, he positioned himself as horizontally as possible, and plummeted downwards without flailing about.

This isn't so bad, he thought.

And then he saw a quick flash of light out of the

corner of his eyes, a kind of silvery shine, and heard a crystalline-like eerie sound.

And then someone grabbed him.

He screamed.

"Shhh!" said the voice of the person who grabbed him. "Don't scream. It's me, Virginia."

"Virginia?!" Luke asked, panicked.

"Yeah, it's me. I got you."

"But if you've got me, who's got *you?*"

"Feel my back," she said.

He felt her back and found two large protuberances, bony and leather like. They were her wings.

"Wings!" he shouted.

"Yes," she confirmed. "I have reached my full vampiric potential. I am *beautiful!*"

"OK," Luke said, having mixed feelings about being saved by the Millennial vampire he had completely forgotten about.

"But you killed all those people," he said.

"And I just saved you from this bottomless pit," she argued.

"Well, thanks. I guess."

"Should I take us back up to the top? I feel like I'm just gliding around in circles."

"Yeah, I need to have a word with Lucifer. I don't know if this is his idea of a practical joke or what."

"Alright! Can do!"

Virginia began flapping her big goth wings and

they started ascending the pit to the surface.

After a while, Virginia asked,

"How long is this going to take, anyway?"

"I don't know, Luke answered. "It felt like I was falling for a few hours, but it could have just been minutes."

"So, it should be a while, then."

"Yeah, thank god you're a vampire and probably have super strength and all kinds of endurance and shit."

"Exactly," she agreed.

Then Luke got a worried look on his face.

"Hey… you don't need to feed, do you?"

"Maybe…" Virginia smiled.

Luke tightened up.

"So," he said, trying to change the subject. "You wouldn't believe who's gay!"

"Who?!" Virginia asked, excited.

"Wait till you hear about this…" Luke started.

"So, while your cards from Belphegor have not been revoked or anything, I just needed a little more of your time—*oh, do try to keep up!*" Lucifer yelled, still jogging, making the teens jog with him.

"Why?" Jasin asked, out of breath. Which is impossible when you're dead, but it seems that human habits die hard.

"It's from high up," Lucifer said. "We're trying to catch an escapee."

"And Luke?" Steve asked.

"Bait."

The group came around a corner and Lucifer slowed down. They stopped, relieved the jog was finally over. It seemed like it had gone on for an eternity. Or 666 minutes. Or like they had run around the block 13 times. But it had probably lasted just under an hour.

"Please," Lucifer said, motioning toward his house. "Come inside."

They followed Lucifer into his home, a big '50s-style cottage that looked like it belonged in Beverly Hills.

As they came in through the front door, Lucifer's maid greeted them.

"Good morning, Mr. Lucifer! Would your guests like coffee?"

Surprisingly, Lucifer's maid was a blonde white woman, not a Mexican stereotype.

"I'll take a wheatgrass smoothie, and as for my guests," he cocked his head at them. "Would any of you like coffee?"

"Sure!" Jasin said.

"Would love some!" Steve agreed.

"I don't have a face," Sandy frowned. That is, if she had a face to frown with. But she didn't. Blame Nietzsche. His poetry was as damning as his name was hard to spell.

The maid promptly returned with a tray of drinks,

put coffee cups on the coffee table in front of each teen, and handed Lucifer his smoothie.

He took a swig, and then spit it everywhere.

"THIS IS KALE!" he shouted.

"Oh, sorry, Mr. Lucifer!" the maid apologized.

"*NYRRRREAGH!*" the devil screamed. He stood up and flexed, becoming more beast-like. He grew black crooked horns, and a third eye popped up on his forehead, but with an eyebrow that furled so you could tell it was angry. And then more eyes popped up on his face, which turned red as his ears became pointed. Razor-sharp claws extended from his fingertips, his legs bent backward, and his feet became hooves. A long, pointy tail fell out of the back of his gym shorts.

The teens blew on their hot coffee as they watched the sickening metamorphosis, preoccupied with cooling their coffee down.

Lucifer's mouth opened wide, flashing pearly white vampire-like fangs, and a serpent rose from his throat. He pulled on the head, and hand-over-hand, removed the slithering snake from his maw. It lashed its tongue, forked in the middle, sensing the heat in the room.

Lucifer grabbed it with both hands and swung the serpent at his maid, hitting her in the face with it.

She screamed. Lucifer held his snake tight.

"Mr. Lucifer! Sorry! No!" she pleaded.

He hit her with the snake again. It whipped across

her stomach, knocking the wind out of her. The group sipped their coffee and watched, anxious to see how it was all going to end.

The maid fell to her knees and clutched her stomach. She reached up to Lord Lucifer as if to beg for an end to her torment.

"Mr. Lucifer! Don't! I work so hard for you!"

Lucifer smacked her in the side of the head with the snake. The fat cobra hit her so hard that her eyes popped out of their sockets, and dangled there like testicles, jiggling all around as she fell over.

"*Noooo!*" she screamed.

Lucifer put his snake away, god knows where, and composed himself. He suddenly reverted to normal "human" form.

The maid writhed on the floor, contorting, slowly withering away. When she was just a dry husk, a new maid appeared from the kitchen. And asked, "Can I get you anything, Mr. Lucifer?"

This time she was a Mexican.

"Yes," Lucifer said, sitting down, and already putting clean socks over his cloven hooves. "A wheatgrass smoothie, please."

"Right away, Mr. Lucifer!" the maid said, eagerly.

"Sorry about that," Lucifer said to the group.

"Don't be!" Steve said. "That was totally *awesome!*"

"I couldn't even see anything," Sandy said, "and,

like, I could totally tell."

"Seemed a bit mean if you ask me," Jasin added, taking another sip of his coffee.

"Jasin," Lucifer said.

"What?"

"What did you think about me torturing my maid?" Lucifer asked, as if he hadn't heard what he said.

The question caught Jasin off guard.

Lucifer cleared his throat, and asked him one more time, "I said, *what did you think about me torturing my maid?*"

"Oh," Jasin said. "It was pretty cool, I guess."

Lucifer smiled devilishly, just like Belphegor had smiled a chapter or two ago. Devilishly. Because they're like devils and it makes even more sense.

"Now who's the Prince of Lies?" he grinned.

Jasin looked down, embarrassed.

The new maid brought Lucifer the correct beverage. He took a sip out of it, and went, "*Mmmmmm!*"

He wiped his mouth, looked back at the group, and said, "Alright, now who wants to fuck?"

They all looked at him shocked. No one wanted to have sex with Lucifer, but they were afraid they were going to have to now, or be punished.

"I'M JUST KIDDING!" Lucifer laughed, slapping his knee jovially.

"Oh, thank god!" Sandy said.

Lucifer's demeanor changed seriously, and he menaced

the girl.

"Except for you, No-Face Girl," he said.

Sandy gasped.

"I'm going to take you in the back and fuck the shit out of you."

Steve and Jasin were glad they didn't say anything.

But then an alarm rang out over Lucifer's intercom system. Lucifer sighed.

"Saved by the bell, I guess."

Sandy let out a sigh of relief.

Virginia looked as demonic as Lucifer had moments before when he killed his maid by whipping her to death with a puke serpent. Her skin was also devil red, her teeth pearly white fangs, feet and hands clawed, and her giant leathery black wings were hooked at the edges and extremely flappy-like. She still wore her human clothes, a plaid schoolgirl dress and a tattered t-shirt of the band Kittie. She looked like the poster child for the "Friends of Danzig" extremist group, who had recently bombed a White Stripes concert.

She was sucking Luke's blood, draining him dry, until he replenished all of his blood, and she could suck it again. She sucked him harder and harder until he was a ghostly pale white. It totally sucked.

"You lied to me!" he screamed.

She didn't respond, lost in a vampiric feeding frenzy. She hadn't fed in a while. This was the exact type of thing that Luke was trying to stop back on Earth. He wasn't a vampire hunter or anything of the sort, but he was a peace-keeping officer of the law. When the exsanguinated bodies started popping up all over town, in dumpsters or rest stop bathrooms or wherever, he was the one who had the hunch that it was probably one of those goth punks in town who hung out in front of the Dairy Queen. In the '90s it was metalheads who had been causing all the cattle mutilations in town. He figured goths might be taking the vampire-wannabe culture a little too far, and were just staging their murders to look like a vampire was to blame. They might've been trying to start a new trend in serial killing, or just wanted to scare the town into thinking the vampires had returned. One of the reasons "the force" didn't alert the Philadelphia Avengers to the case were that they had recently eradicated all the vampires. They even had to sacrifice one of their own members, a half-vampire/half-human named Rapier, so the wound was still fresh.

But here Officer Lucas Kapowski was, being bled dry in Hell by a teenage goth vampire, who was supposed to kind of be his friend. Knowing that he would regenerate was a little comforting, but they had an important mission. He needed to get back to it.

They had come back from the depths of the abyss into this circle of Hell. Virginia burned under the scorch of Lucifer's artificial sun. Not because she was the type of vampire who would burn up in the sun, but because it was hot and uncomfortable enough to have a negative effect on anybody, including a daytime vampire. So, she dragged Officer Kapowski with her into the shadows, on the porch of a nice island-style bungalow. At first he just thought she needed the shade that bad, and was exhausted from all the flying and needed a rest, but then she attacked again. And he was the perfect victim, just regenerating plasma as his body needed it. It was like he was an all-you-can-eat buffet.

When Lucifer arrived on the scene with Jasin, Steve, and No-Face Girl (Sandy), he was taken aback a little. Not only had he not seen a vampire in ages, but he had been the only one to harm a sinner in his circle since... *forever*. His neighbors who cowered in their home, looking out their front window at the horrifying scene of horror, were the ones to set off the alarm. It was the main protocol when something like this happened. But it was usually triggered by drunken low-level demons crashing into his circle from another. Not vampire girls.

And Virginia was obviously the escapee from Hell that there was an inferno alert out on. Only high-level demons such as lords or princes got such notices. It came straight down from the top. It even excited Lucifer a little, because he was able to play the role of "Hell Cop". It was fun to be in a different type of authoritative role. He liked the sound of it too. "Hell Cop". He had an idea for a *Hell Cop* movie once when he was working in Hollywood. But then someone else came out with a movie called "Maniac Cop", which was pretty much the same thing. Lucifer was so furious that he murdered the screenwriter of that movie, and he was now his neighbor. Every once in a while Lucifer broke into his house to strangle him to death, just like he had so many years ago on Earth. But most of the time Lucifer would just come by when he wanted someone to talk about film with. They were kind of friends—if you had a friend you could murder anytime you wanted.

And this is what Virginia seemed to be doing to her victim, her idle plaything, a bottomless blood-bag. Lucifer chose Officer Lucas Kapowski as bait because he had the most pleasant, rosy-cheeked color out of anyone in the group. And the fact that Kapowski was an officer of the law, gave him a good excuse to roleplay "Hell Cop" a little further. Lucifer loved to roleplay. He pulled out a pair of aviator shades and put them on, followed by a police cap that said "Hell Dept." Lucifer pretended his hand was a gun and pointed it at Virginia. A small flame ignited on the end of his gun finger, just like a lighter.

"OFFICER KAPOWSKI!" Lucifer shouted. "ARE YOU IN NEED OF ASSISTANCE?!"

Luke looked up wearily and saw the Hell Cop and his friends standing vigilantly in the gravel driveway.

"Uh…" he said weakly. "*Yeah…*"

"WE HAVE AN OFFICER DOWN!" Lucifer shouted, to no one in particular. "I REPEAT, WE HAVE AN OFFICER DOWN!"

Luke writhed in Virginia's vampiric embrace.

"CEASE AND DESIST IMMEDIATELY!" Lucifer warned. "OR THERE WILL BE *HELL* TO PAY!"

Virginia took her fangs out of Kapowski's neck and looked up to see what the hell was going. Then she remembered what she was supposed to be doing. Her mission from the mirror world that she had to complete so she could get revenge. And here she was getting distracted by the hot guy from school and all of his delicious blood! She cursed herself, and then cursed out loud.

"Oh, shit!" she said. "Lucifer! Not *you!*"

"Who were you expecting," Lucifer smiled, holstering his imaginary gun. "The Easter Bunny?"

"Goddamnit, Lucifer!" Virginia fussed. "You're going to ruin *everything!*"

Virginia spread her wings and hissed.

"COME AT ME, BITCH!" Lucifer taunted, arms outstretched.

Everyone watched with interest. This was the most entertaining showdown since The Phillie Phanatic was finally taken down by The Fresh Prince. After what the baseball mascot did to all those kids, he more than had it coming.

Virginia flew at the devil like a bat out of hell, claws primed to scratch out his eyes, and fangs dripping with hot anticipation. Lucifer transformed into The Beast much quicker this time, and caught her midair by the hands, which he squeezed in his, cracking the bones. Her black wings were impaled on his long, pointy black horns. She screeched in agony. And it was a demonic screech too, not just some whiny goth girl's cry. Between Lucifer's mighty horns, her head stuck tight, and his face pressed against her. Lucifer opened his mouth to retch out a serpent. It slithered out of his mouth and into hers, diving down her throat, filling her innards, and taking a big shit.

Lucifer tore her off of him and threw her aside like a rubber toy bat. She bounced off the pavement and landed flat on her face, which became a bloody mash. She tried to pull herself off the ground, but Lucifer walked over and kicked her in the stomach so hard that the serpent flew out of her ass like a shit missile. It flew through the neighbors' front window, shattering the glass, and thrashed around on the floor. One of the occupants let out a blood-curdling scream.

Virginia was on her back, trying to crawl away from Lucifer on the back of her hands, her skin road-rashed tatters. Lucifer kicked her in the face and she went down once more. Flat on her back, he stood over the dying girl, ready to finish her off.

He stretched his hands out theatrically like a sorcerer, and with a flair of melodrama, said, "DEVIL POWERS, ACTIVATE!"

Rays of blinding white light shot forth from his hands and enveloped the goth vampire girl in a nuclear blast of heat. It was like being eaten to the core by the power of ten thousand suns. Her skin turned black, charred, and sizzled off to reveal the bloody framework of muscle, tissue, and bone. Her melted screams were inaudible. Her scorched body burst outward like a supernova, and a plume of ash exploded skyward and rained down on them like it was from a volcano.

"WOAHHH!" Steve wowed. "That was the best thing *ever!*"

"What happened? I can't see." No-Face Girl (Sandy) asked.

Jasin put his hand on her shoulder and said, "I'll tell you later, Sandy."

In the aftermath of the chaos, Lucifer returned to human form and ran over to Officer Kapowski's aid. The fallen officer still lay flat on the porch, pale white, looking like the life was about to fade from his body.

"KAPOWKSI!" Lucifer cried, cradling him in his arms.

"Lucifer? Is that you?" Luke asked weakly, looking up at the demon lord.

"That's Officer Lucifer," he whispered to him. *"But that's OK."*

"Oh."

Lucifer shed a tear, slipping back into character.

"You're going to be OK, Luke! I swear."

"OK…" Luke said, closing his eyes. The blood was returning to his face.

"STAY WITH ME KAPOSKWI!" Lucifer pleaded.

Luke coughed, and opened his eyes again.

"Do you want a cigarette?" Lucifer asked him.

Luke shook his head.

"Hold on," Lucifer said, wiping away a tear. "I think I have one right here."

Lucifer put a cigarette in his mouth and lit it for him. Luke inhaled, and coughed.

"I don't smoke…" Luke protested.

"YOU'LL ALWAYS BE MY BEST FRIEND, LUKE!" Lucifer shouted, hugging him tight.

"I'm actually feeling a lot better…" Luke said, trying to breathe through the tightness of Lucifer's strong bear hug.

"WHY DOES IT ALWAYS HAVE TO BE THE YOUNG ONES?!" Lucifer screamed to the sky.

"You can let go of me now, I'd like to get up…" Luke protested.

"YOU HAD SO MUCH TO LIVE FOR! WHY?!?!" Lucifer shook him. "*WHY?!?!?*"

"Don't worry, I'm fully regenerating. It's fine."

"USE THE FORCE, LUKE!" Lucifer screamed. "*USE THE FORCE!*"

"I'm totally better, dude."

Lucifer finally looked at him. He was really all better. His rosy cheeks were back. He was restored to full health.

Lucifer scowled at him.

Luke became very, very afraid.

"No," Luke said, like he knew what was coming, and shielded his face. "No! *Don't do it!*"

Lucifer slashed Officer Kapowski's throat with his razor-sharp claws. Blood gushed out of the wound in buckets. Luke became pale white again and slumped back into Lucifer's arms.

"OFFICER DOWN!" Lucifer shouted.

Tears welled up in the demon lords eyes again.

"STAY WITH ME, OFFICER KAPOWSKI! *STAY WITH ME!*" he wailed.

This went on for some time.

CHAPTER 666
PART NINE – 7ᵀᴴ CIRCLE
MAMMON

The group was sent on its way after Lucifer packed some nice lunches, all vegan, with some wheatgrass tea and ginger snaps. They also were the lucky recipients of some "I HEART LUCIFER" t-shirts. When Jasin inspected the tag, he was a little dismayed it said, "Made in Chinese Hell". But it was still a nice shirt, and he wasn't about to belittle their hard work by not wearing it. Besides, it wasn't like anyone in school was going to see him in it. He was dead now. He was actually trying to think of a way out of it though, the whole being-dead part. He had been listening in on the thoughts of a lot of demon lords to look for clues.

Lucifer thanked them wholeheartedly for helping

take care of the Hell escapee, their vampire friend Virginia. But when Lucifer mentioned her, they had no idea who he was talking about. Even Luke, who he had used as bait to catch the monster. As far as Luke remembered, he had spent the *whole* time with Lucifer, cradled in his arms, not hers. Luke even looked at Lucifer like he had developed a little bit of a crush on him. Lucifer didn't know how he felt about that, but Luke even seemed sad to be leaving. He kind of just wanted to stay at Lucifer's house. He could simply lie by the pool all day, hang out, and hear all of Lucifer's fun stories and various juicy tidbits of Hollywood gossip. But it wasn't to be. The foursome had a mission that had to eventually conclude at some point, probably in several thousand words or less, and it was time to get back to it. And whoever the vampire goth girl was, well, maybe it was just for the best that they couldn't remember her.

Lucifer walked them to the back gate to the next circle and they all said their goodbyes before he handed them off to their armless demon guide, *The Nameless One.*

"Come back and see me sometime," Lucifer said as he waved goodbye. "Don't be strangers!"

"Oh, I would *love* that Lucifer!" Luke said. "Is there anything to rent here?"

"Goodbye!" Lucifer dismissed him.

Luke was pushed along with the group and they disappeared in a neon yellow flash of the gate's doorway.

Virginia was back in the mirror world. But you couldn't see what was going on, because it was in another dimension. One thing was for sure though—she was no longer a vampire.

"What could be taking so long?" Belphegor said to himself, checking his watch. It was 6:66 o'clock, as usual. They should have been back by now.

"Maybe they've failed, Belphegor," Marvin taunted, still duct taped to his chair in the boardroom.

"Shut up," Belphegor said, dismissively of him, and got back to some work on his desk. His desk lamp illuminated the nearby wall, which had his election poster pinned to it. It read "VOTE BELPHEGOR, AND *BE COOL!*" and had a picture of the demon wearing a pair of Ray-Ban sunglasses and pretending to wail on a Warlock guitar.

Marvin looked over at where Belphegor had put his gun. It was all the way on the other side of the boardroom table. It was not only far out of reach, but a long way around the large, rectangular-shaped obstacle. Even if he could get Belphegor out of the room for five minutes, it'd be almost impossible to scootch himself in the chair all the way over to it, and try to grab it somehow with his arms and legs still duct taped. But this happened all the time in movies, so he was pretty confident. The prisoner always got free and escaped.

But maybe Belphegor was counting on that.

The crew fell several feet from the gateway portal onto the ground below, stumbling and tripping over.

"Ow! I twisted my ankle," Steve yelled, grasping his injury.

"Don't worry," Luke said. "It will heal in a minute."

"Speaking of healing," Sandy said, reaching for her face. "Is my face back yet?"

"No," Jasin said. "No face."

If Sandy could frown she'd have been doing it.

Jasin tried to think of something to comfort her. And then he had an idea.

"Hey, Nameless One," he said, talking to their demon guide.

"Yes?" he asked, still armless, but doing his job.

"Didn't you say something about some magical way to get a name?"

"I'd settle for new arms instead, but yeah," he confirmed.

"If you got a name, and some arms, do you think Sandy could get a new face?"

"You have to ask *him.*"

"But who is he really?" Jasin asked. "Am I supposed to believe there's some kind of mystery overseer, watching our every move, and affecting the outcome of everything we do?"

"Yes," the Nameless One said. "Just have to believe."

"I wouldn't mind asking this guy a few questions myself," Luke said.

"But what's the best way to ask?" Sandy asked.

"Maybe we can ask Satan!" Steve suggested, feeling that his ankle was totally healed.

"But Satan isn't even around here," Jasin noted. "We haven't seen him the whole time. We don't even know what he's like."

"Yeah," Luke agreed. "We don't need Satan anyway. Other people like Lucifer and Belphegor have been way cooler to us anyway. Especially Lord Lucifer."

Luke smiled and stared blankly for a while, thinking of the Lord of Light smittenly.

"Who even knew there were other devils?" Sandy asked. "Hell is so interesting!"

"But you guys don't even know what you're talking about!" Steve pouted. "I met Satan in a magical doorway way back in the Second Circle of Hell! It was when we all got separated. He was the coolest one of them all! If we should ask anybody for help, we should ask Satan!"

"Eh," The Nameless One said. "Satan cares not these days. Waste of time. You ask President Leviathan. Leviathan in charge now."

"But can Leviathan give me my face back?" Sandy

asked, wondering about her face.

"We can ask, but me don't know. Leviathan is... *very big fish.*"

The Nameless One said that as if the president was just too important to ask such things.

"Anyway, we move on now. Mammon's place over the way."

The Nameless One tried to point, but decided to just take the lead again. He still tried to move his stubs around sometimes in a certain direction but it had no noticeable effect.

They followed him up the hill.

"Mammon?" Luke asked.

"Mammon," The Nameless One replied.

"OK, then," Luke said. "I guess we'll just show this one our *'Get Out of This Circle of Hell Free'* cards too and be on our way, hopefully without any drawn-out, wacky side adventures."

When they reached the top of the hill and looked upon Mammon's circle of Hell, it didn't look like there were going to be any wacky side adventures.

It looked like there was going to be nothing but death.

Belphegor had been in the bathroom for over five minutes, and Marvin decided to finally make his move. He was too scared to try it earlier because he didn't know if the demon lord would just return at any second. But enough time had passed that he figured he'd better take the chance now or it would be too late. He surmised that Belphegor would probably be in the bathroom for 666 seconds, which gave him around two more minutes.

It only took Marvin a minute to scootch his chair over to where his weapon was. It took him another twenty seconds to free himself and grab it. By the time Belphegor returned from the bathroom, Marvin sat at the demon lord's desk with his gun pointed right at him.

"Hold it right there, big guy," Marvin said, like he was the one in charge now.

Belphegor just smiled, and clasped his hands together.

"Splendid! I knew you could do it, Marvin!"

"You wanted me to escape?" Marvin was confused.

"Oh, I want you to do much more than that."

"And what's that which you want me to do?"

Belphegor flashed a devilish smile again, as if this was all going exactly according to his plan.

"Why, I want you to kill the president."

"What's in it for me?" Marvin asked greedily.

"Anything you want," Belphegor offered. "Anything beyond your wildest dreams."

"Well, how about a cheeseburger?" Marvin asked. "I'm about to have a Big Mac Attack over here."

"As you wish."

Belphegor snapped his fingers, and a plate of McDonald's cheeseburgers appeared in front of Marvin.

"Wow!" Marvin grabbed a cheeseburger and unwrapped it from the yellow paper, and had a bite. It was the most delicious taste in the world.

And it was totally worth killing someone over.

Especially the president.

The 7th Circle of Hell was occupied by thousands of protestors. They gathered as far as the eye could see in front of a towering skyscraper—which was literally the end of how far their eyes could see.

"This is going to be a long walk," Luke said, looking down at the sea of sinners carefully.

"We'll never make it!" Steve said.

"Yeah," Jasin agreed. "Even with my superhuman frog powers, I don't know if I could play leapfrog over that many people, if you know what I mean."

"What do you mean?" Luke asked.

"What do you think I mean?"

"I think it sounds like you're going to fuck them all in the ass."

Jasin got red-faced and embarrassed, and quickly disagreed: "No! That's not what I meant at all! I meant jumping over them. You've seen how high I can jump, how far! I just meant I don't think even I could get across that sea of people! I don't think any of us can!"

"I think we can!" Sandy said, reaching into her backpack, retrieving the mystical cloak that Belphegor gifted her. "I'll just turn invisible and walk on by them all!"

"Holy shit!" Steve said. "I forgot about the stuff we got!"

"Oh yeah!" Luke said, remembering.

He reached into the backpack he got from Belphegor (not the backpack from Lucifer, they threw those out already because the food sucked) and retrieved his light sword!

He brandished it about like a Jedi.

"I'll cut those hippie fuckers down to size!" he threatened.

Jasin reached for his shield, inspecting it.

"And I guess this could be used as a weapon, or a battering ram."

Steve looked at his mystical item, Belphegor's autobiography, which was also the story of their journey. He still could look into it at any time to find out what happens to them, but he just couldn't do it. Maybe in the direst of circumstances, but probably not even then.

"Uh…" he said. "I'll just follow close to you guys."

"And I'll stand around like a useless paperweight!" The Nameless One said.

"OK, see you later!" Luke said, and they left the armless sentry on the hill, sure to see him later on if they made it through the sea of sinners.

These particular sinners hadn't bathed in months, and they reeked so bad the odor permeated everything around them. Shantytowns made of tarps buzzed with flies and the muddy ground beneath their feet was just excrement, more than likely. A wide assortment of hippies, hipsters, and homeless people comprised the sea of anger, which surged with hatred. They pounded their fists in the air, feral-faced, screaming their slogans, such as "OCCUPY HELL!", "DEATH TO THE 666%!", and "FREE GREENPEACE!"

Sandy sneaked by the crowd stealthily in her invisible cloak. Luke and Jasin did not take the stealthy route. Luke screamed like a warrior as he hacked through the crowd with his green sword of fire, cutting them down to size. He had his own battle cry too –

"*DIE, HIPPIES, DIE!*"

Jasin was decapitating tons of them at once by throwing his black metallic pentagram shield. He ran across the crowd on top of the headless mens' neck stumps with froglike dexterity, retrieving his shield wherever it landed with his tacky tongue. Steve fended off trashcan intellectuals by swatting them away with his book. But he was quickly becoming overwhelmed.

"HELP ME!" Steve cried.

Sandy heard him and came back to his aid.

"STAY WHERE YOU ARE, STEVE! I'M COMING!"

"WHERE ARE YOU?! I CAN'T SEE YOU ANYWHERE!" he pleaded.

"I'm right here, silly," Sandy said, revealing herself close to Steve by pulling her hood down.

"Sandy, no!" Steve cried, trying to warn her, but it was too late. The horde grabbed her once she appeared. Her cloak was gone, in the hands of some suddenly invisible vagrant. And then she was torn to pieces by bums who were trying to reach into her pockets for change.

"*NOOOOOOO!*" Steve screamed in horror.

Meanwhile, Jasin and Luke grew weary from the battle. They met briefly on the ground at the protestors' ankle-level.

"We need to think of a plan," Luke told Jasin.

Jasin smiled.

"I know, Luke! We can use *the Force!*"

Luke was annoyed. If he had a dime for every time he's heard that…

"Look, kid, do you want to die out here?" he asked the young superhero.

"But we can't die. Not really."

"Exactly. That's my point. Do you think if we died we'd just end up at the beginning of this Circle?"

"I'm not sure. For all we know, we could reappear at the end. Who knows how this works."

"Yeah, it's totally nothing like a video game," Luke said.

"What are you talking about? It's totally like a

video game. Maybe not one of your stupid Nintendo games from the Eighties where you didn't even have a save feature, but definitely like a real game. Like Halo."

"Why you little shit!" Luke yelled, extremely pissed off that the kid would dare dis Nintendo, or the '80s.

He grabbed him by the throat and started strangling him and bashing his head against the ground. Jasin retaliated by jumping with Luke against him. They flew into the air together, but Jasin couldn't keep any kind of balance with Luke's hands still around his throat. They fell to the crowd below and surfed atop them in mortal combat.

"LET... GO!" Jasin pleaded.

"NEVER! I'M TRYING TO KILL YOU!" Luke shouted.

"OH!"

"JUST LET IT HAPPEN, KID!"

"OK! BUT WHAT ABOUT YOU?"

"I'LL THINK OF SOMETHING!"

When Jasin's light left his eyes, Luke tossed the boy's body aside and addressed the crowd.

"MY NAME IS DONALD TRUMP! COME GET ME, YOU FUCKERS!"

The horde tore him to pieces in an instant like rabid dogs.

666

Luke rematerialized in the skyscraper's lobby, safe from the horde outside, protected by walls of impenetrable glass and security demons. He saw to his relief that Sandy and Jasin were already there. But someone was missing.

"Where's Steve?" he asked.

Sandy frowned, but no one knew because she didn't have a face.

"He didn't make it…"

"So he's still alive?" Luke asked.

"Yes."

Luke shook his head and looked down at the ground.

"That poor bastard."

Jasin looked out at the horde.

"Do you think he's still out there?" he asked.

"He's gotta be," Luke said, putting his hand on Jasin's shoulder as if to comfort him. "But there's nothing we can do for him."

Sandy sniffled, holding back a cry, probably only thinking she was because of the whole no-face thing she still had going on, and said, "Maybe we'll see him… on the other side…"

"We can only hope, Sandy," Luke said. "We can only hope."

The group held each other for comfort as they looked at the horde of chaos beyond the shiny walls of Mammon's tower. The mob still slung their verbal arrows, *"FUCK THE POLICE!"* and *"OCCUPY MY*

MOM!", and such, but they could not hurt them any more. They were in a safe place now. They only hoped that Steve would end up in a safe place too somehow.

A pretty, black-horned executive assistant came for the group, looking down at a clipboard.

"Lucas Kapowski, Jasin Jackson, and Miss Sandy Hook?" she asked.

"That'll be us," Jasin shrugged.

"Mammon shall see you now."

They followed the assistant to the elevator, where they ascended to the 666th floor, where Mammon, the Lord of Greed, dwelled.

Steve cradled himself in the fetal position beneath a tarp he had managed to pull down on top of himself for safety. Protestors still trampled above him, but it was hardly a bother. He knew *he* would come for him. He knew he just had to say the right words.

"Satan," Steve said.

And then he repeated.

"Satan."

And repeated again, rocking himself back and forth.

"Satan."

He was sure that if he just said Satan's name 666 times, the demon lord would come for him and save him from his misery.

"Satan, hear my call. Please, save me."

And then Steve winced. He was sure he had to start the count back at zero now because he said other words in the litany that were *not* Satan.

"Christ!" he said, cursing the name of god.

And then Satan appeared from out of nowhere, and said,

"Now, *that* guy owes *me* money."

"SATAN!" Steve yelled, smiling. "It's you!"

"The one and only. How can I help you, Steve?"

"I need to find my friends. We're on a mission, and we have to meet the demon lord Mammon."

"Sounds rough. So, you want to hang out with me for a while?"

"Yeah, that sounds great!"

"OK, but I gotta get something out of it."

"Like what?" Steve asked.

"What you got?"

Steve looked at the book he had in his clutches. Surely he couldn't give it to Lord Satan!

"Ah!" Satan's eyes widened. "Is that Belphegor's autobiography?"

"Yes," Steve said. "But it's kind of magic. And he gave it to me. I don't know if I can part with it."

Satan licked his lips. He knew what was in the book. He had to have it.

"But you want to give it to Lord Satan, don't you, Steve?"

"I can't," Steve frowned, looking down and afraid

to let Satan see his disappointment.

"It's alright, Steve," Satan said comfortingly. "Look at me."

Steve looked up at the demon lord and met his eyes. Satan's glowed red and put Steve in a sudden trance.

"Give me the book, Steve," he suggested.

"Yes, Lord Satan," Steve obeyed. "As you wish."

Steve handed Satan the book. Satan thumbed through it a little, and clasped it shut in one hand, then smiled.

"EXCELLENT!"

Steve shook his head nauseously like he had just been pulled out of a dream.

"Now get in, Steve!" Satan smiled, motioning him in through the doorway of the portal. "We're going to have a great discussion, you and I."

Steve followed Satan into the doorway and it closed and flickered out of the 7th Circle of Hell and into a different dimension.

"FLAKES, LOSERS AND MISCREANTS!" Mammon shouted.

Then he shook a fist at the window.

"OCCUPY A *JOB!* LOSERS!"

"But aren't these *your* sinners, in your hell for you to punish?" Luke asked, wondering.

Mammon shook his head.

"No... no they're not, sadly. I would torture the

fuck out of these fucking fuckers if they were mine. But alas, they're not."

"Where'd they come from then?" Jasin asked. Luke gave him a glare as if to say, *the adults are talking*, and Jasin rolled his eyes. It seemed like Luke was still pissed off about the Nintendo remark.

"They've bled over from other circles of Hell. First it was Astaroth's with his legion of hipsters, and then Sonneillion's with his legion of haters."

Uh-oh, Jasin thought. *That might all be our fault.*

His thoughts were mind-broadcasted to the rest of the group.

Hey genius, Luke thought back. *How come you haven't used this power more? Sure as hell would've come in handy more times than I can think of!*

Leave Jasin alone! Sandy mind-screamed. *He's doing the best he can with what he's got!*

Frogs aren't even supposed to be telepathic anyway! Luke argued. *Your powers don't even make any sense! And as for you not thinking of using this ability earlier— it's just another indication of your generation's laziness and stupidity!*

Jasin knew what Luke was going to think next before he even thunk it, and thought back, *Don't you even think it!*

But Luke thought it anyway, *You never would have been good enough to be a Philadelphia Avenger!*

"NYEARGH!!!" Jasin screamed, and leaped at Luke with his frog-hopping power.

"STOP!" Mammon commanded, and extended his arms all wizard-like. The two froze in place.

"Lord below, it's like Sonneillion hatred got up your ass!"

Mammon released his magical hold, and Jasin dropped to the ground and Luke fell backwards on his ass.

"Look, while I appreciate your problems, and I usually *love* watching quarrels, but I've got my own problems. And if you're not even going to listen to me go on a rant about them, I would prefer it if you three would just be on your way. Now let me see those cards."

Luke reached into his pocket and retrieved his Belphegor card and handed it to Lord Mammon, as did the others.

"Very good, very good, everything looks in order here, let's get you off on your way now, complete your mission, say hi to the president for me, move along now."

He almost pushed them through the neon orange-lit doorway that appeared on the far side of his office.

"But wait!" Sandy protested, turning to Mammon to ask him something really quick before he pushed her through the portal.

"WHAT?!" he asked angrily.

"Can you give me my face back?"

"NEVER!" he shouted, and then kicked her

through the door.

She landed with a thud on top of The Nameless One, who appeared to be sitting in the next Circle, already waiting for them.

"You should've asked him for Steve!" Luke yelled at her.

"But I miss my face! One of these demon lords has got to have the power to get it back!" she cried.

"Steve is probably gone forever now," Jasin said. "We're just going to have to move on without him. We still have to complete our mission."

"I think we have a bigger problem," Luke said, looking at the two teenagers lustfully.

"What's that?" Jasin asked.

"I'm really, *really* horny."

Ruh-roh, The Nameless One thought.

He knew where they were and what usually happens there.

It was going to be the most challenging circle of Hell yet.

CHAPTER 666
PART TEN – 8ᵀᴴ CIRCLE
ASMODEUS

"Two more chapters to go!" said Satan, folding a page in the book to mark his place, and then putting it aside. Steve noticed that Satan had already affixed a sticker on the back of the book to claim it as his. It read *"Property of Satan S. Swift."*

Steve had no idea Satan had a last name, but felt excited and privileged to know what it was.

"How is it?" Steve asked, a little curious to see how his story went.

"Pretty good so far," Satan said. "Don't know how it's going to be wrapped up in two chapters though."

"Maybe you should get back to it," a voice said. Satan and Steve looked around the room to see who it was that said that. But there was no one there.

"Woah," Satan said, looking at Steve. "Spooky."

"Who was that?" Steve asked.

"I don't know," Satan replied. "But I can't wait to find out!"

Satan opened the book again, and got back to reading.

The gang gave the gatekeeper their cards from Belphegor. He took them and held them up to his nose, and sniffed them hard and long like some kind of foot fetish freak.

"Ah, the scent of Belphegor!" the gatekeeper said and smiled. "Always smells so sickly sweet! Those pheromones... always gets me going!"

The demon licked his lips and kicked back in his reclining chair and moaned erotically as he sniffed the cards again.

"Uh... *sir?*" Luke asked, trying to get the sexed-up demon's attention.

He leaned back towards the window, and handed the threesome their cards back through the slot in the bottom.

"So erotic," the demon noted. "Don't you agree?"

Luke unbuttoned his shirt a little, it was getting pretty hot in this circle of Hell.

"Sure," Luke said. "I guess."

The demon noticed Luke's chest hair and glared at him sexually.

"Oooh! A hairy chest," he said. "So sexy. You're going to be quite popular in here."

Jasin decided it was the best time to interject, and said, "Look, we're not here to party."

The demon disagreed: "Oh, you will be," he said, then looked at the boy closer. *"You will be."*

Sandy got agitated and decided to get serious as well. "Look, we just need to meet the lord of this circle, and show him our cards, and be on our way," she said, annoyed. "We don't really have time for this."

"Ah, yes!" the gatekeeper said. "You seek Asmodeus!"

He got a map out and unfolded it, flattening it on the table in front of the window. The group got closer so they could see it clearly.

The demon pointed to a place on the map, "OK, it's Blackout Friday, so Asmodeus should be *here* in the main dance club, *Den-O-Sin*. He likes to deejay on Blackout Friday. He plays some of the most extreme dark metal techno in this side of Hell."

"What is this place, anyway?" Jasin asked Luke, thinking he would know because he was older and maybe had more experience with these things. Jasin had never been to a bar or nightclub and probably preferred to keep it that way.

"I think it's a..." Luke said, with a mixture of disgust and anticipation, "...a gay bathhouse."

"*Gay?!*" Sandy said, but not in a homophobic way.

She wanted to get laid too and thought that wasn't fair. She had definitely heard of gay bathhouses before. After all, she masturbated to gay porn at home because all the guys were hot.

"Don't worry, little girl," the gatekeeper said. "This is a bathhouse for sinners of all sexual persuasions."

"Oh," Sandy said, surprised. "That's *awesome!*"

"Sandy!" Jasin shouted, shocked to hear her say that.

"Oh, c'mon, Jasin!" she replied. "Live a little."

Jasin gulped, scared about the possibility of being fucked by some ugly horned demon. She would probably have six tits, a six-inch wide vagina, and a really, really ugly face.

"But…" Luke said. "It doesn't sound like punishment for these types of sinners."

"Oh, it is," the gatekeeper disagreed. "Asmodeus picks the music."

"That doesn't sound so bad," Luke said.

The gatekeeper looked at him seriously, and warned, "You must not have heard Morbid Angel's eighth album."

Luke had not. Jasin and Sandy had never even heard of Morbid Angel though, so they were perhaps in for an even worse surprise.

The gatekeeper got them clean towels and then buzzed them through the locked gate. They all entered, except for their demon guide, who was stopped by the gatekeeper.

"Sorry," he said. "We don't allow cripples in here."

The Nameless One looked down at the stubs where his arms used to be, grunted, and then looked back at the gatekeeper like he agreed.

No one probably wanted to have sex with an armless low-level demon anyway.

Satan closed the book again after dog-earing the page, and looked at Steve.

"Dude," Satan said. "This is getting really gay. You sure are missing out, Steve."

"Hey!" Steve said, insulted. "I'm not gay!"

"The way you're dressed says otherwise," Satan disagreed. "Have you even looked at yourself in a mirror lately?"

"What's wrong with the way I dress?"

"First off," Satan said. "*Everything*. You look like you got all your fashion choices at Hot Topic. And not only that, but it looks like you got your taste in bands solely from their t-shirt selection."

Steve frowned. He kind of had.

"Just look at yourself," Satan said, pulling Steve over to the wall, which suddenly turned into a mirror.

Steve saw himself the same way the Bensalem School Shooter saw him before he killed the teen—as nothing but a poser.

"But," Satan said. "You could look like *this*."

Satan snapped his fingers and Steve's appearance changed in the mirror, clothes and everything.

Steve looked at himself. He did look a lot cooler. All of his fashion accessories were gone, and his black-dyed hair was now just long blond hair, his natural color, straight and almost long enough to reach his belt, which was made out of bullets. He wore brand new camouflage pants, leather boots, and a band t-shirt with a gothic looking old painting on the front and a logo he couldn't read too well. But it had a bunch of pentagrams and upside-down crosses in it, so the band must be pretty awesome.

"What band is this?" Steve asked, still looking at himself in the mirror.

"That's Morbid Angel," Satan said.

"Never heard of them," Steve said, almost surprised. He thought he knew about all the coolest metal bands.

"Well then, maybe we should go back to my room and I'll put them on my record player," Satan smiled delightedly.

"Do you have the one on the t-shirt here?" Steve inquired, still looking at in the mirror.

"*Blessed Are the Sick*?" Satan asked. "Of course. And I'll let you in a little secret…"

"What's that?"

"I *wrote* it."

"Woah, cool! No way!" Steve shouted, excited to hear something that the one and only Lord Satan wrote himself.

"Let's go," Satan said, guiding him away toward the dark tunnel which presumably led to his room. There was a warm glow at the end.

"I have a lot of other bands to show you as well."

"Cool!" Steve said, and turned his back on the mirror to follow.

Unbeknownst to him, a pair of clawed hands reached out of the mirror for him at that second, missing out on grabbing the boy by mere inches.

"Dammit!" Virginia cursed, from the other side of the mirror. "I almost had him!"

The voices spoke around her, all at once.

"You will have another chance soon. You will use the child. You will have your revenge."

Virginia smiled a vampirish grin. She had become a vampire again at some point. But you couldn't see that. Because it happened in a mirror dimension and you can't see in there.

Everyone in the group plugged their ears with their fingers, as if they were in agony.

"THIS IS THE WORST MUSIC I'VE EVER HEARD IN MY LIFE!" Jasin screamed.

"JESUS CHRIST, LUKE!" Sandy shouted. "IS THIS

WHAT YOUR GENERATION LISTENS TO?!"

"SURE AS HELL ISN'T!" Luke yelled. "WE USED TO LISTEN TO HEAVY MUSIC, BUT IT NEVER SOUNDED LIKE THIS TECHNO CRAP! I THOUGHT THIS WOULD BE SOMETHING MORE LIKE WHAT YOU MILLENNIALS WOULD LISTEN TO!"

"WHAT?!" Sandy shouted.

"I THOUGHT THIS MIGHT BE SOMETHING YOUR GENERATION WOULD LISTEN TO!" Luke shouted even louder.

"HELL NO!" Sandy shouted back. "THIS IS WORSE THAN DUBSTEP!"

"IT'S THE WORST THING EVER!!!" Jasin screamed.

Morbid Angel's worst album, the techno-death nightmare known as *Illud Divinum Insanus*, blared through the labyrinth of the gay bathhouse on loud speakers that were affixed in every single hallway, so there would be no escape. The singer, who one could only assume was the gothiest of the gothy goths ever, was shouting something about how he was totally "kool" and "radikult."

It was the worst thing ever.

While the group followed their map as they went down the halls of the massive sex labyrinth, they saw many writhing souls fucking lustfully along the way. Each sinner had bleeding ears, and they often saw a sinner stabbing their eardrums with various sharp implements they presumably crafted themselves out of items from the labyrinth's sex shop. You could see them stopping their forays of sexual carnage whenever their ears healed, screaming in agony until they were able to pierce their eardrums for any amount of temporary deafness they could devise, and then went back to fucking.

At one point the group stopped in a massive orgy room, a little lost, and asked for directions. A couple of horny sinners immediately began hitting on Sandy. They said something along the lines of '*Man, she has a rocking body!*' and '*I know, right? But her face…*' and '*What face? She doesn't have one!*' They high-fived, and started rubbing against her, trapping her on each side and grinding her with friction. She threw her arms in the air and danced between them in rapture, losing herself to the carnal pleasure.

"Luke!" Jasin yelled, "Sandy is having underage sex with two perverts! What should we do?"

But Luke couldn't hear him. When Jasin looked back at the middle-aged police officer, he was against the wall moaning in pleasure while he was getting a blowjob from a cute twink, who felt up his manly chest hair while masturbating. Luke's ears were bleeding. He had totally pierced them and was losing himself in the ecstasy this circle had to offer much like Sandy.

Then a group of horny naked nymphs encircled

Jasin. His first instinct was to leap out of the way, but when he noticed how smoking hot they were, all he could think was, *BOOBIES!*

The thought came across the mind of every sinner in Asmodeus's circle of Hell, and the sum totality of the damned cheered, regardless of sexual persuasion.

Jasin let the babes undress him and he lay down on the floor and relaxed as they had their way with him.

He listened to the gay Morbid Angel the whole time. Even the worst album ever made wasn't enough to prevent him from experiencing the best orgasm of his entire life.

Steve sat Indian-style on the floor of Satan's man-cave, thumbing through his vinyl collection. They had already listened to the first two Morbid Angel albums, and Satan had just put on the third—*Covenant*. It was pretty much the best album Steve had ever heard.

"This album has some of the greatest drum work of all time," Satan said, inhaling a big drag of Hell weed, before handing the joint to Steve. "Some say it's the death metal drummers' bible."

Steve took a drag of the joint too, and coughed a little as he handed it back to the devil. It was some of the best weed he'd ever smoked.

"Yeah," he agreed. "I never even listen to the drums

in any of the bands I listen to. They don't even stand out. This stuff, on the other hand, is blasting my fucking face off. It's almost inhuman. I'm surprised the drummer didn't die of a heart attack when they recorded it."

"He's the best," Satan said, exhaling a big cloud of unholy pot smoke. "Just goes to show that a human being can do anything on their own as long as they practice. They don't need performance-enhancing drugs, or even the power of Satan. They just have the talent."

"But I thought you wrote the last album we heard," Steve asked, wondering if he was remembering that wrong. He was pretty stoned.

"Oh, I did," Satan said, and then tilted his face up and narrowed his eyes confusingly like he was trying to remember as well.

"Well... *kind of*," he said. "I helped out with a lot of the lyrics and wrote all of the keyboard parts."

"Oh, cool!" Steve said.

"Did you write any more on this album?" pointing to Satan's die-cut limited edition double vinyl of *Covenant*.

"No," Satan said, but then smiled. "But they did give me a producer's credit."

Steve looked through the lyric booklet until he found the credits. And there it was, right there at the end: *Produced by Satan S. Swift.*

"Woah, cool!" Steve said, really impressed.

"Thanks!" Satan said, putting out the joint.

And then Satan pulled out Belphegor's autobiography, *Belphegor and Lovin' It!*, and flipped back to where he left off.

"I'm going to see where we're at right now," he said. "Just kick back and relax and listen to the rest of the album."

"Way cool!" Steve said.

Satan smiled at the boy, happy he was able to turn him on to some true metal. He didn't mention that only the late '80s to mid '90s era of the band was good. Maybe the young man would never find out what happened to the band in their later years.

None of that would have happened if Satan was still in office. Sadly, he was only allowed to run for re-election 666 times.

He blamed President Leviathan completely for the state of music today.

The threesome finally arrived in Asmodeus's dance club—*Den-O-Sin*. They discarded their towels near the door and took their clothes from their backpacks and put them on (it was a rule in the sex labyrinth that you had to be wearing nothing but a towel the whole time you were there. Which was convenient because you were often getting naked to have sex.) Luke double-checked to see if they all had their Belphegor cards in their pockets, and seeing that they did, they flashed the cards to the bouncer and gained entry to the club. They went inside.

It was a typical gay dance club. Dark, with lots of flashing lights, it was occupied by throngs of dancing partiers who seemed like they were all on methamphetamines rather than simply being drunk. But still, the line for the bar seemed endless. It was almost too loud to hear anyone speak, so talking was pretty much pointless, unless you screamed into their ear. But no one in the room seemed to have pierced their eardrums. No blood trickled down the necks of any of them. They must've been enjoying the music. And on closer inspection, none of the denizens of *Den-O-Sin* were sinners—they all appeared to be various types of demons, ghouls, and fairies. They were mostly clad in black leather. The smell of sex and sweat was near-overpowering.

And then they noticed Asmodeus in the center of the room, way up on a platform on top of a steel cage that held conjoined twins, *naked*, and making out with each other lasciviously. The cage was suspended from the ceiling by metal chains. But it didn't rock or sway in place, even though Asmodeus danced maniacally to throbbing techno-death.

It was hard to see what he looked like at first, because he appeared to be made out of so many shapes, and too many moving shadows cast over him from the bar's twirling light arrays. But when the song finally reached its end, and it also appeared to be the end of the Satan-forsaken Morbid Angel album (thank god), the demon lord stopped, and was illuminated by the spotlights aimed at him.

The sight of Asmodeus was shocking, to say the least. He looked like no demon they had ever encountered. The demon lord had three heads—one was of a bull, one was of a sheep, and the center one was of a man, which would've looked normal if it weren't for the fact that it was constantly spitting fire. And below was a man's muscular, defined chest, with a perfectly manscaped chest-hair pattern that was surely the envy of all men (even Luke noticed and was a little jealous). But as Asmodeus's treasure trail of sex hair went down his belly and disappeared into his tight pink short-shorts, they were greatly distracted and unnerved by the fact that one of his legs was nothing but a large, thick penis. It was the biggest dick anyone had ever seen. And perfectly shaped too, even for a leg. If you shrank Asmodeus's penis leg down to size, say even to just 9 inches, and put that between your legs, you would be quite popular in this kind of club, to say the least. Asmodeus appeared to have a third one at first, a flesh colored and long wagging penis, but of a normal-sized width. But on closer inspection—it was not a penis.

It was his tail. But it was literally a serpent. Its forked tongue flickered in and out of its mouth, which could have easily been mistaken for the head of a penis.

Asmodeus seemed to have a lot of weird stuff to play with if you wanted to have the most bizarre sex of your life.

The demon lord called to his steed—a lion with wings and the long neck of a dragon (of course), and jumped off of the platform onto its back. Then he rode up to the threesome.

"GREETINGS!" the demon lord greeted, from the mouth of his sheep head.

And then his bull head spoke, "My name is Asmodeus, and I'm a sex addict!"

The man's head just went *"BLEARGH!"* and kept spitting fire.

"Uh…" Luke said. "*Hello.* I'm Luke."

"And who might these two delicious young specimens be?" Asmodeus asked.

"We're Belphegor's," Jasin said quickly, perhaps disgusted by the beast, and then handed him his card.

The demon lord grabbed it and sniffed it disturbingly.

"Ah, Belphegor," the demon lord said. "That sure brings me back."

The Lord of Lust would've looked like he was thinking of him longingly, if he didn't have a goat, a bull, and a man spitting fire for heads.

"So," Luke said. "If everything is in order then, we'll just be on our way."

But then Asmodeus crumpled up the card like it was worthless.

"Oh," he disagreed. "You three are not going *anywhere*."

Holy shit! Jasin mind-screamed to the other two. *Is he supposed to be able to do that?*

Apparently so! Luke thought, panicking.

And then Sandy, almost unconcerned with what was happening, as if she was already pretty complacent in her position as one of Belphegor's minions and didn't think anything bad could happen to them, added, *What does this guy look like, anyway?*

Sandy still couldn't see, because she had no face. She did have *'the sight'*, but it didn't always work on every demon or part of Hell. She was wondering if Asmodeus might just look like the hottest gay man ever.

Oh, Jasin thought, trying to save her from the disappointment. *You don't want to know.*

Asmodeus started snapping his fingers at them, and said, "*Helloooo*, Earth to Belphegor's lapdogs."

Uh-oh, Luke thought. *This can't be good.*

They all stopped using Jasin's frog-mind hive powers and gave Asmodeus their full attention, fearful of what might happen.

"*Look,*" the God of Lust started. "Me and Belphegor go way back. He's the one who helped me get the seed money to open this nightclub here. So what if I developed a little crush on him? He's kind of amazing!"

Sandy nodded her no-face head in agreement. It was kind of true.

"So, I did a little bit of the creepy stalker thing too much, so sue me! I was in love!"

Then Asmodeus stopped recounting the story nicely and became angry.

"But I have never met a person more incapable of returning affection in my life! Who does he think he is, anyway? The Lord of the Third Circle of Hell?"

"He literally is that though, sir," a demonic gay boy nearby suddenly interjected, correcting the demon lord.

"SHUT UP!" Asmodeus shouted, sending a bolt of red electricity at the low-level gay demon without even looking in his direction. The guy turned to ash and crumbled, leaving nothing behind but a pair of leather pants and a cock ring.

This frightened the threesome even more. Even though they knew they would probably regenerate, being murdered by this demon lord in particular seemed like the last way they would want to go.

"So to hell with Belphegor!" the demon yelled. "Access *DENIED!* You are to stay with me for all eternity, here in my massive sex labyrinth. And we are going to listen to the gay Morbid Angel techno-death album, that weird Cryptopsy album with the keyboards, and EVERY Marilyn Manson album and dance *FOREVER!* And you will damn well LIKE IT!"

"NOOOOOO!!!" Luke screamed. *"THAT'S IMPOSSIBLE!"*

Luke just could not deal with that prospect.

And then, suddenly, a familiar voice came from out of nowhere.

"Hey ugly."

The demon Asmodeus peered in that direction,

"Who-?" he asked, caught off guard.

The group turned to see Marvin McMelvin, the Bensalem School Shooter, their *murderer,* standing there free and pointing his gun right at Asmodeus's, uh… *one* of his heads.

"MARVIN!" Jasin shouted.

Marvin ignored him, and stared intently at the demon lord.

"IT'S A GOOD TIME FOR THE GREAT TASTE OF DEATH!" Marvin said, quoting McDonald's with his own sinister twist once more, and then shot the demon lord Asmodeus right in the penis leg.

He crumpled, falling down screaming, clutching what would be the knee on a normal being. But it was nothing but a penis leg.

"OW!" Asmodeus cried. "MY PENIS LEG!"

The crowd went wild and panicked, screaming and running in every direction, as if for the lives. The shot scared the fuck out of them.

Marvin turned his attention away from Asmodeus,

distracted by the ruckus, and yelled, "SHUT UP YOU FUCKERS!"

And then he fired into the crowd with his magic death gun. He cut down gay and leather-clad low-level demons like they were nothing.

"NOOOO!" Asmodeus screamed.

"Holy shit!" Jasin yelled. "It's a gay bar massacre. That's *so not cool, dude!*"

"I know, man," Luke said. "First a school shooting and then a gay bar, that's fucked up."

"Yeah," Sandy said, agreeing. "It's like he should be the poster boy for ISIS."

"Why aren't we mind-talking?" Luke asked.

Jasin just stared at him blankly, and thought at him, *I don't know, why can I hear you?*

They could totally hear each other talking.

"KIDS!" Asmodeus yelled, bleeding all over the floor from his penis leg. "COME HERE!"

"I'm not a kid, but OK," Luke said, coming over with the others to hear what the demon lord had to say.

"Who the hell is that guy and why the fuck does he have the Enchanted Weapon of Archangel David?" the wounded demon lord asked.

"The what?" Luke asked, shocked that Asmodeus actually knew what it was.

"The Enchanted Weapon of Archangel David!" he shouted. "It's the only thing that can permanently kill

a being that exists in the afterlife! We always feared that it was part of god's plan to finally get rid of us all somehow! But that's not fair! We may be demons but most of us are just fallen angels! You could say that we're doing god's work as well down here! Punishing the sinners!"

Luke looked around the room at the *Den-O-Sin* gay bar. If you ignored the dead bodies piling high, the screaming demons unable to escape through the exits, it actually looked like a really fun place for everyone. Who was being punished exactly? Maybe it was what they deserved.

"We don't deserve this!" Asmodeus yelled.

OK, maybe they didn't.

"So, what do you want us to do?" Luke asked. "We've got to get out of here before he shoots us too!"

"Yeah," Sandy the No-Face Girl said. "And he's already done that once before."

"OK," Asmodeus spoke from his bull head. "The weapon must have been given to him by an angel. It could have been anyone on Earth, angels are good at disguising themselves. Him gaining the weapon, the massacre, his entry into Hell—it all must have been part of god's plan. You must reach President Leviathan and tell him everything! He'll know what to do!"

"We were kind of already going to do that anyway," Luke said. "So if you never had tried to stop us in the first place…"

"Forget that now! Now *go!*"

A pink neon light began to emanate from a suddenly materializing door that appeared across the room.

"Go through the gate!" Asmodeus shouted. "Fly!"

The group ran to the other side of the room trying to reach the gate in time.

But Sandy 'looked' back at the fallen demon lord, and asked, "You can't give me back my face either?"

"You look better this way," Asmodeus said.

Sandy turned back and went through the portal, catching Asmodeus's last words before the gate closed: "Tell Belphegor I'll always love him!"

And then Marvin was in front of Asmodeus, the Lord of Lust, gun pointed at... one of his heads as he lay on the ground, helpless.

"Look for the Golden Arches," Marvin said, cocking his gun.

"*...OF DEATH!*"

He fired, blowing off Asmodeus's man head. The bull head snorted and the sheep head let out a terrified bleat.

It took a while, but after the Bensalem School Shooter shot Asmodeus in his bull head, and his sheep head, the Demon Lord of Lust was finally dead.

Dead forever.

CHAPTER 666
PART ELEVEN: THE FINAL CHAPTER – 9TH CIRCLE PRESIDENT LEVIATHAN

"What happens now?"

"Who said that?" Jasin asked, looking around. It wasn't him, Luke, Sandy, or even The Nameless One, who lay on the ground bleeding from his bloody stumps.

Sadly, the *Den-O-Sin* Gay Bar Shooter had shot off both of his legs.

"It is he," The Nameless One said, weakly. "He who makes word."

They all looked skywards again, wondering where *he* could be, or if *he* even existed.

"If *he* is real," Jasin asked. "Why doesn't he help us?"

"Why doesn't he give me back my face?" Sandy wondered.

"Or make it so we were never even killed in the first

place," Luke said, making the most sense.

"And I my legs, my arms," The Nameless One said, sadly. "Would have if him only give me a name."

They all kept searching the sky, standing around, wasting a lot of time instead of moving on to advance the story.

"FINE!" I shouted, looking forward to getting pizza at the Beach Bite before they closed at ten, which wouldn't be possible if these damned kids were waiting around all night for me to name their stupid demon pal.

I went to the window, brushing the Halloween spiders out of the way, and opened it in the storm. Whipping winds and rain peppered my face. I shouted into the night,

"AZAZEL!"

The lights flickered like they were going to go out, but then brightened again. Back in Hell, Azazel smiled.

"My legs!" he exclaimed. "My legs grow back!"

And then he noticed the growing protrusions coming from his sides.

"And my arms!" he said. "My arms come back!"

The group marveled at the ecstatic transformation.

"WOW!" Jasin said, witnessing the magic unfold, like the rest of the group.

Sandy felt for her face, thinking that it would have returned. But she felt nothing. She still had no face.

"*DAMMIT!*" she yelled, really disappointed.

Azazel stood, and checked out his new body. It was

exactly the same as before, so it was only *kind of* new. In a sense.

"Check you out, Azazel!" Luke said, smiling. "Lookin' good!"

"Yeah, dude!" Jasin agreed. "You look just like you did when we first met, all those hours ago."

"Yeah, but they seemed like *days*," Luke kidded.

"I can't see!" Sandy whined, probably never seeing anything again in her life.

"Azazel happy," the demon guide said, wiping a tear from his eye.

"Hey guys, did you forget about me?" a voice said from out of nowhere.

"STEVE!" Jasin said excitedly, since it was Steve who said that and not Marvin McMelvin, Gay Bar and School Shooter.

"Where have you been?" Luke said, rushing over with the rest of the group to greet him.

Steve hung out of a portal suspended in mid-air, sitting halfway inside it comfortably.

"Oh," he said, braggingly. "I've just been hanging out with my pal *Satan!*"

"Hey guys!" Satan said, poking his red head out of the portal from behind Steve. "It's me! *SATAN!*"

"OH MY GOD! SATAN!" Sandy yelled. "I'm a huge fan!"

Luke went to shake his hand.

"Officer Lucas Kapowksi. Pleased to meet you, Satan."

Satan winked at him as he shook his hand.

"Yeah," Jasin said. "Thank you for saving our friend, Steve."

"Not a problem!"

The group smiled all around (except for Sandy, who had no face, making that impossible). Steve climbed out of the portal to join.

"So long, Steve!" Satan said, saying his farewell to the boy. Satan felt like he had done a good job with him. The kid was into some true metal now, dressed like a real headbanger, and didn't look like a total poseur anymore. Satan grabbed his copy of *Belphegor and Lovin' It!*

"Hey kid!" he shouted, calling back Steve.

Steve finished hugging his friends and turned back to Satan.

"Don't forget this," he said, handing it back to him.

Steve grabbed the book from Lord Satan and smiled.

"You're going to *love* the ending," Satan smiled back, happy to leave the boy with a parting gift.

"Uh, Satan?" Sandy spoke up, kind of sheepishly.

"Yes, little girl?"

"Can you give me my face back?"

Satan smirked, and said, "No."

And with that, he leaned back into his portal and

disappeared with it, leaving the group on their own.

"Dammit!" Sandy shouted, and then muttered under her breath, "I should have gotten his autograph."

"Well," Steve said. "What happens now?"

"Hell House," Azazel suggested, pointing in the general direction of it. He was able to do that this time, because he had clawed fingers on his hands that were attached to arms that were attached to his torso, instead of the naked stumps that he used to have there.

They looked at the horizon, and over the hill, or just generally over there somewhere—at what could only be described as an exact replica of the American White House in Washington, D.C., complete with a green-grassed lawn and red, white and blue flags flapping in the breeze under a clear blue sky, sat there in the 9th Circle of Hell, awaiting the group.

"I guess we get our asses over there and complete our mission," Luke said.

"Yeah," Jasin agreed. "And we better get a move on. Marvin is probably hot on our trail."

"I have a thing or two to say to this President Leviathan," Steve said, anxious to meet him.

"Maybe he can give me back my face!" Sandy said, with a hopeful sense of excitement.

The boys laughed at her.

"Sandy, *c'mon*," Luke said. "If you haven't gotten your face back by now it's doubtful that you're ever going to."

Sandy frowned, but not really. Because she had no face.

"Alright, then," Luke said. "Jasin! Can you keep us in contact the whole time with your frog hive-mind?"

"Sure can do, Officer Kapowski!" Jasin replied, trying to sound all official-like.

"Good," Luke said, looking towards the Hell House.

"I have a feeling things are about to get very fishy…"

The group stood in the Oval Office of Hell, which was more like a pentagram shape, so you should probably call it the Pentagrammatic Office or something. Azazel was not with them, though, because he was not let past security. They had had no problem whatsoever walking across the final circle of Hell's… uh, *White House lawn* and gaining access to it to see the president. They didn't even have to flash their Belphegor cards. They were expected.

President Leviathan was sitting in his pentagram office's desk chair, with his back turned to the group. He was apparently putting his tie on using the mirror on the other side of his desk. When he finished, the satanic demon lord of Hell spun around in his chair to face the group, and what they saw shocked them.

President Leviathan was nothing but a big wet fish in a business suit. Not even like a humanoid-like fish. He was just like a giant trout that was shoved sideways into a suit like a sardine. Only one side of his head faced them, and his big grotesque fish eye reflected the ceiling lights in its dead blackness. Facing them this way, his mouth appeared like it was on the top of his head, pointing upwards. His fin, or arm (?), protruded from a short sleeve in the middle of his chest. He still had a nice blazer that hung on his 'shoulders' somehow. Jasin looked under the desk to see his wide fish-fin tail coming out the bottom of his super-wide pants, which he only had one leg of on his body. The tail moved around down there mermaid-like. It was astonishing that he could even sit in a chair.

"GLUB GLUB GLUB!" President Leviathan said to the group.

"Uh…" Luke said, not knowing what to say. "Excuse me?"

"GLUB GLUB GLUB!" President Leviathan said again, but this time slapping his arm-fin against the desk furiously.

It went *SLAP! SLAP! SLAP!* and made wet squishy noises. A drop of fish oil splattered across his desk and some hit Steve in the eye.

"OW, MAN!" Steve shouted. "My eye!"

"GLUB GLUB GLUB!!!" President Leviathan pressed on, as if he was extremely angry with them.

"Maybe he just needs to be in the water," Sandy suggested.

Luke thought that she might be onto something.

"Is that it, Leviathan?" he said, like he was talking to a cute puppy dog. "Do you need to be in the water? Huh? Do ya?"

"GLUB GLUB GLUB GLUB GLUB!!!" President Leviathan shouted again, smacking his fin against his desk more furiously.

"Where are we going to even find water in Hell?" Jasin asked.

"I don't know, man!" Steve shouted. "But we better save him!"

The group started approaching the president like they were going to save him, whether he liked it or not. They were fully prepared to drag the president out onto the Hell House's front lawn, and find a pond or maybe even a garden hose just to hose him down with or whatever. It had to be done. The president was a fish out of water and he had to be saved.

But then Virginia suddenly emerged from the mirror behind President Leviathan and grabbed him from behind.

"REMEMBER ME?!" she said like a woman scorned, claws pointed at Leviathan's belly like she was going to gut him.

"No," Luke said. "Are we supposed to?"

"Yeah," Steve said. "We've kind of met a lot of other demons on this journey, so…"

"It's me!" she said, all pissed off. "VIRGINIA!"

"Does that ring a bell, anyone?" Jasin asked, looking

around at the group.

"No," Sandy replied. "Sure doesn't."

"*NYEAARGH!*" Virginia yelled, and then sunk her long vampire fangs into President Leviathan's neck.

"GLUBGLUBGLUBGLUBGLUBGLUB!!!!!!" President Leviathan screamed frantically, flapping his fin against his desk in agony.

"LEVIATHAN, *NO!!!!!*" Jasin shouted, and then leapt across the room to come to his aid.

But he was smacked out of the way by Leviathan's tail, which was flailing about uncontrollably. He hit the wall with a loud crack and slumped to the ground, broken.

"Quick, guys!" Sandy said. "Think of something!"

"My light sword!" Luke remembered, retrieving it from his backpack.

He ignited it just by taking it out. Its green fire shone like the weapon of a true officer of Hell. He gripped the handle with both hands, flexing his biceps and taking an attack stance. He actually took fencing at the academy. He wanted to add a lot of useful things to his skill set in case he ever found himself in situations like this.

Luke was going to decapitate that vampire bitch and get rid of her once and for all. Yes, he remembered her.

"HOLD IT RIGHT THERE," a voice said from behind him. And then he felt a gun being pressed against his temple.

"*Goddamnit,*" Luke muttered under his breath.

"Hi, Marvin."

Luke lowered his sword without even being told to. It was like he was already defeated. If only he could use the Force...

"But we have to save him!" Sandy pleaded.

Virginia was still tearing into the president's neck with her razor-sharp teeth, sucking all of the fishy, oily blood out of his body. It smelled really, *really* bad.

"*Glub! Glub! Glub. Glub. Glub... glub... glub...*" the president went, hardly protesting anymore. His fin was barely slapping against the desk anymore as well.

"But he's dying!" Steve shouted.

Marvin smiled, and said, "I know... I'm *lovin' it.*"

And then he kicked Luke out of the way and pointed his gun at the president, ready to fire, vampire on his back and all.

But then Marvin felt a gun pressed against the back of *his* head. He grimaced.

"Drop it or I'll drop you," a stern voice said.

Marvin grinned, and said, "But I'll just regenerate."

"Oh really? You think so?" the voice said. A click was heard as the weapon cocked. "Go ahead and try me. See what will happen."

Marvin began to wonder if he should begin to worry or not.

And then the perpetrator put their mouth against his ear and whispered—"*I know what you did last summer.*"

Marvin dropped his gun.

It clattered to the floor.

"Grab that!" the voice commanded, and Luke retrieved the weapon and pointed it at Marvin.

From across the room, Jasin regained consciousness. What he saw shocked him.

Their savior cracked the Bensalem School Shooter across the back of the head with her weapon, and he fell to the floor instantly unconscious from the mighty blow. And that's when everyone finally got a good look at who it was.

"HILLARY CLINTON!?!" they all shouted in unison.

"That's *Vice President* Hillary Clinton, thank you!" the former U.S. Secretary of State said, badassingly.

Everyone smiled. She was just *so fucking cool.*

"Luke," she said. "Hand me the weapon."

"Yes, ma'am!"

"And take mine, but keep it pointed at this stupid fucking McDonald's employee. We'll deal with him in a second."

"Can do!" Luke said, happy to be helping out the *vice president.* He was hoping that this could turn into a full time job, even. Maybe he could be part of *Satan's Secret Service!*

"Ah!" Hillary Clinton said, inspecting the weapon. "Just as I thought—*The Enchanted Weapon of the Archangel David!*"

She pointed it at Virginia, and said, "Get away

from him, you *bitch!*"

Virginia put up her hands in surrender, and backed away from the president. She was surprisingly terrified at the sight of Hillary Clinton, which was strange because Virginia still looked like a big malevolent vampire, demonic wings and all.

"Glub?" President Leviathan asked.

Hillary Clinton met his eye with hers, and then looked back at Virginia. A vengeful look overtook her face, and Vice President Hillary Clinton pointed the weapon at Virginia the vampire and said, "Glub."

And then she pulled the trigger.

The bullet pierced through Virginia's black, dead heart and she instantly exploded in flames. Little black ashes rained down upon the group, dissipating before they could land. Jasin swore that they were shaped like tiny hearts.

Hillary Clinton blew the smoke from the barrel of the gun, and holstered it, as if she always carried a gun on her. (*She did. Trump supporters…*)

"Now that that's that," she said. "Let's get to business."

She recognized the young superhero and called him by name.

"Ah! The Frogger!"

Jasin smiled.

"I'm a big fan," she said.

"Why thank you President Clinton!"

"That's *Vice* President Clinton," she smiled. "I'm not president. *Yet...*"

She winked at him after she said that, like it was supposed to be their little secret.

"Anyway, young man," she readdressed him. "Would you mind applying first aid to President Leviathan? He looks a little worse for wear."

"Sure thing, Vice President Clinton!"

Jasin leaped over the president's desk and sat crouched on it, frog-like, and started making a slimy secretion with his mouth and spitting it on President Leviathan's wounds.

"*GLUBGLUBGLUB!!!*" the president shouted, flapping his fins up and down energetically. You couldn't really tell if he was grossed out by the boy, or all excited to be safe now, or what. The president of Hell was just a big burbling fish.

Everyone could see who the *real* president of Hell was—*Hillary Clinton.*

"And you two," she said, addressing Luke and Steve. "Can you please get this man tied up tightly and then throw some water on his face to wake him up?"

"No problem, Vice President Clinton!" Luke said helpfully, and he and Steve got to work.

"And young Sandy," Hillary Clinton said, looking for the girl. "Where are you?"

"Right here, Mrs. Clinton," Sandy said, pulling

down the hood on her invisible cloak. "I got really frightened so I decided to hide until it was all over."

Vice President Clinton smiled, and said, "No problem! Now come here, I have a surprise for you."

Sandy walked up to her, and Hillary flashed her hand at the girl really fast as if she was going to push her face in with the palm of her hand.

"IN YOUR FACE!" the vice president shouted all of a sudden, taking the young girl by surprise.

Sandy screamed and stumbled backwards, having no time or warning to have dodged the sudden attack.

Hillary Clinton laughed.

Sandy righted herself, and then felt for her face.

"My face!" she gasped. "My face is back! Oh my god! Thank you! Thank you, Mrs. Clinton!"

The vice president of Hell walked up to her, and removed the young girl's glasses from her face.

"There we go," she said. "You won't be needing *these* anymore. You're quite the pretty girl, you know."

The vice president wiped the hair out of Sandy's face, and the young girl blushed.

"Why... *thank you,* Mrs. Clinton! You are the kindest person ever!"

Sandy beamed, not only happy to have her face back, but thrilled that she would never have to wear glasses again. (She actually didn't need to do this the whole time, just like how she didn't need her inhaler anymore. Her asthma was gone since she died. But Sandy didn't know that. She was like a living plot hole. A literally *dead* girl, but living plot hole. A big enigma wrapped in a bundle of stupidity. I'm sorry she wasn't killed off, actually. I'm sick of having to write witty excuses for her.)

"Alright!" Hillary Clinton said. "Let's get back to business!"

Luke and Steve had Marvin McMelvin tied up and ready for her, and he was finally coming to. And Jasin had completely healed the satanic fish president with his superhuman saliva, and the deep-sea demon flapped his fins happily, going *glub glub glub!*

Hillary Clinton smacked the Bensalem School Shooter across the face. *"WHERE DID YOU GET THIS, YOU SON OF A BITCH?!"*

She was holding onto the weapon in her holster so he could see that she had it.

"OK, *OK...*" he said. "I'll tell you the truth, but you might not believe me."

Hillary looked around the room, and saw the fish president, the frog kid, and the pile of ashes that was once a goth vampire, and remembered the fact that they were also all in the 9th Circle of Hell, and said, "Try me."

Marvin McMelvin smiled and his eyes lit up, like he was about to tell her the most fantastic thing ever.

"Ronald McDonald gave it to me."

"Jesus!" she cursed. "I knew it!"

"What?" Luke asked. "Ronald McDonald, the McDonald's clown?"

"Yes," Hillary Clinton said. "Or better known as— *Jesus Christ the Son of God.*"

Marvin smiled, and said, "I love Jesus."

"Really?!" Steve asked, dumbfounded, as they all were.

"Jesus Christ was really just Ronald McDonald this whole time?"

"Yes," Hillary Clinton confirmed. "And he was sent to Earth from heaven almost a hundred years ago, to open a burger franchise and convert *billions* to his fast food cult."

"Woah," Steve said, mind blown.

"Wait," Jasin asked. "If Ronald McDonald is Jesus, then who is god?"

"Eh," Hillary Clinton replied. "He's just god. Same as he's always been. A bit of a megalomaniac, but who isn't these days."

"And he will smite you along with every other McDonald's-hating sinner upon the face of the Earth!" Marvin spewed venomously. *"As in Hell as on Earth!* JUST LOOK FOR THE GOLDEN ARCHES! BLESSED BE HIS NAME, RONALD MCDONALD! THE ONE AND ONLY TRUE GOD!"

Marvin was gleaming, looking upward like a raving lunatic. He was definitely two fries short of a Happy Meal.

"Hey Marvin," Hillary Clinton said, pressing the gun against his forehead. He tried looking at her but just ended up cross-eyed as he stared down the barrel. "When you see the Golden Arches, tell 'em Hillary sent ya!"

And then she put a bullet from the Enchanted Weapon of the Archangel David between his eyes, and bright yellow streams of light poured from cracks opening on his body and he exploded, raining secret sauce all over them like it was what he was made of.

Everyone shielded their eyes, but then found themselves licking the sauce off of their hands because honestly, it did taste really good.

"OK," Hillary said. "Now that that's solved, let's get you kids on your way."

"Uh," Luke protested. "But I'm not a kid. I'm a 35-year-old man."

Hillary Clinton snapped her fingers.

"Not anymore you're not."

Luke magically lost twenty years of aging in seconds, reverting to how he looked when he was an actual teenager.

"I'm young again!" Luke shouted, kind of unsure how he felt about that.

"So," Jasin said. "I guess it's back to Lord Belphegor. We belong to *him* now."

"Pish-posh," Hillary Clinton disagreed. "You've all completed your mission, and then some."

"But he'll be waiting for us," Sandy said. "He might get angry…"

"Oh, he's *angry* all right…" Hillary said.

"Guards!" she snapped. "Bring him in."

Two demon Secret Service men dragged Belphegor into the pentagram-shaped oval office. He was shackled at the legs by unbreakable mystical chains, which just looked like normal chains since you didn't know how magical they were.

"Drop him!" Hillary Clinton commanded.

Belphegor fell to his knees in shame in front of the Vice President of Hell.

"BELPHEGOR?!" the group all shouted in unison, totally surprised to see him.

"Uh…" Belphegor said sheepishly, hardly able to look at the group. "Hey guys."

"Belphegor? Heh. More like *USURPER,*" Hillary Clinton accused.

"*Wha?*" Sandy said, a little confused by this turn of events.

"Belphegor was just using you all along as bait, *fish bait*, if you will, to have President Leviathan assassinated so he could take the throne in the Hell House! He even released Mr. McMelvin *on purpose*, knowing he would follow you all here. He's still sore about losing the election, aren't you, you poor little *SORE LOSER?*"

Hillary Clinton imitated him by pouting and

rubbing away fake tears rolling down her face.

Belphegor sneered,

"THE THRONE IS *MINE!* I DESERVE IT! I MADE THE MOST MONEY THIS QUARTER! I'M THE RICHEST DEMON IN HELL! THE *RICHEST!!!*"

"You should know by now that money doesn't buy power!" Hillary Clinton said, and then tapped her finger against her temple.

"*Brains* do."

Lucifer shook his head angrily at her, sneering so hard he looked like his head was going to explode.

"*CURSE YOU, HILLARY CLINTON!*"

Hillary just smirked at him.

"Take him outside, boys," she commanded the demon agents. "Chain him up out front near the house. I think President Leviathan has a brand new *water boy!*"

"*GLUBGLUBGLUB!*" the fish lord shouted excitedly, flapping his fin hand around in joy.

"And as for you all," Hillary said as she turned to the crew. "You're going back to Earth."

"What?!" Jasin said. "*Really?!*"

Hillary Clinton smiled.

"Yes, really."

"NO. FUCKING. WAY." Steve said.

"Consider it a reward for putting up with '*Lord*' Belphegor," Hillary rolled her eyes for a second. "I'm sorry, excuse me, I mean 'Lord of my *ASS*' Belphegor."

The crew laughed. That was funny as hell. The vice president ruled.

"You all were never supposed to go to Hell anyway. You were all just pawns in Belphegor's game. You all should've been up near the Golden Arches eating double cheeseburgers for the rest of eternity instead of getting caught up in *this* mess."

A bright blue light slowly appeared across the room, growing brighter, as the frame of a doorway manifested. The gateway opened, and bright blue light splashed across their faces. It smelled like the ocean. It was Earth. They were going back home.

"So I guess this is goodbye," Luke said, about seven inches shorter now that he had regained his youth. Hillary Clinton had to kneel a bit when she hugged him. She is like 6 foot 6 in Hell.

"Be good, Lucas Kapowksi," she said as she embraced him. "Don't forget to use the Force!"

Luke smiled as he turned away to exit through the door out of Hell. He would. He would use the Force. *And* he was going to get to see *Star Wars Episode VIII*! That was going to be the best thing ever!

"Goodbye, Vice President Clinton!" Jasin said, and Hillary hugged him tightly.

"Oh, my little Frogger!" she said, and then looked at him with a smile. "You're going to be one of the best

Philadelphia Avengers ever!"

"Really?" Jasin asked, starry-eyed.

"Really, kiddo. Now go!"

Jasin followed Luke out the door and back to his future, which was apparently going to be everything he had ever dreamed of.

Sandy nearly ran at Clinton to give her a hug, and hit her with a bit of a thud.

"UMPH!" Hillary said, wrapping her arms around the girl.

"Thank you, Mrs. Clinton!" Sandy cried. "Thank you for giving me back my face!"

"Oh, that reminds me", Hillary said, reaching for some things in her pocket. "You're going to need these."

It was Sandy's inhaler and glasses.

Sandy frowned.

Hillary pouted for her, and said,

"Sorry, kid. But that's the way the cookie crumbles."

Sandy reached for a smile, found it, and showed it to Hillary, like it was going to be OK.

"It's OK, Mrs. Clinton," she said. "I'm just happy to be alive."

"Stay safe, kiddo!"

Sandy Hook followed her friends through the doorway, curious whether or not they would just appear right back at school before the shooting or what. Maybe they would come back in real time, who knows? She couldn't wait to see.

Steve followed right behind her.

"Steven S. Stevenson!" Hillary shouted.

Steve turned around and said,

"Yes, Mrs. Clinton..." He looked at his feet, embarrassed.

"Get over here, you're not leaving without a hug either."

Steve went up and hugged her, and she said,

"I know it's hard to say goodbye, but we all have to leave the nest sometime."

"It's not that, Mrs. Clinton. I was just hoping that..." he discontinued, out of fear of offending her. "You know... I just wanted to say goodbye to..."

"*SATAN!?*" Satan asked, suddenly appearing from out of nowhere.

"SATAN!" Steve yelled, running over to give his hero a big hug.

Hillary smiled at them, having planned this surprise reunion all along.

"STEVE!" He hugged him back tightly, and then smiled at the kid. "I told you you were going to *love* the ending!"

"I couldn't have imagined, Satan! I'm so glad I didn't skip ahead!"

"Good things always come to those who wait!"

"They do, Satan! They do! *All. Good. Things.*" Steve started to tear up, but then stopped, because he didn't want Satan to see him cry.

"It's OK, Steve," Satan said, comforting him. "I know you're not a pussy."

"Thank you, Satan!"

"Now run and join your friends! I think you're going to like where you end up." Satan winked at him.

"OK, Satan! But I'll miss you!"

"I'll miss you too, kid!"

Steve turned to go out through the portal, and into his future. He turned back and said, "Thank you, Mrs. Clinton. Thank you for giving me a second chance. A second chance at *life.*"

"You're welcome, Steven! Have a good time."

Steve smiled back at her.

"Oh, and Steve!" Satan said, like he suddenly just remembered. "One more thing!"

Steve looked back at him excited to hear what he was going to say.

"Morbid Angel is going to start putting out good albums again, just you wait!"

"*REALLY?!* No way!"

"Yes way."

"Are you going to be involved?"

"I might just have something to do with it..." Satan grinned and winked at him.

"Now get back to your friends, Steve! And you all be good to each other!"

"Goodbye, Satan! I love you!"

And with that final farewell, Steve stepped through the magical portal in the "White House" of the 9th Circle of Hell—the *final* circle, and back onto Earth, his life returned to him.

He put one foot on the sand, and then the other. The bright sun almost blinded him, so he briefly shielded his eyes. And then he heard the ocean.

"Where are we?" he asked his friends, who he could tell were nearby.

"NEW JERSEY! WHOO-HOOO!" Luke said, like it was the best place on Earth.

"And it's July!" Sandy said. "School's out!"

Steve noticed the people frolicking on the beach together, having fun in the sun.

"I'm going to need *a lot* of sunblock," Jasin said, smiling. "But I *can't wait* to hit the water!"

"WHOO-HOO!" Steve shouted, and pounded his fist up in the air, "BENSALEM TOWNSHIP HIGH SCHOOL FOREVER!"

They all jumped up in the air like it was going to be the best summer of their lives.

And that was the story of how five completely different people—a goth, a headbanger, a cop, a geek, and a *frog-person*—died in a massacre at their high school, went to Hell, met Satan, got involved in a pyramid scheme, defeated Belphegor, and saved the president.

They might have been young (*Millennials*, they called them) but they proved they were tomorrow's future, and that they were going to make that future a bright one.

Oh, and they all had Philly accents the whole time.

THE END.

POSTLOGUE

Azazel, our formerly nameless demon guide, was waiting in a room or something for the teens to come back.

"Hello? Guys? Where go?"

Azazel was sad. And alone.

"They were my favorite sinners I ever had. They not even say goodbye. No new ones could ever replace them."

Azazel had a tear in his eye.

And then suddenly, a bright black light (like, blacklight-colored) appeared and burst forth with a new sinner.

The damned soul hung in midair until the light disappeared, and then fell to the ground in a heap. They got up off their knees and dusted them off. The sinner saw Azazel and smiled.

"Hi! Is this Hell?!"

"Yes," Azazel replied, looking at the man (or woman?) curiously. "This Hell."

"*Wonderful!* My name is *Marilyn Manson!* And I guess I've come to keep you company!"

Marilyn Manson put his arm around Azazel's shoulder. One of his fake tits hit Azazel in the eye.

"We're going to be the best friends ever! I can *feel* it!" the goth singer said.

Azazel frowned, and screamed, "NOOOOOO!!!!!"

THE END, AGAIN.

Azazel will return in… *AZAZEL AND THE SPACE MONSTER ON FIRE*

ABOUT THE AUTHOR

Vince Kramer has lived in exactly three cities that start with
a P: Philadelphia, Phoenix, and Portland. He is the author of
four "word" novels – *Gigantic Death Worm*, *Death Machines of
Death*, *Deadly Lazer Explodathon*, and *Hell of Death*. He is one
of the few gay authors who is actually good looking

To Win Her Back

A Players Series Novel

Mackenzie Crowne

LYRICAL PRESS
Kensington Publishing Corp.
www.kensingtonbooks.com

First Electronic Edition: January 2017
eISBN-13: 978-1-60183-996-1
eISBN-10: 1-60183-996-0

First Print Edition: January 2017
ISBN-13: 978-1-60183-998-5
ISBN-10: 1-60183-998-7

Printed in the United States of America

For the talented and intense gridiron warriors who feed my football hun-

ger year after year.

Go Pats!

Chapter 1

"All right. Last item. I want Samuel Fitzpatrick, people, and I won't take 'no' for an answer."

Victoria Price choked, nearly spewing a mouthful of sparkling water over the half-dozen paper-pushing office jocks seated at the long conference table. Every eye in the room turned her way. She gasped, struggling to drag in a lungful of oxygen as the air in the Manhattan Marauders' well-appointed conference suite suddenly evaporated.

Attempting to disguise her dismay, she pasted on an apologetic smile and blindly set aside the bottle in her hand. Unfortunately, the thick binder in front of her ruined her aim. She bolted forward as the bottle tipped, fumbling to catch it before the contents spilled onto the glossy teakwood.

Beside her, Tom Walden leaned in and whispered, "You okay, V?"

She shot the Marauders' players' liaison a sidelong glance. The concern in his blue eyes made her wince before panic set in. God. Did he know about her and Sam? How? And since when?

The answer smacked her in the forehead like a flat palm. *Jake, that son of a bitch.* She was going to strangle him and bloody his big mouth.

No. That couldn't be right. She was simply being paranoid. Guilty relief eased the panic as quickly as it had come. Tom and Jake might have been friends since before she'd followed Jake to New York, dragging her battered heart behind her, but he wouldn't blab about something so private. Jake wouldn't do that. Not to her. He wouldn't dare.

She forced a smile, nodded at Tom, and shot a nervous glance down the table. At the far end, Caroline Wainwright quirked a quizzical brow.

"Sorry. Clumsy." V offered the team's owner a sickly smile then quickly looked away. She set the bottle to rights and, feigning a casualness she wasn't close to feeling, snatched up her copy of the afternoon's meeting schedule and scanned the bullet points. The blood drained from her head as her gaze stalled on Sam's name.

Holy hell! How the hell did I miss that? Her heart performed a manic thump-and-roll in her chest, and her fingers jerked involuntarily on the page.

Across from her, George Tipton, the team's general manager, leaned on his elbows and shook his head. "I thought Fitzpatrick had been scratched from the list. He's still under contract."

With a manicured fingernail, Caroline tapped out three staccato beats on the tabletop. Determination narrowed her keen green eyes. "Not for long. His contract runs out in less than two weeks and, from what I understand, negotiations have stalled. Bob Duggan insists Fitzgerald is the best man to replace him. I agree." She shifted her gaze to V. "I want you to take the lead on this."

V's stomach muscles clenched, and she stared at the woman she considered a friend as well as her boss. In the seven years since Caroline had acquired the Marauders franchise, she'd shown an uncanny knack for assembling winning teams, both on and off the field. Three trips to the big game had netted two rings for her players and staff, and made her a force to be reckoned with across the league. With very few exceptions, Caroline got what she wanted. V had no interest in handing her a rare defeat.

Despite herself, she couldn't help the rush of pride over Caroline's recognition of Sam's talents. With several Division Two championships on his résumé, he definitely had the chops to take over as the team's offensive coordinator when Bob left. But, damn it! Their disastrous history made V the last person on Earth who should be negotiating his hire.

And there was no freaking way she was admitting that in front of the office jocks or Caroline.

V wracked her brain for a believable excuse to decline the task, one that wouldn't send up any red flags with her friend, and came up with zilch. Still, it wasn't in her to back down. "I'm your PR consultant, Caroline, not one of your scouts."

"You grew up in the same town. You know him."

Well, yeah, but…. "I knew him a long time ago, and we weren't exactly friends." Guilt weighed down her heart. There was a time she and Sam had been good friends. More than friends, in fact. Then she'd gone and screwed up. Big time.

"He knows you, and that's what counts." Caroline flicked her hand in a dismissive slash, and shards of brilliant color shot from the customized Super Bowl diamond gracing her finger. "Anyway, the offer has nothing to do with friendship. It's a business proposition, and you're part of this business."

True, and V loved her job far more than she'd expected when she'd been offered a position with the team. After twelve years of scrambling to keep Jake Malone's image out of the crapper, her lifelong friend and famous client had traded in his playboy status for the family plan, and his cleats and helmet for wingtips and a microphone. She'd long since limited her client list to him alone and their association had left her wealthy enough that jumping back into the cutthroat world of representation held little interest. Retirement, however, was out of the question. She'd needed a new challenge, and Caroline had stepped in to provide it.

However, approaching Sam Fitzpatrick with an offer to come to Manhattan was more of a challenge than V had bargained for.

She mentally clamped down on the rush of alarm threatening to engulf her and held Caroline's steady gaze. "Does he know the Marauders are looking at him?"

"He will when you tell him." The team's owner pushed to her feet and held out her hand to the ever-present assistant waiting at her back. Accepting an envelope, she slid it across the table to V. "Our offer and all the incidentals are inside. Bob's in his office. He's expecting you. He'll answer any questions you might have. In the meantime, Fitzpatrick is accepting some kind of award during the half-time ceremonies tomorrow night at your old high school. Your flight for Texas leaves at ten AM."

V bit back a panicked groan, and any argument she might have made died on her lips as Caroline swept from the room with her assistant on her heels. The office jocks gathered binders and cups, then wandered off to their cubicles throughout the complex. Teeth gritted, V slid her flight itinerary from the envelope and sighed. At least she wouldn't be spending the night.

Barlow, Texas.

She squeezed her eyes shut. What were the odds she could slip in and out of town without the residents finding out? Her throat went dry and she swallowed against the invisible layer of east Texas dust she'd never been able to completely scrape off her tongue.

As if going back wasn't bad enough. The thought of facing Sam....

She refused to throw up.

Eighteen hours later, her stomach was still giving her fits as she slowed her rental car to a stop in the parking lot of Barlow High's football stadium. She glanced around and couldn't help a reminiscent smirk. The field on the edge of town had been ground zero for the football-crazy citizens of Barlow since before man had walked on the moon. Calling the place a stadium, however, was a stretch.

A faded blue, polyurethane oval circled the battered grass field. Perched atop the far set of bleachers and emblazoned with a fiery red rocket, the two-level press box sported a new coat of white paint, as did the concession stand at the far end of the field.

It was early yet, with more than an hour until kickoff. The parking lot and stands sat mostly empty, but the home team boys went through their warm-ups on the field. Smoke curled from behind the gymnasium, suggesting the boosters were on hand and had fired up the grills. Soon the enticing scents of grilling burgers and popping corn would greet the crowds streaming in for tonight's gridiron battle.

The late afternoon sun hung low on the horizon. To V's left, heat waves shimmered off the empty, time-dulled metal bones of the home-team bleachers. She eyed the spot beneath them where she'd unwillingly lost her "kiss cherry" to Brian Hayes during the last quarter of the homecoming game in her junior year. She flexed the fingers of her right hand and her lips thinned at the memory. The shock on Brian's face after her fist had connected with his eye had been worth the bruised knuckles.

Rolling her shoulders, she squinted through the windshield. She ignored the uniformed teenagers doing calisthenics on the fifty-yard line to scan the gathered crowd of adult males stalking the sidelines. Unfortunately, she found no sign of the muscular form that insisted on haunting her dreams.

She sighed. From what she knew, Sam's parents had remained in Florida after he'd graduated, and the home he'd grown up in had been sold long ago. Presenting the team's offer to him in private would be preferable, but with no idea where he now lived, she'd have to take what she could get. She could either wait until he showed up at the game and hope she'd get a moment to speak to him privately, or swing by the gossip central counter at the Barlow Inn and inquire after his address.

She stiffened her shoulders against a shudder. *No way in hell.* Esther Gimmly not only ran the only motel in town, she chaired the local chapter of the chamber of commerce and had been president of the town's unofficial grapevine since before the advent of the cell phone. She was also V's mother's best friend and would no doubt inform Anita Price of her daughter's reappearance in Barlow before the bell on the Inn's front door stopped chiming.

On the passenger seat, V's leather Gucci satchel buzzed. Shifting into park, she pulled her phone from the outside sleeve. She growled deep in her throat at her mother's name on the screen. For God's sake. She'd driven into town three minutes ago and had yet to speak to a single soul. Had the chamber of commerce installed satellite surveillance?

Shaking her head, she slid from the car, shut the door, and tucked the phone into the pocket of her blazer. Unanswered. If she was going to speak to Sam after all these years, she needed to do so with a clear head. She'd deal with Mom later.

She slumped against the hood. Sam was supposedly receiving his award at half time, but she knew damn well he wouldn't disappoint the townsfolk by missing a single second of the game. He'd be in his seat before the coin toss. All she had to do was wait—and ignore the nerves ricocheting around in her belly like pinballs on crack.

Five minutes later, sweat had begun to pool between her breasts. She swore beneath her breath. It figured a heatwave would accompany her on this fool's errand. Slipping open the button on her blazer, she flapped the lapels to create a breeze. She'd chosen the sleekly sophisticated suit because the crisp cut and creamy color pronounced her a serious businesswoman, and the heavy weave would protect her from the chill winds that usually blew this time of year. More importantly, the skirt and blazer held no resemblance to the worn jeans and football jersey she'd worn the last time she'd seen Sam.

When she'd literally added insult to injury by walking out on him wearing his number emblazoned on her back.

The all-too-familiar spiral of bittersweet memories and regret twisted her insides into knots, and she yanked the blazer off her shoulders and down her arms. What would life have been like if she hadn't been such a coward? If she'd been upfront with him from the beginning? The instant chilling of her blood took care of the clammy sweat.

Even fifteen years later, the thought of baring her soul to him, to anyone, left her cold. And damn it, exposing the vile secret she'd kept locked away in the dark recesses of her mind hadn't been necessary. Not with Sam. When he'd touched her, the past hadn't mattered. To her utter surprise and joy, the warm touch of his lips brushing hers had banished the memories of hot breath stinking of whiskey. His big hands were gentle, his touch sensual instead of sickening. And far from frightening, the press of his solid body against hers was exciting.

She'd moved beyond the terror while surrounded by his protective arms, and for a short, sweet time, the gleaming light of normalcy had shimmered before her. Knots of tension pulled her shoulder muscles tight. The harsh truth was, she'd reacted instinctively and cruelly when that light was extinguished in the blink of an eye, but not even the warm promise of Sam's love had been able to quell her panic at the thought of returning to Barlow once his dream of a pro career was dashed.

She tossed her blazer onto the hood beside her. *Water under the bridge.* As cowardly as she'd acted, she'd made her decisions and there was no going back. Still, if she were a better woman, one whose heart hadn't been hardened to coldness by the cruelties of life, she'd have found a way to apologize for any regrets she'd left *him* with when she'd run.

But she wasn't that woman. Never had been and never would be.

"Everything around here seemed so much bigger when I was seventeen."

With a soft yelp, she jolted away from the hood and spun around. Staring into Sam's familiar, slate-gray eyes, dizziness swamped her. She staggered slightly on her heels. He shot out a hand to steady her. The heat from his broad palm seared her ribs through the silk of her shell top. Her nipples pebbled in helpless welcome. She bit down on a dismayed groan and took a wide step back. His hand dropped away as she snatched the blazer from the hood and held it before her chest like a shield.

Flustered, she shot a darting glance at the field. The coaching staff and players had yet to notice his arrival. The moment of privacy was one she hadn't expected, but it worked to her advantage. It wouldn't last long, however. The quicker she delivered Caroline's offer, the sooner she could leave Barlow and its memories behind.

"Sam, I—"

She stumbled over what to say as she catalogued every nuance of his six-four frame. Starved for the sight of him, she slid her greedy gaze over the muscled body she'd known so well for too short a time. Cowboy boots had always been his preference, and she nearly smiled at the scuffs marring the toes. Her gaze climbed over the faded denim encasing his long legs. The soft fabric stretched tight over muscled thighs and cradled the bulge of the impressive package she remembered. She swallowed and jerked her gaze higher, past the tweed suit jacket covering shoulders and a chest that were wider than they had been at seventeen.

The laugh lines bracketing his mouth and spraying out from the corners of his eyes were deeper, and a smattering of gray wove through the jet-black hair at the temples. Neither detracted from the rugged appeal of his familiar face.

Oh, God. He was wrong. Not everything had been bigger when he was seventeen. Back then, he'd been larger than most of the boys his age, but he'd still been on the cusp of manhood. He stood before her now, broad-shouldered and proud, a man fully grown, and the soft gray eyes that used to look at her with love held nothing but disdain.

His lips curled in a sneer. "You're the *last* person I'd expect to find in Barlow. Slummin' it, V?"

She stiffened her spine and refused to wince at the sarcastic bite of his words. His animosity was no more than she'd expected. No more than she deserved.

That didn't mean she had to like it. If he'd expected more all those years ago, so had she. Her dreams had been crushed right along with his when he'd blown out his knee. And wasn't life a bitch? Hell. *She* was a bitch, or so she'd been told on a number of occasions. Sam obviously agreed. She snorted inwardly. She'd take the title of bitch over victim any day.

She jacked her chin to an extra snotty angle. "Normally, I wouldn't be caught dead in this dump of a town, but since you're here and I need to speak to you, here I am."

"Speak to *me*?" He crossed his arms. "That's a complete turnaround from the last time we saw each other."

Since his mocking claim was true, she'd give him that one. She pasted on a fake smile. "I have a business proposition for you."

From the far end of the field, one of the coaches called his name. Sam lifted his hand in a silent wave, then turned back to her. Though he was a foot taller and topped her by nearly one hundred pounds, she'd never been afraid of him. Yet, the way he stepped forward, crowding her against the car, made her nervous. She refused to flinch as he lowered his head until his face was less than an inch from hers.

"Baby, any *business* we might have had together was finished a long time ago."

The direct hit was like a blow to her belly. She absorbed the pain. Embraced it. Put it behind her, the way she always had, and focused on the business at hand. While a pop in his nose would be more satisfying, in her experience, a dangled carrot normally delivered better results. Sam's hostility might be justified, but he was still a man, and a competitive one at that. She'd bet her favorite Louis Vuitton bag he wouldn't let her walk away without finding out why she'd come.

With a careless shrug, she pivoted away. "Suit yourself."

He stepped back as she opened the door and slipped into the seat, then prevented her from slamming the door in his face by propping a forearm on the window frame.

"That's it?" He leaned down to meet her gaze, his broad chest and shoulders filling the crack of the open door.

"That's it." She pushed the sunglasses down her nose to fry him with a pointed glare. "Now, if you don't mind...." She let the unspoken suggestion he go to hell dangle in the air between them.

"It happens I do mind." An angry crease marred the tanned skin of his brow.

"Sucks to be you." She tugged on the armrest, but he held the door firm.

His voice vibrated with an impatient growl. "What's the proposition?"

She could just imagine how much it stung him to ask, since he'd cut off his throwing arm before he requested anything from her. Guilt softened her voice. "A job offer."

His mouth twisted in a derisive smirk, and his eyes traveled over her body in an insulting survey before he lifted his gaze to hers once more. "I've sampled what you have to offer, *Red*. No thanks."

Now he was just being nasty, and the old pet name, spoken in such a cutting tone, hurt enough she was tempted to tell him to go fuck himself. Instead, she tossed out Caroline's dream offer, and hoped like hell he was too angry to accept. "Not even if the job is offensive coordinator for the Manhattan Marauders?"

He snapped straight and his eyebrows shot to his hairline. They quickly lowered to a dangerous tilt. "Last I heard, you were a sports agent, not a recruiter for the pros."

She tossed her head. "Caroline Wainwright offered me a job as the Marauders' public relations coordinator when Jake retired from the field." Tugging the envelope from her satchel, she held it out.

He hesitated for a moment before snatching the thick envelope from her fingers. "Bob Duggan—"

"Was recently diagnosed with cancer."

He stared at her in silence and the hostility in his eyes eased with the pained grimace wrinkling his brow. "Damn. I hadn't heard."

She hardened her heart against the rush of empathy tightening her throat and lifted her chin. "Not many have."

His shoulders sagged. "How bad is it?"

"Bad enough he's retiring as soon as his replacement is found." The team had kept the well-loved coach's diagnosis out of the press so far, but that wouldn't last long. Not with the Marauders searching for his replacement. If Sam accepted the position, he'd learn the details soon enough. Still, he hadn't taken the job yet. "That's privileged information, by the way." She bumped her chin toward the envelope. "Since those papers represent an official offer of employment, and they're technically in your custody, we expect you to keep Bob's condition, and every other detail contained in the offer, to yourself."

Affronted irritation sparked in his eyes, but he dipped his chin once in a curt nod.

She snapped on her seatbelt with a click. "Bottom line, Bob Duggan and Caroline Wainwright want you in the position once he leaves."

He remained silent for a moment, his gaze sliding over her face as if searching for the lie in her claim. "And you?"

"I want you to take your hand off my door."

Surprisingly, he did so. He stepped back, and she slammed the door shut. Twisting the key in the ignition, she jammed the shifter into drive and nearly ran over his toes as she tore out of the lot.

Chapter 2

"Son of a bitch." Sam sent the town's mayor and his wife a final wave and climbed into his truck. Blowing a frustrated breath, he shoved the key into the ignition. Four hours of shaking hands and making small talk when all he could think of were the contents of the envelope in his pocket—and the woman who had delivered it—had been an exercise in torture.

His hand shook as he slipped the Marauders' offer from the inside pocket of his suit jacket. Angling the sheaf of papers toward the glow from the parking lot lights, he began to read. His pulse accelerated with each page until his heart jackhammered against his ribs. His breathing quickened and his palms went clammy.

Jesus. She'd been telling the truth. Offensive coordinator for the Marauders.

Adrenaline surged, and he pounded his fist against the steering wheel in a half-dozen celebratory thumps. From the day he'd made that lateral cut, tearing his ACL so badly he would never play football again, he'd worked his ass off, earning his degree at an accelerated pace, with one goal in mind: to get his foot in the door with a pro team. But he hadn't allowed himself to hope for the door of the reigning Super Bowl champs.

Dropping his head against the rest, he stared at the emptying field and stands. The underlying reason for Bob Duggan's retirement made him sick to his stomach, but with the playoffs about to begin, the Marauders couldn't afford to leave the job open. If Sam didn't take his place, someone else would. And, damn it, he'd earned the position.

Hard work, lucky timing, and a palmful of local celebrity had gained him his first low-level coaching position at East Texas U. He'd made the most of the opportunity, rising through the ranks of the Division II program to head coach. In the six years since, he'd delivered two championship titles. He'd fallen short this year, but considering the lack of talent on the current roster, he was proud of what they'd accomplished.

It happened sometimes, at every level of collegiate sports. Players graduated, leaving the coaching staff to rebuild. His record was solid, however. Solid enough to gain the interest of the Marauders. Thanks to the college administration dragging their feet over his contract, it looked as if he'd won the timing lottery again, along with a second chance at his dream.

And how fucking ironic the chance would come via the woman who hadn't loved him enough to stick by his side when his dream had come crashing down around him?

Ignoring the rare band of anger compressing his chest, he tucked the offer back into the envelope, slipped it in his pocket, and started the truck. Damn. He couldn't believe his eyes when he'd spotted V leaning against her car like a vision from the past. For a split second, he'd been back in high school, exiting the locker room after a game to find her propped against the fender of his old pickup. His reaction was the same as it had been all those years ago, but unlike in high school, the insistent twitch of his cock was an unwelcome development.

He shoved the truck into gear and joined the parade of vehicles exiting the lot. In a perfect world, Victoria Price's sultry shell would match her cold heart, but even at seventeen, she'd had an earthy quality that grabbed the male of the species by the balls. Though petite, she was built, with curves that didn't quit and a mane of dark red curls that had sent his teenage hormones rampaging with thoughts of steamy windows and sweaty sex.

That obviously hadn't changed.

The packaging, however, had been false advertising, or had been back then. With the exception of Jake Malone, who had lived in the trailer next to hers on the Double J Ranch on the outskirts of town, she'd barely spoken to the boys who constantly sniffed after her. In fact, she'd blackened the eye of the one boy who'd tried to steal a kiss. Brian Hayes had taken a shitload of razzing when he'd shown up at school on Monday. He'd suffered a second shiner when Jake learned how he'd gotten the first.

Word was, she and Jake were doing the dirty, but Sam had never bought the rumors. Perhaps because he didn't want to. The way he saw it, Jake treated the quiet little redhead like a sister, not a girl he'd gotten naked. Pursuing V had risked Jake's friendship, but Sam had never been one to walk away from something he wanted. He'd wanted V until he couldn't think straight, and from the shy smiles and blushes whenever he caught her between classes to say hello, the attraction wasn't one-sided.

Still, it had taken perseverance and charm to finally convince her to share a cone with him at the Dairy Barn three months before he left for college. The next morning, Jake had shown up at the garage where Sam worked part time and promised to break his throwing arm if he did anything to hurt her, but their friendship survived.

Before long, everyone in town knew V was his girl. They'd dated throughout the spring and early summer, and with her irresistible mix of shyness and quirky humor, she'd had him eating out of her hand in no time. For a single smile, he would have promised her anything, and had.

He dragged a palm down his face. She'd made promises as well.

Against her mother's wishes, she'd followed him to Florida State that fall, delaying her own plans for higher education. Working two jobs, she'd found a small apartment near campus and had accepted his marriage proposal the night he'd taken her virginity while staring into her incredible bedroom eyes.

She'd disappeared without a word six weeks later.

He grunted. The bedroom eyes hadn't changed, but the screw-you jut of her chin was new. Apparently, the shy girl who had once captured his heart had grown some sharp edges. She wasn't alone in that. He'd developed some as well.

Up ahead, the town's one-and-only traffic light switched from yellow to red. He slowed to a stop and, drumming his fingers on the steering wheel, he eyed the street sign glowing in the beam of his headlights. When the light changed, he yanked the wheel to the left onto Cholla Drive instead of heading straight home. Driving past a half dozen well-tended homes, he pulled the truck to the curb in front of a small Craftsman-style home.

Frustration fired on all cylinders as he stared at Anita Price's empty driveway. He should have known V wouldn't stick around, even for a short visit with her mother.

When V had first taken off, he'd been too raw, too angry, and too embarrassed to object as friends and neighbors alike raked V over the coals for being a heartless bitch. With time and maturity, he'd put the embarrassment behind him and the anger had eased with his acceptance of a lesson well learned, but the damage to V's reputation was done.

With very few exceptions, the citizens of Barlow considered her a pariah and weren't shy about voicing their opinions. Then again, she hadn't given them a lot of opportunity to do so to her face. Anita was another story. Over the years, she'd shown him nothing but kindness; had even become a friend of sorts. Yet, living in Barlow, there was no escaping the nasty criticisms and snide remarks. Anita loved V, and his gut gnawed with guilt over the humiliation she continued to suffer on her daughter's behalf.

As far as he knew, V had only been back to Barlow once, when news reached town her estranged father had died. Sam had returned home from coaching a road game to find the citizenry abuzz over how V had met Anita at the bank to sign some papers and left again before the ink was dry.

She hadn't been back since. Until today.

He propped his forearms on the steering wheel and ground his teeth. Damn it. What was he doing here, anyway? The ache of hurt had dulled long ago, as had the regret. Victoria Price wasn't worth regrets, and he'd discovered what real hurt was during the long months of rehabilitation as he worked to regain the ability to walk.

It was just as well she hadn't hung around. He had no interest in being topic number one on the town grapevine, and if he gave into temptation and strangled the Marauders' PR consultant, he could kiss their offer goodbye.

He curled his fingers around the shifter, preparing to go, then cursed as the front porch light winked to life. Anita pushed open the screen door and stepped outside. She raised her hand in a hesitant wave, and Sam's spine tingled with a sense of déjà vu. The neat little house was a far cry from the small trailer where V had grown up, but the stark sadness on her mother's face was the same as on the day he'd finally swallowed his pride and had come looking for answers—and found none.

"Fuck." *Great going, Fitzpatrick. Now you get to explain to Anita how her daughter was in town and didn't bother to stop by. You're an asshole.*

He twisted the key in the ignition, climbed from the truck, and crossed the lawn to the foot of the steps.

Anita spoke before he could. "If you're looking for V, she's not here."

He hid his surprise by scrubbing a palm over his chin. "She came by to see you?"

A pained smile tweaked her lips. "She called from the airport. Congratulations, Sam. She told me about the job offer."

He shuffled his feet and searched for an excuse for being here that wouldn't make him sound like a sap. "With the game about to start, there wasn't a lot of time to discuss the details. I was hoping to catch her before she headed back to New York."

Eyes full of apology, Anita shrugged. "You know V."

He'd thought he had once, but he'd been wrong. She'd fooled him completely with her claims of love. In truth, he'd been nothing more than a one-way ticket out of Barlow. The moment that ticket was canceled, she was gone.

Anita glanced at his truck then back. "Have you told Lucy yet?"

Christ. He *was* a sap. Rattled by V's appearance, not to mention the job offer, he hadn't stopped to consider how his daughter would react to having her life uprooted yet again. "No. I came straight from the game." He shoved a hand through his hair. "She's not going to be happy."

"Kids are resilient, Sam. Lucy especially. She might just surprise you."

A harsh laugh rumbled in his chest. "When doesn't she surprise me?" He dropped his arm to his side. "She dyed her hair yesterday. Bright purple."

Anita's face softened with her laugh. "I saw it this afternoon when she showed up for dance class."

He shook his head. "I swear, she's deliberately trying to drive me crazy."

Understanding darkened her eyes. "She's expressing herself, which is a big improvement over the sad little girl she was only months ago. Don't you think?"

He grunted, but she had a point. Lucy had barely spoken in those first few months after she'd come to live with him. Not that he could blame her. Confused and grieving over her mother's death, her life had been tipped on its head, and he hadn't been a lot of help. Out of his element, he'd had no clue how to go about being a father to a scared fourteen-year-old he'd never known about, much less met.

As if she'd read his mind, Anita rested gentle fingers on his arm. "It'll all work out, Sam. You'll see." She dropped her hand to fiddle with the button on her sweater. "Well, I'll let you go, but if you need me to talk to Lucy, I will."

"I appreciate that." But whether or not he took her up on the offer would depend on Lucy. She tended to get spooked whenever he tried to have a serious conversation with her.

Anita dipped her chin in a nod, and he waited until she'd gone inside before retracing his steps to the curb. He clenched his jaw as he started the truck, then swung it around toward home. Life was full of irony. What little headway he'd made with Lucy was due in large part to the friendship she'd developed with Anita. Yet, thanks to Anita's daughter, and the delivery of the Marauders' offer, the familiar refuge Lucy had found in the dance classes Anita gave at the rec center was about to be taken away.

His stomach plummeted as he slowed at the light. Dance classes were the least of his worries. The light turned green and he hung a left, sucking air through his teeth. With a little luck, Lucy would see the move to Manhattan as a positive development, but he wasn't holding his breath. The truth was, any progress they'd made had stalled the moment the court insisted on that Goddamned DNA test.

In the month since, Lucy had withdrawn, as if she expected him to tell her a mistake had been made and he was sending her away. That wasn't going to happen. He might have no idea if he was Lucy's father or if some other man held that distinction, but however the test came out, his name was on her birth certificate. More importantly, he'd made a promise to Maggie. He meant to keep it. Convincing Lucy of that was something else, however, and until the legalities of their situation were settled, the fear and confusion in her young eyes would continue to gut him.

Five minutes later, he pulled into his driveway. Sliding from the truck, he crossed the lawn to the back porch. He unlocked the door, dodging Daisy's licking tongue when the exuberant lab attempted to greet him. Lucy sat cross-legged on the kitchen counter beside the stove, a pizza box at her hip. He flicked a glance toward the kitchen table as he hung his keys on the hook beside the door.

"Something wrong with the chairs?"

Daisy returned to her spot on the floor in front of Lucy, nose in the air as she waited expectantly for dropped scraps. Lucy shrugged a thin shoulder and plucked a melted lump of cheese and pepperoni from the slice in her hand. The blob disappeared into her mouth and she chewed. "I put the pizza on your tab."

"Of course you did." He crossed to the refrigerator and opened it in search of a beer. "How many times do I have to tell you, no takeout deliveries when I'm not here?"

She hopped from the counter, picked up the box, and brought it to the table. "I was perfectly safe, Sam. Daisy was here and Cody Thompson from next door made the delivery."

Sam shut the refrigerator and turned with an arched brow. "That's Dad to you."

She shot him a dismissive smirk. "Are you sure? Did the test results come back?" She didn't wait for a response. Didn't have to. He knew she'd been checking the mail twice a day since the test was taken. She'd grown more and more anxious each day the results didn't arrive. Sliding onto one of the chairs, she sat with one leg folded beneath her and slipped the dog a crust.

With an inward sigh, Sam opened a cabinet and grabbed a couple of paper plates. Crossing to the table, he set one in front of her and took an open chair. Using his given name was one of her favorite jabs, when she wasn't testing him, trying to elicit a reaction with her outrageous demands. He'd shot down her tattoo request last month and merely laughed when she insisted she be allowed to pierce her nose. She'd waited a week to pay him back. He eyed the deep purple streak flowing through the dark hair at her left temple and hoped it wasn't permanent.

"Who won the game?" She picked up her can of pop. "And where's the award you were supposed to be getting? I expected you to bring home a trophy or something."

He slid a slice of gooey cheese and pepperoni onto his plate, then pushed Daisy's head away from his lap as the dog turned her focus onto him. "It's a plaque. The coach is putting it in the trophy case at the high school. And speaking of the game, I need to talk to you about something."

Her lips turned down in a mulish frown. "I told you I have a term paper due when school starts up again after Christmas. Besides, football is boring."

He twisted the cap from his beer, took a deep swallow, and settled deeper into his chair. "That's because you don't understand the intricacies of the game."

She snorted and set aside her pop to pick up her pizza. "What intricacies? It's just a bunch of sweaty boys chasing a ball and patting each other's butts."

He couldn't help his smile. "It's a lot more complicated than that, but football isn't what I wanted to talk to you about. Not directly." He resisted the urge to shift uncomfortably and studied her profile. "An old…friend showed up at the game tonight with a job offer."

She froze with the slice an inch from her lips. "You already have a job."

He nodded and watched her closely. "I do, but my contract with the college is up and, so far, the administration and I haven't been able to come to an agreement. This new offer would be a promotion of sorts."

She dropped her gaze to the table and lowered the pizza to the plate. "So, you'd get more money?"

"Among other things." He slammed the mental door on the image of russet curls and flashing blue eyes shimmering in his mind. *Get a grip, pal. The "V" chapter of your life ended long ago.*

Lucy remained perfectly still, except for her fingers. She curled them into fists. "What's the job?"

"Offensive coordinator for the Manhattan Marauders."

Her head jerked up and fear widened her cocoa-brown eyes. Twin flags of color erupted on her pale cheeks. "You're moving to Manhattan?"

"If I take the job, yeah." What color had remained leached from her face, and he swore beneath his breath. "But I wouldn't go alone. You'd come with me."

The panic in her eyes eased only slightly. As if sensing her anxiety, Daisy pressed against Lucy's thigh. She looked down and rested a hand on the dog's wide head. "The court—"

"Screw the court." Sam covered his concern over the court's potential ruling with a negligent shrug. According to the lawyer he'd hired, things could get sticky if the test came back negative, but with Maggie dead, tracking down a nameless man from fifteen years ago would be next to impossible.

Lucy chewed her bottom lip. "What about school?"

Back on safer ground, he smiled. "They have schools in Manhattan, and New York City is big when it comes to the arts. I'm sure we can find a studio where you can continue your dance lessons."

Her shoulders rolled in a stilted shrug, as if to say her lessons didn't matter. He knew better. She played down her interest in ballet, but she spent every hour she could in the dance studio with Anita.

He sighed when she remained silent. "I've got a game to coach tomorrow afternoon. It's the last of the season. After that, I'm free. The Marauders want me in Manhattan for a meet-and-greet on Sunday and a tour of the complex Monday. What do you say we stay on for a few extra days and check things out?"

She stared at the table and swallowed, then spoke in a small voice. "You want me to come with you?"

"Hey." He waited until she looked up. She peeked at him through a thick fringe of dark lashes, and the doubt in her eyes wrenched his gut. "No matter what happens, I'm not leaving you behind." He shoved the plate aside to lean his elbows on the table. "But I'm not going to lie to you, either. This job is a big deal. One I've been working toward my entire career. I want it. So badly I can taste it, but whether or not I accept the position isn't my decision alone. We're in this together, kid. You're going to have to sign off on it, too."

The surprised flash of hope in her eyes was painful to witness. She covered it quickly with the derisive smirk she employed most days. "So, if I say no, you're not going to take it?"

He narrowed his eyes, but was relieved. Call him crazy, but he preferred the snarky brat to the frightened little girl. "Oh, I'm taking it." He straightened and picked up his slice. "And, like it or not, you're going with me."

Her lips turned down at the corners, and he expected a further argument.

He would have preferred one to her taunting drawl. "What about Patricia? Is she coming, too?"

Aw, shit.

Chapter 3

"What kind of gentleman wakes a woman at the crack of dawn to dump her over the phone?"

"I never claimed to be a gentleman, Patricia." Sam shifted the phone to his other hand and opened the refrigerator. "Considering you're floating around on the Caribbean, you're lucky I reached you at all, and *dump* isn't the term I would use."

"You're telling me it's over between us. What else would you call it?"

Correcting a mistake came to mind. He didn't think she'd appreciate the candor, however. The truth was, their on-again, off-again affair had lost its appeal long ago—for both of them, if her extended trip to Italy was any indication. In his experience, that was to be expected. For him, the fleeting pleasure of sex inevitably took a back seat to football and ambition. With Patricia, the lure of the next conquest was the irresistible draw.

The no-strings arrangement had suited them both for a time, but had fallen flat since Lucy arrived in his life. She and Patricia were like oil and water, and he didn't see that improving anytime soon. If ever. Now, with the Marauders' offer…. Hell, even if the Marauders hadn't come calling, Lucy came first and, frankly, the convenient sex wasn't worth the headaches that went along with it.

He plucked a beer from the fridge. "I'd call it a courtesy between friends."

Patricia's harsh laugh coughed in his ear. "That's a nice sugar coating, but our relationship is a little more complicated than simple friendship."

"You're right. We're friends who sleep together when neither of us is involved elsewhere."

"There is no need to be crude, darling."

"Just speaking the truth." With a sigh, he twisted off the cap on his beer. "We've both known for a while this was where things were headed. Look at it this way. With me out of the picture, you won't have to feel guilty for staying a little longer with whoever is currently warming your berth on that yacht."

"You can be a real bastard, you know that?"

He chuckled at her petulant tone, but noted she hadn't denied the charge. "Admit it. You're just pissed you didn't think to dump me first."

"I thought you said this wasn't a dumping," she purred.

"Touché." He smiled as the sound of a key in the kitchen door drew his attention. Daisy broke into a round of happy whining as TJ Burke let herself inside. Eying the phone pressed to his ear, she held up a bag of take-out and mouthed, "Sorry. I brought food."

His smile morphed into a grin as he ran his gaze over her. TJ was a mess, as usual. A stubbed needle of hay protruded from the long black braid falling over one shoulder. The left elbow of her button-down flannel shirt sported a tear, and both knees of her jeans bore stains of a questionable source. She looked as if she'd come straight from someone's barn. As the town's only veterinarian, odds were, she had.

Although the concern in her tired smile set off warning bells, he was too relieved at the interruption to heed them. "I've got to go, Patricia. Someone's at the door."

An irritated sigh floated through the phone. "This conversation isn't finished, Samuel."

Across the room, TJ mocked sticking her finger down her throat. She batted her lashes, then bent to scrub her hands over his excited dog.

"What is there left to say?" He snagged a second beer from the door of the fridge. "We agreed going in, neither of us were looking for long term. I'm saving us both time and aggravation."

TJ jerked straight. Her green eyes sparkled with gleeful anticipation. "Oh, please tell me you're finally dumping the snooty cow."

He squinted at her in warning. She shrugged, unapologetic, and set the take-out on the counter.

"I assume that's TJ." Patricia didn't wait for affirmation. Her cultured voice slid into a sneer. "Tell your bovine-loving cousin, if anyone would know about cows, it's her."

He rolled his eyes toward the ceiling. As usual, whenever his cousin and Patricia clashed, things tended to head toward a catfight in a hurry. "Goodbye, Patricia. I'm hanging up."

"Wait, Samuel—"

He thumbed the screen and ended the call. With a frustrated sigh, he tossed the phone onto the counter and met his cousin's waiting gaze. "Don't say it."

Daisy nosed TJ's hand and she rubbed her fingers over the dog's head. "Okay, but if you recall, I told you jumping into bed with Barlow's Oil Princess would come back to bite you in the ass."

"Thanks for not saying it."

She smirked at his dry tone and caught the beer bottle he tossed her with practiced ease. Screwing off the top, she leaned her hip against the counter. "Word around town is, you've had a busy night."

He cursed beneath his breath. Obviously, she was referring to more than his international phone call. To his knowledge, V hadn't spoken to anyone but him and Anita during her short stay earlier. Still, this *was* Barlow. Strangers stuck out like neon signs, especially curvy redheaded pariahs in cream woolen suits.

Which would explain why TJ was in his kitchen at midnight when she was clearly exhausted. More than a cousin, she was his best friend. She'd had his back during the dark days after his injury, and despite there no longer being a need, the habit remained. Like a hundred-ten-pound warrior, she'd appointed herself as his protector and champion—and she carried a major grudge where her ex-friend V was concerned.

"I guess you've heard."

She sipped daintily and swallowed. "About you and Victoria Price squaring off in the parking lot before tonight's game?" He frowned and she nodded. "I spent the last eleven hours out at the Double J. They had three mares drop foals. One of them breech. Because I was starving, I stopped by the café before going home. Esther Gimmly was there."

Of course she was. Gleefully spreading the word of V's appearance, no doubt.

TJ's kelly-green eyes studied him over the rim of her beer. "You okay?"

"Why wouldn't I be okay?"

A sardonic arch of her brow was her only answer.

Oh, for fuck's sake.

He crossed the room in three long strides. She arched back as he slapped his hands onto the counter, caging her hips, and leaned in until they were nose to nose. "It's been fifteen years, TJ. I moved on a long time ago. It's time you did, too." Dropping a kiss to her forehead, he reached past her for the bag of takeout. Daisy danced around his feet and followed as he crossed to the table and straddled one of the kitchen chairs.

"Please." TJ tore off several squares of paper towel and yanked open the silverware drawer. "Moved on to what? Bimbos like Patricia Amandola?"

It was an old argument. One he wasn't interested in hashing through for the hundredth fucking time. Daisy nosed his arm in a blatant beg for attention and he thumped her side. "I happen to like bimbos."

"That's because you're a slut." He grinned and nodded his agreement, and she frowned. "You're also thirty-five years old with a steady job, every woman you meet thinks you're hot, and you have all your teeth."

He chuckled. "Is that an occupational observation? I'm not a horse, cuz."

She waved him off. "You know what I'm trying to say."

He curled his lips in a leering grin because he knew it would piss her off. "You're trying to say I'm a catch."

She stalked to the table and set several forks down before sliding into the chair across from him. "You're a definite catch, but because of V, the only women you even look at are party girls who are only in it for the sex."

He laughed, ignoring the reference to V, but TJ wasn't finished.

Leaning forward, she chewed her lip, a definite warning he wouldn't like what she was about to say. "But I'm talking about your heart and that family you always claimed you wanted when we were kids."

His grin slipped and he jerked his head toward the hallway. "My *family* is asleep down the hall in her bedroom."

That took some of the wind out of her argument. Her chest swelled on a shuddering sigh.

He sat forward and grabbed the bag of takeout. "I love you, TJ, but I'm a grown man, responsible for my own choices. I don't need you protecting me from V or any other woman, any more than I need you telling me how I should live my life. I get enough of that from Mom." He tore open the bag, revealing two plates of his favorite Tex-Mex barbeque sandwiches and a large side of cole slaw. "So, unless you're prepared to have me sticking my nose into *your* love life, I suggest we change the subject."

She tilted her chin stubbornly, but backed down…in her own way. "I don't want her to hurt you again."

"She hasn't had the power to do that in a long time. You're going to have to trust me on this."

"Okay." She sniffed and dropped a paper towel on her lap with a nod. "But what was she doing in Barlow? What did she want?"

"Not me, I can promise you that. At least, not on a personal level." He smiled at the memory of V's nervousness and slid one of the plates toward his cousin. "It turns out, she heads up the Manhattan Marauders' public relations department these days."

TJ peeled back the foil cover on her plate and sniffed appreciatively at the fragrant steam. "I thought she represented Jake Malone."

So had Sam. He'd talked to Jake a number of times since he'd moved over to the broadcasting side of the sport at the end of last season, and the ex-pro hadn't said a word about V taking a new job. Then again, since Florida, they'd respected an unspoken agreement to steer clear of the subject of V. Sam shrugged. "Once Jake retired from the field, she moved on."

"Well, there's a big surprise. Moving on is V's specialty."

He couldn't argue with TJ's assessment but, strictly on principle, he cocked his head and pinned her with a cautioning stare.

She rolled her eyes and picked up her sandwich. "Fine, but you haven't answered my question. Why did she come back?"

Renewed excitement fired in his veins. "Apparently, the team is looking for a new offensive coordinator. She came to offer me the job."

TJ froze with her barbeque-stuffed roll hovering an inch from her lips. A mix of surprise and disbelief widened her eyes. "Get. Out!"

He shrugged, but couldn't help his satisfied smile.

"Oh my God. Holy shit. Sam, the Marauders. Oh my God." Her lips slowly curved in wide grin.

"I know." He shook his head. "Jesus. I keep thinking I'm going to wake up and find it's all a dream. I'm trying not to get ahead of myself. I only found out this evening the position is opening up. I haven't said yes, yet."

She waved him off. "But you will, of course."

Damned straight, he would. "From what I've seen of the contract, I'd be a fool not to."

"I'll take that as a yes. When do they want you?" Her stomach growled and she bit off an enormous bite of spicy beef. An appreciative moan rumbled deep in her throat.

"From the sound of it, I'll be expected in Manhattan as soon as possible. I'll know more once I've met with Caroline Wainwright. She owns the franchise. The team is flying me out for Sunday's home game."

TJ's gaze cut to the hallway. "What about Lucy? Do you need me to pack a bag and stay with her?"

"I'm taking her with me, but I was going to call and ask if you'd take Daisy for a few days."

"You know you don't have to ask." TJ nodded, and they ate in silence for several moments. He glanced up when she cleared her throat.

"Will you have to work with her?"

He should have known she wasn't finished grilling him on the subject of V. "Damn it, TJ."

"What?" Eyes wide with feigned innocence, she spoke around the bite of cole slaw she shoved into her mouth. "I'm just curious about your new job."

He sighed and picked up his beer. "She works in the front office. I'll be on the field for the most part but, yeah. Some, I guess."

"Ugh." Her eyes glittered with heat. "Maybe you should make it a stipulation of your hiring that they can her ass."

He laughed and shook his head. "I'm not sure requesting they fire their PR consultant is the first impression I want to make." An image of V tearing out of the parking lot like her hair was on fire filled him with satisfaction, and his smile was keen. "But, don't worry. I can handle Victoria Price."

Chapter 4

"When I said Sam Fitzpatrick and I weren't exactly friends, I should have added he hates me."

Caroline frowned. "Hate's a pretty strong word."

"Yeah, well. He has his reasons."

V turned away to stare through the window overlooking the stadium at the Marauders' Sports Complex. Six levels below, two men walked from the field. Sam, with his dark hair and broad shoulders, moved at Coach Duggan's side toward the tunnel and private elevator leading to the administrative offices.

"Do I want to hear them?"

V glanced over her shoulder. "They're of a personal nature."

"Are there any other kind?" Caroline studied her face as if dissecting her brain. "He's here, V. Obviously, he's not letting the past affect his future. You shouldn't, either."

V turned and leaned against the credenza fronting the window. A lump of anxiety solidified in her belly. She'd purposefully missed yesterday's game, which she never did, but avoiding Sam as she'd intended would be impossible if she were forced to follow Caroline's latest directive. "I don't intend to, but there has got to be someone else who can do this. What about Tom Walden? He's the players' liaison and part of the good-old-boy network."

Caroline shook her head. "Tom is in the middle of several key negotiations and doesn't have the time. We're in a bind with Bob leaving. With Christmas next week and the playoffs the week after that, we need Sam on the field, not bogged down with details someone else can handle. The best hope of achieving a smooth transition is to send someone to Barlow to help him with the logistics of resettling here in the city."

"You've already signed him?" V's lungs constricted as her last hope Sam would turn down the job writhed in a death roll.

"No, but I will. He had no issues with the generous package we offered. The only hurdle left is his finding satisfactory living arrangements, which the team will provide." Caroline eased back in her chair. "Look, V, you're my friend and I value your contribution to the team, but if you can't work with the man, tell me now."

She didn't add, "so I can find your replacement." She didn't have to. V knew the drill. When it came to her team, Caroline didn't screw around, and their friendship made no difference. The people Caroline hired either pulled their weight or they were gone. End of story. Normally, V appreciated her boss' straightforward style, but these circumstances were anything but normal.

She met Caroline's watchful gaze and hoped she wasn't telling a whopper. "You have nothing to worry about."

As if she'd expected no less, Caroline nodded briskly and slid open a drawer. She held out a binder. "My real estate broker put together a list of six homes that meet the specifications Sam gave us yesterday. You should be able to view all of them before heading to Barlow Wednesday morning. The broker will meet you at the first house on the list in an hour. In the meantime, Sam's daughter is waiting in the lounge. Why don't you go introduce yourself?"

The breath caught in V's throat. "His *daughter*?"

Sam was a father? He was married? She mentally shook herself. Of course, he was married, or had been at some point. Why wouldn't he be? Even as screwed up as she was, she had been tempted by his sense of humor and kindness. Granted, she'd seen no evidence of either last Friday, but wouldn't expect to. Not with their history. Still, women had always flocked to Sam, and a wife and kids had been a big part of his master plan. He'd have had no problem finding a healthy, normal woman to share his life with.

And the painful spear of jealousy had no freaking business jabbing her in the heart.

"Her name is Lucy."

V blinked free of her musing to squeak, "Excuse me?"

Calculation gleamed in Caroline's eyes and a shrewd smile tugged at her lips. "Fitzpatrick's daughter. Cute kid. You'll get a kick out of her."

V swallowed. "Why is that?"

Subtle laughter hummed in Caroline's throat. "You'll see."

She'd see? What the hell did that mean? The smile V offered was pained, but it was the best she could manage. She took the file and left the office suite.

On leaden feet, she walked toward the lounge at the end of the hall. Sam had a daughter. How she was supposed to feel about that, she wasn't sure. After all, if she hadn't screwed things up between them, the little girl she was about to meet might have been hers.

The idea of a daughter of her own brought a familiar pang to her heart. She quickly shoved it away. A child, children, weren't in the cards. Not for her. She'd accepted that reality long ago and hadn't looked back. She wasn't about to start now. Besides, Jake and Gracie's brood, not to mention Tuck and CC's little guy, provided all the outlet she needed for her latent maternal urgings.

With conscious effort, V stiffened her spine. Keeping her job was her only concern and, at the moment, she needed all the concentration she could muster. House hunting, for God's sake. For Sam and *his* family. Talk about cruel and unusual punishment. Apparently, karma had caught up with her, and it was definitely a bitch.

Her steps slowed as she neared the lounge and spotted a thin girl curled on one of the couches with her nose in a book. As if she sensed V's approach, she lifted her head. Heavy black liner enhanced the dark chocolate eyes dominating her narrow face, but it was the two-inch thread of bright purple running through her dark hair that caught V's eye.

She blinked and her heartbeat quickened. She'd been expecting a small child, not a half-grown girl in her teens. If this was Sam's daughter, he certainly hadn't wasted any time finding that normal woman to fill V's shoes. A tendril of contempt curled in her belly and bumped up against the guilt she'd carried for years.

Caught in her own thoughts, she jumped as a muscled arm dropped across her shoulders.

"Hiya, beautiful."

She dragged her gaze from the teenager and turned her head. Wyatt Hunter wore his usual lazy smile.

He swirled his fingertips over the ball of her shoulder. "I've got twenty-four hours free and a bottle of white chilling at my place with your name on it."

She rolled her eyes. It had been almost a year to the day since he'd asked her out the first time—and she'd turned him down flat. He'd gone on to have the best game of his career that evening, throwing for four touchdowns and running in another. Notoriously superstitious, he'd attributed his record-breaking game to her refusal. In the twelve months since, including the off-season, he'd either stopped by her office or called her once a week to repeat his request. The one time he hadn't, the Marauders had suffered their only loss of this year.

She bared her teeth in a bland smile. "Damn. If only I didn't have to wash my hair."

"I've got plenty of shampoo." He waggled his brows and dropped his voice into the realm of pure wickedness. "Especially if we share."

She couldn't help her snicker. The team's sinfully handsome quarterback was five years her junior and completely fickle where women were concerned. Wealthy, talented, and a confirmed bachelor, he scored as often off the field as on. The only son of Oklahoma's popular governor, he seemed to revel in shocking his parents' political sensibilities with his infamous playboy lifestyle and, for some reason, he'd included V in the pool of females he saw as potential bed-mates. He was harmless, however, and considering her lack of a sex life, his half-assed pursuit was a pleasant stroke to her ego.

She patted his cheek. "I don't think so."

His smile slipped into a practiced look of disappointment. "You always say that."

She grinned. "And I always mean it, too."

Several feet away, the elevator doors whooshed open and Coach Duggan and Sam stepped from the car. Sam glanced between her and Wyatt. His eyes narrowed, and the grin died on her lips. As if she'd been caught fraternizing with the enemy, she jerked from beneath Wyatt's arm, then gritted her teeth at the unconscious reaction. Coach Duggan simply shook his head.

Sam looked away, shaking the hand Bob offered. "I appreciate the vote of confidence, Coach."

The older man smiled. "You're the right man for the job. I'll see you when you get back next week?"

Sam nodded, and Bob turned down the hall in the opposite direction. V tensed and braced herself as Sam faced her and Wyatt. Caroline was right. Sam would sign, and any hope V had had that he wouldn't had been nothing more than a foolish pipe dream.

He looked past her as if she wasn't there, his gaze flicking to the girl on the couch before sliding back to Wyatt.

"Hunter." Sam dipped his head in greeting.

Wyatt grinned. "Sounds like congratulations are in order."

The smile curving Sam's lips didn't reach his eyes. "That's the way it looks."

Wyatt winked at her and she opened her mouth to cut him off before he could make introductions. She wasn't quick enough.

"This is the team's PR genius, Victoria Price. V, this is—"

"We've met."

At Sam's snarled interruption, Wyatt shot her a questioning glance. Warning bells clanged in her head, and she forced a smile. She'd promised Caroline she could work with Sam, but hadn't considered the fallout if he refused to work with her.

Oh, hell. Not good. Not good at all.

Somehow, they were going to have to find a way to work together, at least on the surface. If they couldn't, *she'd* be out of a job.

She held up the binder in her hand. "Yes, we have and we've got a lot on our schedule today." She offered Sam a tight smile. "Are you ready to go?"

His gaze skidded back and forth between her and Wyatt. "If the two of you have plans, I can meet the realtor on my own."

Wyatt laughed before she could respond. "If it were up to me we would have plans, but the lady keeps turning me down." He shot her a leering smile. "I'll convince her to change her mind, eventually."

He touched two fingers to his forehead in a jaunty salute and walked away. She rolled her eyes, but when she shifted her gaze to Sam, the chill in his nearly made her shiver. She sighed and tucked the binder to her chest. With the future of her job front-and-center in her mind, she offered an olive branch.

"I know I'm not your first choice to work with on your move, but—"

"Nor my second."

Well, damn. Of course he wasn't going to make this easy, but if he expected her to cave beneath his steely gaze, he was mistaken. Though their situation was more than a bit awkward, he wasn't the first angry male she'd had to handle.

She cocked her head in a nod of acceptance. "Understood, but I have a job to do, and so do you. Since it appears you'll be a part of the Marauders' family, you need to understand something. Caroline Wainwright doesn't tolerate contention in the ranks. Not between members of her staff, and especially not between coaches and players."

He crossed his arms. "Well now, *Red*. I don't recall seeing your name on the roster."

She bared her teeth in a patently false smile and ignored both his use of the pet name *and* her short-circuiting heart. He could toss out all the personal barbs he wanted. She wasn't about to rise to the bait. Dealing with the larger-than-life egos prevalent in the world of pro sports required patience, cunning, and a thick skin. She'd developed all three over the past fifteen years.

She also understood the game, and it was about time Sam knew it. "Funny."

Satisfaction gleamed in his eyes and his lips twisted in a humorless smile.

She lifted her chin and looked him dead in the eye. "You can hate me all you want." She spoke over his derisive snort. "But here's the deal. With the exception of the next week, week and-a-half at the most, we won't be working together. In fact, you'll barely know I'm here. In the end, how we feel about each other isn't important. If you take this position, the only thing that matters is your relationship with the players. And the most important relationship you'll have will be with the man you just snarled at."

He held her gaze for a long moment, then turned his head and glanced down the hall where Wyatt had disappeared. A scowl darkened his eyes when he looked back. "I don't snarl."

She raised a brow at his growling tone, and his lips thinned in annoyance. With a sigh, she softened her voice. "I know what this opportunity means to you, Sam. Please don't let my presence here ruin it for you."

Surprise lit his eyes before they hardened once more. "I don't plan to."

Relief loosened the muscles of her neck and shoulders. "Good." She stuck out her hand. "Then I suggest we call a truce."

He hesitated as if he meant to refuse. Finally, he wrapped his fingers around hers.

Mistake!

She knew it the second his palm met hers. Deeply buried memories swirled to life and caught her off guard. His fingers entwined with hers as they licked ice cream from a shared cone. The happy laughter in his eyes as he yanked her from her beat-up Chevy the day she'd arrived in Florida. The irresistible mixture of safety, love, and lust she'd found in his arms, and the intoxicating pleasure his wide-palmed hands had coaxed from her body each time they'd made love.

The satisfaction and possessiveness in his eyes the night she'd promised to become his wife.

Slapped by the harsh hand of reality, she jolted and tugged her hand free of his. She stepped back and his arm dropped to his side, but his gaze held her pinned in place. Short-circuit, hell. She couldn't catch her breath. He dropped his gaze to the ragged rise and fall of her chest, and his Adam's apple jumped with his swallow. Something hot and dark flashed in his eyes before he looked away.

He cleared his throat and held out his hand to his daughter. "Lucy. You ready?"

V dragged in a stealthy breath as the girl unfolded from the couch. Yeah, touching him in any way was definitely a mistake. She pressed her thighs together against the unexpected and completely unacceptable pressure humming between them. Good Lord. He was like kryptonite, and she was a masochist. That was the only explanation. The man detested her and, yet, with a single touch, he'd made her wet.

That wouldn't do. Wouldn't do at all.

Suck it up, V. Like you said. How you feel about each other doesn't matter. A week. Two at the most and you're in the clear.

If only her racing heart believed that.

Rolling her shoulders, she focused on Lucy. Though she searched, she found little resemblance to Sam, other than the girl's black hair. Thin and nearly as tall as V, she moved with a subtle grace as she crossed the room toward them. Her cheekbones were high and delicate in a face that held the promise of beauty in years to come but at the moment, she appeared more child than adult, despite the heavy eye makeup.

Lips puckered in a stubborn bow, she stopped beside her father. "I'm hungry."

"You're always hungry." He turned and his intent gaze met V's. "My daughter, Lucy." The girl opened her mouth, but he spoke over whatever she'd been about to say. "Lucy, this is Victoria Price. She's going to show us some houses this afternoon."

"Price?" Lucy's wide-eyed gaze ping-ponged to Sam, then back again. "*You're* Miss Anita's daughter?"

Nerves fluttered in V's stomach, and she nodded.

"Oh, wow." A dimple formed along with the smile that softened Lucy's mouth. "That's so cool."

V swallowed and avoided Sam's watchful gaze. "You know my mother?"

"Well, yeah. She's my dance instructor." Lucy cocked her head. "Do you dance?"

"God, no." V's laugh was self-deprecating. "I was born with two left feet, much to my mother's dismay. I take it you do? What style?"

"Ballet." Lucy's smile dimmed, then disappeared. "My mom danced, but she didn't do ballet like me. She was in a whole bunch of music videos."

Danced? As in past tense? Curiosity curled like a fist in V's belly, but she wasn't about to ask. She offered Sam's daughter a smile. "It's nice to meet you. I love your hair."

Sam grunted. V ignored him, intrigued by the impish smirk twisting Lucy's lips.

"Sam doesn't like it. He says it makes me look like a punk."

V might have laughed at Sam's immediate scowl if she wasn't stuck on Lucy's use of his given name. "You call your father Sam?"

"He's—"

"Hungry, too." Sam shot Lucy a hard glance that looked like a warning to V. The girl fluttered her lashes innocently, but whatever their silent communication was about, she didn't say another word.

V checked her watch. "We're supposed to meet the realtor in forty-five minutes, but the complex has an okay cafeteria. We could grab something to go."

Lucy's eyes lit up. "Do they have pizza?"

"You had pizza twice this week," Sam complained.

"I like pizza."

Sam opened his mouth, but V cut him off with a smile for Lucy. "We'll skip the cafeteria. I know where they make the best pizza in town, and it's on our way."

Chapter 5

Over the next few hours, it became abundantly clear to V that wherever Lucy's mother was, she was no longer in the picture. At least not as far as Sam was concerned. Not that his marital status mattered, but what woman would let her husband and teenage daughter choose their new home without her? And hire live-in help to watch over Lucy when Sam traveled with the team? That wouldn't be necessary if he had a wife stashed away somewhere.

In addition, it appeared Sam had given Lucy the final say on where they lived. Much to the real estate broker's frustration, Sam's daughter had turned up her nose at the first two houses they'd toured. Her watchful silence, however, since they'd arrived at the third, was telling. V couldn't blame her. If the choice were up to her, the search would be over.

Built in the twenties, the three-story house had recently been renovated to include all the modern amenities buyers expected while maintaining old-fashioned details not found in newer buildings. Thirty minutes by car to the city, the neighborhood had a small village feel and was a magnet for young families. In fact, Jake and Gracie Malone were among its residents. Their historic farm house sat less than a mile away on the far end of the sprawling park and golf course at the end of the street.

Aside from the conveniences, like the train station two blocks over and the many restaurants and shops within a short walk to Main Street, the house itself was beautiful. While V had secretly lusted over the chef's dream that was the kitchen, and cooed over the original hardwood floors and intricate crown molding, Lucy lost her heart on the third floor. The moment the teenager stepped into the large attic bedroom, helpless pleasure replaced the perpetual look of boredom she'd worn most of the day.

"The third floor has its own separate heating and cooling system." The real estate agent moved past V and Sam to a curtained doorway. He held the drapes aside. "There's additional space through here. It's large enough to act as a small fourth bedroom or a private seating or storage area. The previous owner had a teenage daughter. I believe she used it as a large walk-in closet."

Lucy glanced through the doorway, but it was obvious the canopied bed and reading nook had claimed her interest. "Does all this stuff come with it?"

Sensing victory, the real estate agent smiled. "All the furnishings are included." He turned to Sam. "The house is move-in ready, per Caroline's instructions. Of course, you'll have your own things and if there is anything you don't like, it can be removed or replaced."

In silence, Lucy roamed about the room. As if greeting the space through touch, she dragged her fingertips over the surface of the antique roll-top desk, then crossed to the bed to test the mattress with several healthy bounces. Wrapping her hand around one of the cherry posts, she rose and moved toward the oversized chair and ottoman tucked into the dormer. A slight whimper escaped her lips as she slipped into the chair.

V glanced at Sam and arched a brow. Unless she misread Lucy, the Fitzpatricks had found their new home.

He crossed his arms. "Well, kid. What do you think?"

Lucy affected a bored shrug with a roll of her thin shoulders. "I guess it's okay, but what about ballet?" She shot Sam an accusing stare, then turned to meet V's gaze. "He promised."

V smiled as Sam sent the broker a questioning glance. "There's bound to be a class somewhere in town."

The man nodded. "The village has a top-notch studio three blocks from here and the den off the pantry can easily be converted into a nanny's quarters."

"Housekeeper," Sam quickly corrected before Lucy could voice a complaint.

The man smiled and cleared his throat. "If you've made your decision, I'll walk you through the security system. All you'll need then are the keys, which I happen to have in my briefcase downstairs."

Sam glanced at Lucy with a raised brow. "Have we made a decision?"

She shrugged, but there was no missing the excited anticipation in her dark eyes. V's heart constricted as Sam dipped his chin and winked at his daughter, then turned to the real estate agent.

"I'll take those keys."

Sam descended the stairs behind the man, but Lucy was slow to follow. Her gaze trailed him until he disappeared. Once he had, her shoulders sagged and she blinked. Her gaze went stark as she glanced around the room.

Concerned and unsure of what had stolen the girl's excitement of a moment before, V walked over and sat on the edge of the ottoman. "What's wrong? I thought you liked the house, but if you don't, there are others we can look at."

"How could I not like the house? It's beautiful." Her dark eyes flicked to V and she shook her head. "It's just...everything is happening so fast. I'm afraid I'll wake up and find out this is all a mistake."

V smiled softly. "I'll bet it feels that way. Things move pretty quickly in the world of pro sports, especially during the playoffs, and this is a big move. For both of you."

Lucy lowered her head. With her fingernail, she drew designs on the chair next to her hip. "Sam said this job is a big deal. That he wanted it so bad he could taste it."

His second chance at the pros.

V didn't have to imagine how much this opportunity meant to him. She'd witnessed his devastation when he'd lost his chance to play with the pros. She cleared her throat against the sudden constriction in her windpipe. "Well, it sounds like he plans to take it. Once he signs the papers it's a done deal, and things will slow down when you're moved in and settled."

"I hope so." Eyes full of an almost painful yearning, Lucy glanced around the room once more. Rising to her feet, she headed for the stairs, leaving V to follow.

When they reached the first-floor landing, Sam waved Lucy to his side so she could listen in as the agent explained the workings of the security panel beside the front door. V's phone vibrated in her pocket and she tugged it free. Jake's picture showed on the screen. She excused herself and slipped into the kitchen.

"I've got some news you're not going to like," Jake said instead of a greeting.

V slumped against the granite island in the center of the room. "If it involves Sam Fitzpatrick, I've already heard."

"You knew the Marauders were courting him?"

"Since last Thursday."

"Well, hell. Thanks for telling me."

She bristled at his grumbled tone. "He's *your* friend. If he wanted you to know about the offer, he could have told you himself."

"V—" Disappointment deepened his voice.

"I know." She squeezed the bridge of her nose. She knew they'd remained friends over the years. Which couldn't have been easy. Not with her between them. But though he'd disapproved of the way she'd treated Sam, Jake had never given her a reason to doubt his friendship or his support. "That was a bitchy thing to say. I'm sorry."

He didn't respond for a moment, then he coughed. "Excuse me? I thought I just heard you apologize. We must have a bad connection."

She dropped her hand and a small smile tweaked her lips. "Shut up."

His chuckle vibrated through the phone. "How you doing?"

Guilt tightened her throat and she glanced around toward the mumbled voices floating from the foyer. "How do you think?"

Several heartbeats passed, then he spoke softly. "I think it's been a long time. Long enough for you and Sam to deal with whatever happened and put it behind you."

Fifty years wouldn't be long enough to do that, and after so much time, what would be the point? "Jake. Please." She steered the conversation into safer waters. "How did you hear, anyway? He hasn't actually signed yet, and I know for a fact the press release hasn't gone out because I haven't written it yet."

He let the diversion stand, but his sigh said he saw it for what it was. "Gracie and I spent the weekend at the lake house. I called Tom when I spotted Sam in Caroline's box while watching yesterday's game. Have you seen him yet?"

"If I walk around the corner, I can describe what he's wearing." But she didn't need to take a step, or rely on her mind's eye to recall the faded jeans hugging his muscled thighs, or the gray sweater, so soft it begged to be stroked, molded to the plains of his broad chest. Sam appeared in the kitchen doorway, and she fought the urge to slap her hand over her eyes.

Definitely kryptonite.

Sam cocked his head and eyed the phone in her hand. "We're ready to go when you are."

"Is that him?" Jake demanded in her ear.

"Um. Yeah."

A second voice sounded in the background through the phone and Jake laughed. "Put him on. Gracie wants to talk to him."

"Oh, I don't think so." Jake might never have followed through on his threat to lock her and Sam in a room together so they could hash things out, but Gracie was another matter. Several years ago, V had made the mistake of attending "Girls' Night" with Gracie and company. Thanks to a ridiculous game of Truth or Dare, and several bottles of chardonnay, V had named Sam as the one that got away. Too embarrassed later to admit she'd actually *thrown* him away, she'd never corrected the record. With him in town, V wouldn't put it past her friend to play Cupid.

Sam arched a brow, and she swallowed. Hard. After Florida, she'd promised herself she wouldn't take the coward's way out ever again, so lying was out, but for God's sake, wasn't this situation bad enough already?

Her lips curled in a pained smile. "It's Gracie Malone. She wants to speak to you."

Genuine pleasure softened his features, and he stepped forward. V held out the phone, her arm stretched as far as it would go. No freaking way was she letting him close enough to touch her again.

He studied her face and, as if he'd read her mind, brushed his fingers over hers as he accepted the phone. She dropped her arm and curled her tingling fingers into a fist.

"Hiya, gorgeous." Subtle laughter sparkled in his eyes, but V wasn't sure if his humor was directed at her or at the woman on the other end of the connection. She held firm beneath his steady regard—and wished to hell she could hear what Gracie was saying.

"Yeah, since yesterday. We've been looking at houses all afternoon." His lips quirked at one corner as he listened. "I doubt she volunteered."

The taunting gleam in his eyes left little doubt to whom he was referring. V turned away and wandered to the French doors overlooking the deck.

"I think this last one might do." He was silent for several seconds. "I'm not really sure, since I don't know the area. Somewhere in Flushing. There's a golf course down the street."

Even at a distance, V heard Gracie's excited exclamation, and glanced over her shoulder.

"You're kidding?" Surprise wrinkled his brow. "No, our night is free. Sounds good. We'll see you as soon as we finish up here." He thumbed the screen and ended the call.

V's stomach dropped in a free fall at his sardonic smile.

"You didn't mention Jake and Gracie were so close by. I hope you don't mind, but they're expecting us at their place for dinner."

The warning bells returned in a nearly deafening clang. Oh, hell no. She made a show of checking her watch. "It's late and I've got to get back to the city. You can take the SUV. I'll call a car."

Sam shot a pointed glance at the kitchen doors. Late afternoon sunlight streamed through the glass. Challenge gleamed in his eyes when he met her gaze once more. "You're the one who suggested a truce." He held out her phone. "We'll be boarding a plane together in a couple of days. Are you telling me you can't handle dinner with friends?"

Chapter 6

"She's beautiful, Sam."

Sam slid his gaze to the foyer, where Lucy and the Malones' ten-year-old adopted twin daughters clomped up the staircase, and shook his head. New to the parenting game, he already knew how difficult it was. He couldn't imagine raising one set of twins, never mind two, but Jake and Gracie made it look easy. The chubby toddler in Lucy's arms gummed a smile and patted her cheek. His twin brother squealed and attempted to break the hold of one of his older sisters. Their giggles and laughter were nearly drowned out by the barking of Murphy, the family's rangy dog.

Sam chuckled and turned to Gracie. "She looks like her mother." He winced. "Except for the purple hair."

Eyes full of understanding, she smiled. "It's just a phase. She'll grow out of it."

Jake winked at his wife. "How much do you want to bet the girls demand a trip to the store for a box of hair color in the morning?"

She tossed her head and returned his wink with a teasing smile. "Hair wars are your responsibility this week, Malone."

Jake groaned, and she patted his knee with a laugh.

"Speaking of Lucy's mother, will she be joining you when you move to Manhattan?"

All eyes swung to V. She sat poker stiff on one of the den's wingback chairs. Her eyes were wide with horror, as if the question had slipped from her lips against her will. Sam choked back a sardonic laugh as she brought her wine glass to her lips and swallowed deeply. He'd wondered when she'd get around to asking about Lucy's mother. The girl he remembered would have done so immediately, but she hadn't blinked an eye when he'd introduced Lucy, whose age clearly put her conception within months of V's departure from his life. Instead, she'd exhibited a remarkable lack of curiosity all day. He'd chalked it up to a lack of interest. The proof she wasn't completely unaffected was as surprising as it was gratifying.

Drumming his fingertips against his knee, he held her embarrassed gaze. He carried no guilt for those months after he'd blown his knee and she'd walked out. His entire world had fallen apart, and he'd survived the only way he knew how. Maggie had been only the first in a long line of women, but he refused to make excuses for the way he'd chosen to live his life. The fact was, he didn't give a fuck what people thought, including V.

"Lucy's mother and I haven't been together for a long time. She was diagnosed with ovarian cancer last year. Lucy came to live with me when Maggie died four months ago."

"I'm sorry, Sam." Gracie's voice was heavy with pain and understanding as her gaze flicked toward the staircase. Jake tightened his arm around her shoulders.

Sam winced, remembering the custody battle Jake and Gracie had fought over the twin girls when their father died. Their mother, Gracie's sister, had succumbed to cancer several years earlier. Sam struggled for something to say. He didn't get the chance.

"I'm sorry, too."

He turned his head at V's soft voice. Sober and still, she held her wine glass in clenched fingers. The genuine regret in her eyes hit him like a sledgehammer. His heart thumped against his ribs as his mind superimposed another apology over the simple one she offered. Christ. What he would have given to hear those words back when they still mattered. He told himself they no longer did.

With a derisive snort, he turned away. Guilt he shouldn't feel slammed into him as he met Jake's disappointed stare. Gracie's narrowed gaze fell closer to condemnation. She cleared her throat and stood. Sam pushed forward to do so as well.

She waved him off. "Sit. Visit. I'm going to put the boys to bed."

"Can I help?"

The note of desperation in V's voice drew Sam's attention, but she ducked her head. Her dark red curls shielded her face as she set her glass on the coffee table and joined Gracie.

"Are you kidding?" Gracie's smile appeared forced to Sam, but she laughed and tucked her arm through V's, pulling her toward the stairs. "Roll up your sleeves, sweetie. Bathing the octopuses is like being waterboarded."

V's low laugh sent a lash of heat straight to Sam's groin. He cursed beneath his breath even as his gaze clung to the slow swing of her hips as she climbed the stairs. He shifted in his chair. Damn it, what the hell was wrong with him? He'd put V behind him a long time ago, but it was painfully obvious his dick hadn't gotten the memo.

The constant shift of emotion in her eyes wasn't helping. Her *guilt* he could understand. If anyone should be apologizing, it was her, but he hadn't missed the flash of feminine awareness when he'd taken her hand to accept her truce, and then again as he'd returned her phone.

Though she talked a good game, he could tell he made her nervous. Why that was, when she'd been the one to walk away, he didn't know and shouldn't care, but like a dog on the scent, his head insisted he sniff out the reason.

"Awkward."

He met Jake's wry smile, then coughed a dry laugh. "Tell me about it."

The humor slid from his friend's face. He leaned forward to prop his forearms on his knees and stared at the floor. "Any possibility you could cut her some slack?"

Sam frowned at the unexpected request. "I didn't ask to be thrown into this situation."

"Neither did she." Jake looked up. The intent gleam in his eyes was the same one he flashed all those years ago, when he'd arrived at the garage to deliver his warning after Sam and V's first date.

Sam sat forward to set his wine glass on the table. "We're not in high school anymore, and the shit that went down between V and me is a lot more complicated than sharing an ice cream cone on a Saturday night."

Jake nodded. "That's true, but like you, V is my friend. I don't want to see her hurt."

"I wouldn't worry about V. From what I can tell, she's developed a hard shell." His laugh was a harsh bark. "Or maybe it's always been there, and I was just too blind to see it back then."

"You know better than that."

"Do I?"

Jake sighed. "You obviously didn't think that way when you asked her to marry you."

Sam frowned. He didn't need to be reminded of that foolish move. Although he'd never admit it to TJ, his cousin was right. The memory of his naiveté with V had played a key role in keeping him single all these years.

He sat back. "I wasn't the first eighteen-year-old to be blinded by sex. I mistook it for love."

Jake cocked his head and his smile was full of challenge. "I don't recall you proposing junior year when you slept with Jeanette Parker. Or a few months later when Celeste Howl caught your eye. Then there was—"

"Damn. What were you doing, keeping tabs?"

Jake chuckled. "We're talking about Barlow, buddy. Knowing which girls put out was essential with such a limited playing field."

Sam shook his head, but couldn't help smiling. "Does Gracie know about your hound-dog past?"

"It's one of the things she loves most about me." Jake grinned. "She says reformed man-whores make the best husbands."

That sounded like Gracie. Sam laughed, and the lessening of tension was welcome. Unfortunately, it was also short-lived.

"My point is, I was there, Sam. I saw how the two of you were together. Like everyone else in town that summer, I could see how much you loved her, and you weren't alone in that. V loved you, too."

Sam scoffed a laugh and picked up his glass once more. "Then you were as blind as the rest of us. I was nothing more than a meal ticket. When the promise of my pro career went down the tubes, she had no more use for me."

Jake sipped his wine, his gaze intense. "You wouldn't say that if you'd seen her when she arrived from Florida."

Though he'd overcome the bitterness over her leaving years ago, resentment tightened Sam's chest, and it pissed him off. "Yeah, well. How could I, when I'm the one she ran from?"

Jake studied him silently for a long moment, then shook his head. "I don't think *you* were what she was running from."

"What the hell is that supposed to mean?" Angry and embarrassed by her betrayal, he'd refused to call Jake for answers upon learning she'd followed him to Boston College. When they finally spoke several weeks later, Jake hadn't volunteered any information, and Sam hadn't demanded any. After all these years, pride insisted he should no longer want to know why she'd left, but his heart thudded wildly at the possibility he might finally learn without having to ask.

Jake glanced toward the empty staircase and sighed. "I'm not exactly sure. I know V, probably better than anyone, and even I don't know what happened to make her run. When she first arrived in Boston, I tried to get her to talk, but she refused. A couple months later, she finally opened up, but only to say she'd made a mistake and it was too late to fix it, so I should quit asking."

Frustrated disappointment heated Sam's gut. "She made a mistake all right, by not counting on an injury derailing her plan to bag herself a pro athlete."

Jake's eyes went hard. "If she's the gold digger you claim she is, she sucks at it. She worked three jobs to put herself through school and earn her degree in sports management. As an agent, she's handled a half dozen all-pros over the past ten years and, in the process, she's become one of the most powerful women in the world of pro sports. Combine that with her looks, and she could have had her pick of dozens of rich jocks."

The memory of her petite frame all but surrounded by Wyatt Hunter's big body flashed in Sam's mind, and he shifted in his chair.

"Instead, she's remained single and alone, with only her job for company." Jake glanced toward the stairs. "Shit, in all these years, I can count the number of dates she's had on one hand. Why is that, do you think?" He looked back at Sam, but didn't wait for an answer. "From the moment the two of you walked in the door, the tension has been crackling like an electrical arc. You want to know what I think?"

Sam narrowed his eyes, but Jake wasn't finished.

"I think that shit you mentioned is still an issue, my friend. For her definitely, and from the way your eyes continue to follow her every move, for you as well." He slid a hand over his chin. "So, my question is, why haven't *you* ever asked her why she ran?"

Sam tensed at the blatant dare. "She never gave me the chance. She took off while I was still recovering in the hospital, and I was a little busy learning how to walk again to chase after her."

Squeals and women's laughter sounded from the second floor, and Jake smiled. He studied Sam with shrewd eyes. "Well, now's your chance. Her life is here, and I can guarantee you she won't be doing any running this time."

* * * *

Perched on the side of the large tub in which her twin sons splashed and shrieked, Gracie turned off the water and looked at V. "I'm sorry, sweetie. That little snub Sam gave you wasn't like the man I've met, but grief can sometimes come across as anger."

Jaw clenched, V leaned against the vanity. God, what had she been thinking coming here with Sam? Letting him goad her was a mistake. To hell with his taunting challenge; she should have called a car. And asking him about Lucy's mother? Obviously, she'd lost her mind and, in the process, opened the door to questions she had no intention of answering. Knowing Gracie, slamming that door shut again would be next to impossible.

"Whatever." V folded her arms over her stomach. "It doesn't matter."

Eyes narrowed, Gracie dug in. "Why didn't you tell us he was coming to town?"

Hoping to head off the inquisition, V shrugged. "What was there to tell? The Marauders offered him Bob Duggan's job. He accepted. End of story."

"End of story?" Disbelief widened Gracie's eyes. "I distinctly recall you saying he was the one who got away, and now, here he is, back in your life."

V uncrossed her arms, trying to look indifferent. "He's not back in my life, he's simply taken a job with the Marauders."

"Where you'll be working with him every day." Gracie brushed bubbles from one of the twin's cheeks.

V bit back a frustrated groan. "We won't be working together every day. Caroline gave me little choice about helping them with the move to Manhattan, but once he and Lucy are settled, I'll barely see him."

"Then you need to move fast while you have the chance. Hand me a face cloth, will you? They're on the top shelf."

Grinding her teeth, V pushed off the vanity to search through the linen closet.

"He's also moving into a house less than a mile away and, at the moment, he's downstairs in the den. You know, the den you spend almost as much time in as Jake and I do?" Mischief sparkled in Gracie's gaze. "He and Jake are friends, and you know as well as I do, he'll be back. I'd say that puts him smack dab in the center of your life."

"Gracie, you're not listening." V handed her the cloth. "Nothing is going to happen between Sam and me."

"Why the hell not? If you tell me you're not attracted to that man, I'll call you a liar." She dipped the cloth in the soapy water and fought little Tommy's flying hands to scrub his neck and shoulders.

Denying an attraction to Sam would be a waste of time. Gracie was a hopeless romantic, and she'd obviously slipped into Cupid mode. "Whether or not I'm attracted doesn't matter. We have a history, Gracie. One that ended badly." V shook her head. "In case you missed it, he doesn't like me very much. With good reason."

Gracie paused in her scrubbing to look up. "Jake told me you were once engaged."

"Oh, he did, did he?" V scowled at the closed door, and Gracie laughed.

"Don't blame Jake. After you mentioned Sam at our girls' night, I badgered him for details. You know how persuasive I can be." She smiled dreamily. "He's so easy."

V groaned. "Ew. I don't want to hear how you got him to talk."

Laughter gleamed in Gracie's eyes. "I'd use a different tactic on you, but the results would be the same, so you might as well tell me what happened."

V crossed her arms. "You know, I liked you a hell of a lot better when you had your own secrets to hide and weren't so pushy."

"Secrets, huh?" Gracie snickered and attacked Jake Jr. with the cloth in her hand. "Do tell."

V winced at the memory of the argument she'd made when Gracie and Jake had been locked in their custody battle over the girls. As V had predicted, the secret Gracie had been hiding eventually got out, but being the illegitimate daughter of a famous pro was one thing. The secret that had sent V running and cost her Sam's love would only cause more hurt if told.

Gracie grinned over her shoulder. "Who was it that told me secrets have a way of getting out eventually?"

V met her grin with a bland smile. "That must have been your husband. I never would have uttered such a cliché."

Gracie laughed, diverting the looming water battle with two rubber duckies from the basket beside the tub when the twins dove after the same toy.

"Well, whoever said it was spot on." Tommy dunked his ducky. It popped to the surface, making both boys giggle, and Gracie smiled. "I thought keeping my father's identity to myself was the right thing to do. In the end, all I'd accomplished was to miss out on the years Tom and I could have had together."

V sighed. "It's not the same, Gracie. I had my chance with Sam, and chose my career instead. Let it be."

Chapter 7

With the simple scrawl of his name, Sam's lifelong dream of making it to the pros came one step closer. Setting the pen on top, he spun the contract to the Marauders' owner and slid both across the glossy desktop.

Excitement and an unexpected case of nerves collided low in Sam's gut as Caroline picked up the pen. He lifted his gaze to the framed painting hung strategically behind her head. Although he was no art expert, he knew a Picasso when he saw one. He twisted his lips to stop a wry smile. As if anyone meeting with Caroline Wainwright would need a reminder of her success or power, especially here, at the complex where there was no mistaking who held the home field advantage.

The scratch of the ballpoint recaptured his attention, but didn't come close to drowning out the thunder of his heartbeat pulsating in his head. With a final, looping flourish, she added her name to the last page of the document, set aside the pen, and looked up.

Satisfaction was keen in her smile. "Welcome to the Marauders, Sam."

He closed his fingers around the hand she offered him. Thankfully, none of the nerves threatening to unman him showed as he blew a shaky breath. "Thanks for the opportunity."

"You've earned it, and trust me, you'll continue to. Beginning next week. The Marauders are the odds-on favorite to win the Super Bowl, and I won't be satisfied with anything less."

Anticipation slammed him in the chest and took care of his nerves. He tried to control his eager grin, but failed. Eyes twinkling with approval, Caroline withdrew her hand and stood. Sam rose and walked with her as she rounded her desk and led him from the office. She paused in the open doorway and he followed her glance down the hallway toward the lounge where Lucy and V waited.

"Did you and your daughter have a chance to see some of the city while you were here?"

"Not really." He turned back and met Caroline's questioning gaze. "And unfortunately, any sightseeing will have to wait. The moment we settled on the house yesterday, V rescheduled our flights. We leave for Barlow tonight."

"V is nothing if not efficient." A tight smile tugged at the team owner's lips. "We're rushing you and, with Christmas on Thursday, that makes the situation worse, but it can't be helped. Until Bob announces his retirement, we'll be keeping you and your name under wraps. We have a bye next week, and V will make sure you don't run into any delays in the meantime." The smile disappeared. "But, her organizational abilities aren't the only reason I requested she return to Barlow with you. With her handling the logistics of your move, you'll have the time and the opportunity to tie up any..." As her words trailed off, she studied him closely as if discerning his reaction. "...*personal* loose ends."

Shit. He schooled his face to a blank mask. Well, damn. He'd wondered why Caroline was handling the signing of his contract when that job usually fell to the GM, and now he understood. There was no mistaking the intent behind her comment, or its personal nature. The loose ends she was concerned about had nothing to do with his resignation from East Texas U and everything to do with V.

He clamped down on a disgusted snort. For a woman who garnered nothing but ill will from the people of her home town, V didn't seem to have had any trouble racking up champions in her new life. Still, he shouldn't be surprised. Before coming to New York, he'd done his homework. From all accounts, Caroline and V were more than just business associates. They were also close friends and had been since Jake Malone had signed with the team eight years earlier.

God knew what kind of bullshit she'd fed Caroline, yet if the team's owner had concerns about him, why sign the contract before they were addressed?

The answer wasn't hard to figure out. With the playoffs beginning next Saturday, she didn't have the time. Winning games was Caroline's first priority, but she was too savvy a businesswoman to ignore a potential problem that could come back to bite her on the ass.

Sam shoved his hands into the pockets of his slacks. With frustration searing his blood, he curled his lips into what he hoped was a reassuring smile. "I'm sure between the two of us, we'll make it work."

Satisfaction gleamed in her smile. "Exactly what I wanted to hear. We'll see you on Monday then." With a curt nod, she turned and disappeared back into her office.

The moment the door closed, he dragged a palm over his face. His cell buzzed in his pocket, and he pulled it out, then frowned at TJ's picture on the screen. With a flick of his thumb, he dismissed the call, just as he had her others. There would be hell to pay when he got back to Barlow, but his cousin's frustration over a few unanswered calls would be nothing compared to the shit storm he was going to face when the town learned he'd shown up with V in tow.

Christ, what a cluster fuck.

He stalked down the hallway toward the lounge where Lucy sat on a couch next to V. According to Jake, V's job was her life, and God knew Sam wouldn't do anything to jeopardize his new position. They'd already agreed to disagree, and that should be the end of it but, clearly, the Marauders' owner wasn't satisfied with their truce.

Caroline expected him to clear the air with V, which meant he no longer had a choice. Doing so, however, would prove difficult if V refused to talk to him. She had barely glanced his way once she and Gracie had come downstairs last night, and except for answering Lucy's occasional question, she'd remained coldly silent on the ride back to the city.

Not that he couldn't find a way around her temper. Thanks to Patricia, he had plenty of experience dealing with stubborn females, and as hard as V's new tough shell was, he'd seen the signs of cracks. He made her nervous. A definite advantage he'd have no qualms exploiting, but there was an easier route to breaking through the barriers surrounding her like a fortress.

V had always had a soft spot for kids. Though she might have decided the best way to deal with *him* was to pretend he wasn't there, Lucy was a different story. V would quickly learn his daughter and he were a package deal.

Entering the lounge, he approached them from behind as V's words reached his ears.

"I Googled the dance studio the realtor mentioned yesterday. He's right about it being a top-notch outfit. Three of their advanced pupils are featured dancers in the Nutcracker with the New York City Ballet this year."

"Really?" Lucy shifted on the couch, tucking her feet beneath her in her favorite sitting position.

"Really. And I was thinking, since we don't have to be at the airport until six, we could make the matinee. If you'd like."

"If I'd like? Are you kidding?" Lucy's voice was breathless with anticipation.

Sam came to a stop behind them as V turned her head. Even in profile, her wide smile was evident. He did his best to tune out the pull of her low laugh.

"I have a contact with the company who can score us last-minute seats. You'd have to get your father's permission, of course, but he'll be busy for a while. I don't see why he'd object."

Of course she wouldn't. She probably figured he wanted to spend as little time with her as she did him, and she'd be right. But he wasn't about to let an opportunity slip by when one landed in his lap.

He cleared his throat. "Object to what?"

V's shoulders snapped so tightly, he was surprised the blades didn't slice through the soft silk of her blouse. She slowly turned to face him, the smile of a moment ago long gone.

Lucy spun around and rose to her knees. "V said she'd take me to see the Nutcracker."

Sliding his gaze from V's wary eyes, he crossed his arms and squinted a warning at Lucy. "Last time I checked, her name was Miss Price."

Lucy huffed. "She said I could call her V. So, can I go?"

He'd rather have his gums scraped than attend the ballet. Still, he had some fence-mending to do before he could put Caroline's command into action, and the pleading in Lucy's eyes sealed the deal. He met V's gaze. The wariness was still there, but the stubborn jut of her chin went a long way in lightening his vicious mood.

On second thought, clearing the air between them might prove more entertaining than he'd previously considered. He offered her his most innocent smile. "Sure. If I can tag along."

Surprise flashed in V's eyes before she looked away and rose to her feet. "Lucy and I will be fine on our own if you have something you need to do here at the complex. We can meet you at the airport after the show."

"No need for that. With the team flying out this afternoon for their Thursday night game in Atlanta, the complex is empty and my time is free."

She jerked her gaze toward Caroline's office. "But the contract—"

"Has been signed." Satisfaction surged in his veins, and he winked at Lucy. "Starting Monday, we'll be New Yorkers, kid."

Lucy's smile wasn't as bright as it should be, and he hated that she still had doubts. However, there was nothing he could do about that at the moment. Only time would ease her fears. V, on the other hand, looked as if she'd just gotten a whiff of something foul.

He was impressed at how quickly she wiped the distress from her face and twisted her lips into a totally fake smile. "I had no idea you were a ballet fan, Sam." She added a suggestive hum. "All those men in tights."

Oh, hell yeah. Definitely entertaining. He answered her intended jab with a toothy grin. "Don't underestimate men who make their living in tights. Tell her, Lucy. Ballet dancers train as hard as pro athletes."

"Harder." Lucy smiled smugly and uncurled from the couch.

A wrinkle creased V's brow, and he could just imagine the strain on her brain as she searched for a valid excuse to leave him behind. He smiled, which no doubt added to her frustration. Color flooded her cheeks.

"Well, then." She glanced at her watch, then turned toward the hallway. "I'll meet you back here in ten minutes."

"Where are you going?" he called to her back.

"To my office. My coat and purse are there, and I need to call my friend about the tickets."

Sam rounded the couch, following her. "We'll come along."

Lucy almost ran into V when she stopped short and turned her head. "Oh, I don't think—"

"You can show me my new office along the way."

From the flat line of her mouth, she'd rather show him the exit. She walked away, saying over her shoulder, "I have no idea where your office is. You'll have to ask someone else."

Lucy shot him a confused look before hurrying to catch her.

"Then I'll have to be content seeing yours." He could have sworn he heard a low growl. Choking back a pleased chuckle, he fell into step behind them.

V led them past Caroline's office to the end of the hallway and stopped before a closed door. Despite the tense line of her shoulders, she made her tone inviting. "Come on in." Once inside, she crossed the room and rounded an antique oak desk. "Are you thirsty, Lucy? I have water and I think there might be some juice." She lifted the handset from the desk phone and waved her free hand toward the mini-fridge in the corner.

"I'm good." Lucy wandered inside and plopped onto the floral print couch across from the desk.

Sam propped a shoulder against the doorjamb and glanced around while V placed the call to her ballet contact. Smaller than Caroline's sprawling owner's suite, V's office had a much warmer feel. Looking more like a personal den than a business office, the room was decorated in soft tans and burgundy. The deep couch and matching love seat must have cost a bundle, but the overall effect was one of comfort. There were plenty of personal touches as well, like the colorful throw pillows and the Oriental rug covering the floor. His gaze swung to the photographs crowding the credenza in front of the window overlooking the field.

Jake and Gracie Malone were prominent in several, as were their kids. In one shot, Kevin Tucker, the Marauders' number-one wide receiver and last year's MVP, grinned at the camera. A petite blonde was tucked to his side, a chubby baby in her arms. Sam recognized country music legend, Jessi Tucker, and assumed the muscular tough guy at her side was her new husband. The center frame held a close up shot of Anita's smiling face.

None of the photos included V.

"Thanks, Heather. I owe you." V disconnected the call and punched in another number. Tucking the handset between her shoulder and ear, she slid open a desk drawer. "Yes, I need a car." Retrieving her purse, she set it on the desktop. "Two passengers. Picking up at the Marauders' Sports Complex. They'll need to stop at their hotel on forty-seventh, then on to Lincoln Center." She listened for a moment, then nodded. "Thank you. They'll be at the front door of the complex in ten minutes."

She replaced the handset, and Sam shoved off the doorjamb, moving into the room. "Change of plans?"

"You're not coming with us?" Disappointment was ripe in Lucy's voice.

V's face softened as she looked at his daughter. "Of course I am." She slid her gaze back to Sam. "I'll meet you at the will call window. You can store your bags there during the show."

"Why aren't we riding together?"

Slipping her coat from the back of the chair, she hung it over one arm. "Because you need to pick up your bags and so do I. The curtain rises in an hour. We won't have the time to stop by both your hotel *and* my condo beforehand, and we'll be cutting things very close if we wait until after."

A logical explanation, but the way her eyes shuttered as he walked toward her said expediency wasn't the only reason she preferred traveling in two vehicles. He was only too happy to derail her plans. "No problem. Our bags are downstairs at the reception desk."

"Oh." She blinked. "You've already checked out?"

"This morning." He reached out his hand and couldn't help his smile when she visibly tensed. Plucking the coat from her arm, he held it out and waited for her to turn around. He slid the material over her shoulders, stepping closer until his chest brushed against her stiffened back. Dipping his head, he spoke quietly in her ear. "Relax, Red. You're safe...for now. Don't you remember? I only bite during sex."

Her soft gasp sent an arrow of heat straight to his cock.

New hard shell, hell. Like taking candy from a baby.

Circumstances had conspired to send them back to where it had all begun. For the next few days, she'd be on his turf, and if he had to wade through the past to secure the promise of his future, he'd damn well get something in return. He'd be playing with fire if he acted on the enticing scenarios for evening the score that were playing through his mind, but what the hell? He could handle the heat and, at the very least, he'd be getting some answers.

Chapter 8

Sam pulled the truck to a stop in the driveway. His kitchen door opened before he'd even cut the engine, and TJ stepped outside holding tight to Daisy's collar. Lucy climbed out the passenger door. Her stuffed backpack bumped against her spine as she hurried across the lawn to Daisy. Stretching his arm over the back of the seat, Sam grabbed his duffle bag and got out to join them.

TJ met his gaze with an anxious frown, but spoke to Lucy. "So, Luce, how'd it go?"

Lucy straightened from petting the whining dog and shrugged. "Okay, I guess. Sam found a house."

"*We* found a house," Sam corrected behind her as he approached.

"A house? Does that mean what I think it means?" TJ's eyes were owl-wide and she held her breath.

A helpless smile stretched Sam's lips. "I start with the Marauders on Monday."

TJ squealed, let go of Daisy's collar, and launched off the stoop. He stumbled back a step as she slammed into him, and wrapped his arms around her to keep them from tumbling to the ground. He laughed as she shoved out of his arms and swatted his shoulder.

"You jerk! Why didn't you answer your phone? I've been going crazy!"

"I was kind of busy." Hoisting his duffle over one shoulder, he scrubbed a hand over Daisy's head when she bumped against his knee. "Hiya, Mutt." He straightened with a final pat and climbed the steps to open the door. "Did she give you any trouble?"

Lucy followed him inside, with Daisy and TJ bringing up the rear. His cousin shut the door and turned. "Daisy's a good girl. She never gives me trouble but, if you're looking for some, your mom left six messages on your machine. Apparently, she saw you and Lucy on TV at the game Sunday."

Sam glanced at the answering machine on the counter and grimaced. "Shit. I need to call her."

"Ya think?" TJ arched a brow. "She doesn't have your cell number?"

He dropped his duffle next to the door. "It's better for my sanity if she can't reach me twenty-four seven."

TJ grinned and turned to Lucy. "So, did you do anything besides football stuff while you were in New York? I'm so jealous. I've always wanted to see Manhattan."

"We went to the ballet." Lucy dumped her backpack on the table. "We saw the Nutcracker. It was amazing." She walked to the fridge and opened the door. "V got us tickets. In the second row!"

TJ's head snapped around to stare at him, and he ground his teeth. *Shit.* He needed to explain about V *and* Caroline's demands, but he'd prefer that conversation happen when Lucy was out of earshot. He shook his head slightly and squinted at TJ in warning.

Her lips flattened in a tight line and she turned back to Lucy. "V?"

Lucy shut the fridge and screwed off the top of her water bottle. "She works for the Marauders. Her real name is Victoria, but she likes V better. *And* she's Miss Anita's daughter. You know. My ballet teacher?"

TJ shot him a sidelong glance. "I know Miss Anita."

Lucy scrunched her nose and cocked her head. "Then you must know V. She grew up here."

"We've met." TJ's smile was strained, but if Lucy noticed, she didn't say.

"Well, V has a friend who works at the Lincoln Center and she said she can get me tickets to the ballet whenever I want."

"That's great, Luce."

Lucy turned to Sam, hope shimmering in her eyes. "Do you think she'll come see me dance while she's here?"

TJ made a choking sound. Sam refused to look her way. "If you ask her to, yeah. You can do that tomorrow, but it's late. Time to hit the hay, kid."

Lucy glanced at the clock on the wall and frowned. "It's only ten-thirty."

"Yeah, but we've got a lot to accomplish in the next few days, which means no sleeping in. I'm counting on you to help with the packing."

He expected an argument, but to his surprise, she strode to the table and scooped up her backpack. She did, however, get in the last word. "He thinks I'm slave labor." She tossed TJ a rare grin and swept from the room with Daisy on her heels.

He delayed looking at TJ until he heard Lucy shut her bedroom door. Facing her, he wasn't surprised by TJ's crossed arms. He sighed. "Thanks for not flipping out in front of her. Regardless of what you and I, or anyone else, think of V, Lucy likes her."

TJ glanced down the hallway before meeting his gaze with an unhappy frown. "That's obvious, and understandable considering V bribed her with ballet tickets. God, that woman is something else."

An image of V hurrying down the hallway toward her office flashed in his head, and he couldn't disagree. She probably considered the navy blue business suit proper armor for a woman in her position, but the tailored cut did little to disguise her luscious curves. Shaking his head, he did his best to banish the enticing vision of her fine ass and toned legs beneath that pencil-slim skirt.

As for TJ's charge of bribery, from what he'd seen, enticement had nothing to do with it. However, TJ would never attribute a simple act of kindness to V. Arguing the point would be a waste of time.

He cleared his throat and opened the fridge. "You want a beer?"

"Don't you have anything stronger?" He grinned, and she flopped into one of the kitchen chairs. "What's going on, Sam? When is she arriving and why?"

"She's already here. She flew in with Lucy and me." Plucking two long necks from the fridge, he approached the table, handed TJ her beer, and slid into an open chair. "Taking care of our move was part of the Marauders' incentive package. V's here to expedite the process and handle any unexpected details." He twisted the lid off the beer bottle and grunted. "Among other things."

TJ's eyes went hard. "What other things?"

After taking a long slug from his beer, Sam leaned on the table and filled in TJ on Caroline Wainwright's not-so-veiled demand.

"So much for requesting V be fired," TJ grouched when he'd finished.

He chuckled and sprawled back in his chair. "That was never going to happen."

TJ sighed. "What are you going to do?"

A slow smile tugged at his lips and he couldn't help teasing her. "What do you think? I'm going to sleep with her, of course."

"That's not funny."

He grinned at her disgruntled tone and sour expression. "Caroline is concerned the tension between us will affect our ability to work together. Haven't you heard? Sex is a great tension reliever."

"Yeah, well, sex between the two of you didn't work out so well the last time." Her scowl disappeared behind the beer bottle she brought to her lips.

He chuckled. "Relax. I was kidding. This isn't about sex, it's about putting the past behind us once and for all."

She huffed, and he sobered.

If Jake was right—and after spending the last few days with V, Sam was beginning to believe he might be—he'd been reading the situation wrong all along. From the beginning, V had experienced the same unprecedented pull as he. The stark awareness in her eyes as he'd whispered in ear yesterday proved that hadn't changed.

Jake claimed she didn't date as a rule, which fit the woman Sam remembered. She'd also never been the kind of woman to grab at cheap sexual thrills. For V, sex had gone hand-in- hand with her heart. She may not like it, may be fighting it for all she was worth, but after all these years, a spark remained.

The realization had hit him like a blitzing linebacker and, while his head insisted he was wrong, his gut disagreed. As for his heart....

He swallowed. *Put the past behind them?* How could they...shit, how could *he* when those embers that had burned so fiercely years ago insisted on flaring in the present?

The fact was, he couldn't. Not without knowing the truth, anyway. The question remained, why would a woman who reacted to a man so completely and honestly, disappear without a word? The only logical answer was something had spooked her, and whatever it was had been enough to make her turn her back on them. It was time he found out what that something was.

V had made it clear she intended to avoid him once he and Lucy were settled in Manhattan, but if he was to find a way past the protective walls V had erected, he couldn't let that happen. Ironically, Caroline had provided the perfect solution to the problem.

Professionally, he had nothing to worry about. He'd double-checked his contract and, barring unsatisfactory performance or any dangerous or destructive behavior toward the organization on his part, his position with the team was iron-clad. Caroline obviously knew that. The contract was hers, after all. Yet, she'd been the one to inject a personal agenda into the situation by insisting he and V *work out* their issues.

That was exactly what he was going to do. Sitting forward, he leaned his elbows on the table. "If I have to make nice with V to...ensure the future, then that's what I'll do." He bumped his chin in TJ's direction. "And you're going to help."

She choked on her beer, then dragged her hand across her mouth. "Me?"

"Yes, you." He sat forward. "From what I've seen, V is as uncomfortable with the situation as I am. I don't expect an argument from her, especially when I explain Caroline's concerns, but easing the tension between us won't work if she has to deal with hostility from everyone else in town. Most importantly, Lucy cares about Anita and, by extension, V. I don't want her exposed to misplaced aggression over an event that happened years ago and has nothing to do with her feelings for either of them."

"I would never do anything to upset Lucy."

The hurt in TJ's eyes stung, and he sighed. "I know you wouldn't. Just promise you'll be on your best behavior while V is here. It's only for a couple days." She nodded without hesitation, and he smiled. "It will go a long way toward convincing the people of Barlow that V and I have settled our differences if they see you've forgiven her, too."

"Now you're pushing it."

He smiled, relieved at her grumbled complaint. "The two of you used to be good friends. How hard could it be to pretend you are again?"

"Really pushing it." She cocked her head. "You'll owe me."

Tapping his beer bottle to hers, he laughed. "Add it to my tab."

* * * *

V picked up a box full of linens and headed down the hall toward Sam's living room. The movers she'd hired before leaving Manhattan wouldn't arrive until Friday morning. They would handle the furnishings and incidentals, which left Lucy and Sam's personal items. V and Lucy had made an impressive dent in that chore over the past five hours. Tomorrow was Christmas, which meant they'd lose an entire day, but with a little luck and perseverance, V would be back in Manhattan earlier than she'd predicted.

Her departure couldn't come soon enough, but not because of the nasty welcome she was bound to receive from the residents of Barlow. Booking a room thirty miles away in Tyler had delayed word of her return from getting out so far, but she could handle the dirty looks and even the insults once it did. The Marauders' new offensive coordinator was another matter.

Since meeting with Caroline to sign the Marauders' contract, Sam's entire demeanor had changed. V wasn't sure why and didn't like it. Broody and suspicious she could deal with. The sexy smiles and charm he'd been employing for the past twenty-four hours made no sense and knocked her off balance.

I only bite during sex. Lord, what was that about?

To her relief, he'd left for East Texas U to tender his resignation shortly after she'd arrived this morning. She didn't expect him to be gone all day, but a smart woman didn't look a gift horse in the mouth. The morning had passed with relatively little stress, and she was grateful for his absence.

As she had several times throughout the morning, she paused outside the closed door to Sam's bedroom. So far, she hadn't been able to bring herself to enter his private domain. Each time she'd talked herself into opening the damn door to pack up his things, her mind had conjured one unpleasant scenario after another. Like Sam returning home at the precise moment she stood in his closet with her nose pressed to one of his sweaters, sniffing for signs of the woodsy musk cologne he still seemed to prefer.

Or worse, finding some faceless woman's lingerie tucked into a drawer.

As if she had any business contemplating Sam Fitzpatrick's sex life. She was here to do a job, nothing more. She squeezed her eyes shut. Geez, how the hell had she gotten here? Obviously karma was having a good laugh at her expense. One day she was making million-dollar deals, and the next she was packing up her ex-lover's boxers.

Her eyes popped open and she gritted her teeth. Not in this lifetime. She might love her job, but she drew the line at Sam's underwear drawer.

Hitching the box higher in her arms, she stalked down the hallway. Lucy turned her head as V stepped into the living room. On the floor in front of a media cabinet, the teenager sat with her legs folded beneath her, a half-filled box by her hip. She'd sorted CDs into two piles, and a dozen books and binders were scattered on the floor around her.

Lucy chewed casually, then swallowed, and V eyed the remains of the donut in her hand. Sam had left a dozen on the counter in the kitchen and, by V's count, the chocolate-covered pastry was Lucy's third since he'd left.

Her lips quirked in a guilty smile. "I got hungry."

V shook her head and carried the box to the stack near the front door. "Do you know how much sugar is in those things? Lord, if I ate one I'd have to spend a week in the gym."

Another bite disappeared. "Why do you think they taste so good?"

V laughed and shook her head. "Metabolism is wasted on the young." She squatted beside Lucy. "What have you got there?"

Lucy shoved the last bite of donut in her mouth, then plucked a binder from the shelf. "Books and stuff. Some pictures."

V selected a photo album from the top of one pile. "Did you look through them?"

"A little. Mostly it's football stuff."

V opened the album and, sure enough, each page contained photos of various players on the field. Sam stood amongst the coaching staff in several team pictures. From the uniforms, she assumed they were from his years at East Texas U. After placing the binder in the box, she selected another and opened it, then froze. Her heart clenched as she stared at a close-up of Sam mugging for the camera in a garnet-and-gold uniform.

"Is something wrong?"

She glanced sideways to find Lucy watching her. Dropping her gaze to the picture, V sucked in a stealthy breath. "Just remembering. This was taken before Sam's first game in college." She'd arrived in Tallahassee at dusk the night before and had been horrified when he snuck her into his dorm room, afraid they'd be caught and he'd get into trouble. He'd laughed and said a little trouble would be worth it to hold her through the night. An hour later, he'd proposed. Neither of them had slept a wink.

"You were there?"

Shaken by the memory, V nodded. "I took the picture."

"Did you know my mom?"

The breathless excitement in Lucy's voice and eyes made V's heart throb almost as much as the question. "Your mother? Did she go to FSU?"

Lucy shook her head. "No, she lived in Tallahassee. She and Sam met in the hospital after he hurt his knee. Mom was a volunteer."

V's stomach muscles clenched. Oh, God. For three days, she'd remained at Sam's bedside while hospital staff came and went. Had she actually met Maggie? Spoken to the woman Sam had so quickly replaced her with? Or had Lucy's mother and Sam met after V had panicked and fled town?

Breathing became difficult. She closed the binder and set it aside. "No, I'm afraid I didn't." She softened her voice. "Sam said she passed away."

Lucy ducked her head. "She had cancer."

"I know." V brushed her fingers over Lucy's arm. "I'm sorry."

Lucy nodded, then looked up. "But, are you sure you didn't know her? You knew Sam."

V swallowed. She was tempted to ask why the girl used Sam's first name instead of "Dad" simply for a chance to change the subject, but the memory of his reaction the other day stopped her.

None of my business, anyway.

"I grew up in Barlow. Everyone knew your father." She jerked her chin toward the CDs. "Are these sorted for a reason?"

Disappointment flashed in Lucy's eyes at the obvious shift in conversation, but she pointed to the first pile. "Those must belong to his girlfriends. Sam doesn't listen to anything but country."

"Girlfriends?" *Lord, would this day ever end?* The thought of facing dirty looks and snide remarks from Sam's friends and neighbors was beginning to sound almost pleasant compared to this bizarre peek into Sam's virtual black book.

"TJ says he's dated half the women in Smith County, Texas, but the only one I've met is Patricia." Lucy's lips turned down in a frown. "Her daddy owns an oil company."

Patricia Amandola? Sam was dating the Barlow Oil Princess? V stiffened against the stab of pain piercing her heart.

Suck it up, V. You made him a free agent a long time ago and have no right to question whom he spends his time with.

"You don't like her?" V plucked one of the CD's from the "girlfriend" pile. The cover featured a well-known pop artist in his early twenties who had been slammed by the press just last week for a drunken tirade on YouTube.

She grimaced and returned the case to the stack.

Lucy shrugged. "I've only met her once, so I don't really know her. Sam likes her, but she seems kind of snobby to me."

V held back a smirk. The word she'd use to describe the princess of Barlow was far grittier. Patricia and her "It Girl" minions might have spared V the derision they'd aimed at so many of her female peers, but only because of her close friendship with Jake. Any pretense of acceptance, however, had vanished the day after her first date with Sam. Patricia had shown her true colors throughout that spring and early summer, and they were all shades of bitch green.

The irony of Sam turning his eye Patricia's way shouldn't sting so much, but it did. Pointing out his horrendously bad taste in women would help ease the bite, but wouldn't say much for V since she'd once been one of them. She would never do that in front of Lucy, however, and singing Patricia's praises was equally impossible. V settled for diplomatic and hoped she didn't gag in the process.

"It takes time to get to know new people. Given time, you may like Patricia as much as Sam does."

Lucy's face closed up like a door slamming shut. "Maybe, but I don't see the point when I won't be around much longer."

What the hell? V knew what fear looked like. She'd seen it reflected in her own mirror often enough as a child. Lucy's eyes simmered with it.

V dipped her chin. "I'm not sure I understand, sweetie."

Lucy looked away. "Forget it. It's stupid, anyway." She leaned forward, picked up the binder V had set aside, and opened it to flip through the pages. "Maybe there's a picture of my mom in here. If you see her, you might remember."

Oh, for heaven's sake. Apparently V wasn't the only one who knew how to direct a conversation and, for some reason, Lucy was intent on sticking with the subject of her mother. V bit back a sigh and began loading Sam's CD's into an empty box. He could sort out the "girlfriend" disks himself.

"Hey, this is *you*." Lucy looked up from the photo album, her eyes wide with surprise. "Why were you kissing Sam?"

V's stomach did a spinning roll as she jerked her gaze to the picture on the page. She remembered the day the photo was taken like it was yesterday. FSU was flying Sam to Florida that morning, and she and her mother had a terrible fight. The plan was for V to leave the next morning and drive to Tallahassee, meeting him at the end of the week. Anita was convinced V was ruining her life, and to keep that from happening, she'd hidden the keys to V's rat-trap car.

V rode to town on a bike she'd borrowed from the rancher's wife so she could kiss Sam goodbye. The next morning, after collecting her spare keys from Jake, she'd left Barlow for good—and Sam's daughter didn't need to know any of that.

"That was nothing." She waved her hand airily. "Just a case of friends joking around."

She'd been clinging to him like she'd never see him again.

"Then what happened? Why aren't you friends anymore?"

The question surprised her, but before she could come up with a reply, Sam spoke from the kitchen doorway. "Who says we're not friends?"

Chapter 9

V's heart thudded in triple time when she turned her head to find Sam wasn't alone. TJ Burke stood at his side, her lips pulled up at the corners in what V figured was supposed to be a smile. The attempt looked more painful than pleasant.

With the exception of Jake, friends had been rare for V as a girl, but TJ had been one. Though they hadn't had the type of friendship that included weekend sleepovers, TJ often accompanied her uncle on his veterinary rounds at the Double J. Together, she and V would follow him around as he checked on the animals. When they were in high school, TJ's uncle had occasionally made arrangements with the rancher to allow V and TJ to ride on the ranch's trails.

It had been TJ who had cajoled V into accepting Sam's request for a date. A half-dozen times that spring, TJ and her boyfriend at the time had double-dated with V and Sam. Despite their friendship, or perhaps because of it, TJ had taken V's betrayal harder than most. Their friendship had died when, not knowing what to say, V had refused to take TJ's calls in those weeks after she'd arrived in Boston.

TJ glanced at Lucy before her eyes settled on V. "Hello, V. It's been a long time." The coolness in her tone said it hadn't been long enough.

Curling her lips in a smile, V rose to her feet. "Yes, it has. You're looking well."

"Thanks. You, too." TJ's fake smile morphed into a genuine one as she faced Lucy. "Hey, kid, I'm headed out to the Double J to check on those foals I delivered the other day. Want to ride along?"

"Yeah!" Excitement lit Lucy's face, and she scrambled to her feet.

V tensed, not so much at the mention of the ranch where she'd grown up and become friends with TJ, but at the idea of being left alone with Sam. She flicked a peek his way. His intent gaze clashed with hers as if he'd been waiting for her to look his way. Her stomach sank with the knowledge that TJ's invitation to Lucy wasn't an arbitrary one. For some reason, Sam had decided he and V needed to be alone, and TJ had agreed to assist him in whatever mischief he had up his sleeve.

V cleared her throat, hoping to derail their plan. "Don't worry about me if you want to go along, Sam. I can finish up here and lock the doors before I leave."

He shook his head. "That won't be necessary. This is my house. My stuff." A dimple creased his cheek beside a predatory smile." I wouldn't dream of leaving you all alone to pack it up by yourself. I'll stick around and help."

Right. He was definitely up to something and, whatever it was, odds were the results wouldn't be helpful. Not for her, anyway.

TJ adjusted the strap of the small backpack on her shoulder and addressed Sam as if V weren't there. "Don't forget the Christmas Eve open house tonight. Dinner is at five sharp. If you're late, I'm not covering for you with Mom."

He grinned and tugged on the inky black braid hanging over her shoulder. "Have I ever failed at charming my way out of trouble with Aunt Kay?"

TJ slapped at his hand and glared at V. "There's a first time for everything, cuz."

Sam narrowed his eyes at his cousin, while V mentally rolled hers. She might be guilty of a lot of things, including the death of her and TJ's friendship, but spending time alone with Sam was the last thing she wanted to do. She refused to accept responsibility for any hypothetical trouble he might get into with his family because of it.

TJ slipped Daisy's leash from the hook and fastened it to her collar. "Lucy and I will meet you at Mom's."

Sam nodded. "Sounds like a plan."

Lucy paused as she put on her coat and turned to V. "Wait. What are you doing for Christmas Eve? And Christmas?"

Enjoying a quiet glass of wine back at her hotel sounded perfect for tonight, but she doubted Anita would agree. As for tomorrow, V had specifically selected her hotel because of the five-star restaurant on the top floor. She'd be doing her best to convince Anita that room service and a football marathon in front of the large flat screen in her room was the ideal way to spend the holiday.

Charmed by the obvious concern in Lucy's eyes, V smiled. "I'm covered, sweetie. Mom and I will probably grab something to eat for dinner tonight, and we'll figure something out for tomorrow. Which reminds me." She walked to the entry table near the front door and pulled a small box from her purse. Ignoring Sam's questioning gaze and TJ's frown, she held out the box to Lucy. "Merry Christmas."

Pleasure danced over Lucy's face as she accepted the box, plucked off the ribbon, and opened it. She cooed with delight and held up a delicate silver bracelet with its blinged-out dance-shoes charm.

Lucy looked up at V. "I saw this in the theater gift shop."

"I know." V returned her infectious grin. "I thought you should have it as a reminder of your first theater experience in New York."

Unprepared for Lucy's lunge forward, V almost stumbled as the girl slammed into her and wrapped her arms around V's shoulders in a tight squeeze. A huffed snort came from TJ, who spun away to walk out the open door.

No surprise there. Knowing TJ, she probably thought the gift was some kind of bribe aimed at manipulating the teenager's affections. Though TJ's low opinion of her stung, V had no one to blame but herself. Since there wasn't a damn thing she could do about it, she shoved the hurt from her mind. Sam's opinion, however, was a different story. Whether she liked it or not, they had to work together, and she hoped she hadn't made that more difficult by crossing an imaginary line.

Hesitantly, she met his gaze over Lucy's head, but the judgment she expected to find wasn't there. Not at first, anyway. He briefly dropped his gaze to Lucy's arms, clinging to V, and the pain in his eyes hit her like a fist to the belly. He swallowed audibly and his jaw tightened, as if he'd gritted his teeth. She didn't wait from him to look up. After returning Lucy's squeeze, she let go and stepped back.

Lucy looked embarrassed. "I didn't get you anything."

Still shaken by Sam's reaction, V managed a small smile for Lucy. "That hug you just gave me is the best gift I'll get this Christmas. Go on. TJ's waiting. Have some fun with the new foals, and would you do me a favor and take some pictures? I'd love to see them."

Lucy nodded, grabbed her phone off the coffee table, and disappeared out the front door.

As soon as the door shut behind Lucy, V turned to Sam. "There is no secret agenda behind the bracelet. I saw her drooling over it in the gift shop before the ballet and thought—"

"I didn't think it was part of an agenda." Sam moved deeper into the living room.

O-kay. Then what was up with the clenched jaw? "TJ did."

She watched as he peeled out of his coat and tossed it over the back of the couch.

"My cousin is overly protective of the people she cares about." He turned to face her and shrugged. "Plus, she doesn't like you very much."

"There's a news flash." V bared her teeth in a saccharine smile. "You don't have to sugarcoat things with me, Sam. By all means, be blunt."

He chuckled. "I thought I was." Slipping the button on his suit jacket, he dropped to sit on the arm of the couch, his thighs spread wide in one of those blatantly male postures that wreaked havoc on a woman's system.

V tried not to stare, but with faded denim molding various muscles and one very impressive bulge, it was almost impossible not to. She jacked up her chin. "Then why the ruse to get Lucy out of the house?"

"It wasn't a ruse, exactly. TJ really does have a few new foals to check on."

"And Lucy?"

He propped his palms on his thighs and sighed. "She likes you, V. I've got no problem with that. In fact, I'm glad she has at least one other person in New York she feels comfortable with."

An unexpected flood of pleasure tightened her chest—which wouldn't do. He hadn't arranged to speak to her alone so he could hand out compliments, and she preferred he get to the point. "I assume there's a 'but' coming."

A small smile tugged at one corner of his mouth, then quickly disappeared. "But, because she cares about you, I didn't think she should be here for this conversation."

Pleasure crashed beneath a wave of trepidation. "That sounds ominous."

He cocked his head and held her gaze with an intensity that only made her apprehension worse. "It doesn't have to be."

Her heart had begun to pound, and her legs were suddenly weak. She slid into the wingback chair across from him. "Why don't you just say whatever it is you have to say."

"Fair enough." He dipped his chin. "Caroline thinks the two of us need to clear the air."

Definitely ominous. Crap. She swallowed. "Clear the air, how?"

He crossed his arms, causing his thick biceps to strain his jacket sleeves. "You tell me. Obviously, the two of you have spoken about our... previous association. Caroline signed my contract, then told me one of the reasons she was sending you here to Barlow was so the two of us could, and I quote, *tie up any* personal *loose ends*."

She winced. *Oh, geez, Caroline. Are you kidding me?*

Horrified, she shook her head. "You have nothing to worry about. I'll take care of it. I'll talk to her the moment we get back."

"Not good enough." He dropped his arms and sat forward with his forearms braced on his thighs. Combined with his growled tone, the position was sufficiently intimidating. "I'm not willing to risk my career over shit that happened more than a decade ago. It ends here. Before we go back to Manhattan."

"I agree—"

"What did you tell her?"

Oh, shit. Sure, he was worried about his job, but he didn't need to be. Caroline never would have signed him if she had any real doubts. Then again, in all the years she and Caroline had known one another, V had never expressed concern over dealings with any man. If a player or coach, or a complete stranger, for that matter, caused V grief, she had no trouble handling the problem herself. Unfortunately, Sam's reappearance in her universe had left her too rattled to realize Caroline would see V's reaction as an issue to be handled.

"Relax, Sam. Caroline and I might be friends, but neither of us are the type of women who share the intimate details of our private lives."

"And yet, she somehow knows enough about our history she felt compelled to warn her new offensive coordinator that he'd better fix whatever he'd done to upset her *friend.*"

Yikes. Was that how Caroline had put it? No wonder he was pissed. V attempted to diffuse his growing anger. "You have nothing to fix."

"Damned right, I don't."

She grimaced at his snarled. "I doubt she meant it as a warning."

His eyes narrowed in barely contained anger. "Then you'd be wrong. What did you tell her, V?"

She crossed her arms. "I didn't tell her what happened between us, if that's what you're thinking."

A muscle twitched in his tightly clamped jaw, and he sat up straight. Silence hung between them for a long moment, as if he were struggling for control. Slowly, the wrinkle of his brow eased and his chest wall expanded on a deep sigh. "Maybe we should start there."

His quiet tone made the hair on her arms stand up. She fidgeted in the chair. "Start where? I don't understand."

"I've never asked, and I probably should have...." She wanted to look away, but his laser-like gaze held her paralyzed. His deep voice dropped another octave. "What, exactly, *did* happen between us?"

Nausea bubbled in her belly as her most desperate dream and worst nightmare collided. She'd dreamed of the chance to make things right with him. To tell him the truth and be understood. To shed the dark secret that had destroyed her dreams and reclaim the life and love she'd thrown away. She longed to beg his forgiveness and have it given. But, even if by some miracle that should happen, it wouldn't matter.

Baring her soul to him wasn't an option. Not fifteen years ago, and not now. The time for truth had passed long before she'd lost her heart to him and dared to dream she could have what his love promised. Then, as with now, grabbing her chance at happiness would mean destroying her mother's soul. How could she do that and survive?

She couldn't, which left her with one option. Convincing him she was the bitch he believed her to be all these years wasn't something she could do sitting down, however. She shoved to her feet and, curling her lips into a bland smile, she cocked her head.

"You know what happened. Considering the extent of your injury, Jake's rising star was a much better bet to get me where I wanted to go."

A muscled ticked in Sam's jaw, and she could have sworn that was hurt in his eyes. His tone, however, was pure irritation. "Yeah. That's the way I remember it."

She held firm beneath his angry regard. "I admit, taking off without a word wasn't a very kind thing to do, but really, what could I have said to make what I was about to do sound better? Bottom line? I wanted things you could no longer give me."

"That much is obvious." His brows dropped over narrowed eyes, and he stood. She stiffened, but he didn't step any closer. Instead, he crossed his arms. "And you've gotten many of those things."

Adrenaline spiked her pulse at the suspicion gleaming in his eye as if he hadn't believed a word she said. Unsure of where he was leading her, she refused to back down. "I won't apologize for being ambitious."

"I wouldn't expect you to. I know all about ambition. Without it, I wouldn't be standing here."

She lifted her hand, palm up. "Exactly, and I—"

"But there was a time you included *me* in the list of things you wanted."

The claim hit her like a physical blow, and it took all her concentration not to flinch. Denying she'd wanted him wasn't something she could do with any conviction and they both knew it. Running her gaze down his big body, she hid her dismay beneath pure bluster. "You're a fine-looking man, Sam. Wanting you was never the problem."

"I'm glad to hear you still feel that way. That'll make things easier."

The fine hair on the back of her neck prickled when he suddenly dropped his hands to his sides and stalked toward her. "Wait. What are talking about?"

"It's simple." He closed the distance, and she stumbled backward. Stiff-arming him did no good. He gripped both her arms and held her in place. "You claim you walked away from me to get what you wanted. If that's true, as far as I'm concerned, I dodged a bullet fifteen years ago. I'm perfectly happy to let that be the end of it."

Some of the tension eased from her clenched muscles. He may have his doubts but, thankfully, he wasn't going to press her on them.

"But, it appears providence has other plans." Her tension returned tenfold as he released one of her arms to slip his hand around her waist. Calculation darkened the blue of his eyes. "Because of our past, my position with the Marauders is shaky when it shouldn't be." He slid his hand down her spine and tugged her against him until her breasts smashed flat against the solid muscle of his chest. "Caroline made it clear she expects us to put our personal differences behind us. What better way to convince her we have than to return to Manhattan as a couple?"

She opened her mouth to protest, but only succeeded in aiding him as he lowered his head and crushed his mouth to hers. His tongue slid into her mouth with practiced ease. Familiar and irresistible, his woodsy scent and spicy flavor wrapped around her, seeping into her taste buds and absorbing into her skin like a well-remembered balm.

Her knees went weak and, although she struggled to keep her feet beneath her, it was no use. She hung in his embrace, off-balance and unable to care, and curled into him as if returning home. His guttural groan was a rumbling vibration against her breasts, and she reveled in the knowledge she wasn't alone in her madness.

He shifted his head, taking the kiss deeper, and time retreated. Mistakes, secrets, and years of regret vanished until only pleasure and heat existed. Desperate for more, she fought her arms free to slide her hands up over his chest and neck, and plunged her fingers into the thick pelt of his hair. She was rewarded by the quick thrust of his hips and cried out at the delicious friction of his erection pressed against her lower belly and mound.

A whimper of disappointment caught in her throat as he lifted his head suddenly. She opened her eyes and regret swiftly slid into alarm at the heated confusion in his. Lord, what were they doing? What was *she* doing?

Frightened and completely flustered by her reaction to his unexpected kiss, she shoved at his chest, and he let her go. "Are you insane? You hate me, remember?" She stumbled back a step, forgetting about the chair behind her. Tumbling sideways, she ended up with her legs draped over one of its arms.

His gaze lingered on the length of leg exposed by the hike of her skirt, and she yanked at the hem. He reached down and adjusted the hard-on straining the front of his jeans. "All evidence to the contrary."

Heat infused her cheeks as a blush spread from her chest to her face. "You have a girlfriend."

"Says who?"

"Have you forgotten Patricia?"

His brows jumped to his hairline before he cleared his throat. "Patricia was never my girlfriend. We've dated occasionally, but that's all it ever was, and it's over now."

Relief she couldn't deny tangled with disgust. She sat up, straightening herself on the chair, and waved her hand. "Regardless, you can't be serious about the two of us pretending to be a couple."

"Oh, but I am." Leaning down, he propped both hands on the arms of the chair, caging her in, and smiled when she shrank away from him. "You did what you had to do to achieve your goals. Now, it's my turn, and you're going to help. I checked my contract and there is no anti-fraternization clause. Until the season is over, you and I are going to play the happy lovers, because I can't do the job I was hired to do if I'm hamstrung by Caroline's concerns over our personal relationship."

"She'll never believe it. Nobody will." Lord, Gracie would blow a gasket. And Jake? No. Sam was nuts and so was his ridiculous plan.

The anger was gone from his eyes, but the odd light that had replaced it wasn't something she could place. Holding her gaze, he straightened. "Then you'll have to convince her and everyone else. You owe me, V, and that's my price."

Chapter 10

Sam knelt among the spider web of cords behind the cabinet holding TV components and unplugged the Blu-ray player. Winding the cord, he slapped one of the preprinted labels V had made around the end and tossed it into the box at his hip. He glanced toward the other side of the room, where V was nearly finished packing the last of his books.

She hadn't said a word in three hours, not since he'd gotten off the phone with Anita. As a friend of Kay's, V's mother was among those typically present at his aunt's Christmas Eve celebration. With V in town, she'd obviously made other plans for the evening. She'd sounded as shocked as V when he suggested she arrive early for the family dinner, since her daughter would be attending with Sam and Lucy.

No doubt Anita, along with his family and the friends attending the open house, would think he'd lost his mind, and they wouldn't be far off. But hell, a man couldn't be held responsible for the depraved workings of his brain when all the blood in his body had taken up residence in his cock.

Pretend to be a couple? He rolled his eyes.

Caroline might have opened the door to the possibility, but there had to be some other way to ensure V didn't succeed in her plan to avoid him. Unfortunately, the moment he'd slipped his arms around her, his brain had gone blank.

Christ. He'd forgotten what it was like to hold her. The way her curves fit against him like a puzzle piece sliding home. Forgotten her quick-fire response to his touch. And her taste…. Her vanilla-sweet flavor lingered on his tongue. He licked his lips and called himself a fool. This business would burn him alive if he weren't careful.

Demanding she play along with his nutty facade had to be one of the craziest ideas to ever come out of his mouth. Yet, once his raging hard-on had subsided to simple discomfort, and he'd recognized the fear in V's eyes at the thought of facing his family, guilt wouldn't let him back down.

No matter what her reasons for running had been, their relationship had been no one else's business. His failure to put his foot down with the residents of Barlow had turned what should have been a private matter between the two of them into a public lynching that never ended.

And that was on him.

Not once in the months he'd been falling for her had he heard an unkind word leave V's lips. Nothing to indicate she was anything other than the sweet-but-shy girl who'd stolen his heart. Yet, he'd attributed the worst to her when she'd left, without trying very hard to find out the truth. Worse, he'd accepted the unwavering support of family and friends as if it were his due, while she had faced the animosity of those she'd considered friends without complaint.

His mind supplied a picture of her as she'd accepted TJ's obvious disdain earlier without comment. He knew how much his cousin's friendship had meant to V, and yet she'd stood there and quietly taken TJ's contempt as if she deserved it. Up until a few days ago, he would have agreed with that assessment, but something wasn't right with this picture.

If he hadn't been consumed with proving to himself and others he was over her, he would have questioned her silence in the face of the town's collective condemnation. A cold-hearted bitch who didn't give a rat's ass wouldn't have taken the shit the townsfolk had dished out all these years. She would have told them to go fuck themselves and been done with it.

Instead, V had kept silent, and the slings and arrows had continued. And she wasn't the only one who'd been pierced by the barbs. Anita had as well. That ended today. If nothing else, their supposed reconciliation would allow him to right that wrong.

As for him and V…. He licked his lips once more, then shoved a hand through his hair. Pulling off his ruse without ending up with blue balls would be a miracle.

"You almost ready? TJ wasn't kidding when she said Aunt Kay will be mad if we're late." He stood and stretched his back.

V turned her head and fried him with a heated glare. "Caroline is one thing, but I don't see what my attending your family's Christmas party will achieve. Other than giving the entire town heartburn."

He fought a smile. "It's been a long time, V. They might surprise you."

Her face went blank, and she held his gaze.

"Okay, maybe not, but they aren't going to say a word against you with me at your side. Wouldn't you like the chance to snub a few of them?"

She climbed to her feet and dusted her hands. "I would prefer not to see them at all while I enjoy a nice glass of wine in my hotel room. Alone."

Hotel room? He paused in the act of collecting his coat from the couch. "You're not staying with Anita?"

She shrugged and turned away, shoving the full box of books against the bookcase. "I like my space. Mom understands."

He picked up his coat while staring at the ramrod-stiff line of her back. "You think walking through the lobby of the Barlow Inn will be any easier than facing my family?"

Her laugh was dry and humorless. "Like I'd step one foot inside the Barlow Inn."

Shoving his arm into a sleeve, he frowned. "Wait a minute. If you don't have a room at the Barlow Inn, where are you staying?"

"At the Marriott in Tyler."

"Jesus, that's a thirty-mile drive."

"Which is why I'm staying there."

Well, shit. It wasn't as if a room in the Barlow Inn meant she'd have to sleep with one eye open—in case the lynch mob showed up in the middle of the night—but it was close.

Guilt jabbed him in the gut. He grunted and shrugged the coat onto his shoulders. "My aunt's parties usually run late. Maybe you should bunk with your mother tonight."

V passed by him without a glance. "You may have blackmailed me into agreeing to your stupid plan, but I'm a grown woman. Where I choose to sleep is my business."

And that right there was why he was suddenly questioning everything he'd thought he knew. She didn't have a problem slapping *him* down verbally, so why hold her punches when it came to everyone else? The contradiction didn't make sense.

She snatched her coat and purse from the coat tree, her agitation evident, and he sighed. "Wait, V."

She turned to meet his gaze with an arched brow.

"Look, I know you want no part of tonight, but your attending with me isn't just about convincing people we've buried the hatchet."

She opened her mouth, presumably to tell him where and in whom she'd like to bury said hatchet, and he held up his hand. "Yeah, I know. The best place for the blade is in my thick skull."

"Glad to see we're both on the same page."

He squinted in warning, then nearly laughed at the satisfied twist of her lips. The girl he remembered had had a quirky sense of humor he'd found charming but, he had to admit, now that the initial shock of seeing her again had eased, he found those sharper edges of the woman she'd become more than a little intriguing. Not to mention sexy as hell.

Shit. Quit thinking with your johnson, pal.

He cleared his throat. "What I'm trying to say is, you haven't been treated very well by the people of Barlow."

Suspicion flickered in her eyes. "Noticed that, did you?"

"Actually, I hadn't. Not really. Not until recently."

Suspicion morphed into surprise. She hid it with a careless shrug. "No biggie. What they think of me doesn't matter."

He doubted that, but pointing it out would be a waste of time. Dipping his chin, he pinned her with an intent gaze. "It matters to Anita."

That took some of the starch out of her spine. Her shoulders sagged a bit, and she busied herself by pulling on her coat. "Nothing I can do about that now. I made my bed, as they say, or more precisely, abandoned *yours*." The zipper on her coat sang as she yanked it up to her throat. When her gaze met his, her eyes were a hard crystal blue. "In this town, that's a capital offense."

He fought a wince at the truth of her words and softened his tone. "It matters to me, too."

She stared at him in silence as several moments stretched, then her brow wrinkled in a frown. "Who *are* you? Because you sure as hell aren't Sam Fitzpatrick."

He smiled at her dry tone, but quickly sobered. "When you took off the way you did, I was hurt and angry. I can't deny that. But, I'm no longer an eighteen-year-old with a case of wounded pride. I could have stopped the gossip and innuendo at any time with a single word. I didn't, and I'm sorry about that."

Her stunned expression poured salt in an already guilty wound, and he swallowed an inward curse. "If life has taught me anything, it's that shit happens. While I can't help thinking there was more to your leaving than you're willing to say, whether or not you choose to be upfront with me after all this time is up to you."

If he had any doubts her explanation for leaving was a load of bull, the way her face closed up killed them dead. Although he waited, she refused to meet his eyes and didn't say a word.

Finally, he sighed. "You've moved on, V. So have I. We're different people than we were back then, but with a little bit of effort, we might manage to be friends again." Her gaze jerked to his. "Since we'll be working together, that's something I'd like."

Several heartbeats passed. "I'd like that, too."

The sadness in her tone scraped at him, and he forced a smile. "Okay, then. When I said it ended here, I meant it *all* ended. Not just the distrust between the two of us, but the condemnation of everyone in town who felt the need to rip into you in support of me."

She blinked. "I'm not sure I understand."

"I'm talking about a little shock and awe to set the citizens of Barlow straight."

Her eyes widened, and she swallowed. "Oh, that's really not necessary."

"It is for me. What do you say? You with me, Red?"

It took a moment, as if she were calculating the odds of his plan backfiring and blowing up in her face, but then she shrugged. "Damn it, I'm probably going to regret this but, what the hell. They can't hate me any more than they already do."

* * * *

As if afraid she would bolt, Sam's muscled arm tightened around V's shoulders as they approached the wreathed door of Kay Burke's sprawling ranch house. V dug her elbow into his side in a quick jab, then rolled her eyes at his quiet chuckle.

Though he couldn't possibly have known for sure, he had good reason to be concerned. She'd considered leaping from his truck about fifty times on the ride from his house. Luckily for him, she wasn't interested in experiencing road rash first-hand.

As frustrated as she was suspicious, she cast a furtive glance at his smiling profile. The boy she remembered had been so easy to read, like an open book, but the man....

He was a puzzle she couldn't figure out. His moods changed quicker than a quarterback's hand-off, angry one moment and teasing the next. He did it on purpose, she was sure, to keep her off-balance, and it was working, damn it. Why else would she be tripping up his aunt's sidewalk, when this was the last place she wanted to be?

She lay the bulk of the blame on his shocking kiss. How the hell was she supposed think straight when he'd melted her circuits and scrambled her brain? And like the seasoned competitor he was, he'd delivered a one-two punch by following up with that apology.

Why would he do that when he'd done nothing wrong? God, the genuine regret in his eyes when he said he should have put a stop to the gossip and innuendo had slayed her. She'd left him without a word and *he* was sorry? Talk about piling on the guilt.

Still, he couldn't possibly believe he had any say over the way the citizens of Barlow had treated her. Football was practically the town religion, and he'd bagged the Holy Grail by winning the state championship his senior year. Even Jake, who was a shoo-in for the Hall of Fame, took a back seat to Sam in the hearts and minds of the citizens of Barlow.

No one screwed with their ultimate hero and got away clean.

She couldn't help the niggling doubt hovering in her mind, that all of this was a ploy for revenge. That today was nothing more than a long-awaited judgment day. That Sam's surprising offer of friendship was a sneaky way of softening her up, so he could lead her to the slaughter without a fight.

If that was his game, so be it. She did owe him, just as he'd said, and she'd faced worse than a bunch of petty insults from people she cared little about and survived. Her heart, however, yearned to take him at his word. Through her own actions, the only man she'd ever loved had been lost to her. Nothing real or permanent could ever come from what Sam had proposed, but a chance to regain a small piece of him through friendship would be well worth a few hours of discomfort.

He paused before the door, and she stiffened her spine. She'd give him the benefit of the doubt and if she were wrong.... Well, she hadn't gotten where she was in the world of pro sports without knowing how to play a few games of her own.

"Ready?" He dipped his head to meet her gaze.

"As I'll ever be, but I don't want to hear a word when I say 'I told you so.'"

He laughed and squeezed her arm. "Trust me."

She wanted to. Very much, and that was the problem.

He opened the door and guided her inside. Curling her lips in a polite smile, she prepared herself to face the firing squad. Instead, she met a smiling Kay Burke.

As Anita's friend, Sam's aunt had never jumped on the *We Hate V* bandwagon like so many others. Still, V hadn't been sure what to expect. Kay had always been close to Sam, treating him more like a son than a nephew, and she had to know others wouldn't be happy with today's shocking development.

If Kay had a problem, however, she didn't show it. Her lips puckered in a soft coo of pleasure. "V. Your mother said you might show up. I'm so glad you did." She pulled V out from beneath Sam's arm and into a warm hug, and pressed her lips to V's ear. "It's about time you and my stubborn nephew made up." She stepped back and winked.

"Oh, but we hav—"

Kay spun away to face the room and cut V off with her announcement. "We have company, everyone."

V noticed the crowd for the first time. Anita stood at the edge of the kitchen, unease tightening her smile. The various members of Sam's extended family wore a range of expressions from welcome, to confusion, to outright shock. TJ looked as if she'd swallowed a bug.

Chapter 11

Several hours later, Sam slid his gaze over the thinning crowd of friends and neighbors and found V standing with Lucy at the kitchen island. His mouth quirked in a wry smile as he eyed Anita and Kay fussing about the kitchen when there was no need. They hovered several feet away, as if they didn't want to make it obvious they were standing guard. As they had throughout the evening, they flanked V like middle-aged sentries, daring anyone to comment on her presence. So far, no one had been brave enough to try.

V leaned her head close to Lucy's, but the distance was too far for him to hear what she was saying. Lucy snickered, grinning widely. Sam rubbed a hand over his chest. Caught up in securing his future with the Marauders, he hadn't considered how his daughter would react to his fictitious relationship with V.

From the surprised pleasure on her face when he'd arrived with V as his date, Lucy approved. Things were bound to get sticky, however, when the season was over, and he and V *broke up.* He'd need to explain. Lucy wasn't a small child and she deserved the truth, something he'd promised he'd always give her. What to tell her was the problem. Unfortunately, in this case, V was the only one who could provide the complete truth. Unless he could convince her to trust him the way she used to, he'd never know what that was.

Rebuilding their friendship was the key, and tonight they'd made a good start.

There hadn't been a doubt in his mind his family would follow his lead. They'd accepted V's inclusion in the evening without complaint, even if one or two had to bite their tongues in the process. The real test had come later, when people had begun to arrive for the open house.

He lifted his beer to his mouth to hide his satisfied smile. V had stood stiffly at his side when the first guests had arrived but, as he'd predicted, no one had dared to voice a complaint. However, this was V's hometown, too, and if they were ever going to truly put the crap of the past fifteen years behind them, more than the town folks' silence was required. She needed their acceptance.

To that end, he'd made sure to include her in every conversation as friends and neighbors offered him their congratulations. He had to hand it to her. Although the small talk was often stilted, and her strained smile said she expected to be blindsided at any moment, she hadn't backed down.

The flicker of pride warming his chest left him itchy, but he couldn't help it. More than one tough-guy jock would have caved under much less pressure. The shy teenager had transformed herself into one hell of a formidable woman and, despite the shit between them, he was proud of her.

He lowered the beer as she turned and headed toward the back door. Shit. He'd spotted TJ slipping outside several minutes ago. His cousin had promised to be on her best behavior, but that was before he'd pushed things into the realm of crazy by bringing V along this evening. So far, TJ had kept her distance, and the two had yet to speak privately. God only knew what TJ would do when once they did.

He crossed the room, meaning to head off the potential disaster. Kay blocked his path five feet from the door. Tucking her hand through his arm, she tugged him toward the empty den.

"Well, my boy, you certainly are full of surprises."

He cast a worried glance over his shoulder at the closed door. "Aunt Kay—"

"Leave them be. It's about time the two of them worked things out, don't you think?"

"Long past time, but you know TJ. I was hoping to make it through the evening without having to call in the SWAT team."

Kay laughed. "My daughter can be a pill, but she knows my rule about no bloodshed on the premises." She squeezed his arm, then stepped away and slid onto the loveseat. "I'm proud of you, Sam. You may be a little slow, but it's good to know you eventually do the right thing."

He winced as guilt jabbed him in the gut. Unlike her daughter, Kay had maintained her belief that the pursuit of money hadn't sent V running, arguing there had to be a logical explanation for her actions. A romantic at heart, Kay claimed he and V were meant for each other, and had never understood how he could let her go without a fight. She'd eventually given up pestering him, but her sense of romance was offended by his refusal to track V down and claim his happily-ever-after.

"Tonight isn't exactly what you think, Aunt Kay."

Dipping her head, she studied him over her glasses. "I'm not blind, Sam. It's obvious the two of you still have things to work out, but she's here. You've been given the gift of a second chance." The lifelines in her face deepened with her wistful smile. "Those don't come along often."

Setting his beer on the coffee table, he sat on the loveseat and picked up her hand, entwining his fingers with hers. "I love you, Aunt Kay, but you're reading more into this than there is. The second chance I've been given is with the Marauders. The only reason V is here is because—"

"I know. You and V are *playing nice* to placate the Marauders' owner." She waved her free hand dismissively when he frowned. "TJ told me all about your plan, but smoothing things over with your new boss would hardly require you standing up for V here in Barlow." She squeezed his fingers. "That came from your heart. The same heart that, despite the years and the pain she caused you, recognizes that girl in the backyard as *the one*."

He shook his head, but couldn't help a chuckle. "You need to cut back on the romance novels, sweetheart. They're fogging your brain."

Her smile went sly. "Don't you dare dis my romances. Your Uncle Henry, God rest his soul, swore they were man's best friend. Many a night, he went to sleep a happy man thanks to my choice of reading material."

"Jesus, Aunt Kay." Sam tugged his hand free with a grimace. "Don't say another word. You and Uncle Henry reenacting fictional sex scenes isn't an image I want imprinted on my brain."

Satisfaction smoothed out her smile. "Then don't try to tell me this thing with V is only about a job. If that's all you were concerned about, you would have told this Caroline Wainwright you had no problem working with V and that would have been the end of it."

Because Kay was right, he didn't bother arguing. Rising to his feet, he shoved his hands into his pockets and paced.

She crossed her hands on her lap. "Instead, you came up with a plan that allows you to get close enough to V to get inside her head. Have you asked her what happened yet? Why she left without a word?"

"I asked her straight out."

"And?"

"She confirmed everything I've thought all these years."

"But you don't believe her." It wasn't a question.

Dropping his head back, he stared at the ceiling and sighed. "No, I don't. Not anymore."

* * * *

"Your mother should have named you 'Cat.'"

V flinched and spun around to blink into the shadows of Kay's rose-trellised gazebo. As her eyes adjusted, a pair of denim-covered legs and scuffed boots came into focus. The wooden blades of the rocking chair creaked on the oak floor as it swung forward, and TJ's face came into view.

Feet propped on the wrought-iron table in front of her, she arched a brow. "Sorry, did I startle you?"

The sardonic twist of her lips said she wasn't sorry at all. V clenched her teeth. For heaven's sake. For the last three hours, Sam had dragged her around his aunt's house with his arm around her shoulders like a manacle, laughing and joking with people who would just as soon poke their dessert forks in her eye as look at her. Her jaw hurt from holding a smile, and she had a headache. All she'd wanted was a moment or two alone, not an altercation.

Ignoring TJ's taunt, she cocked her head. "Cat?"

"It appears you have an uncanny ability to land on your feet. From what I've heard, you made a fortune wheeling and dealing for the jocks you represented. That's a far cry from the east Texas girl who skipped town in a rust-bucket Chevy."

"Thanks. Yes, it is."

"That wasn't meant as a compliment."

Like V would think so with all that sarcasm dripping from every word. "No? Well, my bad." She bared her teeth in a counterfeit smile. "I'm sorry I disturbed you. I didn't expect to find you out here." She started toward the gazebo opening.

"And I didn't expect to find you in Barlow." The chair rocked backward violently as TJ jerked to her feet and moved into V's path. "So, how's the *date* going?"

With her route blocked, V had no choice but to stop. "This isn't exactly a date."

TJ's eyes gleamed cold as emeralds in the low light of the garden lamps. "Just checking to make sure you understood that."

Well, shit. Of course, Sam would have told TJ his plan when he asked for her help getting Lucy out of the house.

V's tensed shoulders dropped with her sigh. "I guess he told you what's going on."

"About you bad-mouthing him to the Marauders' owner, and her insisting he make nice with you if he wants the job? Yeah, he told me."

TJ's accusing tone sliced at V, but she should have expected it. Sam might have been a little more diplomatic in his word choice, but he'd said much the same thing. And if that was how he truly characterized the situation, everything he'd said was nothing more than a business tactic. So much for his claim of wanting to rebuild their friendship.

She forced a smile. "Well, then. Looks like I don't have to keep up the pretense, do I? If you'll excuse me—"

TJ didn't take the hint, and instead spoke in a low voice. "Please, tell me you didn't agree to all of this because now that you've seen him again, you realize you're still in love with him."

V hid her flinch by crossing her arms. Her speeding heartbeat thumped against her ribs. "Yeah, I'm still in love with him. That's why I badmouthed him to the team's owner." The wry laugh she attempted garbled in her throat and sounded more like a grunt. "Neither of those accusations are accurate."

TJ squinted at V. "Are you saying you aren't trying to sabotage his job with the Marauders?"

"I couldn't do that even if I wanted to. Now, if you don't mind?" She stepped forward, but TJ stood firm.

"Sam said—"

"I know what he said, but he's wrong. The team's owner didn't ask him to *clear the air* with me because *his* job is on the line. He's the right man for the job and Caroline knows it. She asked him fix things between us because she's my friend and doesn't want to have to fire *me* if we can't find a way to work together in peace."

Surprise lit TJ's eyes, quickly replaced with suspicion. "Do you really expect me to believe that line of bull?"

"Not that I care what you believe, but Caroline's a business woman and the team is her life. Friendship comes in second to the success of her Marauders."

"That's a pretty cynical attitude."

V rolled her shoulders in a shrug. "The world of pro sports is brutally competitive. If you're not all in, you go home a loser. Caroline doesn't like to lose."

TJ remained silent for a long moment, her gaze intent. "If you don't still have feelings for Sam, then what is there to fix?"

"Oh, for God's sake." V dropped her arms to her sides. "You're like a dog with a bone. I'm not in love with your cousin, okay?" She shook her head. "I dumped him, remember?"

"You didn't dump him. You ran."

V stiffened then arranged her face in a bland look of acceptance. "Same difference."

TJ coughed a disdainful laugh. "Not at all. Dumping a guy means the relationship has ended."

"I've been gone for fifteen years. I'd say that qualifies as ended."

"Yet, after fifteen years, here you are because your *friend* thinks you and Sam have things to work out. She obviously knows something you aren't willing to admit."

TJ had a point. What the hell was V supposed to say? Before she could think of anything, TJ slumped against the gazebo's post.

"You were my friend, V. You might have convinced everyone else you never loved him, that you'd just used him for what you could get, but I know better." The haunted look in her eyes arrested the defensive comeback on V's tongue. "I remember every detail of that day Mom and I got to Florida after Sam was injured."

So did V. Sam's parents had been beside themselves with worry, and she wasn't much better. She'd been so relieved when TJ and Kay had finally arrived. Then Sam had announced he had a coaching job waiting for him back in Texas when he was done with school, and V had panicked.

A gust of wind tossed a loose strand from TJ's braid into her eyes and she tugged it free. "Did you think I couldn't see the hell in your eyes that day? A woman doesn't look like that over a man she's using. Then, all of a sudden, you went white, like you'd seen a ghost or something, and you took off, claiming you had to get to work before I could ask what was wrong."

And instead of driving to her job at one of the college-town cafés, V had raced to her apartment to pack up her meager belongings and head north. Jake had spoken to TJ several times when she'd called shortly after V had arrived at Boston College, but she'd been too screwed up to talk to her friend. After a couple of weeks, the calls had stopped.

The way she'd treated TJ was one more regret V had carried for years. An apology now was too little, too late, but it was something. "I'm sorry, TJ. I should have called you back, but…." She held out her hands, then dropped them to her sides. "I didn't know what to say."

TJ pushed off the post. "How about, 'Hi TJ. I'm in trouble and I don't know what to do about it?' Did you think I wouldn't listen? Think I wouldn't have found a way to help? I love Sam like a brother, but you were my friend, and you dumped me right along with him."

Tears stung the back of V's nose and throat. "I don't know what you're looking for."

"You could tell me what scared you enough to turn your back on Sam. On me."

And this. This right here was the main reason she'd stayed away from Barlow even after learning of her father's death. Not the insults or the dirty looks. Those she could handle, but Sam's questions and the pleading in TJ's eyes were razor-sharp stakes piercing her heart.

Brushing an errant tear from her cheek, she gave the only answer she could. "There's nothing to tell. Even if there was, it no longer matters. I made my choices and I've learned to live with them."

Disappointment dulled TJ's eyes, and her chest rose on a frustrated sigh. "You're wrong. It still matters. Sam got over you, but you were his first love. Now, here you are again, and the two of you are playing a dangerous game. I no longer care if *you* get burned in the process, but Sam is another story. If you break his heart again—"

"That's not going to happen."

TJ's eyes flashed with heat. "It did once."

"Only because I was stupid, thinking I could have things I couldn't. I know better now." Heart in her throat, V softened her voice. "I'm not here by choice, TJ. I've got a job to do, just like Sam. Besides, after what I did to him, I couldn't break his heart again even if I tried."

Chapter 12

Sam set the foil casserole dish on the stovetop and glanced at the clock. According to Lucy, turkey with all the fixings followed by a movie marathon had been her and Maggie's Christmas tradition. With the kitchen packed up for the move, he'd been forced to improvise, but the frozen store-bought lasagna was one of Lucy's favorites. Plus, he'd never cooked a bird in his life, never mind all the stuff that went with it.

Opening the fridge, he eyed its meager contents, and retrieved the bagged salad. Second thoughts flickered through his mind as he dumped the pre-measured greens and Caesar salad dressing into a large bowl. He probably should have accepted Aunt Kay's invitation to Christmas dinner. That would have been easier. This was the first Christmas since Maggie had died, and being surrounded by a crowd might have helped to dull Lucy's grief.

On the other hand, he and Lucy would need to form their own traditions from here on in, and the sooner they started that process, the sooner she'd see her life with him wasn't a temporary arrangement. The Marauders would be taking the field in Atlanta in twenty minutes, followed by several other games, but there would be movies later. He slid a knife through the pasta and cheese, cringing at the titles she'd chosen when they'd stopped by the RedBox.

She'd picked out one action-adventure—to keep him sane, she'd said. He'd need it after the three chick flicks on the agenda. He plucked several heavy-duty paper plates and plastic cutlery from the box of temporary supplies V had left on the counter, and grunted. Caroline was right about V's organizational skills. She'd thought of everything.

He scrubbed a hand down his face. Upon arriving home last night, with V in tow so she could pick up her rental, Lucy had slipped out of the truck as soon as he'd parked. After a quick "Merry Christmas" to V, she'd rushed inside, then practically pressed her nose to the kitchen window, no doubt hoping to catch a glimpse of their good-night kiss.

Another taste of V was a temptation he'd found almost impossible to resist, but one look into her eyes had overruled his baser instincts. They were dulled with exhaustion, with good reason. Kay's party couldn't have been easy for her, but she'd gone through with it. The question was why?

Her life was in Manhattan. In a few days, she'd shake off the dust of Barlow once again and return to the life she'd built, where the opinions of her former friends and neighbors couldn't touch her and didn't matter. Why then, had she said yes?

The only logical explanation was she'd done it for him. Because he'd said she owed him, and she agreed. That didn't jibe with the image of selfish bitch he'd painted her as all these years, any more than her reaction to his kiss fit that of the cold-hearted woman who'd agreed to marry him one day and disappeared the next.

Leaning his hands on the counter, he dropped his chin to his chest. He'd told TJ not to worry, that V no longer had the power to hurt him, but she could sure as hell still tie him in knots. He'd stared into her tired eyes last night, and the urge to hold her and beg her to tell him why she'd left had nearly seared his soul. In the end, he'd pressed a chaste kiss to her forehead with the reminder to drive safely.

Lucy had retreated to her room by the time he'd watched V drive off, giving him no opportunity to explain what was happening between them. That needed to be done. Today. The problem was, he had no idea where to begin.

Straightening, he tore open the bag of croutons for the salad with more force than was necessary, then cursed when most of them ended up on the floor. Gritting his teeth, he carefully opened the small package of grated cheese and dumped it in the bowl.

The spicy scent of their Christmas meal wafted past his nostrils, and he wondered where V had packed the antacids he normally kept on the shelf in the bathroom. The coming conversation was bound to give him a raging case of heartburn.

"Come and get it, kid!"

* * * *

By the end of the first quarter, the Marauders were up by ten. Setting his empty plate beside Lucy's on the coffee table, Sam sprawled back into the couch and turned his head. "I need to explain some stuff about me and V."

"What's to explain? You like her, and she likes you. Anyone can see that."

The sudden compression of his chest felt an awful lot like pleasure, and he frowned. "What do you mean, anyone can see that? What do they see?"

"The way you tease her, for one." The tab on her can of pop twanged as she plucked at it with her thumbnail. "Boys always tease girls they like."

His lips quirked with his smile. "They do, do they?"

"It's a product of genetics."

"Huh?"

"Human development. I studied it in school. In the early days of man's development, the cave man simply took what he wanted, and the female put up with it because a strong mate increased her odds of survival. With the advent of modern understanding, females became less inclined to respond to that type of thing, and the male of the species was forced to come up with more acceptable courting behaviors, but they're guys. Their skills are still basic."

He must have looked like he'd been hit over the head with one of those cave man's clubs, because she rolled her eyes. "It's true."

"What the hell was the name of this class? Male Emasculation?"

She snickered. "Social Studies."

"Taught by a woman, no doubt."

"Miss Marston. She's studying for her master's in women's studies at ETU."

"That explains it." He shook his head, but then a thought occurred. Lucy was only fourteen, but a school-girl crush could be a powerful thing. Was there a boy she'd miss when they left for Manhattan? "Is there a particular boy who teases you?"

"Get real. There are only two things the boys in my class are interested in. Football and the captain of the cheering squad. Jasmine Harris is the prettiest girl in school."

He studied his daughter's narrow face and large doe eyes. She was pure Maggie, with the exception of her midnight hair. Even with the shock of bright purple marring her sleek dark locks, the boys at school would have to be blind not to see how pretty she was. "I know Jasmine and her family. She's a sweetheart and she is cute, but you're just as pretty, and you've got brains as well."

"Thanks for the confidence builder, Sam, but boys aren't attracted to brains." She glanced down at her dancer's body, all slim lines and small breasts. "They can't see beyond Jasmine's boobs."

Sam cleared his throat. They'd gotten off track and, fuck, the last thing he wanted to discuss were women's breasts. Especially his teenage daughter's. "You said V liked me, too. How can you tell, and when did I tease her?"

"About coming with us to the ballet. She didn't want you to, you know." Of that, he was certain.

"You whispered something in her ear while you were helping her with her coat. She blushed. Girls blush over boys they like. That's genetic, too." Nodding, she brought the can of pop to her lips. "She likes you."

That was definitely pleasure warming his chest cavity, but he thrust the emotion aside. "I like her, too, but last night wasn't what you think, and I don't want you reading too much into it."

"I don't understand."

His gut twisted in knots, and he briefly considered abandoning this discussion to go in search of his missing antacids. "Have you heard anything about V and I dating back in high school since you've been in town?"

"You did?" Clearly curious, she curled her leg beneath her and turned to face him more fully.

He nodded. "The summer before I left for college."

Understanding flashed in her eyes. "That's why you were kissing her in that picture."

Startled by the unexpected comment, he stared at her. "What picture?"

She tossed her head toward the boxes stacked against the wall. "It was in one of the photo albums V and I packed yesterday. She got all nervous when she saw it, then said it was nothing. That you were just goofing around and someone snapped the picture, but it didn't look like that to me."

Shit, he'd forgotten about the photo albums. They contained more than one picture of the two of them together. Had she browsed through the others? And what did it mean that seeing them made her nervous?

"It was more than just fooling around. The fact is, I asked V to marry me shortly after she followed me to FSU. We'd planned to marry as soon as the football season was over."

"Then what happened? Why didn't you?" Lucy's eyes shot wide. "Oh my God. You met my mother that fall."

He held up a hand. "Hold on, Luce. I didn't meet your mother until after V and I had broken up." Immediately after, but that was a detail she didn't need to know.

"Why did you break up?"

That was the million-dollar question, and one he couldn't answer. Only V could do that. He shook his head. "Honestly, I don't know. You know the story about how I hurt my knee early on in my first season at FSU. V left Florida a couple days later." He shrugged. "Sometimes relationships don't work out, and obviously V's and mine was one of those. To make a long story short, I was pissed and hurt, but life goes on."

He dragged a hand through his hair as the second half kicked off on TV. "Your mother and I met about that time, while I was recuperating from my second surgery. A couple of weeks later, I learned V had moved to Boston. We never saw each other again until last week, when she showed up with the Marauders' offer."

Lucy sat quietly for a moment, then asked, "But why did V leave?"

"That's something you'll have to ask her."

He went on to explain about Caroline and her concerns about him and V working together, and his plan to put the team owner's fears at ease. He didn't bother mentioning the way the people of Barlow had treated V all these years. Lucy liked V, and the truth would only upset her. Somehow, she'd escaped the gossip, and they were leaving for Manhattan in a few days, so what would be the point?

"So, you're pretending you and V have worked out your differences by making everyone believe you're a couple?" She closed her eyes and shook her head as if something had gone loose inside. "Miss Marston was right. Guys are idiots."

The incredulous tone of her voice made him cringe. Spoken out loud, the plan sounded ridiculous, even to him, and it was a good thing they were leaving town or he'd be paying the high school a visit to set Lucy's ultra-feminist social studies teacher straight.

He sat forward and propped his elbows on his knees. "The job isn't the only reason, though that's a big part of it. We have to work together, and I'd prefer we do that in peace, but we didn't break up, Lucy. V just took off one day. Without a word."

Her nose wrinkled in offense. "I don't know her very well, but she's nice. That doesn't sound like something she'd do."

Her instant defense of V pricked at his guilt. He'd known V better than anyone and, yet, he'd let his pride blind him to what he should have seen all along. "No, it doesn't." He straightened. "I was supposed to love her. Hell, I'd planned to grow old with her, but when she left, I didn't do a thing to stop her."

He sat back and shut his eyes. "Fifteen years ago, I let hurt and anger keep me from doing what I should have done. I should have tracked her down and stuck by her side. I should have helped her deal with whatever problem she was facing." He opened his eyes and met Lucy's stark gaze. "I finally got around to asking her what happened yesterday."

She spoke in a whisper, as if fearful of his answer. "What did she say?"

"She fed me a BS line about money and ambition, but I got the feeling, whatever sent her running still has her scared."

"Then you have to help her."

Sam barked a laugh at the militant gleam in Lucy's eyes. "That's my plan, kid."

"I want to help, too. What can I do?"

His heart throbbed in his chest, and he sent a silent "thank you" out into the universe and hoped it reached Maggie. Circumstances beyond his control had conspired with his own regrettable decisions to rob him of the life he'd planned for himself. With the Marauders' offer, he'd grabbed hold of the career golden ring, but he'd long since given up on the dream of a family. As Kay had said, he'd been given a second chance with V, but regardless of how that turned out, Lucy was his. God help anyone who said she wasn't.

He held out his hand, and she immediately grabbed his fingers. Surprised by the tiny prickles stinging the back of his nose and his eyes, he squeezed her hand and smiled.

"Just be her friend, Luce. That's what I plan to do, too."

Chapter 13

At seven sharp on Friday morning, V pulled her rental to the curb in front of the rec center. Like much of downtown Barlow—if a quarter-mile of storefronts could be considered a downtown—the architecture of the building was dated. Birthed out of the oil boom of the late fifties, Barlow hadn't changed much in the sixty years since.

When V had left town, Thompson's Bakery had been housed in the glass-fronted space that made up the center today. Old Man Thompson had retired nearly a decade ago, and his only son, Howard, hadn't wanted anything to do with the business. Neither, apparently, had anyone else. The elder Howard had closed his doors after fifty years and donated the building to the town.

V spotted her mother through the curb-to-roof glass window as she bent to assist a girl in a pale pink leotard. Struck by the easy smile on her face, V shut off the car. She remembered Anita's excitement the day she'd called to say the town fathers had accepted her proposal to provide dance lessons to the local kids, and had asked her to run the program.

Even though she'd been thrilled for her mother, the guilt had nearly strangled V. Dancing was Anita's passion, and teaching her joy. Because of V, she'd been robbed of both for too many years. And yet, abandoned by the man who had promised to love and honor her, then failed at both, her mother had never once complained. Not even on the day she'd had to walk away from the job she'd loved so much.

How many times had V heard her father complain that her mother's dancing didn't pay enough to keep the lights on? He'd never understood that, for Mom, it hadn't been about the money. She would have done it for free. But he was right. After he left, the lessons she gave at the small studio two towns away weren't enough to buy groceries, never mind keep a roof over her and V's head.

Her mother had been grateful to the owners of the Double J. Not just for the job they'd offered her as housekeeper and cook, but for the home that came with the position. The ancient trailer behind the foaling shed might have put a roof over their heads, but for V, it had also been a constant reminder that while her prayers had been answered, Anita had paid the price.

Swamped by guilt and terrified of saying something that would expose her filthy secret, V had withdrawn. Keeping Anita at arm's length had quickly become a habit, and had shielded her from the ugliness but, as if caught in a self-imposed, vicious circle, V's remorse was compounded by the hurt in her mother's eyes.

The moment V's commission check from Jake's first pro contract cleared the bank, she'd spent the entire amount in an effort to pay her mother back. Anita had balked the day V's lawyer arrived at the Double J with the keys to the house on Cholla Drive and a bank book reflecting a balance that would allow her to quit her job and not look back.

Ironically, less than six months later, V was able to hand Anita enough money to purchase her own dance studio if she wanted. She'd shot down the idea, saying she was a dance teacher, not a businesswoman. As far as V knew, the money was still sitting in the bank. Mad money, Mom had called it, in case the two of them decided to go on a world tour someday. So far, that hadn't happened and never would.

Not on that money. Those funds hadn't come from answered prayers. God and his angels had nothing to do with it. Just the opposite. That money had come through evil forces, in reply to the desperate and dark cry of V's heart as she lay curled on her bed in a frightened ball the night of her eleventh birthday.

Hush money, left to her upon her father's death.

Although Anita had insisted V keep it, she couldn't touch a penny. She'd flown into Barlow, signed over the check, and left on the next flight out.

Funny, she'd thought learning Edward Price was dead would free her, but she was wrong. Although the memories came with less frequency, the sickening fear still woke her on occasion. Drenched in sweat, she'd lay frozen in bed, waiting for the moment when Daddy opened her bedroom door, knowing this time he wouldn't stop, and she'd be shattered.

In the distance, a freight train whistle echoed and she startled. Glancing around, she blew a ragged breath and, shoving the memories back into that dark place in her soul, climbed from the car. The weather had turned cold, and she tugged her coat closed.

Inside the rec center, Lucy stood at the bar in first position. She turned her head and the serenity on her face morphed into a smile. With her arm above her head, she waggled her fingers in a wave. V smiled and waved back, then hurried inside.

She'd been surprised by Lucy's call this morning. Barely awake, V had rolled over at the sound of her phone and, for a moment, she hadn't known where she was. Recall came quickly as Lucy asked if she would like to stop by the center before heading to the house to finish packing. This was her last dance lesson with Anita before they left for Manhattan, and would V like to see her dance? She would have said yes, anyway, but the chance to delay seeing Sam for even an hour was a bonus she hadn't expected and couldn't turn down.

The soothing notes of a classical piece filled the air as V closed the door behind her. She glanced up and grinned at the jangle of the small bell announcing her arrival. As the story went, Mr. Thompson's young bride had hung the bell there on the day they'd opened the bakery—to remind her of the church bells that had rung the day they were married. For V, the musical chime conjured up memories of Mrs. Thompson's double-chocolate cupcakes and sweet scents.

In addition to Lucy, only four girls were present. All of them were younger, perhaps nine or ten. Anita called out instruction as, lined up behind Lucy at the bar, they seemed to be following her lead.

Anita turned, and pleasant surprise widened her smile. "V. You're here!"

V ventured farther into the room and stopped at her side. "Lucy invited me to come see her dance. I hope I'm not disturbing the class."

"Oh, heavens no. They're almost finished. I'm so glad you stopped by. I have two classes this afternoon and wasn't sure I'd get to see you again before you left town."

They'd celebrated Christmas yesterday in V's suite in Tyler. The five-star restaurant had lived up to its rating with a delicious meal of roasted squab, red potatoes, and grilled asparagus as the Marauders added another W to their win column. In a long-standing agreement, Sam was one of those topics they avoided. After V's *date* on Christmas Eve, skirting the elephant in the room had made the day even more uncomfortable than usual.

With the movers arriving in an hour, the last of Sam and Lucy's belongings would be on the road no later than three this afternoon. V had booked them all on a six o'clock flight.

"I'd planned to come by this afternoon before heading to the airport, but this is so much better. I'm excited to see Lucy dance."

"She's very good. I'm so glad she'll be continuing her lessons in Manhattan."

V smiled. "I don't think that was ever in doubt. She's very passionate about ballet."

"The best always are." Anita turned toward Lucy, and her smile faded. "She has the talent and the drive, but she's had so much upheaval in her life. This move will be good for Sam. I'm hoping it works out for her, too."

Mrs. Thompson's bell chimed before V could ask why it wouldn't. She turned her head as several women stepped inside. All three looked vaguely familiar and were, if the surprise in their eyes that quickly turned to disapproval was any indication. A fourth passed by the front window, head dipped against the wind.

V braced herself for an altercation, but one never came. The music faded to a stop and Anita clapped her hands. "Excellent job, ladies. Be sure to bundle up before going outside. It's freezing out there."

Lucy immediately crossed the room. She greeted V with a hug, then stepped back and smiled as the younger girls scrambled for their coats and bags. "Thank you for coming."

V's heart squeezed at the genuine appreciation in her dark eyes. Minus the usual black makeup, soft flecks of gold stood out in the irises, making them shine. "I wouldn't have missed the chance to see you dance for the world."

A faint blush of pleasure bloomed on Lucy's cheeks. One by one, the girls from the class approached to hug her goodbye until she was surrounded by all four. V was reminded that today marked another new beginning for Sam's daughter. According to him, she'd only come to live with him four months ago. Yet, here she was, facing more of that upheaval Anita had mentioned with their move to Manhattan. Lucy's dancing wasn't the only thing that would be affected. Once again, she'd be starting over. V knew how difficult that could be, which must be what her mother had meant by things working out for the girl.

Not much taller than the younger girls, Lucy draped her arms around them in a group hug. "I got a new laptop for Christmas, and Sam helped me set up my own MyWorld account. Miss Anita can give your mothers the web address so you'll be able to follow me and see what I'm doing, okay?"

Anita was briefly inundated with requests for Lucy's MyWorld address but, within a few minutes, the studio was quiet and empty except for the three of them. Anita pointed V to a chair where she'd be out of the way.

Lucy stepped to the center of the wooden parquet floor and dipped into a *plie* as Anita cued the music on the studio's sound system.

Soaring notes filled the room. Lucy rose to the toes of her shoes, seemingly suspended for several heartbeats, then burst into motion. Delicate one moment, powerful the next, the dance defied the laws of physics. Confident joy radiated from her face as Lucy utilized the entire space of the room. Swaying. Bowing. A graceful leap followed by a dizzying spin. V watched in awe as Sam's daughter became one with the music, speaking in visual words of raw emotion. The graceful stretch of her arms pleaded with longing. The toss of her head as she turned away suddenly was full of rejection and disdain. She began to spin, her slim body riding the music to its crescendo, then dropping to the floor in abject defeat as silence returned.

V's instinct was to leap to her feet in a standing ovation, but she was too overwhelmed to move. Her mother was wrong. Lucy wasn't good. She was exceptional. One of those dancers who came along only once in a century. The Manhattan dance community didn't have a clue what they were getting, but they would soon, if V had to see to it herself.

She pressed a hand to her chest as Lucy uncurled from the floor and sat up. Sweat dampened her brow and darkened her leotard like a bib at her chest. She met V's gaze and sighed.

"Oh, Lucy. That was...." She shook her head at a loss for words. "That was beautiful."

Anita wore a grin and handed Lucy a towel. "I tried to tell you."

V stood as Lucy rose to her feet. "Brilliance can't be expressed in words, Mom. It has to be seen to be believed."

Chest heaving from exertion, Lucy mopped at her face, but that didn't hide the raw pleasure still shining in her eyes. "Your mom helped me with the choreography."

V smiled when Anita shook her head as if to say it was all Lucy. "Then maybe Mom should come to New York, too. Together, you two will take the Big Apple by storm."

Lucy grinned, but Anita dismissed the idea, as V knew she would. Over the years, she had occasionally suggested Anita move to Manhattan, only to be relieved when she rejected the idea. Sadness darkened Anita's eyes as she repeated the same answer she always gave V. "I'm a small-town girl and always will be." Dropping her arm around Lucy's shoulders, she squeezed. "But, I expect front-row seats for your first prima performance at the Met."

Lucy laughed. "It's a deal."

Ten minutes later, after a teary goodbye, Anita shooed them out the door so she could prepare for her next class. Before they'd taken two steps toward the car, a teasing glint sparkled in Lucy's eyes. She motioned toward the donut shop at the end of the block with a jerk of her head.

"Oh, no. After that performance, protein is what you need, not sugar." V rounded the hood.

Lucy paused beside the passenger door. "But Sam likes donuts."

V squinted and held Lucy's hopeful gaze over the top of the car. "Sucks to be him, then. Get in. We'll pick up a few egg sandwiches on the way to the house."

Sitting at the window in the drive-thru lane at the Dairy Barn, V laughed and caved when Lucy leaned over to instruct the teenage attendant to add a chocolate shake to their order.

Lucy had devoured half of her sandwich by the time they'd gone a block. V stopped for the red light and glanced her way. "Has your father started the paperwork to enroll you in school yet? I hadn't thought of it before but, after seeing you dance, one of the city's arts academies might be a better fit than a traditional high school."

Lucy's cheeks caved in as she sucked from her straw, then swallowed. "Sam checked out a couple of places where dance is part of the curriculum. He said he'd contact them if I wanted, but," she shrugged, "I don't think so."

The light turned green and V stepped on the gas. "A diploma from one of the academies will help open doors you'll want to walk through later. Why wouldn't you want to take advantage of that?"

From the corner of her eye, she was aware of Lucy's stiffened posture. Turning her head, V was surprised to see the flash of fear in Lucy's eyes before she turned to look out the passenger-side window. She lowered her shake to her lap, clenching it in both hands.

"The tuition at those places is really high."

"Oh, sweetie. Your father can afford it. Believe me, the Marauders pay well."

She shook her head. "That's what he said, but I couldn't stand it if I started there, then had to leave."

"Why would you have to leave?"

"Because *I* don't have any money. If the DNA test says Sam's not my dad...." V's fingers involuntarily clenched around the steering wheel as Lucy turned her head and met her gaze. Though no emotion showed on the girl's face, hell screamed in her eyes. "Why would he invest that kind of money in a kid who isn't even his?"

Chapter 14

With Daisy in her crate in the van's cab, and Sam's truck on a car hauler behind it, the movers pulled from the curb to begin their two-day drive to Manhattan. Sam stood at the open front door and watched Lucy climb into the back seat of the next door-neighbor's SUV. Alice Walker's invitation to the Dairy Barn, to thank Lucy for being such a great babysitter these past four months, had produced little more than a tepid "okay." However, the two-year-old girl on Alice's hip, holding out her arms and squealing "Woocy," was apparently impossible for Lucy to resist.

Something was off. With the moving van pulling away, leaving the house virtually empty, he was a little out-of-sorts himself, but he didn't think that was the cause of Lucy's funk. She hadn't been in Barlow that long. Didn't feel the same attachment he did for the place.

Something had happened this morning. Lucy had been quiet since they'd arrived at the house after dance class, and V had been avoiding his gaze.

When the SUV turned right at the end of the street, he shut the door and went in search of V. He found her in the kitchen. Bent at the waist, her head and shoulders inside the fridge, she scrubbed at a spot on one of the shelves. He propped a shoulder against the doorjamb and took a moment to enjoy the view of her denim-covered ass.

No skirt today. She'd arrived carrying a garment bag he assumed contained the sophisticated business armor she'd don for their flight later, but she'd come to work. Her russet curls were pulled back in a plain ponytail, and the soft, pale peach sweater and faded jeans brought back memories of the girl who used to ride shotgun in his old pickup on humid summer nights.

Those days were long past, however, and they had more important issues to tackle than choosing between the bonfire at the old mine or cuddling up together at the drive-in. He cleared his throat.

V yelped and straightened with a start, banging the back of her head on the open freezer door. Sam grimaced and pushed off the doorjamb as she turned accusing eyes his way. "You scared me, you jerk." She felt her scalp and winced. "I'm going to have a lump."

"Let me see." He stalked forward, and she scooted to the side to avoid him. He stuck out his arm to trap her. Pinned between the open fridge door and his forearm, she had no choice but to comply.

Moving her hand away, he slid his fingers into the silky hair above her ponytail and felt for a wound. There was no contusion, but she was right, there was already a slight swelling. Glancing around, he reached for one of the clean rags on the counter, then scooped up some ice from the cooler of water bottles he'd put together that morning. He folded it into the rag and held up the makeshift ice pack.

"Have a seat."

"Where, exactly?" She glanced around the empty room. He rolled his eyes.

"Right. We'll have to improvise." Stepping in front of her again, he handed her the pack, then cupped her waist to lift her.

"Wait. Stop." She grabbed his shoulders, fumbling the rag full of ice.

He plunked her down on the counter. She narrowed her eyes in silent warning, but damn. She felt so good under his fingers, he was slow to remove his hands. He took the rag and rewrapped it, then handed it back. "Keep that on the bump for a few minutes."

As she lifted the rag to her head, he leaned his hands on the counter on both sides of her hips and stared into her eyes. Her pupils were dilated, but they were the same size.

She arched away from him. "What are you doing?"

He bent forward, keeping the distance between them constant. "Checking for concussion."

She slapped him in the chest with the ice pack and shoved until he straightened away from her. "Back off, Fitzpatrick. I didn't hit my head *that* hard."

"Safety first." He twisted his lips into his most charming smile.

"More like 'annoying' first." She reapplied the ice-filled rag.

He chuckled at her snarky tone, then crossed his arms. "Now, tell me what happened at the dance studio."

Her eyes immediately went wary, but up came her chin. "I watched Lucy dance."

"And?"

Mackenzie Crowne

Her entire posture softened, along with her eyes. "And she's incredible, Sam."

"So your mother tells me."

The hand holding the ice pack dropped to her lap. "Mom told me, too, but God. I had no idea. I certainly didn't expect what I saw. Lucy comes alive in pointe shoes."

Anita had told him much the same thing, but she was Lucy's teacher. Hearing the awe in V's voice, he couldn't help the swell of pride filling his chest. "I'll take your word for it."

Surprise widened her eyes. "You haven't seen her dance?"

"She hasn't invited me yet. I was respecting her space. Now, back to my question. What happened? The two of you showed up here this morning looking like you'd just walked out of a slasher movie."

She started to slide off the counter, but he crowded close, keeping her where she was. After a long stare down, she sighed. "Fine. Lucy told me something that obviously upsets her but, while she didn't swear me to secrecy, I'd like to respect her privacy."

"She's my daughter, V. Don't you think I should know if something has her upset?"

From the way she froze, her face a mask of uncertainty, he knew exactly what they'd discussed. Dropping his head to hang chin to chest, he propped his hands on his hips. "She told you about the DNA test."

"Yes, she did."

Cursing beneath his breath, his arms fell to his sides. With his chest heaving in fury, he bent over the cooler and threw open the lid to grab a water bottle. He needed something in his hands. He was pretty damn sure the real estate agent he'd hired to sell the house wouldn't appreciate a row of holes in the walls.

"Don't be mad at her."

He jerked up his head. "Is that what you think? That I'm mad at Lucy?"

V held out her hand, and the compassion in her eyes only made the desire to rip something apart worse. "I don't think she meant to tell me. We were talking about schools and…it just slipped out."

Slamming the cooler shut, he straightened. "I'd like to take a flamethrower to the fucking courthouse, but I'm not mad at Lucy." V's shoulders sagged as if in relief, and he shook his head. "I've told her the test results don't matter, but she doesn't believe me."

V slid from the counter and set aside the ice pack. "You can tell me this is none of my business, Sam. I'll understand."

He was inclined to do just that, but it was a little too late to shut this particular door. And maybe her knowing the truth about him and Lucy wasn't such a bad thing. He'd need her trust if he was ever going to discover what happened all those years ago. Trusting her in return was a good place to start.

"It appears Lucy feels differently." Shoving his hand through his hair, he sighed. "To my knowledge, she hasn't discussed her fear over the DNA test with anyone. Even me. She throws it in my face every chance she gets, but refuses to talk about it when I try to bring up the subject." He shook his head. "I don't know. She likes TJ and she's opened up some to Anita but, for some reason, she obviously trusts you."

V's smile was a little surprised, a little sad. "I like her, Sam."

He dragged his hand around the back of his neck. "I know you do. It shows."

She swallowed hard, a sure sign she was uncomfortable with what she was about to say. "*Is* she your daughter?"

Bingo. Nothing like going straight for the jugular. He needed her trust, but Jesus. He hadn't been prepared to open a vein to get it.

"As far as I'm concerned, she is." He slumped against the counter. "But fuck. I just don't know. Maggie and I were only together for a couple of weeks. She left town with a guitar player headed for California." He rolled his shoulders in a shrug. "The timing is close enough Lucy could be his."

"Do you know his name? How to find him?"

Crossing his arms, he shook his head. "No on both counts, and I have no intention of looking for him. I get the feeling there was a revolving door of men in Maggie's bedroom. While I'm in no position to judge her for the way she lived her life, that doesn't prevent me from being pissed at the impact her lifestyle had on Lucy. The kid doesn't have an ounce of trust in the concept of stability. She believes I'll send her packing eventually, and goes to bed every night in fear of what comes next. That's no way for a kid to live."

V's eyes flashed with a starkness that was painful to witness, before she dropped her head to stare at her feet. "Will you? Send her away if it turns out she's not yours."

The question pissed him off. He shoved from the counter, bending his knees to meet her gaze. "No way in hell. My name is on her birth certificate. That makes her mine in my book."

The last thing he expected was for her to step forward and slip her arms around his waist. She briefly pressed her forehead to his chest. "I'm glad, Sam. Don't let her go. Ever." Sliding her arms free, she moved back, and damned if there weren't tears in her eyes. "She needs you, and I think you need her, too."

"Damn, Red." He cupped her cheek in his palm and swept his thumb across her soft skin. "Don't cry."

She pressed her lips together in a stubborn line. "I never cry."

She attempted to pull back, but he brought his other hand into play, lifting her face for his study. Gravity left behind twin streaks of wetness as her tears spilled.

"I can see that." Testing her, he dipped his head and brushed a kiss over her temple. "That's not a tear." He expected her to jerk from his hold and, when she didn't, he moved to the other side and repeated the caress. "Neither is that."

"I must have gotten something in my eye."

Her breathy excuse fluttered in his ear. He kissed his way across her cheek until his lips hovered over hers. "Yeah, that must be it."

He covered her mouth with his, and the gentle shudder of her body was an elemental siren's cry he was helpless to ignore. He dropped one hand to the small of her back and eased her closer. He needn't have bothered. She pressed against him, her fingers sliding over his waist to his chest.

Tilting his head, he took the kiss deeper, and she met him move for move. His eyes nearly rolled to the back of his head as she captured his tongue with hers and sucked. He repositioned his hand on her back to bring her into more precise contact with his erection and couldn't hold back his deep groan.

All his senses firing, he burrowed his hand beneath the hem of her sweater and traced his fingertips over her ribs to the heavy lower swell of her breast. She gasped, breaking the kiss, and he recaptured her mouth with a hunger that could only be satisfied by a complete plundering. He devoured her, sinking his tongue deep, and she hummed her approval.

Reason fled. The silk of her bra was cool, but the firm mound beneath was warm as he peeled back the material to slip his hand inside. Tight with carnal need, her nipple stabbed at the center of his palm, and she squirmed against him.

Releasing her mouth, he dipped his knees, lifting her sweater at the same time. Her chest rose and fell on heavy breaths. Eyes full of need, she threaded her fingers through his hair, guiding his mouth to her bared breast. Like a man starved, he took her into his mouth, swirling his tongue around her nipple.

Her scent was honey and vanilla mixed with the heady musk of her arousal; a familiar combination he'd gone without for far too long. She bucked against him, jerking her hands to his waist to bury them beneath the hem of his sweatshirt. Cool fingers explored his ribs, pecs, the balls of his shoulders, then traveled lower, over his abs and lower still until she cupped his painfully rigid length in her palm. Squeezing gently, she slid her palm down, then up, measuring him.

Sweet Jesus, in another moment, he'd explode. His head spun and his ears began to ring. He thrust his hips helplessly, and the top of his head nearly came off at her throaty moan. The sights and sounds, tastes and scents, all so familiar, threatened to unman him. The ringing in his ears grew louder. With a final stab of his tongue he released her breast and lifted his head.

"My ears are ringing."

Her eyes slowly slid open as if she were waking from a dream, and he groaned at the unabated lust staring back at him.

Then she whimpered. "Mine are, too."

The sound of her voice doused the X-rated fire racing through his body. Reason snapped back into place and his mind cleared. He glanced around, and glared at the lighted face of her phone on the counter beside them. He dropped his forehead to hers. She automatically lifted her mouth, and he was tempted to say fuck it, and take her right where she stood.

That wouldn't be wise, however. Lucy wouldn't be gone long, and doing the dirty on the floor of his empty kitchen would only complicate an already fucked-up situation.

"V." He lifted his head. Her eyes had closed again. "V," he repeated. "It's not our ears. It's your phone."

Like she'd been doused with a jug of cold water, she jerked back and bumped into the counter. She looked down, then whimpered and yanked her sweater to her waist, covering herself. Eyes wide with embarrassment, she avoided his gaze and skirted out of his arms. She tucked her chin to her chest and, turning her back, picked up the phone, then moaned.

"Who is it?"

She didn't turn around, and didn't answer immediately. "Gracie Malone."

Chapter 15

"You going to answer?"

V scrunched her eyes shut. Answering Gracie's call when she was still vibrating with lust was a bad idea, but it would give her an opportunity to escape Sam's presence for a few minutes. God. If her phone hadn't rung, they would have both been naked in under a minute.

"Um. Yeah." She opened her eyes, spotted the back door, and headed straight for it.

"Where are you going?" The slight edge of humor in his voice grated on her over-sensitized nerves. How he could possibly find anything remotely funny about what they'd almost done was beyond her. She didn't answer. Yanking open the door, she stepped outside.

"You might want to put on your co—"

She slammed the door behind her as she thumbed the screen of her phone. "Hello, Gracie."

"I'm considering revoking your girlfriend card."

"Excuse me?" Damn it. She'd forgotten how cold it had turned. Hunching her shoulders against the chilly wind, she hurried toward her rental.

"You and Sam are seeing each other and you didn't think that was something I'd want to hear about firsthand?"

She froze with her hand on the car door. "What?"

"One of Jake's buddies from Barlow called this morning and mentioned you and Sam had shown up together at some Christmas Eve party. And by together, I mean *together*."

V groaned, opened the car door, and slumped into the front seat. There was no point in denying it. Apparently, the Barlow grapevine was alive and well, and it had connections in Manhattan. Gracie wouldn't believe her, anyway, and once they were back in Manhattan and Sam put his plan in action for Caroline's benefit, Gracie would see for herself what happened to V whenever Sam got within ten feet.

"I'm screwed, Gracie." V dropped her head against the headrest and stared at Sam's house.

"Screwed as in you've gotten naked and sweaty with the Marauders' new offensive coordinator? Or screwed as in, holy shit, I'm in big trouble?"

V blew a windy sigh. "Both."

"Get. Out!" Gracie lowered her voice. "You slept with him? You've only been there three days. Damn, girl. You work fast."

A pained laugh worked its way up V's throat. "I haven't slept with him. Yet. But it's only a matter of time. When I'm around him, it's like my brain cells malfunction."

Gracie's sigh floated through the phone's earpiece. "Don't you love when that happens?"

Not particularly and definitely not in this case. "I don't have a lot of experience with this particular phenomenon." *Except with Sam. Only with Sam.*

"Then it's time you got some, my friend. But you said 'both.' What's the problem?"

Squeezing her eyes shut, V told Gracie a condensed version of the conversation she and Sam had had about Caroline and her concerns, and Sam's plan to address them.

Gracie snorted. "You're making this up to toy with me, aren't you?"

"I wish I was."

A long pause, then, "Okay. This isn't an accusation or anything. You know I love you and only want you to be happy, but why would you agree to such a thing unless you were hoping something real would come of it?"

V sighed. "Because Sam was right when he said I owed him. I threw his proposal, along with his love, in his face when I walked out on him without a word."

"You were, what, eighteen? We're talking ancient history, V. Give yourself a break. You were a kid. Kids do stupid things. Granted, you should have faced Sam a long time ago and settled things between you, but what's done is done. The only question left to ask is, if there was a chance to win him back, would you take it?"

In a heartbeat. But how could she after what she'd done? "Yes, but—"

"No 'buts.' There's no time like the present to put the past behind you for good. Apologize, beg him for forgiveness, then jump his bones for real. Everybody wins."

Gracie made it sound so simple, but uncertainty gnawed at V's gut. Although Sam was justifiably curious about the true reason she'd left him, he'd said it was up to her whether or not she told him. Did he mean it? Would he be willing to take a chance on them again without knowing what had shattered them the last time? Or would the past always be there, hovering over them until it eventually destroyed them both?

Wrapping the fingers of her free hand around the steering wheel, she sucked in a breath. When she'd finally come to her senses after leaving Florida, she'd promised herself she'd never be a coward again. Career-wise, she'd kept that promise, clawing her way to the top of her industry with a no-holds-barred attitude. It was time she applied the same to her personal life.

She loved Sam, always had, and she did want him back. If that wasn't to be, at least she could console herself with the knowledge that she'd tried.

Swallowing nerves, she took the plunge. "I wouldn't know where to start."

"Atta girl. Where are you?"

"In my rental car in Sam's driveway."

"Where is he?"

V eyed the plate-glass window of his living room. "He's in the house."

"Is he alone?"

"For the moment. Lucy went for ice cream with the neighbors."

"Perfect. Get out of the car and go inside. When you get there, take off your shirt and say your piece."

V laughed. "I think I can take things from there."

"Good. Make sure you call me the minute you get back to town. I want every single hot detail."

V shook her head. "I'm hanging up now."

Gracie snickered. "Love you."

"Love you back."

* * * *

As it turned out, V didn't have an opportunity to say her piece, topless or otherwise. The neighbors' SUV pulled to the curb, delivering Lucy home before V had taken three steps toward the house. Sam had finished wiping out the fridge when they got inside, and V slipped into the bathroom to change her clothes.

With nothing left to do, Sam locked up the house and joined Lucy and V at her rental. After stowing their bags in the trunk, he dropped his arm around his daughter's shoulders. "Do you think Manhattan is ready for us, kid?"

The trip for ice cream seemed to have repaired Lucy's earlier mood. She turned to him and grinned. "You, maybe, but no way is the Big Apple ready for me."

V's heart was in complete meltdown as she started the car.

Several hours later, their bags were checked, and they boarded their flight. Like a mischievous matchmaker, Lucy maneuvered V and Sam into adjoining first-class seats, claiming she wanted pictures of the Manhattan skyline for her first MyWorld post and the view from V's seat was better. Sam squinted at her as if he saw through the excuse, but he didn't seem upset with the arrangement. V fidgeted at his side throughout the three-hour flight. Although anxious to speak to him, she didn't think the flight attendants would approve if she whipped off her blouse.

Likewise, she found no opportunity to talk to him alone when she dropped them off at their new home. It was late, and it had been a long three days. She said good night and, on the drive back to the city, returned one of Gracie's three missed calls to say Sam's seduction had been postponed to a later date.

When that would be, however, she didn't know.

* * * *

Sam sat on the edge of the couch in his new living room and triggered the TV remote. The seventy-inch flat-screen came to life, and he scrolled through the channels to ESPN. Setting aside the remote, he picked up the package he'd found on the table in the foyer when they'd arrived an hour ago, and peeled back the seal. Along with the playbook Caroline had said would be waiting for him, there were several full-color pamphlets and a handwritten note welcoming him to the team. It ended with a PS:

I asked my assistant to gather some information on the arts academies you mentioned for your daughter. See enclosed. If you should need assistance expediting the application process, let me know.

He flipped through one of the glossy brochures, then lifted his gaze to the ceiling. For a man who faced problems head-on in his professional life, he'd done a piss-poor job when it came to the personal side of things. With V, certainly, but also with Lucy. Her despondency this afternoon only proved he'd been handling the situation with the DNA test all wrong. He'd told V he'd tried to talk to Lucy about it and she refused to listen but, the truth was, he hadn't tried very hard. Anxious himself over what the results would reveal, he'd backed down each time she'd shown the least resistance.

Gathering up the pamphlets, he shoved to his feet and headed for the stairs. V was right. Lucy needed him, and somehow, over the past four months, she'd gone from an obligation he'd felt compelled to accept to the child of his heart. It was time she knew it.

He paused before the open door leading to Lucy's third-floor bedroom and rapped his knuckles on the wood. "You decent, kid?"

"Yeah."

Ducking his head to avoid the dormered ceiling, he climbed the narrow staircase. With a book in her lap, Lucy sat curled on the overstuffed chair near the window. She met his gaze, her dark eyes wary, and he cursed beneath his breath.

"You all settled in?" He walked across the hardwood floor to stand beside the large ottoman at the foot of the chair.

"There wasn't much to settle. All I had was a backpack."

He grunted and sat beside her feet. "Here." He held out the pamphlets. "You need to look through these."

Suspicion flickered in her eyes. She kept her hands on her book. "What are they?"

"Brochures." When she didn't take them, he tucked them between the arm of the chair and her hip. "There are three of them. Each representing one of the arts academies I mentioned the other day."

She looked down and flipped a page in her book. "I told you, I want to go to a regular high school."

"Tough." Her head jerked up, but he didn't give her the chance to speak. "We're at a crossroads here, kid. A new life for both of us, and we're going to clear up a few things before we start. Beginning with you believing I'm going to cut you loose if the results of the DNA test come back negative." He dipped his head for emphasis. "That isn't going to happen, Lucy."

Her gaze skittered away, across the room. "You say that now, but...."

"You're my daughter. You can fight me on that all you want, but it won't change a thing."

She turned her head and looked him dead in the eye. "What about later? It won't bother you, knowing you're stuck raising some other guy's kid?"

"Frankly, I don't give a shit whose blood runs through your veins." Desperate hope darkened her eyes, and he went in for the kill. "But maybe that's the problem. Maybe you think less of me because of that. Maybe you can't respect a man who could love another man's kid as his own."

She blinked at the sudden sheen of tears flooding her eyes, but then her brows bunched together in offense. "That's just stupid."

"Yeah, it is, but it's no worse than you believing I can't possibly ever love you because some other guy might have been your sperm donor." He dragged in a breath and spoke out loud what he'd only admitted in his heart. "I don't know if you're aware, but your mom and I talked for a while before she called you into her hospital room to meet me. She didn't hold back as she told me about her life. About moving from city to city to find work. About the times she left you alone while on a shoot for one video or another. And about the men."

He leaned forward, propped his elbows on his knees, and stared at his dangling hands. "I sat there listening to her describe the same desolate existence I'd let my life become. My job at the college kept me in one place, but I'd spent years going through women the way she had men, and I was just as aimless."

He raised his head to find Lucy watching him, her eyes awash with tears. "Then you walked into the room. I looked into your big, frightened eyes and I felt like I'd been sucker-punched. In your eyes, I saw everything I'd wanted before life had stolen my dreams. Home. Family. But most of all, kids."

He straightened. "I had no idea if you were mine, but it didn't matter. I wasn't leaving you to the system. You needed me, but I needed you just as much. I needed you to help me find the man I'd lost." He jammed a hand through his hair. "Despite the snarky comebacks and the purple hair, you've done that. So, whether you share my blood or not, you're the daughter of my heart and you're not going anywhere, no matter what the court says."

She sniffed, then lifted her chin, and he couldn't help his smile. The move reminded him of V. It struck him funny how they'd only known each other a few days, yet Lucy was already copying her habits. Then she knocked him for a loop.

"I love you, too, so if you're just saying that, I'm going to be really mad."

With the lump in his throat, he found it difficult to speak. "You have my word."

She studied his face for a long moment, then nodded briskly. "Okay." She picked up the brochures, then cast a glance around her large bedroom. "Well, you've got the home...and the kid." She faced him, and her watery smile nearly brought tears to his eyes. "For a family, you're going to need a wife. I know the perfect woman."

The irony of her comment slammed him in the chest like a fist. If not for his injury and V's disappearance, he and Lucy wouldn't be sitting here today. His world had been knocked from its axis all those years ago, stealing the life he'd planned for himself. A life including the pro career, V, and the children they'd have. As if the heavens had recognized their mistake, the stars had aligned to give Sam back each one of the dreams they'd stolen.

Lucy was his, no matter what happened with the court, and the pro contract was signed. All that was left was convincing V to put the past behind them so they could start anew.

His smile started slowly and grew to a determined grin. "Funny. So do I."

Chapter 16

At seven-thirty the next morning, Caroline woke V from a dead sleep to congratulate her on a job well done. Although he was two days earlier than expected, the Marauders' new offensive coordinator had apparently walked onto the practice field a half hour ago.

"I appreciate your efforts in getting him here so quickly, especially since I know the two of you aren't comfortable working together."

V rolled over and stared at the ceiling. Had Caroline spoken to Sam, and if she had, what did he tell her? Not that it mattered, now that V had decided to turn his ruse into reality.

"About that. I wish you had spoken to me before you'd said what you did to Sam. He was under the impression his new job was on the line."

"Nonsense. He's got an ironclad, two-year contract."

"I guess he figured you'd slipped in a clause somewhere he hadn't noticed."

Caroline sighed. "I'm sorry, V. I hope I didn't make your job more difficult. You know me. I'm on the ball when it comes to business, but relationship stuff baffles me."

"Actually, you helped."

"How so?"

"By forcing us to talk." V twisted the sheet around her fingers as nerves cramped her stomach muscles. As Sam had said, the Marauders' contracts didn't contain a no-fraternization clause, but office relationships could still cause problems. "I planned to tell you Monday morning that we've decided to give it another go. I know you don't normally have a problem with that kind of thing within the organization, as long as the two parties keep their private relationship private, but with our past...." She sighed. "You don't have to worry. He's a good man, Caroline, but he's also a professional. So am I, and I'd tender my resignation before I let anything harm the team."

"Relax, V. I know you would, and your word is good enough for me."

Relief loosened V's muscles, and she exhaled a long breath. "Thanks."

Caroline paused, then cleared her throat. "Please, don't take what I'm about to say as a criticism."

Okay, that doesn't sound good. "What is it?"

"I'm actually relieved to hear about you and Sam. On a personal level, you understand. Like I have, you've worked hard and succeeded in an industry where, until recently, women were seen as nothing more than someone to sleep with after the game. But unlike me, you aren't built for a solitary existence. You have a giving heart under that tough exterior, and I've often wondered why there wasn't some man in your life."

Moved, and more than a little surprised by her friend's rare candor involving a personal matter, V didn't know what to say. "Caroline, I—"

"I don't know what went wrong between the two of you, nor is it my business, but after meeting Sam…. Well, I figured I'd finally discovered the reason why you've remained alone. A man like that would be a tough act to follow."

Understanding dawned suddenly and V slapped a hand to her forehead. "So you decided to try your hand at matchmaking? With your brand-new offensive coordinator, whom you just signed to a six-figure contract?"

"And my PR consultant, who also happens to be a friend."

Stunned, V shook her head. "Didn't you just admit relationship stuff baffles you?"

A snort blew through the earpiece. "That doesn't mean I'm not an excellent judge of character. I wouldn't have hired either of you if you were the kind of people to let personal issues spill over into business."

V's laugh was sardonic. "That's not the impression you gave Sam."

"Please, I simply gave him a little nudge and, from the sound of it, it worked." Caroline hummed appreciatively. "That man is hot."

A shocked chuckle gurgled in V's throat. "God, you're spending far too much time with Gracie Malone." V grinned at Caroline's quiet laughter, then sighed. "And, yeah, he is hot." And irresistible.

"Anyway, back to business. Today's practice is closed, so no press is around, but we'll need to put out our release Monday morning. I've got a press conference scheduled for ten AM. Bob is going public with his diagnosis, and we'll be introducing Sam."

"I'll email the packet for your approval tomorrow morning."

"Perfect."

V disconnected the call and stared at the blackened screen. She'd never stopped to consider how others saw her, but did they see what Caroline obviously did? A lonely woman, filling her life with work? No wonder Gracie was so anxious to see her patch things up with Sam. Jake, too, in his own way, had tried to push her toward that same thing over the years.

Did her friends see her as a charity case needing to be saved? God, how pitiful was that?

Shaking her head, she threw back the comforter and sheet. After a cup of much-needed coffee and a banana, she spent the morning bouncing back and forth between what to say to Sam and what to say *about* him to the press. The press release was far easier. There was no doubt in her mind Sam would be a positive addition to the staff, and anyone who read his résumé would agree. With a heavy heart, she listed Bob's career accomplishments, knowing they would be overshadowed by the news he had to deliver.

Her doorbell rang close to noon. She opened the door, not completely surprised to find Gracie's Gridiron Girls standing in her hallway. Gracie, CC Tucker, and Jessi Grayson all wore anticipatory smiles. The only member of their group missing was Kris Tucker, CC's cousin. V flashed back to "Girl's Night," and she made a mental note to lock her wine cabinet.

"Where's Kris, and did I forget an appointment?"

"Kris is overseeing a photo shoot in Boston, and we're here to give you moral support." Gracie swept past her into the condo. "In case you've changed your mind about seducing Sam."

V frowned at CC, who shrugged as if to say this was all Gracie's idea. Like that was ever in doubt. Jessi simply grinned. Holding the door wide, V let them pass, then closed the door.

"I haven't changed my mind, and I don't need moral support."

Gracie turned and gave the T-shirt and sweats V had thrown on the once over. "Get dressed. We're going shopping."

V crossed her arms. "I am dressed, and I don't need to go shopping."

"Oh, really? What did you wear on your last date?"

V opened her mouth to answer, but didn't have a clue what to say. Her last date had been five years ago, and utterly forgettable. She mentally scrolled through her closet for something her three would-be fairy godmothers would find acceptable but, unless the man were a director on some board or an uptight lawyer, nothing she owned would make the cut.

"My periwinkle suit."

"You did not." Gracie rolled her eyes at CC and Jessi. "I was with her last month when she bought it."

CC laughed, but Jessi took the diplomatic approach. "We're just trying to help, V."

"Thanks, but I know how to dress myself. I've been doing it for years."

Gracie plucked a banana from the bowl of fruit on the counter of V's kitchen bar and snapped the top. "I'm sure you've got rows of suits designed to intimidate corporate types, but we're talking a big strapping jock here. You need something with some slink. Something that says 'I put out.'"

"She has a point." CC snickered.

V turned to Jessi, who grimaced. "She kind of does."

V shook her head. "You're all insane. Besides, Sam has a daughter. My best chance of catching him alone will be at the complex. Where slut clothes are frowned upon."

Gracie took a bite of banana. "No, your best chance will be tonight in a restaurant of your choice. Preferably one attached to a hotel."

"But Lucy—"

"Is babysitting for Tuck and me tonight, and she'll be spending the night." CC grinned at Jessi. "Gracie and Jake, and Tuck and I are taking Max and Jessi out to celebrate. Her debut solo album just went platinum."

V smiled widely and squeezed Jessi's arm. "Oh, Jessi. Congratulations. That's incredible."

Jessi's disbelieving laugh was infectious. "Thanks. I'm still pinching myself."

"So, we've cleared the path for you." Gracie skirted the bar into the kitchen to toss her peel into the trash, then immediately plucked an apple out of the fruit bowl. "I still say we need to go shopping, but since you've got that stubborn wrinkle creasing your forehead, that's obviously not going to happen." She crunched off a big bite of Granny Smith. "The rest is up to you, sweetie."

Nervous butterflies swarmed in V's belly. Could she do it? Could she convince Sam to give them another shot for real? Would he even agree to go to dinner with her if she asked? God, she was going to throw up. Shaking her head, she squinted at the apple in Gracie's hand.

"Why are you eating all my fruit?"

Gracie crunched another bite. "Jake knocked me up again. I'm hungry all the time, just like with the boys."

There was a moment of shocked silence before Jessi squealed. "Oh my God. When are you due?"

"Mid-August. It's early yet."

Jessi's smile could have lit up Times Square. "Maybe we can get a package deal at the maternity ward. I'm due August twentieth."

Gracie's mouth dropped open, and she turned to CC expectantly. CC held up both hands. "Don't look at me. Tuck is still grumbling over the two months of forced celibacy the last time. He says baby Huey is going to be an only child, but I'm wearing him down."

Girlish shrieks, hugs, and laughter were exchanged, along with a few tears. Genuinely happy for her friends, V couldn't deny the tug of envy as she joined in the celebration. At thirty-five, her biological clock was running low on batteries. She'd given up on the hope of having a child a long time ago, but now that Sam was back....

He loved Lucy, of that she had no doubt, but he hadn't consciously had any children. She hadn't thought that far ahead, but even if things miraculously worked out between them, there was no guarantee he'd want more kids.

As if Gracie had read V's mind, she pulled her into her arms. "Don't take no for an answer, sweetie. You and Sam both deserve your happily ever after."

* * * *

V picked up the phone for the fifth time, then set it down again.

Just do it already. If he says no, you've got that half gallon of double chocolate fudge in the freezer. You can throw it at his head at the press conference on Monday.

Blowing a breath, she shook her arms, then cracked her neck for good measure. Picking up the phone, she rang Sam's number before she could change her mind. Her hands were already sweating when he answered on the third ring.

"Fitzpatrick."

She had to swallow before she could speak. "Hi, Sam. It's me." She rolled her eyes. "It's V."

"Hello?"

"Hello, Sam?" Masculine laughter sounded in her ear as if he were in a bar.

"Hold on a sec. It's noisy as hell in here."

She waited as the chaos in background slowly faded, then ended with the thud of a shutting door.

"Sorry, hello?"

"It's V, Sam."

"V? Sorry, I was in the locker room. The team is throwing a goodbye celebration for Bob."

"Oh." *Well, shit.* "I'm sorry, I don't want to drag you away from that. Tell Bob I'm thinking of him."

"Wait. What's up?"

"Nothing that can't wait. I'll call you tomorrow."

"I'm here now, and the party is winding down, anyway."

She slapped a hand to her stomach. She really was going to throw up, and she was going to kill all three of the fairy godmothers. "I spoke to CC earlier. She said Lucy is babysitting for them tonight, and...."

"And?" He prompted her when she ran out of breath—and her nerve.

"I was wondering...if you'd made plans." She swallowed and hoped the gulp in her throat didn't echo through the phone. "For dinner."

A long pause. Long enough for the acid in her stomach to reach her esophagus.

"Dinner?"

She squeezed the bridge of her nose. "You know, two people sitting down to eat food?"

Silence. Then, "That sounds more like a date."

The teasing note in his voice grated on her nerves. "Well, we're supposed to be dating, aren't we? That *was* your plan, right?"

"Yeah. I just didn't expect you to be volunteering to plan the itinerary."

The fairy godmothers were going to suffer before they died. "Do you have plans or not?"

A hint of humor deepened his voice. "Sheath your fangs, Red. I was planning to pick up Chinese on the way home." He paused as if he'd checked his watch. "I'm going to need another hour here, but I'll be free by six. Shall I come by your place, or will you be driving yourself to mine?"

"No!" She winced and softened her tone. "I mean, if you don't mind, I'd rather meet you somewhere in the city." *On neutral ground.* He may have just moved into the house in Queens, but it was his and Lucy's home. If V was going to get her vamp on, she'd rather do it where a friendly neighbor, the local Welcome Wagon, or his daughter couldn't unexpectedly show up.

"Where did you have in mind?"

"There's a restaurant on the fourth floor of the Marriott in Times Square." She gave him the restaurant's name and glanced at her kitchen counter and the keycard to room 1620 the courier had delivered fifteen minutes ago.

"Will I need a tie?"

She glanced down at her periwinkle suit, with its improvised lace camisole. "No, it's casual. You might need a jacket, however."

"Got it covered. Will we be dining alone? Just the two of us?"

If she played her cards right, they'd be doing a bit more than dining. And yeah, they'd be alone. "That's kind of the definition of a date, isn't it?"

His deep chuckle sent goose bumps dancing over her skin. "Just checking. So, this isn't a performance for Caroline's benefit?"

For heaven's sake, why was he fishing, and why did she suddenly feel like bait? "No. It isn't."

More silence. "Interesting."

Back came the nerves. "Look, if you'd rather not—"

"I didn't say that. I just like to know the game plan before kickoff."

She had the feeling he was reading her like a playbook, but maybe that wasn't such a bad thing. She'd need him willing if she was going to pull this off. "Then I'll see you at six."

"I'll be there."

* * * *

Sam spotted V the moment he stepped off the elevator. At a table by the windows overlooking Times Square, she gazed out at the blinding lights and flashing neon, and not one of the "holy shit" signs could come close to her for the pure wow factor. She was stunning.

At thirty-five, the years had matured the piquant features of her youth into those of a classic beauty. Not for the first time, he wondered what the hell was wrong with the men who'd crossed her path, and had moved on empty-handed.

Single and alone.

Jake's words that day at the farm echoed in Sam's head. His friend was right about one thing. In the world she moved in, full of confident competitors, she should have been snatched up long ago. So, why hadn't she been? If Sam hadn't known her, had met her on a sideline somewhere, or on the street—hell, at the DMV—he would have moved heaven and earth to win her. And he wouldn't have given up until he had.

He'd won her once, with disastrous results, but providence had given him a second chance, just as Kay had said. They hadn't had an opportunity to talk about what had happened between them in the kitchen yesterday, and he'd expected her to hit him with a list of reasons why it shouldn't have happened and never could again. Clearly, he'd misread the situation. A satisfied smile tugged at his lips. Tonight they'd be taking the first real step toward erasing what had gone wrong in the past, and the fact she'd made the first move was a point in his favor.

The maître d greeted Sam with a welcoming smile and asked if he had a reservation. He waved him off, indicating where V sat waiting, and made his way to the table.

She'd swept up her hair in a sophisticated twist. He eyed the slim column of her neck above the bluish-purple collar of her fitted blazer, and ran his tongue over his teeth. She'd had a spot on the left side, just below her ear, that used to make her toes curl when he kissed her there. He wondered what she'd do if he greeted her by scraping his teeth along the sensitive tendon until he'd rediscovered her weakness.

Probably knock me in the head with the crystal pepper grinder at the center of the table. The concussion would be worth seeing her eyes cross the way they did when he'd had her beneath him, wanton and willing.

And if he didn't put that kind of thought out of his head, he'd spend an uncomfortable hour with his dick poking the underside of the table.

He couldn't resist touching her, however, and ran his fingertips over her special spot. She flinched and turned her head. Surprise gave way to recognition, and in her unblinking eyes was the reaction he'd been looking for.

Oh God. You remembered.

Satisfaction surged, and he slid into the chair opposite hers. "Have you been waiting long?"

A slight blush colored her cheeks, and she toyed with the stem of her empty wine glass. "About ten minutes." She cleared her throat, and her smile appeared forced. "I think the cab driver might have done a few laps at the Indy 500 in a past life."

He smiled and ran his gaze over her face, then lower, past the hammering pulse point at the base of her throat to the deep plunge of the suit's lapels. Classically cut and fitted, tonight's armor would put her at home in any board meeting—until the participants got a close look at the white lace camisole beneath.

He didn't bother trying to hide his interest in the soft swell of her breasts, clearly visible through the sheer lace. She'd dressed with a purpose tonight, and from the look of things, that purpose was seduction. Far be it for him to deny her the expected, and utterly appropriate, response. He let his gaze linger as he dropped his napkin onto his lap.

Though she'd fought it, the way she'd responded to his every touch these past few days made it clear she was helpless against the physical pull that had always been between them. For whatever reason, she'd decided the fight wasn't worth the effort, and tonight, she intended to do something about it. While he heartily agreed with that sentiment, there was a much more important prize on the line than temporarily quenching the fire she stoked in his gut and balls.

Desire was a powerful force and, for the purpose he had in mind, wielding it properly would be his key to ultimate victory.

"That's a dangerous outfit you're wearing, Red." He raised his gaze to hers. "It could give a man ideas."

Her blush flared to a bright pink, and the uncertainty in her eyes said she wasn't completely comfortable with whatever plan she'd set in motion. He shifted in his seat. Her hesitancy worked in his favor, but was little conciliation against the self-induced burn he'd be forced to endure until he achieved his goals. Still, there were other pleasures to be enjoyed in the process. Like the way her eyes flashed when she was frustrated.

Before she could reply, the sommelier arrived at the table. He looked to Sam for their selection. Deferring to V, Sam smiled as the name of the French vintage rolled off her tongue with ease. The girl he remembered wouldn't know a cabernet sauvignon from a cranberry cocktail. Come to think of it, he couldn't recall ever seeing her touch a drop of alcohol, wine or otherwise. Granted, she'd been underage at the time, as had he, but that hadn't stopped him from swilling a few brews on occasion. She'd always declined.

The sommelier returned to fill their glasses before they'd finished giving their orders to the waiter. Once they were alone again, she fiddled with the napkin in her lap, then frowned and straightened the fork next to her plate. When she cleared her throat, he figured it was game on, but as much as he was looking forward to her opening kickoff, he had some tweaking to do first.

"Sam, I was thinking...that is—"

"Practice went pretty well, I think." He picked up his glass. "The guys were antsy, knowing it was Bob's last day, but we managed to accomplish a few things."

She accepted the pause to her agenda with a sad smile. "They respect and like him."

"As they should. He's one of the best. I've got some huge cleats to fill."

She fidgeted with the stem of her wine glass, but had yet to take a sip. "From what I know of your abilities, that shouldn't be a problem."

He fought a grin at the irresistible opening. Leaning forward, he dropped his voice to a husky tone. "What abilities would those be?"

The blush returned, but she was on a mission. She curved her lips in a coy smile. "Your coaching abilities, of course."

He smiled and straightened. Swirling the wine in his glass, he tripped her up with a quick delay of game. "How did Caroline take the news about our reconciliation? I assume she's heard, since you were so anxious we put my plan into motion immediately."

"I...." Sacked at the line, she frowned, then stumbled over her words. "Wait. You haven't spoken to her?"

"I'd planned to stop by her office before I left, but after your phone call, I was...." He paused for impact and dropped his tone an octave or two. "...distracted."

If her relieved smile was any indication, his little innuendo told her she had him back on the right track. "Yes, well, I did speak to her, and everything's fine. In fact, she was pleased."

Sam propped his elbows on the table. "Pleased is good."

She tipped her glass toward him in a flirty salute, then brought the rim to her lips. "Pleased is very good, and I was thinking—"

"But we're supposed to be sleeping together."

She coughed as if she'd choked, and he bit back his smile. "You okay?"

Flapping her free hand in front of her face, she set down her glass. "Went down the wrong way."

She hadn't taken a sip.

Sam nodded and lowered his voice as if he didn't want to be overheard. "But since we aren't really lovers, we're at a disadvantage that might blow the whole thing."

She blinked, and he nearly grinned at the frustrated frown wrinkling her forehead. According to Jake, she'd had only a handful of dates and no relationships since Sam. He supposed one or more of those dates could have ended in bed, but the odds were none of them had. Which meant she had exactly two months of sexual experience. With him. She was a babe in the wilderness when it came to seduction. Hell, he could practically hear the tumblers clacking in her head as she tangled with how to go from "we aren't really lovers" to "maybe we should be."

She shook her head. "I'm afraid I'm not following you."

Of course you aren't, baby. Stick with me. I'll get us where you're trying to go. Eventually.

He sat back. "Real lovers know things about their partners. It's been a long time since we were together. Other than you work for the Marauders, I don't know anything about your life." He sipped slowly from his glass. "Like, what do you like to do on your days off? Do you have any pets? Like to travel? That sort of thing."

The waiter arrived with their meals. V waited until he'd gone again, then picked up her fork. "I like to read when I have the chance. No pets, and I travel all the time with the team. The last thing I want to do is board a plane for a vacation, so I stay home and do some of that reading I don't have time for."

Cutting into his steak, Sam paused and cocked his head. "What about men? I didn't think to ask, but is there someone special who might have a problem with—" he bumped his chin toward her, "you and me and all of this?"

V paused with her first bite of pasta near her lips, then set her fork down without tasting it. "No, there isn't, and about that. I have a question for you."

"Ask me anything, but first, I have a question for you." He slipped a slice of beef into his mouth. In the short time they'd had together, V had been incredibly responsive in bed and a little dirty talk had often been enough to send her over the edge. Time to turn up the heat with one last tweak, before he let her have her say. "If it's out of line, just say so."

Her lips tightened in a flat line, a sure sign of her frustration, and he threw out a question designed to throw her permanently off balance. "I remember a sweet little pulse point on your neck that used to make you melt whenever I kissed you there." V gasped. The lace camisole stretched tight across her breasts, and her pupils dilated until almost no blue remained. He leaned in for the kill. "If I sucked you there now, would that still make you wet?"

She blinked, opened her mouth, closed it, then opened it again. "I—" She swallowed, then straightened her shoulders. "Maybe we should go find out. I got a room."

More than satisfied with her response, he slid a second bite into his mouth, and played dumb. "A room?"

"For us. Upstairs." She lowered her fork to the table, and he followed the movement of her hand as her fingers briefly disappeared into her cleavage. They reappeared clutching a card key. "Sixteen-twenty. I've already checked in."

Sam sat back and studied her face. High color stood out on her cheeks, and her pupils had yet to contract. "Are you inviting me to your bed, V?"

"No!" She slammed her eyes shut, and her chest heaved as if she'd taken a bracing breath. "Okay, yes." She opened her eyes and shook her head. "But only if you'd like to. No pressure. Really. After what happened between us yesterday, I just thought...."

V groaned, and his lips quirked in a slow smile. "Well, now. That's a very tempting offer."

She glanced around at the nearby tables. When she met his gaze again, embarrassment had leaked into her eyes. "An offer you have to know was difficult for me to make. So, are you coming?" He arched a brow and grinned, and she grimaced. "You know I didn't mean it that way."

He chuckled. "Yeah, I did." He glanced at her full plate. "You haven't taken a bite yet."

She glanced down at the food, then up again to accuse, "You and your bedroom voice have got me too rattled to eat." Her shoulders slumped on a sigh. "I didn't mean to blurt that out the way I did, but…I'm sorry. I'm not very good at this sort of thing."

"On the contrary. You're doing just fine, Red." Sam shoved back his chair and stood. He pulled out his wallet and dropped a handful of bills on the table. "Lead the way."

Chapter 17

V stared at Sam where he stood by the bed and every insecurity she'd ever had slammed into her like a wrecking ball. She twisted her hands at her waist. "Now that we're here, I'm not sure I know what to do."

He shrugged out of his suit coat and tossed it over the chair. "Yes, you do. We've danced this dance before, remember?"

"Yeah, but my dance shoes are *really* dusty."

He smiled and held out his hand. She forced her feet to move until she stood in front of him and could cling to his fingers with hers. He guided her down to the edge of the bed, then squatted before her. "It's like riding a bike. It'll come back to you."

"If you say so." V looked up at the ceiling, then over her shoulder at the king-sized bed. Swallowing, she turned back to look into his eyes. "Where do we start?"

His smile softened. "We start with you telling me what you see happening here. I don't want any misunderstandings."

Shadows of the past darkened his eyes, and she understood. She nodded. "I don't either."

"Good." Knees spread, he propped his forearms on his thighs. "Then what are we talking about? Are we here to simply get our rocks off for old time's sake, or were you thinking we could turn this plan of mine into an actual reconciliation?"

Her heart thumped erratically in her chest. "You said you wanted us to try to be friends again."

"A 'friends with benefits' kind of thing, then?"

V was tempted to take that suggestion and run with it. She liked as well as loved him, and he didn't seem like he carried a grudge, despite everything. Having him in her life again, even under limited circumstances, was more than she'd ever hoped for, and would fill a void she'd lived with for fifteen years. Yet, her greedy heart wanted more. He'd said the truth of their past was up to her to share or not, and with that one sentence, he'd made *anything* possible again.

She wanted to put the past and its painful secrets behind her. She wanted what she could have had with him if she hadn't panicked and thrown his love away. The patience in his eyes gave her the courage to ask for it all.

"No. That's not what I want. I want what we used to have. I want you, not just a sometimes lover who happens to be my friend."

Sam opened his mouth, but she pressed her fingers to his lips to silence him. "Before you answer, I need to say this." The deep breath she took wasn't nearly enough to calm the quaking of her heart. "When I walked away from you, I left behind the best thing that ever happened to me because I was a coward, and always had been."

Gone was the carefree friend contemplating their future. Confusion wrinkled his brow and he picked up her right hand. "What does that mean? I don't understand."

"I know you don't." She threaded her fingers through his, needing the contact. "You said it was up to me whether or not I told you the truth about what made me leave, but I can't do that. The best I can do is apologize and hope you can forgive me." She dropped her gaze to their interlocked fingers. "I'm sorry, Sam. Sorrier than I can ever express. What I did to you, walking away at the very moment you needed my support the most, was unforgiveable. If I could go back there, go back in time, I'd do things differently, but that's not possible."

He was silent for so long, she didn't think he was going to respond. When he did, the low timbre of his voice wrapped around her heart like squeezing fingers. "You could trust me."

She looked up and met his gaze. The hopeful intensity in his eyes brought tears to hers. "I do trust you."

His smile held a hint of sadness. "No, you don't. Not really." His chest expanded on a heavy breath. "Not now, but you will." He studied her face, then nodded. "We'll consider this a reconciliation." Rising to his feet, he pulled her up with him. "For now, but time and circumstance change people. I'm no longer that cocky kid you knew, racing toward the future I'd decided was my due. You'll learn I've become a patient man, Victoria Price."

Apparently, he'd decided enough had been said on the subject, and she was more than happy to avoid further conversation. He cupped her face in his palms and pressed a gentle kiss to her lips. Her eyelids slid closed, and she stood pliant as he flicked open the button on her blazer, then slipped the material from her shoulders. His hissed breath drew her attention and she opened her eyes.

Heat blazed in his blue eyes as he stared at her puckered nipples, straining against the stretchy lace clinging to her skin. He turned her to the side so he could examine the back. "How does this come off?"

"There are snaps." Her answer came in a breathy sigh.

He ran his palm down her spine, searching. "Where?"

"At the crotch."

His gaze jerked back to hers. "It's a good thing I didn't know that downstairs. The elevator tape would have been all over YouTube, if we didn't get arrested before we reached the sixteenth floor."

A helpless laugh escaped her. He'd always been able to do that. Make her laugh even as he heated her insides to the boiling point, simply by looking at her with his long-lashed eyes.

Taking a page from his book, V stepped back, out of his reach. "I lost one piece; now it's your turn."

He squinted, but the dimples bracketing his mouth broadcast his humor. "I took off my jacket when we first came in."

"Doesn't count." She flicked a finger at his chest. "Lose the shirt."

"You're bolder than I remember." She stiffened at the reference to the past, but he waggled his brows and slipped the top button of his dress shirt. "I like it."

Tensed muscles easing, she reached behind her waist to unclip the hook on her skirt.

"Slow down." Sam sat on the edge of the bed and continued with his buttons. "I'm multi-tasking. I don't want to miss anything."

She snickered and slowed at her task, but not because he'd asked her to. She simply forgot what she was supposed to be doing as he tugged the tails of his shirt from his slacks and yanked the material down his arms. Roped muscles bulged as he ignored the buttons on the cuffs, tearing one hand free of a sleeve, then the other.

She stared. He was broader than she remembered, in both his chest and shoulders. The dusting of dark hair across his pecs and surrounding the disks of his flat nipples was peppered with gray that did nothing to diminish the overall effect.

He was beautiful. A natural warrior who may have been denied the field, but obviously hadn't walked away from the daily regimen of weights and cardio training she remembered him doing.

He caught her staring, and his smile went dark as he rose to his feet. She had an inkling of what was coming by the twinkle of mischief in his eyes, and she was right. Just as he had in Florida on their first night together, he lifted his arms and struck an Atlas pose, then dropped them to lock his wrists at his waist and made his pecs dance.

He winked as he turned to the side in a third body-building pose. "Admit it. I've still got it."

V laughed, but with saliva pooling on her tongue, saying "hell, yeah, you do," would make her drool all over her lacy tank he seemed to like so much.

He toed off a loafer, then paused. "Hurry it up, Red. I'm one ahead of you."

Feeling more carefree than she had in years, she followed his lead. Dropping her arms to her sides, she abandoned the skirt zipper and stepped from one of her high heels.

Silent laughter sparkled in his eyes, and he kicked off his second shoe. So did she.

He reached for the button of his slacks. She twisted her arms around her back to her zipper. Five seconds later, with their respective garments pooled around their ankles, they stared at one another. He slid his gaze from her face to the junction of her thighs, where the snaps of her lace tank had already gone damp. There was no missing the impressive erection tenting his underwear.

Then he shuffled toward her like an X-rated penguin in blue boxers, and she burst out laughing. His eyes twinkled with wicked intent, but the humor in them died as he stopped in front of her. Lifting his hand, he traced a fingertip over her cheek, then down around her jawline. "You are, beyond any doubt, *the* most beautiful thing I've ever seen in my life."

Her eyes flooded and breathing was impossible. He cupped the back of her neck and brought his mouth down on hers as if he were starving and she his sustenance. Bracketing an arm around her waist, he crushed her to him, compressing her ribs with the strength of his desire.

Lifting her free of her skirt, he kicked free of his slacks and turned. Without releasing her mouth, he lowered his knee to the bed, then eased her to her back. He followed, and the weight of his big body pinning her to the mattress was a homecoming V never thought she'd find.

With hands and mouth, Sam worshiped her. Fingertips spread, he traced a path from her shoulder, across her collar bone, to the swell of one breast. Cupping her in his palm, he brushed the pad of his thumb over her nipple, and she was helpless against the full body shiver as fire raced from her chest straight to her clit.

Releasing her mouth, he shifted his body until he was propped on one elbow above her. He turned his head, his hungry gaze following the path of his fingers. She looked down her body, mesmerized by the sight of his large hand against the white lace covering her. As if relearning her form, he traced a path to her other breast, then between the mounds and up until his palm and fingers encircled the column of her neck.

Through the sheer lace, his touch left a trail of fire behind as his hand moved lower, exploring the shape of her ribs, her waist and belly. He swirled a fingertip around the shadowy indent of her belly button, then traveled lower still, moving ever-closer to the throbbing folds between her thighs.

She couldn't contain her whimper when his hand suddenly detoured and paused at her hip. He turned his head and captured her gaze. The carnal intensity in his eyes made her even wetter.

"Lace becomes you, Red." He slid his index finger beneath the high-cut elastic band of her tank and traced downward. "Strong, yet delicate." The back of his finger brushed over the curls on her mound. "Concealing, yet offering glimpses of the woman beneath." Rotating his hand, he slid his finger between her wet folds. "Cool elegance and burning heat."

He pressed down on her clit, and she couldn't help her gasp of pleasure. His lips curved in a dark smile. Turning his head, he lowered his eyelids to half-mast, and dragged air through his nose in a slow, unapologetic sniff. "The scent of your need has haunted me for years. Hot and musky."

His erection pressed against her thigh, and she needed to touch him. She shifted her arm, but he grabbed her wrist with his free hand. "No, baby. This time is all about you. My time will come later." He burrowed his thumb beneath the lace to join his finger. "Do you still make that little squeaky sound you used to whenever I made you come with my fingers?"

He plucked at her tightened bud, and the combination of his words and touch was all she needed. She shattered into a thousand points of pleasure, and his laugh was low and deep. "I see you do."

Sam gave her no time to recover. Dipping his head, he caught her mouth in a ravenous kiss, before sliding his lips across her cheek and jaw to her throat. He grazed his teeth over the tendon running down the side of her neck, honing in on the spot he'd mentioned earlier. She squirmed, her body lost in a tangle of pleasure mixed with near-pain. Over-sensitized and still throbbing, the flesh between her thighs pulsated as he sucked at her throat in an open-mouth kiss.

Holding back her second orgasm was impossible. Lashes of pleasure whipped over her again and again, and she bucked against his hand.

"Sam." Her plea came out as a throaty cry. Lethargic and heavy, her arms reached for him, but her fingers slid over the firm muscle of his chest and shoulders as he moved free of her grasping hands.

"I'm here, Red."

The bed shifted, and she opened her eyes. The ceiling of the hotel room was all she saw, until she dipped her chin and looked down her body. On his knees, Sam's hot blue gaze was focused on the juncture of her spread thighs. With a flick of his fingers, the snaps of her tank sprang free.

His heavy swallow made his Adam's apple jump. "Fucking beautiful." He lifted his gaze to hers, and his eyes gleamed with carnal intent.

"No, Sam. I can't."

He slid his palms beneath her bottom and lifted her. "Yes, you can." Lowering his head, he brought his mouth to within a breath of her swollen folds. "Come for me, baby. I need to taste your sweet pleasure on my tongue more than I need my next breath."

Closing the distance, he stabbed at her clit with the hardened tip of his tongue. Once, twice, then a third thrust, and she dropped her head to the mattress. He closed his lips over her swollen folds and sucked. Wet heat and pleasure enveloped her and she cried his name as she tumbled over the edge once more.

Chest heaving, her body quivering with the latent spasms of her fading climax, she lay wrecked and shattered. God, how was it possible she'd forgotten how expertly he could play her body? Like a master musician drawing perfection from his instrument, he dragged forth the tune he was after with little more than a brush of his fingers, the tone of his voice, and his magical tongue.

V had to concentrate to open her eyes. When she'd managed the feat, her mind struggled to make sense of what she saw. At the foot of the bed, Sam pulled his wrinkled slacks over his hips.

"What are you doing?"

He snatched his shirt from the floor and straightened. "Getting dressed." Shoving his arm into one sleeve, he tugged the material over his shoulders.

"I can see that. Why?"

He made quick work of the front buttons as he spoke. "I don't think Caroline would be pleased if her new offensive coordinator was arrested for public indecency for walking through the lobby of the Marriott naked and sporting a hard-on."

She pushed up on her elbows. "You're leaving? Now?"

"I've got to pick up Lucy." Tucking the tails of his shirt into his slacks, he tugged the zipper closed. He covered the obvious bulge of his erection with his hand, adjusting himself more comfortably, before closing the clasp at his waist.

Rolling upward, she sat. "She's spending the night at CC and Tuck's."

He stepped into one loafer, then the next. "No, she isn't. I spoke to Tuck on my way to meet you. I told him I'd get Lucy on my way home."

"I don't understand." She shook her head. "If you never planned to stay, then why did you…." A cold chill raced down her spine and made her shiver. She grasped the edge of the comforter and covered herself. "God. If this was some twisted play for revenge, it backfired big time. I had three orgasms and you…" her eyes widened in horror, "you never even took off your shorts."

Disappointment darkened his eyes. "What happened here didn't have a thing to do with revenge." He rounded the bed and sat at her hip, then sighed. "The truth is, I couldn't resist touching you."

She crossed her arms, tucking them tight under her breasts. "You did a hell of a lot more than just touch me."

"And I enjoyed every moment. So did you." He reached out to brush a curl behind her ear. "I told you this time was about you."

A good portion of her panic eased at the genuine affection in his eyes. "Well, yeah but, what about you?"

Sam leaned forward, placing his hands on the mattress so they bracketed her hips. "You still don't trust me, Red. When you do, I'll be inside you before your heart can take its next beat. Count on it. Until then…." He pressed a kiss to her forehead, stood, and turned toward the door. "I'll see you at the complex Monday morning."

Her mouth dropped open as the door clicked shut, and she fell back to stare at the ceiling. "You have *got* to be kidding me!"

Chapter 18

V sent Caroline the press release first thing Sunday morning as promised, then spent several hours swinging back and forth between confusion, anger, and occasionally, a touch of wonder. Finally, she couldn't stand her own company anymore, and drove to Jake and Gracie's farmhouse for some of that moral support her friend had offered.

"He didn't."

"Oh, yes, he did."

Gracie's eyes went dreamy. "You've got to admit. It's pretty romantic."

V scowled. "No, it isn't. It's diabolical. He said it didn't matter, then resorted to blackmail."

"Giving you the option of telling him the truth or not isn't the same as saying it doesn't matter to him. Obviously, it does, but he didn't hold out on you. He held out on himself. How is that blackmail?"

V pinned her with a bland stare. "If Jake gave you multiple orgasms, then walked away hurting in an effort to get you to do something you didn't want to do, what would you call it?"

Gracie screwed up her face in a grimace. "Okay. You're right. He's blackmailing you, but it's still romantic."

V dropped her head to the back of the couch with a groan.

"He asked for your trust, V, not a kidney."

"A kidney would be easier."

Gracie smiled, then stood and crossed the room to fish a ball out from under the bookshelf. Little Tommy squealed and Jake Jr clapped his hands. "Just tell him the truth. The man obviously cares about you. Whatever your big secret is, he's agreed to start over, right? You've already cleared the biggest hurdle."

"Yeah, but—"

A solid knock sounded on the door. Jake walked in. "Sam called. He's on his way to the sports complex. Caroline wants to see you both ASAP."

V sat up from her slump on the couch. "Did he say why?"

"She's in damage-control mode."

"Over what?"

"Apparently there's an online article claiming to have spotted you and Sam cozying up at a hotel in Times Square. It's gone viral."

"Oh, shi...oot." V's heart did a manic flip as her gaze snapped to the twins on the floor.

Jake chuckled. "Nice save."

The Malones had a no-swear policy at the farmhouse, backed up by a row of swear jars on a shelf in the kitchen. Five dollars per infraction. V's was stuffed with enough cash to send one of the twins to college. She rolled her eyes and bolted from the couch, looking around for her purse to check her phone.

"Why didn't Caroline call me herself?"

"I take it she did. A few times. When you didn't answer, she called Sam."

V tried to recall the last time she'd seen her purse. She'd had it in the car, she knew, because she'd had to search through it to find her keys. Flustered over what had happened last night, she must have left it on the front seat.

Gracie whipped out her tablet. "What website?"

Jake made a pained face. "Eye on Sports."

V whimpered.

Gracie scowled. "Ted Jaffrey? He's a chauvinist pig and glorified gossip columnist who doesn't know jack about football."

Jake shrugged at his wife's assessment of the sport's editorialist. "Maybe so, but he's got a following."

While Gracie brought up the page, V tugged on her coat.

"Here it is." Gracie scrolled her thumb over the screen and read out loud. "With the playoffs kicking off this weekend in the wildcard matchups, The Marauders' owner, Caroline Wainwright, has scheduled a surprise press conference for Monday morning." She rattled off the particulars of tomorrow's press conference, and V paused in the doorway, torn between racing to beat Sam to the complex, and hanging around for a few minutes so she would know what they were dealing with before she got there.

"An unnamed source tells Eye on Sports that Bob Dugan, the Marauders' long-time offensive coordinator, will soon be announcing his retirement. Dugan joined the team...blah blah blah." Gracie scrolled her thumb over the screen. "Our source gave no reason for Dugan's decision to the leave the championship franchise on the eve of post-season play, but named his replacement as Samuel Fitzpatrick, a relatively unknown force in the world of football. EOS can independently confirm, Fitzpatrick recently resigned from his position as head coach of East Texas University's football program after a respectable six-year run."

"Where's the part about the hotel?" V returned and slid onto the couch next to Gracie.

"I'm looking. I'm looking. Here's some stuff about Sam in high school...State championship...Sam's injury and his coaching stats." She read in silence for a moment. "Okay, here we go. While on paper, Fitzpatrick's stats make him a reasonable candidate for a position with a pro team in the future, offensive coordinator for the reigning Super Bowl champs might be a stretch. Especially as the Marauders prepare for a tough match-up with Seattle next Sunday."

"Asshat." V winced and shot a glance at the boys. "Sorry."

Jake grinned. "Don't be. I would have said it myself, but you beat me to it. Just don't forget the five bucks for your swear jar."

"I'll get to it as soon as I find my purse."

Gracie continued reading. "The team's owner, Caroline Wainwright, who made her fortune thanks to lucky timing and some questionable investments in the early days of the internet..." She looked up at Jake and snorted, before dropping her gaze to the screen once more. "...has seen unprecedented success since she scooped up the troubled franchise seven years ago. Those in the know attribute her miraculous record over the past seven years to the genius of George Tipton, her general manager. Tipton, who put together a dream team coaching staff for the novice team owner, including Dugan, has brought home four conference titles and two championships in the last four years."

Jake shook his head. "He thinks Tipton has been calling the shots. Moron."

"Shh." Gracie waved her hand and continued. "It appears, however, that someone other than Tipton is making the decisions on staff personnel these days, using a much different criterion than most outfits in the league. According to our source, Fitzpatrick was once engaged to Victoria Price," Gracie ignored V's horrified gasp and continued, "the team's public relations consultant for the past year, and a close personal friend of Wainwright's."

"Oh, no." V's eyes slid shut on a moan.

"EOS was not able to confirm the details of the personal relationship between Fitzpatrick and Price, but the two...Oh, shit."

"Five bucks, babe."

"Shut up, Jake."

V's eyes popped open and she leaned over Gracie's arm to read the words herself. "The two were seen entering an elevator together last night at the Marriott Marquis in Times Square." V slapped a hand to her forehead. "Oh my God. I'm going to be sick."

Gracie patted her knee. "No, you're not." She finished reading the end of the short op-ed. "Which begs the question. Will the Marauders take the field next season with another championship patch gracing their uniforms, or will they settle for wearing their *hearts* on their sleeves?" She dropped the tablet to her lap. "What a dick."

"What have I done?"

Jake eyed V with interest. "While I'd pay a thousand bucks to hear what you and Sam were doing at the Marriott, this isn't about the two of you. Jaffrey's been gunning for Caroline for years."

"I know, but Sam…." She dropped her head in her hands. "He's going to kill me for setting him up the way I did last night."

Gracie coughed, but V didn't bother to look up.

"Maybe, but he's in the pros now, V. Did you think he'd be welcomed into Dugan's position without the vultures questioning whether or not he had the chops?"

She lifted her head to meet Jake's reasoning look with a scowl. "Of course not, but questioning his résumé is one thing. Jaffrey made it sound like his girlfriend got him the job, which is the exact opposite of what happened."

"Sam's a big boy, V, and he can be one tough son of a bitch when he wants to."

"I've got to go." V stood, but Gracie grabbed her arm before she could race out of the house.

"Give us a moment, will you, Malone?"

Jake glanced between them, but then nodded. "Come on, punks. Daddy wants ice cream." The twins squealed their approval. Scooping them up, he tucked one under each arm and strode from the room.

"Thanks for not narcing me out to Jake." Gracie frowned. "He gets pissy when I interfere in his friends' lives."

V cast an anxious glance at her watch, then sighed. "I wouldn't have gone if I didn't want to. You just gave me the shove."

"And you ended up with three orgasms."

V snorted a laugh as Gracie stood and pulled her into a hug. "It's going to be okay, V. You'll see. But in the meantime, I think you should find out who Jaffrey's source is. He may be gunning for Caroline, but considering the information he used to cut her, someone else has it out for either you or Sam."

* * * *

V tapped her foot impatiently, mentally rushing the elevator car upward toward the administrative floor. Having clinched their division several weeks ago, the Marauders' complex was mostly empty. The staff and team were no doubt gathered around their TVs, waiting for the wild card games to begin in fifteen minutes.

Only a handful of cars had been in the private lot, Caroline's Jag among them. The movers weren't due for another day, and V had no idea what Sam was driving in the interim, so she wasn't sure if she'd beaten him here, or if he'd already arrived.

The elevator car slowed to a stop and the doors whooshed open. Stepping out, V spotted Lucy on the couch in the lounge, and detoured that way.

Lucy looked up from her book and smiled. "Hi."

"Hi yourself. How's the new house?"

She shrugged. "It's good. Sam's looking for a nanny." Her nose wrinkled in distaste. "He says it's a housekeeping position, but he's not fooling anyone."

V smiled. "New York is a fun city, but it has its dark side. He'll be on the road a lot and he'd worry if he left you all alone at the house. I don't blame him. I would, too."

Lucy closed her book and her eyes lit up with a hopeful smile. "Maybe *you* could come stay with me once in a while. I'm sure Sam wouldn't mind."

If I'm still alive after he catches up with me.

"Oh. I'd like that." V's smile felt like a clown mask. "Really."

A door opened behind her, and she glanced over her shoulder. Her nerves snapped tight as Sam stepped out of Caroline's office. V studied his face, looking for a clue to his mood. He didn't *look* like he wanted to commit murder, but the tick of his jaw was a dead giveaway.

He stalked toward them, moving straight toward V. She briefly considered running around the couch, but that would be the coward's way out. Instead, she lifted her chin and met his gaze—then blushed as a particularly irresistible image from last night came out of nowhere.

With everything that mattered to her on the line, daydreaming about Sam's wide shoulders wedged between her spread thighs was highly inappropriate and problematic. It was just as well she'd be looking for another job. She lost all sense when he was around, and the staff and team were bound to notice the first time she forgot what she was saying when Sam walked by. She shook her head to clear it as he stopped before her.

Her throat constricted on a painful swallow. "Sam, I'm so sorry."

His gaze roamed her face, pausing on her mouth before lifting to her eyes. "For what? Unless you were Jaffrey's source."

Horrified he'd even consider such a notion, she slapped a hand to her chest. "No, of course not."

"Then you've got nothing to apologize for. If you're not busy later, Lucy and I have a first-dinner-in-the-new-house celebration planned. Isn't that right, kid?" His eyes never left V's face, and she had to drag her gaze to Lucy's.

The arch of the girl's brows said this was the first she'd heard of it, but she was a quick study. She bobbed her head in an exaggerated nod. "That's right. We're having pizza." Sam cleared his throat. Lucy's smile was smug, but then her eyes turned pleading. "Please say you'll come."

V turned to Sam. He leaned over and pressed a hard kiss to her mouth. He straightened, and she blinked, confused by the conflicting signals. The tight line of his jaw clearly broadcast anger, so why was he inviting her to join them for their celebration?

"We'll see you at six." He stepped around her. "You ready, Luce?"

V stared at his retreating back as Lucy hurried after him to the elevator. When they'd disappeared inside, V turned and walked to Caroline's office. The door was open, so she didn't bother knocking.

Caroline held her phone to her ear and waved V into the seat in front of her desk. The moment she disconnected the call, V leaned forward. "This was my fault, Caroline, not Sam's. I'll have my resignation on your desk before the press conference tomorrow."

"Like hell you will. We both know Jaffrey's claims are total bullshit." Caroline sat back and tapped her pen against the blotter. "This is about me, V. Not Sam or you."

Relieved, V's shoulders slumped with her sigh. "I don't understand. What has Jaffrey got against you?"

Caroline twirled the pen in her fingers. "My first cyber platform contained the early framework for the security used by many of today's social media sites. Jaffrey had developed similar code, but his had some issues. They've long since been gobbled up but, at the time, CySec was at the cutting edge of the technology, and they were courting us both."

Her lips quirked in a sharp smile. "Long story short, they bought me out, making me a very rich woman, and he's had a bug up his butt ever since. Jaffrey didn't know a thing about football, but that didn't stop him from launching EOS the month I bought the Marauders. Ironically, he's had far more success with his sports editorializing than he ever did in high tech."

She rolled her eyes and set aside the pen. "Anyway, the only thing your resignation would accomplish is speculation from others, and I'd sell the team before I'd give the little prick that kind of satisfaction."

"Then what are we going to do?" V curled her fingers into frustrated fists. "We've got to comment, or that speculation will grow on its own."

"I agree, and it's taken care of."

V shook her head. "How?" A flash of Sam's clenched jaw as he approached her down the hall made her stomach muscles cramp.

"Bob sent me a copy of his statement for tomorrow's press conference, in which he makes it very clear Sam was *his* choice, not mine. This may sound crass, but considering the seriousness of everything else he'll be saying tomorrow, there won't be a soul alive who will believe Jaffrey's claims after hearing Bob sing Sam's praises."

As painfully cynical as that was, it was true. The football world respected Bob Dugan and, upon learning his diagnosis, not a single broadcaster, player, owner, or water boy, for that matter, would question a thing he had to say.

"As for you and Sam, I'll tell you what I told him." Caroline studied V with shrewd eyes. "Your personal relationship is no one else's business. We won't be denying your connection. First, because I don't want the two of you to feel like you have to sneak around. Others in the organization have carried on relationships without incident, and I won't deny you and Sam the same courtesy. And two. Romance sells."

"Excuse me?" V blinked.

"Regardless of what people think of Jaffrey's take on Sam's relationship with you, the story is out there. There is no shoving it back into the bag. People will talk, especially since Sam is single and a good-looking man. If we experience a little extra buzz because the ladies who love football are intrigued by the idea of a gridiron romance, so be it."

V closed her eyes. "Oh, Caroline, no wonder Sam didn't look very happy on his way out."

"He wasn't happy, but Jaffrey was the reason. Sam wanted to know where to find him."

V's eyes popped open, and she jerked forward in her chair. "You didn't tell him."

Caroline grinned. "I was tempted. That man can be very intimidating, but I explained the Marauders' philosophy is to do their talking on the field. The best revenge against this kind of thing is a win, followed by another win, and eventually, a ring. Sam grudgingly agreed. I simply wanted to make sure we were on the same page for tomorrow's presser. Sam will be reading his statement and fielding a few questions, but I told him I'd take any questions on the subject of Jaffrey's claims."

V blew out a breath. "I'm so sorry, Caroline. The Marriott was my idea. I never even considered anyone would take notice of us. It's not like either of us are recognizable to anyone outside of football."

"No, you aren't. Which I mentioned to Sam. Whomever Jaffrey used as his source obviously knows the two of you."

"I was thinking the same thing." TJ had come to mind first, but Sam's cousin would never belittle his coaching ability by suggesting he'd gotten the job because of V. No, whomever had whispered in Jaffrey's ear obviously had it in for Sam, if not her as well.

Caroline smiled sharply. "It doesn't really matter. By tomorrow afternoon, Jaffrey will look like he has every time he's attempted to cross swords with me. A little man with a big grudge."

Chapter 19

"What's all this?" V sat beside Lucy on the couch and picked up one of the brochures spread across the coffee table.

"I'm trying to decide which one is the best fit."

V read the name of the prominent New York City academy on the pamphlet, and her surprised gaze flew to Sam. Shoulder propped against the archway, he nodded. She jerked her head back around. "You changed your mind about attending an arts academy?"

"Yep." Lucy nodded at the brochure in V's hand and scrunched her nose. "Not that one, though. It has a great reputation, but they expect the students who go there to live on campus in dorms. I'd rather live here." She shifted her gaze to Sam, and the look of awe on her face made V's heart contract. "At home. With Sam."

The breath stalled in V's throat and she turned. Sam had said Lucy refused to talk to him about the DNA test. He'd obviously gotten through to her somehow. The bemused joy in his eyes was enough to make V weep.

"He said he doesn't give a shit what the DNA test results say."

A startled laugh bubbled up in V's throat.

"Luce." The warning in Sam's tone held little heat.

Lucy grinned at him. "It's a new beginning, V." She turned her head and waited until V was looking her in the eye. "We're going to be a family."

Something, either the inflection in the girl's words or the intensity in her dark eyes, sent a shiver down V's spine. Maybe it was a case of wishful thinking, but it sounded to V as if Lucy's "we" had been meant in the collective sense, with all three of them included.

"Lucy, I—" Unsure of how to respond, V was rescued by the arrival of the pizza delivery man.

They ate their celebratory dinner on the long coffee table in Sam and Lucy's living room. V and Sam sat side-by-side on the couch and, claiming she needed pictures for the post she had planned, Lucy squeezed between them to snap a group selfie on her cell. Parked on the floor across from them, she devoured half a pie as she chattered about the merits of the two remaining schools on her list, and wondered at the level of talent in her future classmates.

The despondent teenager from that last afternoon in Barlow never made an appearance, and V marveled at how much younger she appeared. Contentment radiated from her large eyes, clear of the dark makeup she usually wore. And she giggled. Actually giggled and juggled the slice of pizza she'd pulled from the box just out of his reach when Sam attempted to pilfer a disk of pepperoni from the top.

It was as if the weight of the world had been lifted from Lucy's shoulders, but V worried at the role Sam's daughter saw V playing in her newfound joy. From several of her comments—like when she asked what V normally ate for breakfast, then instructed Sam to add bagels, tea, and honey to their grocery list—Lucy expected something permanent to come of V and Sam's dating arrangement.

That had been V's hope as well, and the point of last night's ill-fated adventure. However, after the way he'd left things when he'd walked out the hotel-room door, she wasn't as confident as she'd been when he'd said yes to their starting over. He might have left the decision up to her but, clearly, he wouldn't be satisfied with anything less than the entire truth.

With the pizza mess cleared up and the lights dimmed, Lucy pulled a disk from the selection of movies that had either been left by the previous owners, or provided by the Marauders until Sam's things arrive. Five minutes into the R-rated romance, she raised her arms above her head in an exaggerated yawn. "I'm going to bed." She climbed to her feet and headed for the hallway. "I'm so tired, I'll probably be asleep in three minutes, and I won't wake up until morning." She tossed a pointed smile over her shoulder. "Goodnight."

She disappeared through the archway before either of them could comment.

"Subtle, isn't she?" Sam shook his head but his smile was amused.

"As a matchmaker." V regretted her choice of words the moment they left her lips and searched for a neutral topic. "Uh…it looks like you got through to her about the DNA test. I'm so glad, Sam." With his arm stretched along the back of the couch, he needed only to move his hand to finger a curl at her cheek. Her heartbeat accelerated and she sucked in a breath. "I think the Romanov Academy is the right choice. From what I understand, their dance program is exceptional."

A dimple appeared in his crooked smile and he traced his fingertips along the line of her jaw. "I'm not sure a discussion on the merits of her choice of schools was what Lucy had in mind when she set this romantic stage."

Probably not, but it seemed a much safer subject than the way V's skin tingled beneath his fingers. She tilted her head slightly, breaking the connection. Undeterred, he moved his hand to her throat.

She swallowed. "Manhattan Academy has an excellent reputation as well, but it's at the other end of the island. In addition to the train, she'd have a twenty-minute subway ride. The Romanov facility is a two-block walk from Penn Station."

"Have you been thinking about last night?" Ignoring her neutral topic, he eased his hand around her neck to bury his fingers in her hair at the nape. "I didn't sleep a wink."

Her skin pebbled with goosebumps. "It's your own fault if you couldn't sleep. You chose to leave before I could...before you'd...." She bit back a groan as he massaged her scalp with gentle strokes. "I slept like a baby."

"Bragger." He chuckled, and wrapped his other hand around her arm, then shifted her until her back was pressed against his chest. He lowered himself against the pillow at the end of the couch and dragged her down with him so they were almost prone. "Still, the missed shut-eye was worth it. I lay awake in my bed, hearing that adorable little squeak you made as I fingered you to pleasure."

Damp heat fired between her thighs. "Sam, this isn't a good idea."

He slid his hand from her arm, over her ribs and breasts to swirl a fingertip in lazy circles at the base of her neck. "And remembering the way you shivered when I sucked you." He ran the tip of his finger up the tendon to her weak spot and pressed. "Right here."

Preventing another shiver was impossible, but she brought up her hand to encircle his wrist. "I mean it. Your daughter is right upstairs."

"It's already been three minutes. She's asleep."

Or standing at the top of the landing, listening to see if her romantic stage worked.

V's grip on his wrist made no difference, but then, she didn't try very hard to stop him from touching her. As much as she thought this was a bad idea, his hand roaming over her chest was too tempting to resist. Flattening his palm to her throat, he moved it lower, exploring one breast with its straining nipple, then lower still, over her belly to rest against her mound.

"And I wouldn't be a man if the sweet taste of you on my tongue and the memory of your musky scent didn't keep me awake and wanting."

He was doing it again. Seducing her with his dark silk voice and clever touch. "Again, your fault." His soft chuckle sounded in her ear, and he cupped her through her jeans. She squirmed beneath his hand, meaning to move away, but rubbing against him instead. "I really should go."

His rumbling hum vibrated through his chest to her back. "But you don't want to. You're so hot, I can feel it through your jeans."

"Sam." She sighed his name. If she was burning, so was he. She rolled her head to the side until she could look at him. His long-lashed eyes gleamed with a hunger that matched her own. Lifting her mouth, she swept her tongue across his lower lip, and his body shuddered beneath hers.

"Red." His arms contracted, and he shifted her around so she lay against him. The solid wall of his chest squashed her breasts. His erection jammed against her hip, and he took her mouth in a kiss so scorching, she was afraid she'd combust.

She forgot to breathe as he slipped his hand beneath the hem of her sweater, his spread fingers nearly spanning her waist just above her jeans. Warm and slightly rough, his palm rode her spine to the base of her neck, and he held her there as he explored her mouth with his tongue. Too soon, he abandoned her lips to nibble his way across her cheek.

"Stay, V." He nipped at her earlobe, then soothed the sting with his tongue.

She wanted to. Wanted to so badly she ached. "Sam."

"Take a chance on that new beginning Lucy mentioned." Running his palm down the length of her spine, he molded her butt with his palm. Squeezing gently, he pressed her closer, then groaned. He tucked his face into her neck, his heavy breaths warming her skin. "Trust me, Red, and stay."

Trust me.

The reminder of the price he put on that new beginning doused the red-hot flames of desire burning her to the core. She briefly dropped her forehead to his shoulder. "You don't play fair."

"I play to win."

It took every ounce of willpower she possessed to push off his chest. She stared into his eyes, smoldering with blue fire, and nearly gave in. Dragging her gaze clear of his, she disentangled herself from his arms and climbed to her feet.

He sat up, his gaze following her as she crossed the room to gather her purse and coat. "But this. You and me. It's not a game." He waited until she'd turned to look at him, then stood and stalked forward until he stood in front of her. "Not to me. I'm putting my trust in the hope it isn't to you, either."

She stiffened, his verbal jab slicing at her heart. Holding his hopeful gaze wasn't easy, but she refused to look away. "It isn't, Sam. You have every reason to doubt me, but I don't play games."

He blinked, then stared at her. "Then stay. See this through, and put us both out of our misery."

Despondency dragged at her, and she shook her head. "What you're asking of me is…impossible."

Denial flashed in his eyes, but his hands were gentle as he took her coat and helped her don it. "Nothing is impossible if you want it badly enough." Dropping an arm around her shoulders, he walked her into the foyer and stopped at the door, then turned her to face him. "Whether you had come running straight back to me fifteen years ago, or shown up on my doorstep years later as you have, we would have ended up right where we are at this moment. With me wanting you so fucking bad I hurt."

Tears welled in her eyes, and she shook her head. "The last thing I want to do is hurt you again. I couldn't live with that." Sighing, she dragged her coat closed. "Maybe it would be best if we just left each other alone."

His nostrils flared on a humorless laugh. "I wish it were that easy. Although I'd convinced myself I was over you, it's obvious I was fooling myself. The truth is, I never could resist you. That hasn't changed." He cupped her cheek in his palm. "Up until four months ago, I might have been satisfied with *I'm sorry I hurt you* and taken what you offered no questions asked, but yours is no longer the only heart to claim mine. You were right when you said I needed Lucy. I do, but I need you, too."

He dropped his forehead to V's. "Family is a concept Lucy has never really known. I won't short-change her by building our life together in half measures. I can't do that to her, and I won't do it to myself. We, both of us, want you in that life but, if we're going to work, it has to be all or nothing."

Pressing a kiss to her forehead, he straightened and opened the door. "Sleep well, baby."

Chapter 20

Early the next morning, Sam parked his rental car in the complex parking lot and switched off the ignition. Lifting his hips, he dug his buzzing cell phone from his back pocket. V's name appeared on the screen. He clamped the fingers of his free hand around the steering wheel as the rush of blood quickened in his body.

Her comment about them leaving each other alone had kept him awake a good portion of the night. She hadn't repeated the suggestion, but then, he hadn't given her the chance. Shit, he'd all but proposed and…nothing.

He was probably pushing her too hard. Hell, of course he was, but he was only human. The way she responded to his every touch was burning him alive. If she didn't talk soon, and put him out of his misery, he was going to combust—if he didn't blow a nut first.

Sucking air through his teeth, he thumbed the screen to answer and spoke as calmly as his wildly thumping heart would allow. "Good morning, Red."

"Sam, I was hoping to catch you before you headed to the complex."

No friendly greeting and her voice was pure business, holding no resemblance to the soft tones of the woman he'd held in his arms less than twelve hours ago. Not a good sign. His stomach muscles knotted.

She was going to bail, and he hadn't a clue how to convince her not to.

He eyed the high glass walls of the building in front of him. "Too late. I'm in the parking lot. What's wrong?"

"Nothing's wrong, exactly, but I think we should talk about last night."

He dropped his head against the rest and squeezed the bridge of his nose with forefinger and thumb. "Running away wasn't the answer last time. It's not this time, either."

She hesitated, and he held on to the small chance he'd misread the reason for her call. When she finally responded, her voice was calm and even. "I'm not running. I'm not going anywhere, but I can't give you what you want." Another pause. "Prolonging this…this thing between us, isn't going to change that."

"This thing?" Frustration whipped at him like a lash and his laugh was harsh. "It's called love, V, and no one ever said it was easy." He dropped his hand to his thigh. "Not to me, anyway."

The silence stretched and, with it, his patience. Telling her he loved her over the phone was a lame-ass move, but from the moment she'd walked back into his life, he'd lost all sense of what was normal and what was bat-shit crazy. He was losing his fucking mind.

He sighed. "No response to me admitting I'm still in love with you?"

"Sam."

The way she breathed his name stirred the embers of his frustration into a flame of anger. "You say you can't give me what I want, but you're wrong. I want you. *You*, Red, and so does Lucy."

Professionalism leaked away under hurt. "You're making this more difficult than it has to be."

"*I'm* making this difficult?" His gut clenched and the anger flared over all she was willing to throw away. Again. He curled his fingers into a fist. "The other night at the hotel, you said you'd left behind the best thing that ever happened to you because you were a coward. How is what you're doing now any different?"

She remained silent. He ground his molars so hard, he was surprised his jaw didn't crack under the pressure. "What? No snappy comeback from the hard-as-nails agent?" His laugh was a wry cough. "Oh, right. The agent isn't the one speaking, is she? *She* doesn't back down from anything, no matter how difficult. It's the *woman* who doesn't have the guts to trust that I love her. That I'd stand beside her, no matter what. It's the woman who doesn't have the courage or the conviction to believe the love I have for her is stronger than any dark secret she's hiding."

The sound of her hitched breathing pierced the red haze of his anger. He dragged in a ragged breath. "Shit. V—"

"I can't do this." Her thready voice was a dagger slice to his gut. "Please, tell Lucy I'm sorry."

The call went dead. He tossed the phone onto the dash. Slumping back, he dragged a palm over his mouth and jaw. "Way to go, asshole."

Jesus, he'd made her cry.

No way in hell was he going to lose her again. He couldn't. But berating her wasn't the answer.

He wrapped his fingers around the steering wheel. What the fuck was she hiding that would make her give up what she clearly wanted? Even his mention of Lucy hadn't been enough to make her stop and reconsider.

Think, Sam. Think.

He eyed the nearly empty parking lot. He'd come in early, wanting to refresh himself on the playbook before meeting the team on the field. He checked his watch. Practice wouldn't begin for more than an hour. He sat forward and grabbed his phone from the corner of the dash. Barlow was an hour behind, but Anita was an early riser. She answered on the third ring.

"Hello, Anita. It's Sam."

"Sam." Pleasure permeated her greeting. "This is a surprise. How are you? And Lucy? How is she handling the move?"

"We're good. Both of us. Settling in." He shifted in his seat. "I need to ask you a few questions."

"About?"

His chest rose on a heavy breath. "V."

"Of course. How are things going with the two of you?"

He scraped his palm over the back of his neck. "Not as well as I'd hoped when we left Barlow."

"I'm sorry, Sam. I'd hoped the two of you could reconcile."

"So did I. I still do, but I've done a piss-poor job of convincing her to talk to me so far." *And after that pissed-off performance a few minutes ago, you'll be lucky if she ever speaks to you again.*

Anita's sigh was heavy. "I'll wish you good luck, but I'm not sure it'll do a lot of good. I talk to her at least once a month and don't feel as if I know her at all."

"She doesn't ever tell you what she's thinking or what she wants out of life?"

"Not really." A short laugh sounded in his ear. "There was a time she told me everything. Now she talks to me like I'm a casual acquaintance instead of the mother who dried her tears and tucked her into bed. She tells me what she thinks I want to hear, but she doesn't say a lot. The truth is, she hasn't shared her heart with me in a long time."

Sam stared blindly at the glass walls of the complex. "She did with me, or at least it felt that way back then."

Anita's voice softened. "She was different with you, Sam. More like the magpie she was as a toddler. When she was little, she told me *everything*." She laughed softly. "Most of the time, I couldn't get her to shut up, but then her father left us, and...."

"And what?" he probed as she trailed off into silence.

A long pause, then, "And everything changed. I did the best I could when Edward left, but life was tough for a while. Things improved when I was offered the job out at the Double J, but V never quite bounced back to the happy child she'd been.

"She never acted out the way some kids do when their life falls apart, but she started keeping her thoughts to herself. She was, I don't know, less animated. Quiet. Introspective. Well, you know how she is. As stubborn as the day is long and completely confident in her ability to handle everything on her own."

Anita's tone took on an undercurrent of guilt and pain. "When she told me she was following you to Florida, I told her she was making a mistake. I'm sorry, Sam. I know there was love between the two of you, but you were both so young. Too young to handle the disappointment of your injury, obviously."

Sam didn't think it was that simple. "You mentioned her father. She's never spoken to me about him. Were they close?"

Anita's voice lost some of its softness, going flat. "Very. They did everything together. If he was leaving the house, she wanted to be with him. He called her his little kitten."

Sam drummed his fingers on the steering wheel. "Did she ever get in touch with him after he left?"

"Not that I know of, but I don't think so. She never talked about him and never forgave him for leaving. When he died, his lawyer contacted her to tell her Edward had named her the beneficiary of an insurance policy he'd bought years ago. He left her five hundred thousand." Anita sighed. "That was one of the few times she came back to Barlow. She said she didn't want anything to do with his money and signed every penny of it over to me."

They spoke for a few minutes more but, other than learning her father's abandonment had caused a major shift in V's life, his call to Anita was a complete bust. She certainly hadn't told him anything that shed any light on the problem at hand.

Frustration burned in Sam's gut as he climbed from the car and spent the first day of his dream job feeling like shit. He'd hurt V, and that was the last thing he'd wanted to do. Although every instinct screamed at him to go to her and tell her he was sorry, he hesitated. She'd made it clear she didn't want to see him. He'd give her the space she'd asked for, but there was no way in hell he was giving up on her. Not this time.

* * * *

V stood at her office window, her eyes following Sam as he moved up and down the sideline on the field below. The stadium teemed with activity as the facility staff prepared for Sunday's home game, and the players ran through their last practice of the week. It had been less than five days and she missed Sam horribly.

He'd called her a coward, and he was right. He'd also said he loved her. The admission haunted her, but continuing on as they had been wouldn't be fair to him. Despite wanting to with all her heart, she couldn't give him what he asked for, and spending time with him and Lucy when nothing could come of it was as painful as it was a joy for her. She consoled herself with the knowledge that she'd made the right choice when she insisted they call a halt to their hopeless relationship.

He hadn't been happy, but he'd respected her wishes. After standing at his side at the press conference Monday morning, which had gone exactly as Caroline predicted, V had kept her distance. So had he.

According to Caroline, the moving van had arrived late Monday afternoon with Sam and Lucy's things, including Daisy. With as many hours as he'd spent at the complex, familiarizing himself with the Marauders' system and players, V couldn't imagine he'd gotten a lot done at the house. She huffed a wry breath and turned from the window, reminding herself Sam and Lucy's home, their life, wasn't her concern.

The furor over Jaffrey's claims had fizzled after Caroline's presser, leaving V to focus on her job. She'd declined Gracie and Jake's invitation to spend New Year's Eve at the farm, claiming the trip to Barlow had put her behind. Gracie didn't buy the excuse, but she didn't force the issue. V rang in the new year alone in her condo, planning the victory celebrations should the Marauders do what most of the experts expected and claim yet another conference championship and Super Bowl.

With less than forty-eight hours till kick-off, the city pulsed with anticipation for Sunday's home game. V, however, was exhausted. Despite the early hour, she slid open her desk drawer to retrieve her purse. She shrugged into her coat and headed toward the elevator, looking forward to a glass of wine and an over-the-counter sleep aid.

Her cell phone buzzed as she pressed the down button. Pulling the device from the pocket of her purse, she checked the screen. Her heart did a little flip in her chest. Though she hadn't spoken to Sam's daughter since their pizza celebration, she'd heard through Caroline that Lucy had been accepted at the Romanov Academy. She had started classes on Wednesday. It had been hell resisting the urge to call and congratulate her, but a clean break would be easier on all of them.

V couldn't ignore the girl's call, however. Pleasurable anticipation warmed her chest and a helpless smile tugged at her lips as she swiped her thumb over the screen to answer. "Hello, Lucy."

"V?"

Lucy's whispered greeting sent V's pulse skittering. This was New York, after all, and Lucy was new to the city. "What's wrong? Are you okay?"

"I'm okay, but can you come over?"

Relief washed through V, making her leg muscles weak. She slumped against the elevator's frame. "Over where? Where are you?"

"I'm at our house. I just got back from school and checked the mail." A slight pause. When Lucy spoke again, her voice was breathless. "The DNA results are here."

The double doors whooshed open. V jerked straight, but stood rooted to the spot. "Oh, sweetie."

"Please, don't say no. I haven't opened them yet. I can't."

V entered the elevator, but instead of the street-level button, she cued the one that would take her to field. "I'm just leaving the complex. Sam's down on the field with the team—"

"Please, can you come by yourself? I don't want him here when I look. Just in case, you know?"

Empathy squeezed her heart, but going around Sam with Lucy would violate the line V herself had drawn. "I'll come if you want me to, but not without telling Sam first." Silence met her comment. "Lucy?"

"Okay."

The tears in her voice ripped at V. "I'll try and make him understand."

"I know. Thank you."

The doors opened and V stepped into the utilitarian hallway leading to the field. "I'll be there as quickly as I can, okay? Just breathe."

A strangled laugh came through the earpiece. "I'm trying, but hurry. My hands are shaking and I feel like I have an elephant sitting on my chest."

V couldn't help her smile. "Breathe deep then," she instructed and disconnected the call.

She pushed through the doors leading outside. The early January sunlight hit her eyes. Lifting her hand, she shielded them and scanned the arena for Sam. She spotted Tuck, CC's husband and the team's first-string wide receiver, standing in front of a sideline bench where Sam sat. Tuck nodded at whatever Sam said and turned to lope onto the field.

Like wide-shouldered bookends, Wyatt Hunter and Gabe Tillman, the team's huge center, sat on each side of Sam. He dragged a finger across the screen of the tablet he held. Wyatt and Gabe leaned close and bent their heads to study whatever Sam was showing them.

Hurrying across the outer walkway, she smiled a greeting to several of the coaches and a couple players. As she approached the bench, Wyatt rose to his feet and tugged on his helmet. He turned his head and spotted her, and his teeth flashed in a grin. "Hiya, beautiful. If you're looking for me, you just made my day."

Sam lifted his gaze to hers. A moment passed, then two. His blue eyes, lightened by the sunlight, swept over her face like a soft caress, and he dipped his chin in a silent greeting. Her pulse took off like a greyhound after the rabbit.

Gabe snorted, breaking the spell holding her in its grip, and she looked away. Crossing his tree-trunk arms, he shot Wyatt a smirk. "Get bent, Hunter. She's looking for me. Ain't that right, Ms. Price?"

Blood pressure near stroke level, V met the man's toothy grin with a stern look. "Your agent still hasn't contacted me, Gabe. That endorsement deal won't last forever, and you know I don't like to be kept waiting."

Nearly four hundred pounds of roughhewn muscle, and Gabe still had the ability to blush. Pink tinged the ebony skin covering his high cheekbones. He nodded sheepishly. "Yes, ma'am. I'll call him right after practice."

Sam pushed to his feet and slapped the tablet against the thigh of his khaki slacks. He turned a hard stare on Wyatt. "They're waiting on the field for the play, Hunter."

Unfazed by the sternness of Sam's tone, Wyatt winked at her, then turned to trot out to the fifty-yard line. Sam turned to Gabe next. The team's center cleared his throat, grabbed his helmet off the bench, and hurried onto the field.

V stared at Sam's profile as he followed their progress. A muscle twitched along his jaw. She clutched the strap of her purse with trembling fingers. "Sam, Lucy just called me."

He called out a series of numbers V assumed meant something to the players. They shifted slightly on the line of scrimmage as Wyatt set up behind Gabe. Sam spoke without looking her way. "What did she want?"

Both offensive and defensive lines burst into movement, and Wyatt dropped back into the pocket. Down field, Tuck made a slicing cut. Wyatt sent the ball sailing in a perfect spiral. Sam sidestepped, following the movement of the play.

V kept pace with him. "The DNA test results arrived in today's mail."

That got his attention. He stopped short and whipped his head around to meet her gaze. The flash of anxiety in his eyes hit her like a fist to the belly. "Shit." He briefly squeezed his eyelids shut, then lifted his arm and twisted his wrist to check his watch. "I've got another forty minutes before I can head home."

"She asked if I'd come out and be with her when she opened the envelope."

He lifted his gaze to hers. "What did you tell her?"

She sighed and couldn't resist touching him, resting a reassuring hand on his arm. "I told her I'd be there as quickly as I could."

He lowered his gaze to her fingers. His Adam's apple bobbed on a heavy swallow before he blew a harsh breath. "Thanks. How did she sound?"

"Scared." V dropped her hand to her side.

He scrubbed a hand over the back of his neck, then lifted his head. Some of the anxiety had drained from his eyes, but not all of it. "Tell her I'll be there as soon as we break."

V tried to smile, but the exercise felt forced. "I'll wait with her if she needs me to." She didn't add *if the results are negative.* Sam had relieved Lucy's fears that he wouldn't send her away if they were, but learning she really wasn't his daughter would still be a blow. For both of them and, V had to admit, for her, too.

He blew another breath and nodded. "Thanks, Red."

Her heartbeat skipped at his slip, even as the endearment sliced at her, and she turned away without a word.

Chapter 21

Thirty minutes later, V pulled into Sam's driveway. On the front stoop next to Lucy, Daisy clambered to her feet. The dog cocked her head and eyed V's car. Despite the forty-degree temperature, Lucy wore no coat. A large manila envelope rested on her knees. She looked so small, sitting with her shoulders hunched against the chill. And so utterly lost.

Sympathy compressed V's chest and she sighed, shut off the car, and climbed out.

Daisy bounded from the stoop and loped forward to greet her. She bent to pet the lab, then crossed the lawn, dead with winter, and climbed the steps. Lowering to the step beside Lucy, V waited for the girl to say something. When she remained silent, V slipped the envelope from her lap and read the return address from the medical facility that had run the tests for the court.

"So, these are the results, huh?"

Daisy nosed between them, and Lucy wrapped her arm around the dog. She glanced at the envelope and nodded.

"You okay?"

Lucy lifted her head, and her dark gaze met V's. "I can't feel my lips."

"Probably a case of frostbite." V shuddered in an exaggerated shiver, then smiled and brushed a lock of Lucy's dark hair back from her forehead. "It's freezing out here, sweetie. Why don't we head inside?"

Lucy nodded and stood. She didn't reach for the envelope, just turned and opened the front door. Daisy squeezed inside first, and V followed them. She set the results on the old-fashion hall tree bench, peeled out of her coat, and hung it on one of the hooks.

"I could use a hot cup of tea. You don't happen to have any in the house, do you?"

The ghost of a sheepish smile tweaked Lucy's lips. "I put some in the cart when we went shopping the other day. Sam said you weren't coming back, but I believe in thinking positive."

V couldn't help the little pang of her heart. "You do, do you? So do I." She smiled and picked up the envelope. "What do you say we make ourselves a cup of tea, then we'll see what's what."

Lucy sighed heavily, but she nodded.

V followed her into the kitchen. Setting her purse and the envelope on the table, she slipped into one of the chairs and watched as Lucy gathered cups and the makings of their tea on a small tray. Lucy pulled a bear-shaped plastic jar of honey from a cabinet, and V's lips curved in a sad smile. No doubt the bagels she'd listed as part of her morning ritual had made it into the cart as well.

"I heard you went with the Romanov Academy. How do you like it?"

Lucy turned from the stove where she'd set the kettle to boil and braced a hip against the edge of the counter. "It's different than I'm used to, but the teachers are nice. Especially the ballet instructor. He's a guy and he's young. About twenty, I think. It's kind of weird, since every teacher I've had has been a woman, but he's cool."

V cocked her head and held her gaze. "Is he cute?"

"Really cute, and really gay."

V grinned. "And the students?"

Lucy turned as the kettle began to simmer. "I haven't met that many, but a girl in my economics class is pretty friendly. She invited me to eat lunch with her and her friends." She shrugged. "There's this one boy in ballet class. I don't think he's gay and wow, can he dance."

V arched a brow. "Is *he* cute?"

Lucy rolled her eyes, but she smiled. "He has a big nose and an even bigger ego."

V laughed.

Placing the steaming kettle on the trivet, Lucy approached the table. She set the tray in the center and eyed the envelope. Her smile dimmed as she dropped into a chair.

V reached over and covered her hand. "It's only a document. The results don't matter, remember?"

"I know, but," Lucy looked up, "it's just that...."

"You *want* Sam to be your biological father," V finished for her in a soft voice.

Lucy's eyes slid shut and she nodded. V's throat constricted. She'd spent a good portion of her life wishing she didn't have a father, but Lucy was different. She had Sam. No matter what.

After squeezing her hand, V released her to pour the tea. "That's understandable, but there's no pressure here. In every way that counts, Sam is already your dad."

Lucy opened her eyes, but hesitated to reach for the envelope. When the tea had been poured and V passed Lucy her cup, the envelope still lay untouched. V glanced at the clock on the wall, then stirred honey into the hot brew in front of her. "Do you want me to open it? Sam will be here soon."

Lucy wiped her palms on the thighs of her jeans and shook her head. "No, I need to do it." With a bracing breath, she picked up the report and tore open the seal. A sheaf of documents was inside. V sat silently as Lucy scanned the top page, then set it aside. She read quietly for several moments and, suddenly, her chest shuddered and her breath hitched.

Despair washed over V, and she lowered her tea to the table. *Oh, Sam. I'm sorry.*

Lucy lifted her head and the dark gaze that met V's swam with tears. Then slowly, Lucy's mouth twisted into the most beautiful smile V had ever seen. Chills raced over her skin, raising pebbled bumps and the tiny hairs on her arms.

She had to take a breath before she could speak. "Yes?"

Huge tears spilled over Lucy's lashes and her face crumbled as she started to cry in earnest. Joy and wonder, however, were evident in her sobbing response. "He's my father. Sam is my father."

"Oh, sweetie." V slid from her chair as Lucy slumped forward to lay her head on the table. Bending over her, V wrapped her arms around the girl's shoulders. Tears stung her eyes, and she pressed a kiss to Lucy's head.

Sam and Lucy were going to be a true family, after all. The knowledge was a bittersweet lashing to V's heart. Unbearably happy for Sam's daughter, and Sam, too, her soul cried out in pain and desolation and an overwhelming sense of loss.

Their dream of a family was her dream. Their joy at learning there would be no more doubts between them, her joy. And she couldn't claim either.

The clearing of a throat startled her. She tensed and slipped her arms from around Lucy to straighten, but had no time to school her features into a smile or wipe the tears from her face. Standing like a statue beneath the arched doorway, Sam stared at her, his jaw tight as if he was gritting his teeth. Slicing pain flashed in his eyes before he dropped his gaze to Lucy, then he stepped forward and walked to the table.

"Luce?" Squatting beside his daughter, he rubbed his hand down her spine. "It's okay, kid. It's going to be okay."

Almost dreamlike, Lucy rolled upward, lifting her head to look at him. She blinked and turned in her chair to face him until they were eye to eye. Fresh tears erupted in her dark eyes to roll down her cheeks, and she pressed a palm to his cheek.

Her voice was rough and broken with emotion when she finally spoke. "Hello, Dad."

Wonder lit Sam's face, followed by a slow smile that grew so blinding, V wanted to look away. She couldn't, however, and locked her knees to keep from slipping to the floor and curling into a fetal ball. Sam dropped his forehead against Lucy's, and V bit back a sob.

"I told you, kid."

Lucy hiccupped a laugh. "You were only guessing."

He rocked his forehead against hers in denial. "No, I wasn't guessing. I was hoping. Wishing it would turn out you were mine by birth harder than I've ever wished for anything in my life."

"Me, too." Lucy slid from the chair and into his embracing arms.

V couldn't take it. Couldn't witness her deepest dream coming true while she stood just out of reach. Rounding the table, she grabbed her purse and hurried down the hallway. Ignoring Sam's hoarse call, she snatched her coat from the hall tree and raced out the door.

* * * *

"V, wait."

The front door slammed, and Sam jolted like he'd taken a gunshot to the chest. Lucy's hold around his shoulders loosened, and she pulled back to look at him.

"She was crying."

He stared into Lucy's tear-filled eyes. Jesus, she was his daughter. In blood as well as heart. Joy so big it couldn't be contained threatened to rip through the walls of his chest. He smiled and brushed his thumb over her cheekbone, dispersing the track of her tears.

"So are you."

Her lips curled in a small smile. "Look who's talking." She swiped a fingertip beneath his left eye and held it up for him to see. It was wet.

"Happy tears, kid." He scrubbed a hand down her arm and rose to his feet. She stood as well.

"Mine, too." She glanced away, down the empty hallway. "But V's seemed more sad than happy." She looked back at him. "Our plan to help her isn't working very well, is it?"

"No, it isn't." He tugged off his coat, then twisted around to toss it over a chair.

"But she came when I called."

He slowly turned and met her gaze with narrowed eyes. "And you knew she would."

Up came her chin. "I really did want her here when I opened the stuff from the court, but geez, Dad. How can we convince her to be part of the family if we never see her?"

He froze as she glanced down the hallway again. "Back up a second, kid."

She turned.

"Say it again."

He didn't need to elaborate. If her smug smile was any indication, she knew exactly what he meant. "You're the one who kept insisting I stop calling you 'Sam.' Now that it's official, I will." She grinned. "Okay, *Dad*?"

He nodded, the best he could do with a lump the size of a baseball clogging his throat.

She crossed her arms. "So, about V. We're obviously going to need a little help. The Malones are her friends. I think we should start there."

* * * *

"Well, this is a pleasant surprise." Clutching the family dog's collar, Gracie stood in the open front doorway of the Malone's farmhouse, her violet gaze shifting between Lucy and Sam.

Sam forced a smile. "Sorry to show up unexpected like this. I was hoping to speak to Jake for a few minutes."

Lucy had insisted they visit the Malones immediately so he could talk to Jake, but Sam had the sneaking suspicion his daughter had her own agenda. One that involved V's good friend, Gracie, and that worked for him. Tonight should be about celebrating, and the pleasure of knowing Lucy was biologically his still zinged through him, but she was right. A piece was missing from their family puzzle, and they were going to need all the help they could get if they were going to make the picture complete.

He eyed the smudge on Gracie's cheek and the layer of white powder dusting her hair. "Looks like we came at a bad time."

"No, this is a perfect time actually. Tuck and CC are here, too." Gracie grinned and brushed a hand through her hair, then coughed and fanned at the fine mist of flour she'd dislodged to float in the air. "Our girls are baking cookies for a school thing tomorrow and the boys insisted on helping."

She stepped back so they could enter, tugging Murphy with her. The dog whimpered and wiggled with excitement as he lunged for the hand Lucy held out. Gracie let him go and shut the door.

"I'm so glad you're here, Lucy. CC and I need reinforcements." She winked at Lucy and turned to Sam. "Jake and Tuck are in the den watching film. They're dissecting Seattle's defense in preparation for Sunday." Gracie dropped an arm around Lucy's shoulders and dragged her down the hallway, calling back. "Go on in. Lucy and I will be in the kitchen relieving poor CC in the batter wars."

Sam rolled his shoulders against the nerves pulling them tight, and turned toward the closed den door. He wasn't a man who asked for help. Never had been, but he was desperate. Telling V he loved her hadn't worked for shit, and all his efforts to seduce her into opening up to him had achieved was a raging hard-on that wouldn't subside. But agreeing to stay away from her, giving her a little time and space to consider what they could build together, was the worst move he'd made. She'd gone about her business, leaving him miserable.

He missed her, damn it, and they'd wasted too much time already.

Knocking on the den door, he didn't wait for an answer and stepped inside.

"Look what the cat dragged in." On the couch in front of the TV, Jake paused the screen and grinned.

"Hiya, Coach." Sprawled at the other end of the couch, Tuck bumped his chin in greeting, then turned to Jake. "You don't have a cat."

Jake shoved to his feet with a scowl. "The neighbors do. Damn thing shits in Gracie's flower beds while her dumb-ass dog watches." He stuck out his hand to Sam. "You ready for Sunday?"

Sam shook Jake's hand, then dropped his arm to his side. Now that he was here, he didn't have a fucking clue where to begin. Football was much easier than figuring out how to fix things with V, and he grabbed at the diversion. "The team looks good. Really good. Bob put together an unbeatable offensive line, and the defense isn't too shabby, either."

Tuck crossed his ankles on the coffee table and grimaced. "Nothing personal, Sam, but losing Bob's talents will be a huge disadvantage come draft time. The man has a knack for spotting talent where others don't."

Sam nodded. "No offense taken."

Jake tipped his head toward the TV. "We're watching tapes of Seattle. You want a beer?"

Hell, yes. "Please."

Jake cocked his head at Sam's windy reply and headed to the bar. "Something on your mind?" He bent to tug a longneck from the fridge behind the counter.

Sam swallowed. "Someone."

Jake straightened. "Considering your night at the Marriott last week, that could only mean V."

Sam shot a wary glance at Tuck. The last thing Sam had expected, or wanted, was to bear his heart to Jake while one of his players listened in.

Flicking his gaze between Sam and Tuck, Jake rounded the bar and shook his head. "If you and V are expecting privacy in your personal life around here, you're shit out of luck, my friend. She's a charter member of Triple Gs."

Sam's confusion must have shown, because Tuck laughed. "Gracie's Gridiron Girls. You'll get used to it. We all do eventually."

Sam shook his head. "Gracie's Gridiron Girls?"

Jake handed him the bottle of beer. "There's five of them." He ticked off the names on his fingers. "There's Gracie, and Tuck's wife, CC. CC's cousin, Kris. Kris is married to Tuck's cousin, Tim. Then there's Jessi Grayson, another of Tuck's cousins. She's married to Max, who is a friend of…" he dropped his arm to his side and grinned, "well, all of us. Max and Gracie sort of grew up together." He shrugged. "Long story. Anyway, V makes five." He swept his own beer from the coffee table and toasted Sam. "A friendly warning. Trying to keep the Gridiron Girls in the dark when it comes to their members is not only dangerous, it's impossible."

"I'm not following you." Sam slid his gaze between the two grinning men.

Tuck sprawled back on the couch. "What he's trying to say is, we didn't need to read about you and V in that dumbass article Jaffrey wrote. We already knew about the two of you shacking up at the Marriott because the wives knew, and there isn't one in the bunch who can keep a secret."

Sam frowned.

Jake grinned and thumped him on the back. "I'm glad you took my advice and decided to work things out with her."

He met Jake's smug smile. "Yeah, well don't pat yourself on the back yet. V's proving to be a hell of a lot more stubborn than I remember."

Jake chuckled. "What did you expect? As an agent, V's had to deal with some of the most arrogant assholes in the league, but she's also a woman. Stubbornness is in their genes."

Sam grunted. He couldn't disagree. He could barely walk upright when he'd left the hotel, not to mention the sleepless night he suffered after last Sunday's celebration at his new house. And it wasn't as if V was unaffected. Christ, he'd given her three orgasms at the hotel, and she'd been teetering on the edge with him on the couch. Yet, she'd held her ground, calling him the next morning to say, "Adios, pal."

He jammed a hand through his hair in frustration. "Her stubbornness I can handle, but she's avoiding me now."

"The Sam Fitzgerald I remember never failed to seal the deal when it came to a woman." A teasing glint sparked in Jake's eyes. "Sounds like old age might be taking its toll, buddy."

"Fuck you."

Jake grinned and sipped from his beer.

Tuck wore a smile as he cleared his throat. "She didn't seem to be avoiding you on the sideline this afternoon." Sam sent him a scowl, and Tuck brought his beer bottle to his lips. "Just pointing out the obvious. Maybe you're reading her wrong."

This afternoon on the sideline had been about Lucy. No matter what happened between the two of them, V's soft heart was firmly in Lucy's corner. But the DNA test was no one's business but his and Lucy's, and wasn't a subject he intended to discuss.

Sam shook his head. "That was about…business."

Jake leaned against the back of the couch. "It's been a lot of years. Are you sure she still has feelings for you?"

Sam pinned him with a hard look.

He held up his hands. "Just asking."

"She still has feelings, and aren't you the one who insisted I cut her some slack because there was still something between us?"

"Touché." Jake winced and cocked his head. "Have you asked her yet?"

"I asked her flat out, but no dice. She isn't talking, and that's the problem in a nutshell." Sam rolled his shoulders against the frustration tying him in knots.

"Asked her about what?"

Sam jerked his gaze to Tuck. The question, and the curiosity on his face, proved V and her friends didn't share everything. That knowledge brought him some measure of relief. What had happened between him and V had been the topic of conversation for too many people already.

Jake chuckled. "You might as well tell him. The Triple Gs are on the case. CC will cave, and he'll get the whole story eventually."

Sam blinked and cursed beneath his breath. "Then he'll be one up on me. I don't know the whole story myself."

"Shall I give him the condensed version, then?"

Blowing a defeated breath, Sam shook his head. "Shit. I thought I'd escaped the gossip mill. Gracie and her girls sound as bad as the Barlow grapevine."

Jake's smile went wide, and he rounded the couch to drop to the cushions. "You have no idea, my friend."

Shoulders slumping, Sam sighed. "What the hell? Go ahead." He sat down as Jake turned to Tuck.

"Jaffrey's exposé was a load of bullshit, but he did have one fact right. Sam and V were engaged fifteen years ago, then she took off one day without a word."

Tuck looked at Sam. "Why?"

He propped his elbows on his spread knees. "That's what I'm determined to find out." Turning to Jake, Sam found him watching with the same intensity that had been in his eyes two weeks ago when he'd pushed Sam on his feelings for V. "Which is why I'm here. You were right. There is still something between us, and not just for me. For her, too." He sat up straight. "She asked if we could start again, and I agreed."

Satisfaction lit Jake's eyes. "Shit, yeah. I love being right. So, what's the problem?"

"The same problem I've had for fifteen years. Despite everything, I'm still in love with her, and if it was just the two of us, that would be enough. But that's not the case. Not anymore. I have Lucy to consider."

"Kids complicate things," Tuck said quietly.

Jake nodded his agreement. "How does Lucy feel about the two of you being together?"

An image of the two of them embracing in his kitchen flashed in Sam's mind and his stomach muscles clenched. He'd raced home from the complex with his heart in his throat, then walked in on everything he wanted. His miracle, however, had been short-lived.

He dragged a hand down his face. "She's all in." She'd even used the test results to get V and Sam under the same roof again. A helpless smile formed at his daughter's matchmaking ingenuity. "If it were up to her, V would already be moved in with us."

"But?"

Sam met Jake's question with a sigh. "But Lucy's already dealt with more loss than any kid should. I have to know V's not going to split on a second's notice. Until she comes clean about whatever happened back in Florida, I can't trust her not to do it again."

Jake's mouth twisted into a contemplative line. "It's been a long time, Sam. She may never come clean."

Denial was a knife slicing him in a thousand different cuts. "I can't accept that. She loves me, too. It's there, in her eyes, but something is holding her back. I need the time and the opportunity to convince her to trust me enough to tell me what it is."

The door opened suddenly, and Lucy, Gracie, and CC filed in. Lucy smiled at Sam and sat on the arm of his chair. CC slid onto the couch beside Tuck.

Gracie stopped in front of Jake, and he groaned. "Oh, hell. I know that look."

She grinned and climbed onto his lap. With her arm around her husband's shoulders, she pinned Sam with a sly smile. "Lucy says you're here because you're having a little trouble convincing V to see you."

Sam coughed and slowly turned his head to stare at Lucy. She shrugged, but her smile was serene.

Gracie glanced between Jake and Tuck. "What about the two of you confirmed ex-bachelors? You chased and caught CC and me. Have you figured out how to help Sam get the girl?" Jake rolled his eyes and shook his head. Tuck grinned, then shrugged. Gracie turned to Sam. "Don't worry, Sam. We girls have a plan."

Chapter 22

Sam sipped from his beer and shot yet another impatient glance toward the front door. The girls' plan to put Sam and V in the same room felt a little like an ambush to him, but he'd been overruled. The Triple Gs had spoken.

Apparently, both Gracie and Jessi were expecting and, according to Gracie, V wouldn't be able to ignore their small gathering to celebrate. The farmhouse was out, of course, since V would suspect Jake would invite his good friend, Sam, to any party held there. Tuck and CC had volunteered their Long Island home instead. They hadn't blinked an eye when Sam informed them his cousin, TJ, and Aunt Kay would be in town by party time to attend the Marauders' matchup with Seattle the next afternoon.

The small guest list had been altered by two and, twenty-four hours later, it was game on.

Jessi and Max Grayson had yet to arrive. They'd been tasked with making sure V arrived for tonight's impromptu party. Gracie had something up her sleeve she swore would give Sam the chance to speak to V in private, but the rest would be up to him. A few minutes alone with her was all he needed to put in play the decision he'd made earlier, but that couldn't happen if she didn't show.

Where the hell was she?

"Oh my God. Kevin Freakin' Tucker just poured me a glass of wine."

At the reverently whispered statement, Sam dragged his gaze from the empty foyer to look down at his cousin. He followed TJ's wide-eyed stare to the kitchen where everyone else was gathered.

At the large center island, Tuck held a finger to his lips. He squeezed his arm between his cousin, Tim, and his wife, Kris, to whom Sam had been introduced earlier. CC wasn't fooled. She swatted Tuck's hand as he attempted to snatch a fat shrimp from the tray she was arranging. Jake took advantage of her preoccupation and pilfered two of the shellfish. He handed one to Gracie, and they both grinned at Tuck's scowl.

Sam chuckled and turned back to TJ. "Kevin Freakin' Tucker?" He eyed the glass in her hand. "You gonna drink it or have it bronzed?"

"Shut up." She tried to smirk, but couldn't hold it. Hero worship sparkled in her eyes. "Holy shit, Sam. Tuck! I can't believe you know him, and *I'm* standing in his house."

"He shares the place with the little blonde over there. Her name is CC. She's his wife."

"I know. I just met her. She's nice." A mewling sigh escaped as TJ brought her wineglass to her lips, then she nodded toward Kay and Lucy, who were laughing with Gracie, CC, Kris, and Tim. "Look at Lucy's face. She's so happy."

Sam turned his head and had to agree. She'd smiled more in the last twenty-four hours than she had in four months, and the change dissolved the ball of tension he'd carried since he'd brought her home with him. The lost little girl was gone. Without the haunted look he'd witnessed in her eyes so often, she glowed like a happy fourteen-year-old with a bright future in front of her.

"Have you told your parents yet?"

Sam grunted and turned back to his cousin. "Not yet."

TJ blinked. "Don't you think they'd want to hear Lucy is their natural granddaughter sooner rather than later?"

"I wanted to tell them in person."

"When do they arrive?"

"The last flight tonight. Mom didn't want to miss her weekly luncheon with her girlfriends. She said she had some bragging to do." TJ grinned, and Sam cleared his throat. "Listen, there's something else I have to tell you before the last of the guests get here."

"Who else...V." She muttered the name in defeat.

"Right the first time."

TJ scowled, and he lowered his voice so only she could hear. "These people are her friends, TJ, and tonight is about more than expected babies. I'm trying to convince V we should get back together, for real, and her friends are all here to help me do that."

Her shoulders slumped, but she took his cue and spoke softly. "For God's sake, Sam, wasn't once enough?"

"Apparently not." His chest heaved on a sigh. "I love her, TJ." She groaned and shook her head, and he rubbed a hand over her arm. "That's not what you want to hear, I know, but it's the way things are."

"You said you're *trying* to convince her. I take it that means she's resisting?"

He squinted at the hope in her tone. "A temporary setback. It's... complicated. She doesn't quite trust me. Yet."

"*She* doesn't trust *you*?"

He held her gaze. "I love you, TJ, and understand the way you feel, but this is my life. I'd really like your support."

Color bloomed on her cheeks and, though her eyes held concern, she nodded. "You know I never could say no to you." That brought a wry smile to his lips, and she rolled her eyes. "Not about the important stuff, anyway."

He leaned forward and pressed a kiss to her forehead, then straightened. "Lucy loves her, too."

TJ grimaced, but then sighed. "Of course, she does. V's always been an easy person to like." Surprise shot his brows to his hairline, and she snorted. "She was my friend, too, you know."

He squeezed her elbow. "I know. I'm still working on getting her to tell me what happened but, whatever it was, I get the impression she felt she didn't have any other choice than to leave."

"I hate to admit it, but I sort of got that impression myself." He pinned her with a questioning look, and her mouth twisted into an unhappy line. "On Christmas Eve, when you brought her to Mom's party, V and I had a conversation in the garden."

He dipped his head. "I saw that. You had me worried for a few minutes, yet there wasn't a drop of blood on either of you when you came back into the house."

"Ha! You're a funny guy." She rolled her shoulders. "She told me the reason Caroline Wainwright asked you to fix things with V wasn't because *your* job was at stake. Apparently, Caroline didn't want to have to fire V if things got testy between the two of you."

Sam looked to the front door. Still nothing. "V said that?"

"Yeah." TJ swirled the wine in her glass. "Not exactly the kind of thing a heartless bitch would admit, is it?"

"No, it isn't." He tucked an arm around her shoulders.

TJ sighed. "I'm willing to give her the benefit of the doubt, but if she hurts you again, she dies." She shot a quick glance toward the group in the kitchen. "I don't care how famous or freakin' cute her friends are."

He chuckled and squeezed her close to his side.

"Which reminds me." She tilted her head to look him in the eye. "Patricia's back, and I think she might have been that creepy Jaffrey guy's source."

Caught off balance by the quick change of topic, he shook his head. "What makes you think that?" *Damn.* The possibility wasn't all that far-fetched. If he'd been thinking clearly, he might have suspected Patricia himself. Catty paybacks were her style.

"She blew into town like a fire-breathing dragon in heels the day before the article was posted. I bumped into her at the café the next morning." She twisted her lips in distaste. "You should have seen her satisfied sneer when she asked me if I'd read it. I swear, a puff of green smoke shot from her nostrils."

Sam laughed, but the humor died in his throat as the front door opened and V stepped inside.

TJ twisted her head, briefly glancing over her shoulder. "Well, there's the guest of honor. Looks like it's show time. I assume you and her friends have some sort of plan. What do you want me to do?"

He kept his gaze on V and handed TJ his beer bottle. "Just follow the crowd."

* * * *

Wedged between Jessi and her husband, Max, V stumbled to a stop in Tuck and CC's grand foyer. The blood rushed to her head as she stared across the room. In the corner, Sam stood with…. V blinked. Oh, yay. TJ was here, too.

Sam turned his head. The smile slid from his face as his intent blue gaze locked onto V.

Biting back a whimper, she looked away and spoke out of the side of her mouth. "A double baby announcement party, huh? First thing tomorrow, I'm going online and requesting new friends." Max's deep laugh scraped along nerves gone taut as Jessi squeezed V's arm linked with hers. "Admit it. You wouldn't have come if you'd known he'd be here."

"Damned straight, I wouldn't."

"Which is why we didn't tell you." Jessi smiled serenely. "Damn, I need to pee. Oh, look, he's coming over." Moving faster than V had known she could, Jessi released her to grab hold of Max's arm and hurry him toward the kitchen.

Abandoned and seeing no chance for a graceful escape, V did her best to ignore her racing heart as Sam moved in her direction. She should have known something was up when Jessi insisted she carpool with her and Max instead of driving herself. The reigning princess of country music had conned the world with her sunshine-and-innocence act. She was as devious as Gracie, CC, and Kris.

Sam stopped in front of her. He studied her face for a long moment. "Are you okay?"

She tensed as a shiver ran up her spine. The man didn't play fair, knowing exactly what happened to her when he used that crooning tone. "Why wouldn't I be?"

He reached out a hand, then aborted the motion and dropped his arm. "You were upset when you left the house yesterday. Lucy was worried about you. So was I."

The son-of-a-bitch definitely didn't play fair. She lifted her chin. "It was a big moment. For both of you. I didn't want to intrude."

Disappointment darkened his eyes. "It *was* a big moment, and you belonged right there with us. You know that as well as I do."

"Sam, please." She sighed and glanced around. Suddenly, things had gotten awfully quiet. Leaning to the side, she looked past him toward the kitchen—and blinked. "Um, Sam? Where'd everyone go?"

He looked over his shoulder, then back. His smile was more of a wince. "I'm not exactly sure, but they might be out by the pool."

Her jaw dropped open. She snapped it shut. "It's forty degrees outside."

"Tuck told me he'd set up a bunch of propane heaters."

"Oh my God." She slapped a hand to her forehead.

"Don't be mad at them. They're just trying to help."

She dropped her arm to her side and stared. "Gracie and Jessi are pregnant, for heaven's sake. Did anyone even think to put on a coat before they abandoned ship?" She bent to the side and yelled. "You're all insane." Straightening, she spun toward the door. "I'm calling a car."

Sliding his arm around her waist, Sam stopped her before she'd taken a single step. He moved forward until her back was flush against his chest. "Wait." He lowered his head until his cheek met hers. "I'm sorry for what I said to you on the phone the other day."

"Why?" She stared at the closed door in front of her. "Everything you said was true."

"No, what I said was cruel, and that's the last thing I ever want to be with you." He moved his head, just enough to brush the skin of her cheek with his. "Will you take a drive with me?"

"Sam, what would that change?"

"Maybe nothing." He straightened and turned her to face him. "No pressure, V. I've heard everything you've said, but there are some things

I'd like to say." He glanced over his shoulder, snorted, and turned back. "Without an audience."

Intrigued, she peeked around him, and nearly burst out laughing at the more-than-a-half dozen faces pressed against the kitchen window. Lucy held the center spot, an expectant smile on her face. V straightened and shook her head. "I told you. They're insane. You should probably keep your daughter far away from all of them."

He smiled and held out his hand. She couldn't resist. She placed her fingers in his.

Chapter 23

Fifteen minutes later, Sam pulled his truck into the driveway of his new home. V stared at his profile as he switched off the ignition. He didn't move to open the door. His jaw tight, he flexed his fingers around the steering wheel before turning his head to look at her.

"We can stay right here or go inside. It's up to you."

A muscle jumped in his cheek, surprising her. His obvious case of nerves should have ratcheted hers into the red zone but, for some reason, knowing he was unsettled calmed her.

"I could use a cup of tea."

His chest expanded on a deep breath, and he nodded. Opening his door, he climbed out and turned, then held out his hand. A sense of déjà vu washed over her. How often had he offered her his hand in exactly the same way during that short, sweet summer they'd shared?

A laugh murmured deep in her throat. "I feel like I'm back in high school."

She placed her hand in his and slid over the bench seat to exit through the open driver's door. He held onto her fingers as he eyed the knot of curls she'd wrapped in a scrunchie at the top of her head. Then his gaze moved down, over the casual sweater beneath her open coat to the jeans covering her legs.

He smiled. "Makes sense. You *look* like you're still in high school."

She smirked. "Liar." Lifting her free hand to her head, she fingered the easy hair style. "I thought it was just dinner with friends, but thanks."

His wince made her laugh, and it felt good. She knew where to lay the blame for tonight's agenda. Until lately, she hadn't been a victim of one of Gracie's stealthy matchmaking schemes, but V had witnessed her friend in action several times with CC and Jessi. Gracie was nothing if not thorough. When the Marriott debacle hadn't produced the desired results, V should have seen tonight coming.

"Relax, Sam. Gracie is a formidable force. I know how difficult it can be to derail her once she's taken up a cause."

The tense line of his shoulders eased, and he shook his head. "She doesn't take 'no' for an answer."

"Not very well, anyway."

She instantly missed the warmth of his fingers as he released her and held out a hand to indicate the walkway to the front door. He followed her, reaching around her to let them inside. Light filled the foyer with his flip of the switch, and he shrugged out of his coat. She handed him hers, then trailed him to the kitchen.

As he gathered the makings for tea and flipped on the burner beneath the kettle, her nerves made a vicious comeback. She didn't sit. Couldn't. His continued silence rang in her ears, and she wandered over to stare out the French doors.

Winter moonlight illuminated the deck enough for her to make out the row of dormant planters rimming the inviting space. She pictured them in the summer sun, full of colorful flowers, green herbs, and possibly a tomato plant or two. The low square table edged by four long benches hadn't been there when they'd first looked at the house. A black dome took up its center.

Sam spoke behind her, and she jumped. "Lucy picked out the table. It's got a built-in fire pit." His voice held a wry laugh. "She said, in case I get homesick and needed a little Texas outdoors in the city."

V smiled and glanced over her shoulder.

The humor slid from his face as he met and held her gaze. He spoke in a hoarse facsimile of his usual drawl. "I love you, Red."

The breath backed up in her throat, and she slowly turned to face him.

"When you left, I didn't know what to do." He dropped his hips to lean against the thick, stainless steel handle of the industrial stove. Eyes full of remembered pain, he shook his head. "I was hurt. Confused." He scrubbed a hand across his flat stomach, then dropped it to his side as if he wasn't sure what to do with it.

"I should have come looking for you." The kettle began to whistle behind him. He shoved straight and turned around. Snapping off the burner, he braced his hands on the stove handle and dropped his chin to his chest. "But I was so pissed, I couldn't see straight. A week later, I went home to Barlow to recuperate."

An iron band of self-incrimination tightened around her chest. She couldn't have said a word if she'd wanted to. He'd asked her why she'd left, but she'd never bothered to inquire after what he'd done once she was gone. She figured she didn't have the right but, the truth was, she didn't want to know. Didn't want to hear a description of the wreckage she'd left behind.

He lifted the kettle from the burner. The muscles of his back shifted as he poured steaming water into the teacups he'd set on the counter. "Most of that time is a blur. You were gone. So was football. I still had my scholarship, and getting my degree suddenly took on a deeper meaning, so I went back. They'd scheduled a second surgery on my knee at the hospital in Florida. Maggie was there, working as a volunteer."

V's stomach muscles clamped tight, but not because of Maggie. She was Lucy's mother and V could never feel anything but grateful Maggie had come into Sam's life. The dejection in his voice was another story. "Sam, stop. You don't need to tell me this."

"Yeah, I do." He turned his head to look at her. "Tea's ready."

He snagged both cups in his right hand and, plucking the honey from the shelf above the counter, crossed to the table. She was slow to follow. Sliding into the chair across from his, she wrapped her cold fingers around the cup he handed her.

His eyes were clear, if a little sad. "Maggie was the complete opposite of you. A wild child from the other side of the tracks, she had a chip on her shoulder a yard wide. At the time, so did I, and I didn't say no when she invited me into her bed." He picked up his cup. "I wasn't surprised when I showed up at her apartment a few weeks later and she was packing her bags. All there'd ever been between us was attitude and sex. LA was calling, and she'd found a ride with a musician playing back-up guitar in a bar downtown."

Sam sipped his tea, then set down the cup. Crossing his arms on the table, he looked at V. Really looked at her for the first time in minutes. "I don't regret Maggie. She gave me Lucy and I can never repay her for that. Neither do I regret the women I've been with over the last fifteen years, and there have been a few. I can't regret them because each of them, in their own way, led me back to you."

The love in his eyes tempted her beyond reason, and she dropped her gaze to stare into her teacup. "I gave up the right to question anything you did when I walked away."

"Yeah. You did."

Heart in her throat, she met his waiting gaze.

"But that didn't change the way I felt about you. The way I still do." He shook his head. "I love you. There's nothing I can do about that. The only question is, do you love me?"

Her breath hitched, but denying the truth was impossible as she stared into his eyes. "You know I do."

His shoulders lifted with his deep, indrawn breath, as if he hadn't been sure of her answer, and he dipped his chin in an abbreviated nod. "Then make a life with me. With Lucy. A whole and happy life full of love and the family each of us wants."

God. Didn't he know how much she wanted to? But pronouncing their feelings aloud didn't change the facts and never would. "If only it were that easy."

"It can be, if we choose to make it so." His shoulders heaved in a harsh sigh. "I want your trust. I need it, for Lucy's sake *and* mine, but I can't go on the way we have been the last week, knowing you're within reach and keeping my distance."

He stood suddenly and, slipping his hands over the ribs beneath her arms, he lifted her to her feet. Wrapping his arms around her, he held her gently and buried his face in the crook of her neck. He spoke between sweet kisses.

"I need you. What's more, I love you and you love me." He worked his mouth up her throat to her jaw line. "We've wasted years because neither of us was willing to bend." He shifted his head until his heated blue gaze burned into hers. With his mouth hovering an inch above hers, his warm breath bathed her lips. "I'm bending now, like I should have all those years ago. I'll wait for your trust. Earn it. But I don't want to spend another day without you in my life."

Although she expected his kiss, it didn't come. He waited, making it clear the next move was hers.

She stared into his earnest face and battled the doubts that came at her like flying stones. Could he truly overlook what she'd done to him? Be content to move forward without knowing what had gone wrong in the past? Could they succeed at building the life she saw shining in his long-lashed eyes? Or would her father's insidious legacy fester like a cancer, eating away at their love and killing them both in the process?

Her greedy heart screamed at her to take the chance. He stood before her, offering everything she'd ever wanted. How could she step back and deny her heart's desire? Deny the love in his eyes? And if she did, how could she go on with her life, standing in the shadows and dreading the day she'd be forced to watch him give his love to another?

Lifting her mouth to his, she sealed their fates and prayed they would survive with their hearts intact.

His arms crushed her to him the moment her lips brushed his. A deep groan vibrated through his chest to her breasts, and her feet left the floor. Lifting her, he spun and wasted no time traversing the hallway to the foot of the staircase.

He released her mouth, and the scalding desire in his eyes sent fire coursing through her veins. "Hold onto me, Red. Don't let go." His arms contracted as he began the climb to his bedroom on the second floor.

The irony of his comment drew a wry laugh from her. She'd remained alone for fifteen years because no other man had ever been capable of excising the memory of Sam from her mind and heart. "It seems I never could."

His lips kicked up in a smile. "Neither could I." He slid his right hand down her spine to cup her butt cheek and squeezed. "The feel of you under my hands has haunted me for years."

"It's the same for me. I need to touch you." She slipped one hand under his sweater and spread her fingers over the smooth muscle of his back.

He stopped at the landing and covered her mouth with his in a hard-and-fast kiss. Moving again, he passed through the open doorway to his bedroom. In three long strides, he'd crossed to the edge of the big bed near the window. He lowered her to the mattress, then straightened. "Hold that thought."

A tug and a twist, and his sweater landed on the floor at his feet. Sprawled on her back, she stared at the muscled expanse of his broad chest and swallowed.

He toed off one loafer, then the next. "I can't go slow, Red. Not this first time."

V didn't want him to. When his fingers went to the snap of his jeans, she jackknifed to her knees. She reached out to cover his hand with hers. "Let me. Please. It's my turn."

He dropped his hand, and a slow smile curled his lips. His Texas drawl made an appearance. "My pleasure, ma'am. I'm all yours."

Overwhelmed at the concept, she slid her feet over the edge of the bed. She blinked and leaned forward to press her forehead to his stomach while wrapping her arms around his waist. "Thank God."

"Hey." He tucked his knuckles beneath her chin and lifted her face. "What's this?"

Her arms dropped away, and she shook her head. Staring into his concerned eyes, she battled the sudden tears that wanted to come. "I've made so many mistakes."

A low croon sounded in his throat. Dipping his knees, he squatted until they were at eye level. He took her hands in his. "We both have, but we've been given a second chance. The past can only hurt us if we let it."

That was a truth she knew only too well. If they were to build the life he described, there would be no room for fears and past mistakes. Nodding, she shoved her remaining doubts to the back of her mind and grabbed with both hands at the happiness she never thought she would find again.

* * * *

Relief rushed through Sam. He'd taken a chance, laying it all on the line the way he had. The odds had been fifty-fifty she would turn him down flat, but he hadn't gotten anywhere playing it safe. Committing himself and Lucy when he still didn't know what had sent V running was a gamble as well, but Jake was right. Her life was here. She wasn't going anywhere. He had plenty of time to convince her to trust him, with the added bonus of holding her in his arms every night.

He made a mental note to send Gracie and the Triple Gs a big box of chocolates. Tomorrow.

"There's my girl." He grinned and stood.

The moment he did, V's nimble fingers went to work on the button of his jeans. She tackled the zipper next. He held still as she curled her fingers in the belt loops at his waist and tugged the worn denim down his hips. His jeans hit the floor with a whoosh. He kicked free of them and she blinked, staring at the bulge of his erection tenting the soft material of his boxers.

She lifted her gaze to his. The sultry hunger in her eyes as she traced a fingertip down the engorged length of his cock, then up again, nearly brought him to his knees. She slipped her fingers inside the waistband of his underwear and shimmied the material down until she'd exposed the tip. Sighing softly, she slid from the bed onto her knees, and his rapidly increasing pulse pounded a tango beat in his head.

Rocking forward, she licked the tip of her tongue over the head of his straining erection, paying special homage to the slit. He swallowed heavily against the sudden dryness of his mouth and throat. To keep from dragging her to her feet and burying himself inside her, he tangled his fingers in her soft hair. It didn't help.

Sam sucked a harsh breath in an attempt to slow the inevitable. His self-inflicted foreplay sessions had seemed like a good idea at the time, but they'd left him so fucking primed he was about to blow.

"Red." Her name was a hoarse plea on his lips. "I wasn't kidding when I said this first time would be fast."

"Mmm hmm." Cupping his sac in her palm, she kneaded him. He couldn't prevent his guttural moan, and she looked up, smiling knowingly. "I see you still growl when I touch you here."

His cock jumped even as a pained laugh worked its way up his parched throat. Payback was a bitch. She was killing him, but fuck. What a way to go.

She repeated the caress, dragging another groan from him. The rumbling in his chest had yet to cease when she closed her lips around him. Wet heat sucked at him as she took him deep then drew back, gently raking her teeth over him in the process.

The base of his spine tingled and his balls contracted. He clenched his teeth, and his hiss was loud in the quiet room. Gently tugging on the stands of her hair, he eased her mouth clear of him before it was too late. She lifted her desire-glazed gaze to his, and it was all he could do to speak.

"Inside you. Now."

He bent over her and tucked his hands beneath her arms. Tugging her to her feet with more speed than finesse, he gripped the hem of her sweater. She lifted her arms as he peeled it over her head. If he was in a hurry, so was she. She unzipped her jeans, shoved them over her hips, and kicked the denim aside, along with her heels.

He wanted to take his time. To savor the mouthwatering mounds of her breasts beneath her red lace bra. He needed the feel of her soft skin beneath his fingers as he explored the sweet curve of her hip. Yearned to peel back the triangle of lace concealing the dark curls at her mound and feast on the sweetness of her. All of that would have to wait, however. He had the rest of his life to immerse himself in rediscovering the beauty of her body, but if he didn't slide inside her in the next minute, he'd embarrass them both.

He wrapped her in his arms and lifted a knee onto the edge of the mattress. Without releasing her, he lowered her to her back. He came to rest cradled between her thighs, eliciting a half-crazed moan. He wasn't sure if the sound had come from him or her, but it didn't matter.

Her eyes gleamed in the low light. Shifting her hips, she tucked her hands between them. He lifted slightly so she could tear her panties down her legs. She kicked one leg free of the lacy strip of cloth and wrapped her calf around his upper thighs.

The delicious friction of his cock jammed against the heat of her was nearly his undoing. "Fuck. You're killing me, baby." He closed his mouth over hers, and her tongue tangled with his in a frantic mating. Blindly tossing out his arm, his knuckles rapped against the drawer handle of the bedside table.

V twisted her head away, breaking the kiss. Her chest heaved on erratic breaths. "What?"

"Condom." His fingers closed around the knob, and he wrenched open the drawer.

"Oh. Good." She tangled her fingers in his hair and tugged his mouth back to hers.

Condom in hand, he shifted his hips, shoving his boxers down as far as he could one-handed.

She whimpered in frustration when he lifted his head. "Hurry."

"I am." He tore at the packet with his teeth. Her fingers joined his as he balanced on one elbow to cover himself. Breathing so hard he was nearly panting, he resettled between her thighs.

"Now, Sam," she pleaded.

The appeal wasn't necessary. With a single thrust, he slid home.

Chapter 24

V opened her eyes to the early morning rays of the sun shining through the curtains of Sam's bedroom windows. With his heavy arm draped over her waist, his solid body spooned at her back. He snored softly, his warm breath puffing against the skin of her neck. She smiled and held still, not wanting to wake him.

Today he'd take the field in his first official game as a Marauders' coach, and neither of them had gotten much sleep. They'd dozed some throughout the long night, between bouts of lovemaking. Three of them, if her sex-fogged brain could be trusted in its calculation. At some point, they'd staggered into the kitchen. He'd pushed her into one of the chairs, claiming they needed to refuel, and had devoured three grilled cheese sandwiches to her one.

An image of Sam's wicked smile as he swept their empty paper plates from the table formed in her mind. She mentally adjusted the count to four, and the heat of a blush rose up her chest and neck. God. How was she going to look Lucy in the eye the first time they sat down together at that table for a meal?

V had lost track of the orgasms he'd given her. As if making up for lost time, he'd kept after her until she'd cried exhaustion sometime near dawn. Awash in sensual completion, they'd drifted to sleep with nothing between them but matching, contented smiles.

Twisting her head, she checked the alarm clock on the night stand. Seven-oh-three. They hadn't gotten around to discussing what came next, but there would be time for that later. There were two important games taking place in the league today, and the Marauders were slated for the later one. Sam wouldn't need to be at the complex until noon. She, however, wasn't so lucky.

Caroline expected her administrative staff to be on the job by nine on game days. Her friend and boss might have given a green light to V and

Sam, but arriving at the complex rumpled from a night of debauchery was bound to raise a few eyebrows.

She slid from Sam's arms as gently as she could, and had to bite down on a pained groan. After the excesses of the night, muscles she didn't know she had tightened in complaint as she tiptoed around the room gathering items of clothing. The rustle of cloth drew her attention, and she straightened with her sweater and jeans tucked to her chest and a high heel dangling from her fingers.

"Where are you going?" Sam's bristle-shadowed jaw cracked on a wide yawn.

V stared at him, sexily mussed and sleepy-eyed, and nearly tossed everything over her shoulder to climb back into bed. As if he'd read her mind, his lips curved in a dark smile and he patted the mattress at his hip.

"Come back to bed. It's early yet, and Gracie won't be dropping Lucy off until nine."

Years of professional habit strangled the urge before V could give in to his tempting invitation. She bent to pluck her other shoe from under the bed.

"I've got to be at the complex by then, and I need to run home first for a change of clothes and to shower." His gaze shifted to the open door of the adjoining bathroom, and she laughed. "Not a chance, Fitzpatrick. I can barely walk as it is."

His gaze whipped back and narrowed. "Did I hurt you?"

She stepped close and, balancing her weight on the mattress beside his shoulder, she pressed a kiss to his mouth. "Don't even think it." She tugged the strip of red lace from under his pillow and straightened. "I'm just a little out of practice."

The concern vanished and he sat up, swinging his legs over the side of the bed. "That's not the impression I got last night, but I'm willing to," he shifted his hip and tugged her missing bra from under his thigh, "put in a little overtime to help you out with that."

She snickered and dumped her clothes on the foot of the bed, then stepped into her panties. "I'll take you up on the offer." She held out her hand. He handed her the lace demicup. "*After* you win tonight's game."

He raised his eyebrows and blew a sharp breath.

She grinned and bent her arms at the elbow to snap the back clasp of her bra. "Did you forget today was game day?"

He propped his hands on the edge of the mattress and slid his gaze over her body in a slow survey. "There's a smoking hot, naked woman wiggling into red lace underwear in front of me. I'm lucky I can remember my name."

A laugh burst from her throat, and she tugged up her jeans, zipped and snapped them. She pulled her sweater over her head. "It's Sam Fitzpatrick, and he's due at the complex at noon."

"Oh, shit."

V's head popped out the neck hole and met his gaze. "What?"

"I'm supposed to meet TJ, Aunt Kay, and my parents at their hotel for breakfast."

Her fingers clenched on her sweater. "Your parents are here, too?" Of course, they would be. They wouldn't miss his pro debut. Nerves threatened, and she mentally stomped down on them. If she and Sam could move forward and leave the past behind, everyone else would just have to do the same.

"They flew in late last night."

"Then you'd better get moving." Smoothing the heavy cotton blend over her waist, she stepped forward and bent to kiss him goodbye.

Her plan for a speedy departure was derailed the moment her lips met his and he wrapped his arms around her waist. Twenty minutes later, he finally let her go.

* * * *

Gracie showed up to gloat two hours before kickoff.

"Am I good or what?" Grinning, she slid onto the couch opposite V's desk.

"What you are is interfering and pushy." V sat back and took a second to enjoy the grimace wrinkling her friend's brow, but she couldn't pull off her affected scowl for more than a moment. Not with her heart so full of happiness she was afraid it would burst. "I'm telling you right now, don't you ever, *ever*," she softened her voice, "change."

Gracie squinted. "You are such a *bitch*." She plopped her purse to the cushion beside her. "I really thought you were mad."

V snickered. "I should be. Your massive manipulation could have backfired."

Gracie brought up her chin, and her eyes sparkled smugly. "But it didn't. Did it?"

"No." V grinned. "In fact, it worked like a charm."

"Details." Gracie crossed her legs. "The girls are going to want a full accounting."

"The girls are going to be disappointed."

V batted her lashes, and Gracie smirked. "Oh, you're no fun."

Laughing, V sat forward. "We haven't worked out everything, but we've agreed to give us another shot, with no stipulations this time."

"No relationship is perfect, sweetie, not even the successful ones, and many of them get started with a much weaker foundation than you and Sam have."

"That's just it. Our foundation is what worries me." V tapped her pencil against the legal pad she'd been working on and frowned. "We're starting fresh, but our past isn't gone. It's sort of just…shoved into the closet."

"Hiya, beautiful. Something wrong?"

V jerked her head around toward the door. Wyatt Hunter slumped against the jamb.

"No." She drew out the word while shooting a quick glance at Gracie. Mentally scrolling through their conversation, V couldn't recall either of them saying anything particularly juicy or damaging to Sam.

Wyatt shoved off the frame, walked into the office, and propped a hip on V's desk. "You sure?"

"Of course I'm sure. Why would you ask that?"

"I don't know." He studied her face and his voice held a note of curiosity, as if he were trying to work something out. "But something's different about you today." He winked at Gracie, then turned back and met V's gaze. "Now that I think about it, Fitzpatrick's snarls held a little less heat than usual this morning." A smile twitched at the corner of his perfect lips. "Hell, he even smiled at the end of the pre-game meeting when Tuck congratulated him on finally sealing the deal with you last night."

Gracie snickered into her hand, turning it into a cough.

V's jaw dropped, and she snapped it shut to grind her teeth. She pinned Wyatt with a lethal glare. "Tuck's a dead man, and you're an ass." Wyatt grinned, and she growled low in her throat. "What are you doing up here, anyway? Shouldn't you be downstairs getting ready or something?"

He arched a brow as if he was surprised by her question. "It's game day."

She rolled her eyes. "No."

He squinted and crossed his arms. "That's not how it works, sweetheart. You're supposed to let me ask you first." He picked up the paperweight from the far edge of the desk and flipped it over to read the manufacturer's name. "Marry me and have my babies."

She smirked, but said nothing, and he returned the small glass dome to its spot.

"Okay, *now* you say no."

Gracie laughed outright. "I've heard you were easy, Wyatt, but I didn't realize how easy." She snorted. "That's quite an approach, doing the asking *and* the rejecting yourself."

He smiled and shrugged. "She turns me down every time, anyway, and now I know why."

"I turn you down because I'm too old for you, and I have an aversion to being just another concubine in a man's harem."

"You tell him, girl," Gracie cheered from the couch.

He ignored her. Leaning forward, he propped a muscled forearm on his thick thigh. His gray-green eyes glittered with mischief. "You're ageless, sweetheart, and with that face, you make me forget about every other woman."

V snorted a laugh. "You're so full of it."

His dimples made a reappearance, and he straightened. "So, you and the new offensive coordinator, huh? I guess it's just as well you were able to resist me this past year. With Fitzpatrick calling the plays, I'd be in traction from being sacked on every down because I'd had my hands on his girl."

"Please. Sam's a professional. He wouldn't do any such thing. Besides, you asking and me turning you down is all about your winning streak. You wouldn't have known what to do if I'd ever said yes."

He lowered his lashes and curled his lips into a leer. "For you, Miss Price, I would have taken the chance."

"And you'd have found yourself sacked on every down because you'd had your hands on my girl."

Every eye swung to the open doorway as Sam stepped into the office.

"Geez, it's like Grand Central in here," Gracie purred from the couch.

V stared at Sam as he approached her desk. He looked at Wyatt, but didn't appear angry.

"Heard that, did ya?" Wyatt slipped from her desk to face him.

Sam jerked his head toward the door. "Scram."

Wyatt grinned, winked at V, and walked toward the door, calling over his shoulder. "Same time next week, sweetheart."

"He *is* an ass," Gracie grumbled and stood. She swept up her purse. "And I think I'll head up to the sky box so you can wish Sam good luck in the proper manner." She grinned at V and blew Sam a kiss as she breezed from the room.

V turned to him the moment they were alone. "Sam, Wyatt was only—"

"Making sure he wins tonight's game?" He stepped around her desk. "I know all about his superstitious rituals."

She blinked. "You do?"

He slid his arms around her waist and tucked her close. "A very smart lady once told me the most important relationship I'll have in this job is with my quarterback, and she was right. Hunter and I had lunch after the press conference on Monday. He said he hoped I wasn't a jealous bastard, because until the streak was broken, he'd be asking you out every game day."

She smiled and slipped her arms up his chest to link her hands at the back of his neck. "But you're not a jealous bastard."

"When it comes to you, yes, I am." He nuzzled her neck with nibbling kisses.

"Hmm. Sounds like a problem." She arched her head to the side to give him better access. He licked his favorite spot and she shivered.

"It might have been, but we worked it out."

"You did, did you?"

"He can continue to ask, as long as he does it in front of me. Which is why we stopped by before we headed downstairs." He nibbled his way over her cheek and spoke against her lips. "And when you tell him no, I get to kiss *my* girl."

Chapter 25

With his first professional win under his belt, Sam had been flying high all week. So had V, but for reasons in addition to football. She'd never dreamed she could be so happy. Of course, not everything had been sunshine and roses. At the private post-game party in the complex's visitors' lounge, V had gotten the stink eye from Sam's mother. Unlike his father, who hugged V and said it was about time the two of them found each other again, his mom hadn't taken the news of their reconciliation well. In a surprising show of kindness, TJ had dragged her away to go meet Tuck before she could make a fuss.

Sam shrugged off his mother's disapproval, saying she'd come around in time. V hoped he was right. Their foundation was already complicated enough without her being a source of friction between mother and son.

Lucy, on the other hand, couldn't have been happier. V hadn't technically moved in with them, but some of her things hung in Sam's closet and she'd stayed over five out of the last seven nights. That wasn't good enough for Sam's daughter, however. Apparently, she wanted the matter settled.

Throughout the week, she continued her convince-V-to-move-in campaign. The girl was as bad as Gracie. It also appeared Lucy was getting advice as well as props from her mentor. V recognized Gracie's hand in the candlelit dinner for two waiting in the kitchen when she and Sam arrived at the house last night. The incongruous mix of Gracie's borrowed Wedgewood place settings and the large bucket of Sam's favorite delivery chicken, mashed potatoes, and cole-slaw, made V laugh, but the sweet sentiment also melted her heart.

She smiled at the memory as she stepped off the elevator several hours before kick-off for tonight's game. Everyone on the Marauders payroll, from the players and staff to the stadium personnel, were working long hours. Including V. As soon as the season was over, hopefully with a Super Bowl victory, V would give Sam's daughter her wish.

She breezed into her office, surprised to find Sam and Wyatt waiting. She stumbled to a stop. Her gaze flicked between Sam in the chair behind her desk and Wyatt, sprawled on the couch. Her mouth dropped open and she shook her head. "Oh, for heaven's sake. You were serious?"

Sam rolled the chair back and stood. "A smart man doesn't screw with a winning streak, Red. Especially when he's about to step on the field in a championship game." He shot Wyatt a leer. "Do your thing, Hunter. They're waiting for us downstairs."

Wyatt unfolded his six-foot-three frame from the couch and walked toward her. "He's right. So, what do you say you dump this stiff and run off with me to the Bahamas?"

"No, thanks," she answered in a sugary sweet tone.

Sam chuckled, and she grinned as Wyatt flipped him the bird over his shoulder and continued past her and out the door.

Rounding the desk, Sam crossed the space and folded her in his arms. His kiss was fast and hard, and over way too soon. "Sorry, they really are waiting for us."

"I know." She stepped clear of his arms. "Go help Wyatt win his game."

He squinted and swatted her gently on the ass before he headed for the door. She laughed and walked around her desk.

"Red."

She glanced up to find Sam paused in the doorway. "I left a little something for you in the bottom drawer." With a wink, he was gone.

Surprise and pleasure tickled through her as she dropped into her chair and slid open the bottom drawer on the left. Nothing there but her binders. She checked the one on the right and froze. A small square box sat on top of a folded sheet of paper. Her heart began race and she couldn't catch her breath.

Oh, God.

Her hand shook as she picked them up. Setting the box on her desk, she unfolded the paper and read the simple lines written in Sam's bold script.

This time, we'll do it right.

Starting with a ring.

Please, be my wife.

The breath shuddered in her chest, and she set aside the note to flip open the top of the box. A diamond solitaire sat in a bed of blue satin, winking in the morning sunlight splashing through the windows.

Shivers raced over her skin as she stared at his ring. "Oh, Sam." She eased back in her chair. The silver band and cut stone taunted her, tempting her with all that could be and reminding her of the price to be paid in accepting it. Living with him, loving him, those decisions were easily made, but marriage? Marriage was a promise. A vow to love and honor.

She loved him. Always had. Always would. But any promise spoken by her without giving him the truth wouldn't honor him. Instead, her vow would be a mockery of *his* love.

It has to be all or nothing.

That's what he'd said. What he needed and wanted from her. His ring represented all, yet she'd given nothing. He'd apologized when she'd been the one to blame. He'd compromised his principles, giving her his trust while she'd distrusted him. He offered her everything, and she continued to cower in fear.

Anger and self-incrimination clawed at her heart as the echo of her father's voice whispered in her mind. She clenched her teeth against a whimper.

My pretty little kitten. So soft.

Revulsion shuddered through her. Her skin crawled at the memory of rough fingers slipping beneath the hem of her favorite Barbie nightgown and brushing her inner thigh. She squeezed her legs together in futile denial as the nightmare memory replayed in her mind.

Nausea boiling in her belly, rising up her throat in a burning trail.

I don't like that, Daddy.

Cringing fear gripping her as his fingers rise higher, peeling down her panties to touch her private place.

A sob of terror.

Shh, you'll wake Mama. This is our special secret, remember? She can never know.

Lips clamped together so tightly, her teeth draw blood.

Help me, God. Please. Send your angels to help me.

The crushing weight of his body covering hers. The stench of whiskey scalding her nostrils.

You love your daddy, don't you?

Sweaty, hot naked skin pressing against hers and the foreign stab of something hard between her legs, pushing against her private place.

Daddy loves you so much.

The putrid taste of vomit in her mouth. Gagging. Coughing. Spewing.

Sticky wetness dotting Daddy's face and tangling with the tears in her hair.

Her darkest wish escaping to whisper through the shadows of her bedroom. *I want you to die.*

Horror and fear, mirrored in her father's eyes as he rears back.

A painful hammering in her chest as one heartbeat passes, then another, and one more.

Tears in Daddy's eyes. His fingers ripping at his hair and clutching his head. *Jesus. Jesus, what am I doing?*

Desperate hope as his weight shifts away. The door closing behind him. Freedom. Blessed freedom.

Chest heaving with her stilted breaths, V palmed away the tears streaking her cheeks. The freedom she'd thought she'd found had been a mirage. Freedom had never come. Not after her father had left and never returned. Nor after the countless hours of counseling she'd forced herself to endure. Not even with her father's death. All these years later, his malevolence still haunted her. The shameful, evil memories remained alive, locked in her soul, and there would be no freedom, no love, no marriage unless she found the courage to purge them at last.

"V, I need the list for the owner's suite."

V jumped, her head swiveling toward the door.

Caroline took one look at her and turned to someone in the hall. "Go downstairs and make sure they've started setting up in the visitors' lounge." She closed the door on her assistant's mumbled reply. "What's happened, V? You look like you've seen a ghost."

Embarrassed and horrified, she didn't know what to say. The fact was, she had seen a ghost. One who had been haunting her since she'd turned eleven. Her gaze caught on Sam's ring and note, and she grabbed at the excuse. She indicated the box.

"Sam wants to marry me."

Caroline slid into the guest chair at the edge of the desk, her eyes doubtful. "Don't give me that. I've seen the two of you together. You glow when he's around. There is no way in hell Sam proposing would put that haunted look in your eyes."

But it had. If they'd just gone on the way they were, she could have held it together. Loved him hard enough that the mystery of her past would have lost its importance. Loving him hard wasn't a problem. She did that with every breath.

She shook her head. "It's not Sam. It's some stuff from a long time ago. Complicated stuff."

"Life is complicated, V, but you're one of the strongest women I know. You kick ass and take names, and don't apologize for it. Yet, the man you love asks you to marry him and you fall apart?" Caroline crossed her legs and smoothed the crease in her red power-suit pants. "If you want that man, then fight for him. Can you fix this complicated stuff from your past?"

V's pulse kicked into overdrive. "It's not something that can be fixed, but yes, it can be addressed." *If I can find the courage to say the words out loud.*

"Then do it. Put whatever it is behind you and move on because, I have to tell you, you look like hammered shit and it's breaking my heart."

The comment was typical Caroline. V laughed. Still, her heart clanked against her ribs. Her friend was right. V was strong, refusing to let anything beat her when she wanted something. She wanted Sam. Needed him, and Lucy, and the life they could build together.

The repulsive memories of her father had stolen her dreams and the knowledge she'd continued to let it happen sickened her. Somehow, she had to find the strength to tell Sam the truth. First, however, she needed to speak to her mother, in person.

There was no way V could manage to speak the depth of her father's depravity, but then, she wouldn't have to. Even a watered down version of the truth would leave a hateful stain on Anita's heart and soul.

"I need to go to Barlow. If it's okay with you, I'll leave tomorrow."

Caroline grimaced. "For how long?"

"Twenty-four hours. Maybe less."

Caroline thumbed the screen of her phone then held it to her ear. A murmured voice answered. "Have my plane ready to leave in a half hour. Tell the pilot to set a course for Barlow, Texas. Returning tonight or tomorrow." She disconnected without waiting for a response and stood.

V blinked. "Caroline, I don't know what to say."

"Say goodbye and head to the airport. The Super Bowl is in fourteen days. After we win tonight, things are going to get crazy around here. I need my PR specialist here and happy, and I need my new offensive coordinator smiling. I expect to be fitted for a new ring in two weeks, and Sam and the boys don't need any distractions if they're going to make sure that happens."

Chapter 26

V hesitated on her mother's front stoop. Mother Nature was apparently in a playful mood, teasing the residents of East Texas with an early taste of spring. With the temperature at a comfortable seventy-two, Anita had opened the windows and front door to the fresh air. The murmur of a sports commentator floated to V's ears.

Like everyone else in Barlow, Anita would be watching the game. V's nerves briefly took a backseat to excitement for Sam. The last time she'd checked the team app on her phone, the second quarter had just ended with the Marauders up by thirteen.

She pictured Sam on the sideline, his big body pacing up and down the line as he called in plays. Clinging to the image, she knocked on the wooden frame of the screen door.

"Yes. Coming."

Anita's eyes widened in surprise as she spotted V through the mesh. "V, what on earth?" The hinges squeaked slightly as she pushed the door open, and her happy laugh scraped at V's heart like clawing fingers. "What are you doing here in Barlow? The game is on."

V stared at her mother's smiling face. *Fast and efficient. Like ripping a bandage from a festering wound. That's the only way I'll be able to say what needs to be said.*

"I need to talk to you, Mom."

"Come in, then." Her mother's eyes held simple curiosity as she held the door wider. The band of nerves circling V's chest tightened a notch. Curiosity would soon be replaced with hurt and revulsion.

She stepped past Anita into the comfortably decorated living room. V had only been inside her mother's home a few times, but everything was the same as the first time she'd seen it. Anita had always liked things simple and familiar.

V glanced at the TV. The fourth quarter had just begun.

"It's so exciting. The camera panned to Sam twice." Anita laughed. "You could hear the cheers and shouts from up and down the street."

V blinked at the screen. She'd shut off her phone before she'd come inside, needing to sever any possible source of connection with Sam—as if the evil of what she was about to say would somehow reach him across the miles. The compulsion was stupid and completely illogical. She'd be flying back this evening to face him with her past, but today, this afternoon, was important to him. She cringed at the thought of somehow sullying his pleasure at coaching his first championship game with the pros.

"Would you mind turning it off?"

The curiosity in her mother's eyes took on the sharp edge of concern. She picked up the remote from the coffee table and aimed it at the TV. The screen blinked off. "Can I get you anything? A cold drink?" She indicated the couch with a sweep of her hand.

"No, thank you." The way her stomach was churning, V didn't think she could keep anything down.

"You're starting to scare me. What's this about, V?" Anita sat on the edge of the couch.

Too wound up, V couldn't sit. She stood in the center of the room and dragged in a breath, then another, before she could force the words from her lips. "It's about Dad and what he did to me."

Surprise lit Anita's eyes before a crease wrinkled her brow. "I don't understand?"

"I know you don't." V swallowed. "He...." The word dragged out, blending with her shuddered exhalation. "He molested me, Mom."

All emotion washed from Anita's face, along with the color.

V forged ahead before she could turn and run for the door. "The first time happened a couple months before my eleventh birthday."

A soft cry escaped her mother's lips, and she clapped her hands over her mouth, speaking through her clenched fingers. "The first time?"

"We'd been at a cookout down the street at one of the neighbor's houses. I don't remember whose." V twisted the strap of her purse around her fingers. "You said you weren't feeling well and went to bed. He came into my room. I think he was drunk. His breath smelled like whiskey."

"Oh dear God." Her mother's face tightened and a sheen of tears flooded her eyes.

"He never raped me. I need you to know that, but he came close."

Anita covered her face with her hands, and her thin shoulders seemed to draw in on themselves.

Tears stung at the back of V's eyes and throat. "And I'm not going to share the details with you, because they're disgusting and shameful. I won't be responsible for planting hateful images in your head."

Anita's hands slid to her chest, her face a mask of horror. "They're already there. Oh my God, baby. I'm so sorry. So sorry I didn't see."

The hair on V's arms stood up. She hadn't heard the familiar endearment from her mother's lips in years, and that was V's fault. She'd erected a wall between them when her father left and refused each of her mother's attempts to scale it.

"He didn't want you to see." Her throat convulsed on a painful swallow. "Other than that first night, and the night before he left, he only came after me when you weren't home. I never remembered him drinking when I was little. He hadn't stunk of booze and sweat before, but he did then." She shuddered at the memory. "He was sick and evil, and he said if I told you, you'd blame me and then you'd leave."

Anita shook her head in adamant denial. "Never. I never would have blamed you, baby. I never would have left you behind."

V's breath trembled in her chest, and she squeezed her eyes shut against the tears spilling over her lower lashes. "I believed him. I was too scared not to."

V shivered as her mother's arms suddenly came around her. She tucked her face into Anita's neck and breathed the familiar clean scent of her perfume.

"The night Dad left, I prayed God would send his angels to save me, but they didn't come. He was drunk, so drunk he was slurring his words. I threw up all over him. I think it shocked him." She slid her hands around her mother's back and held on. "Then I told him I wanted him to die."

She didn't know how long they stood there, clinging to each other. Weeping. Eventually, Anita guided her to the couch.

V curled into a ball with her head on her mother's lap. "I'm sorry, Mom. I should have told you right away."

"Shh." Anita sifted her fingers through V's hair, the way she had when V was little. "You were a child, and your...." She hesitated and shook her head as if using the word "father" to describe Edward Price was an abomination. "Predators like him prey on the weak and the young. What he did to you was not your fault."

V knew that. She'd had it pounded into her head by the counselors she'd seen, but her heart had never managed to believe it. "Later, after he left, I couldn't tell you."

"I wish you had."

V burrowed closer. "I couldn't. You worked so hard to take care of us. I didn't want my dirty secret to touch you."

Anita crooned and tucked a curl behind V's ear. "His secret, baby. Not yours." She rubbed her hand over V's hair. "It's a heavy burden you've carried. I'm glad you've finally told me so I can bear some of the load with you, but why now?"

"Sam asked me to marry him."

"Oh, V." Her mother's sigh held a smile. "You said yes, of course."

"Not yet, but I will. I had to tell you first."

They spoke for hours, between tears and laughter, too. V shared her dreams of a future with Sam and Lucy, and the hope of more children. Anita spoke of her students and simple things like the garden she'd planned for when true spring arrived. Drained and exhausted from the emotional outpouring, V drifted off at some point during the evening, safe and warm in her mother's arms.

* * * *

Sam ran along the sideline, his arm pinwheeling in time with Tuck's long strides. The roar of the crowd pulsed in his ears as Tuck crossed the thirty, the twenty, the ten. With eighteen seconds left on the clock, the Marauders' all-pro wide receiver raced toward the goal line in a spectacular sixty-yard run that would, if successful, put the final nail in Arizona's coffin. Two red-shirted defenders barreled toward him in a pincher move that would have worked, but for Tuck's sudden leap into the air. Clipped on the thigh, he spun like a top, but momentum was with him. He came down hard several inches inside the goal line.

The noise was deafening, and Sam raised both fists to the sky in a victory pump. In the end zone, Tuck rolled to his feet to spike the ball and faced the crowd with an Atlas pose. Sam grinned and absorbed the small stab of envy as his entire offensive line piled onto Tuck in jubilant celebration. Amidst helmet slaps and chest bumps, pure elation lit sweat-streaked faces as the players exited the field and the kicking team replaced them.

In the middle of the chaos, Wyatt and Tuck loped toward Sam. Grinning from ear to ear, Wyatt extended his arm in a chopping point as they trotted the last couple of yards. "Fucking kick-ass call, Coach. We caught 'em flat-footed, just like you said."

Tuck extended the ball he carried to Sam. "This one belongs to you. Just don't expect it to become a habit."

Sam laughed and grunted his appreciation around the solid lump of emotion in his throat. The celebration continued on the sideline as the kicking team added another point to the tally.

After the clock had ticked off its final second, the field crowed with players, press, and fans. Sam accepted congratulations and shook hands, gave several interviews. All the while, he kept his eye out for the one face he wanted most to see. Throughout the presentation of the championship trophy, he searched the crowd but, though he found Lucy standing off to the side with Gracie and CC, V was nowhere to be found.

A nagging kernel of doubt grew in his gut until he could barely breathe. Had he fucked up, not getting down on his knee and popping the question in the traditional way? He'd considered it but, with V, the unexpected normally yielded the best results. He'd also wanted to give her plenty of time to process his proposal without the pressure of him standing in front of her with desperate hope in his eyes.

The moment he was able, he slipped through the milling crowd to where he'd last seen Lucy. She spotted him when he was several yards away and ran toward him to jump into his arms.

"Oh my God, that was incredible. Did you see the way Tuck leaped and spun? He should have been a dancer."

Gracie, grinning widely, arrived right behind her. "Be sure to tell him that next time you see him, sweetie. Congratulations, Sam. That was quite a game."

He tucked his game ball under one arm and Lucy under the other. "Thanks." He glanced around. "Have you seen V?"

Lucy shook her head.

So did Gracie. "She never showed up in the skybox. I assumed she was somewhere down here on the field."

Gracie whipped out her phone as a print reporter cornered Sam to ask him a few questions. When the reporter finished a few minutes later, and left to chase after Wyatt, Sam looked at Gracie.

She frowned and lowered the phone from her ear. "I don't know, Sam. She's not answering."

Shit. If V was still in the building, she'd be here on the field like everyone else. The bottom dropped out of his stomach as trepidation ratcheted up his spine.

Jesus. He'd asked her to marry him and she'd run. Again.

Chapter 27

Sam wandered into his kitchen just as the first fingers of the dawn sun streaked across the sky. Jake turned, a sleepy toddler on his hip. At the table, CC and Tuck sipped from mugs. Sam arched a questioning brow, and CC shook her head.

"I'm sorry, Sam. I tried to call her five minutes ago. She's still not answering."

Sam scrubbed a frustrated hand down his face. Morning bristle scraped at his palm. "You should all be at home in your beds. If she doesn't want to be found, she won't be. God knows, she's had plenty of practice at disappearing."

"She hasn't disappeared." Sam turned as Gracie spoke behind him. "There's a logical explanation for all of this. You just need to be patient until she shows up."

Patient? He'd been patient for fifteen years, and look where it had gotten him. "I appreciate the positive attitude, sweetheart, but this ain't my first rodeo with V's disappearing acts."

"She'll be back, Sam. If she didn't plan to return, she wouldn't have taken your ring with her."

There was that. He'd checked her office before he'd really started to panic. She hadn't been there, and neither had his ring. She'd left his note on her desk.

Hurt, confused, and pissed as hell, last night's post-game celebration held no appeal. He and Lucy had left the complex shortly after the official presentations had ended. Much to his surprise and embarrassment, his new friends had shown up at the house in staggered intervals throughout the evening. Max had left sometime after midnight to deliver his pregnant and drooping wife home to her bed, but everyone else had insisted on staying until V was found.

At some point during the long hours of the unexpected mass vigil, Sam had spilled his guts. The Triple Gs had claimed the tactic was romantic when he admitted he'd fucked up with his note and ring instead of waiting until he could ask V to marry him in person. From the smirks and grins of the guys, they knew the truth. He was a sap.

"Coffee?" Jake held up the pot.

"If it's laced with whiskey."

Sam crossed the room and pulled a mug from the shelf. Jake's eyes gleamed with humor and Sam shook his head.

"Just give it to me straight." He held out the mug as Jake poured. "Where's Lucy?"

"She's asleep on the couch with the rest of the kids." Gracie eased into one of the kitchen chairs.

Sam leaned against the counter and sipped at the scalding brew. "Seriously. You guys should head out. I appreciate the show of support, but…." The gong of the doorbell strangled the words in his throat.

Daisy began to bark. Every eye in the room swung Sam's way, and he swallowed. Down the hallway, several thumps were followed by the sound of the door opening.

"Where have you been? Dad's a wreck!" Lucy's voice held more relief than accusation.

Suddenly, chairs scraped and feet slapped the tiles as Gracie and CC abandoned their seats to rush from the kitchen. Tuck was slower to rise. He passed by Sam with a scowl.

"I hate when they're right. There'll be no living with them for days."

Sam's lungs didn't seem to want to cooperate. Jake helped him along by slapping him on the back. "She's back, buddy. Take my advice. Let her talk before you blow your top." He wandered from the room leaving Sam to follow.

He had to force his feet to move, then paused beneath the hall archway. V, looking as tired as he felt, attempted to field the questions flying at her from the women and Lucy. Anita stood behind her. *Her mother? What the hell was going on?*

"I fell asleep. My phone was turned…off." V's voice drifted off as her gaze locked onto him.

Silence fell as, one by one, his unlikely support group turned and looked his way.

"Yes." V held his gaze. "My answer is yes." Her eyes flooded with tears. "If your offer is still on the table after I tell you what happened."

His heart thumped erratically in his chest.

"Come on, everyone." Gracie snapped into motion. Snatching coats from the hall tree, she randomly shoved them into reaching hands. "Breakfast at the farmhouse in ten."

V didn't say a word, just stared at him as sleepy kids were gathered and wrapped haphazardly in whatever covering was handy. Lucy tugged Daisy and Anita outside behind everyone else, and silence returned.

The moment the door shut, V took a step toward him, then stopped. "You said you'd wait. That you'd earn my trust. I need to earn yours."

He tensed as the echo of his words rang in his ears. "You already have it."

"No, I don't. Not yet." She moved closer. One step. "I'm sorry. I should have left you a message, but I expected to be back shortly after the game ended, and...." Uncertainty clouded her eyes. "I spent the night with Mom in Barlow. She deserved to hear the truth just as you do."

His pulse began to race. He'd wanted the answer to why she'd fled from him. Needed to know. But the hell in her eyes gutted him. "Don't, Red. It no longer matters." He started forward, but she stopped him with a raised hand.

"Yes, it does." Another step. "Do you remember the day I left?" Her eyes briefly slid shut and she shook her head. "Of course you remember." Her throat convulsed on a swallow. "Your parents and aunt were there. TJ, too. None of them knew what to say to you, and you told them everything would be okay."

The hair on the back of his neck stood on end as he recalled that afternoon, and he nodded.

"You said you had a job awaiting you at ETU. That we would be returning to Barlow once you'd gotten your degree. I panicked, Sam, but not because your pro career hopes were done." Her chest expanded on a bracing breath. "I didn't run from you. I ran from the thought of returning to Barlow."

One step closer. "It was illogical and stupid, and within a few days, I knew I'd made a mistake. Knew I should have stayed and talked to you. Somehow made you understand. I should have convinced you there were other jobs, other towns or cities, places we could go where we could both be happy, because I couldn't go back to Barlow. Not when I'd lived every moment from the time I was eleven, yearning for the day I could escape to somewhere my father wouldn't know to find me."

Another step and she stopped a foot away. "A place that held no memories of his sick and twisted love."

Chills raced down Sam's spine as he stared into her eyes. It was all there in the teary blue depths. The hell. The fear. Utter loathing for the man she'd adored and followed everywhere, according to Anita. Bubbling acid seared the lining of Sam's stomach. "He molested you?"

A lone tear slipped onto V's cheek. "Yes, and the memories are mine alone to bear. Don't ask me to speak them aloud, because I won't. He's dead, and I refuse to give him the power to hurt anyone else. I've given him enough already by letting him turn me into a coward."

She shook her head vehemently, as if to deny what had happened. "I let him steal my dreams. Let him destroy the pure and honest love I'd found with you." She lifted her chin and her eyes shimmered with pain. "He broke something in me, Sam. Something I've never been able to repair. With you, I come close, but the damage is always there."

Fury curled his hands into fists, and he battled the urge to kill a man who was already dead.

She closed the remaining distance and placed her hand over his hammering heart. The mix of resolve and acceptance in her eyes unmanned him, and his nose and eyes stung.

"Knowing that, if you still want me, I'm yours."

Jesus. He dipped his head to brush a gentle kiss across her lips. Pressing his forehead to hers, he slipped his arms around her waist. He closed his eyes in relief when her body softened against his.

He swallowed past the emotion blocking his throat before he could speak. "Fifteen years ago, on a warm spring day, a redheaded girl with a sultry smile climbed into my truck and stole my heart. I've wanted her ever since. The depravities of a sick fucker can't change that."

He straightened to meet her gaze, and his heart constricted at the tears streaming over her cheeks. "You're my life, Red. My woman. The heart that beats in my chest."

Capturing her mouth once more, he poured all the love he had for her into his kiss. He spoke without words, telling her what she meant to him, and she responded in kind. She slid her arms up his chest and around his neck, and she squirmed closer.

The fire that always flared between them burned the chill from his bones, and he spoke against her lips. "Where's the ring?"

Laughing through her tears, she dropped one arm to slip her hand into the purse hanging from her shoulder. She lifted her mouth to his once more while digging blindly. A moment later, her irritated hum vibrated through her chest to his. She broke away and stepped back.

"Damn it. It's in here somewhere."

He chuckled at her grumbling tone, and stared at the top of her head as she continued her search. Finally, with a frustrated growl, she upended the bag. The contents spilled to the floor and she bent to scoop up the jeweler's box. She held it up, heart in her eyes.

He grinned, took the box, and lowered to one knee. Her tear-filled eyes sparkled like blue gems, and a beaming smile tugged her lips wide as he flipped the top open with his thumb.

"I love you, Victoria Price. Marry me, and put me out of my misery."

"I love you, too, Samuel Fitzpatrick, *and* Lucy."

She held out her shaking hand, and he fumbled to slip the diamond on her finger. Once he had, she pressed her hands to his shoulders and shoved. He landed on his ass and she hiccupped a tearful laugh. Hiking her skirt to her upper thighs, she lowered to straddle his lap and wrapped her arms around his shoulders.

"I'll put you out of your misery and more." She tightened her hold on him and her smile held a teasing twist. "Trust me."

"Oh, I do, Red. I do.

She shrieked with laughter as he spun them around and pinned her to the floor.

Epilogue

"I now pronounce you husband and wife."

V stared at Sam's smiling face and couldn't contain the joy in her heart. She grinned and his smile broadened.

"Kiss the girl already," Tuck grumbled. "We've got a Super Bowl to win."

V blinked and turned her head. The skybox was stuffed to capacity with friends, new and old. Lucy was there, looking pretty as a picture in her salmon-pink bridesmaid's dress. Her dark hair, minus the streak of purple, was swept up in a sophisticated twist that Sam had complained made her look too grown up for his liking.

The Malones and Tuckers, Graysons and Fitzpatricks were all represented along with several others. There wasn't an inch of space left in the glass-fronted suite. Two stories below, Everbank Field in Jacksonville was beginning to fill with fans finding their seats for the season's biggest game.

TJ winced and nodded. "Tuck's right. Kiss the girl. You're holding up the game."

Caroline snorted at the back of the room. "The Marauders don't take the field until I say so."

Wyatt grinned and dropped his arm around TJ's shoulders, making her blush. He sent Sam a leer. "Coach can't kiss the girl until I ask her a question."

V started to laugh and Sam groaned. Gracie snickered and CC, Tuck, and Jake grinned.

V lifted her lips to within a breath of Sam's and sliced her gaze to Wyatt. "Well?"

He opened his mouth, but whatever he said was drowned out by a chorus of "No's!"

Laughter rang in V's ears as Sam captured her lips. He dipped her back in a hungry kiss to the catcalls and whistles of those gathered. As he brought her upright, the love in his eyes brought tears to hers.

Pressing his cheek to hers, he whispered in her ear. "I love you, Mrs. Fitzpatrick."

She smiled against his cheek. "I love you, too, Mr. Fitzpatrick, and I've got my ring. Now, go get yours."

THE END

Keep reading for another great Lyrical Press release!

Fourth Down

Go Big or Go Home.

When her relationship goes up in flames, Holly Funchess jumps straight back into the heat—by becoming a firefighter. Running as far away from her past as she can, Holly trains hard and lands a job with a small San Diego firehouse. With everything to prove, she has no problem putting her love life on the back burner. But where there's smoke…

A former football player with a string of failed relationships behind him, Chase DeMarco has put his all into his Coast Guard career and the youth football team he coaches. He's not about to let anyone distract him—especially Holly, the woman at his gym who seems to relish getting under his skin. But when their skirmishes turn into full-contact workouts—and they face off against the dangers of their jobs—Chase and Holly must choose between letting the clock run down or playing to win…

Chapter 1

Chase DeMarco parked his SUV in front of Pump It Up and grabbed his gym bag from the backseat. Resigned, he climbed out and pressed his key fob to lock the doors, taking in the large two-story building in front of him. It was crazy to come to this gym—a study in concrete, steel, and glass, definitely not his kind of place—instead of his regular gym. But avoiding his friends tonight was more important than his comfort level, and he desperately wanted a workout after a long day at sea. Swallowing a sigh, he jogged up the sidewalk to the entrance.

Just as he reached the doors, his cell phone rang. For a long moment, he hesitated, not sure if he wanted to answer. He had a feeling he knew who it was, and he wasn't in the mood for the conversation. As the ringtone stopped, he pulled his phone from his pocket and looked at the readout. Yup. Right on the money.

As usual, John "Johnny-On-The-Spot" McFarland had lousy timing, always in Chase's face when Chase least wanted him around. He and John had been solid friends for sixteen years—four at the Academy and twelve in the Coast Guard. They had come up through the ranks together, and now John served on the patrol boat that Chase commanded. The phone rang for a second time. *Persistent ass.* Would John not leave him alone? When the phone rang yet a third time, Chase gave a sigh and tapped the screen to accept the call.

"Hey, bud." John's voice rumbled through the connection. "Where are you? Don't tell me you're standing us up tonight. After we sweat for an hour, we're all taking Mancini out to get him drunk and celebrate his engagement. We're waiting for you."

Waiting for him. Great. Unless someone's schedule made it impossible, Chase and three of his friends met at the Coast Guard's fitness center every night to work out. They'd been doing it since they'd all arrived at the San Diego facility. Sometimes they went out afterward, sometimes not. But it was a comfortable habit and he enjoyed it. Except for tonight. He'd told John he wouldn't be there, given him a lame excuse. He should have known his friend wouldn't let him off the hook that easily.

He just hated shit like this. It wasn't just celebrating his friend's engagement that left a sour taste in his mouth. It was the fact that every time one of his friends got hooked up, they wanted to find someone for him. Why was it when two people coupled up they wanted the same thing for everyone else? Couldn't they see he was happy just the way he was? That he did just fine flying solo? He told them often enough. Damn John—and everyone else—for refusing to believe it.

He swam on the surface of the dating pool, never sticking with any one female too long. He always broke it off before there was a chance for someone to get hurt.

He sighed again. "Sorry, buddy. Remember I told you I had a conflict? Text me where you guys end up. If I can do it, I'll catch up with you later."

Not.

There was a long silence.

"Jesus, Chase. Enough already. Get your ass in gear for later. I'll text you where to meet." John paused. "Don't let us down," he warned.

Chase would have answered him, but he was listening to dead air.

His life in the Guard was who and what he was, a man to be respected and admired. It was his anchor in life. Women came and went, but the Guard was always there, steadfast and loyal.

The days at sea were exhilarating, the work he did soul satisfying. Validating.

Validation, the thing he craved the most. It was a counterbalance to the words that never left his head.

"It isn't you, Chase. I just can't stay in this house any more, not even for you. Be good for your dad." His mother's voice seemed permanently lodged in his brain.

Along with that of his high school sweetheart. *"Come on. Unbend a little. We're celebrating graduation, right?"*

And Cheryl, the last straw for him. *"We were just having a little fun. Why are you such a stick in the mud?"*

He'd wanted to ask her if she'd ever heard of a thing called fidelity, but it seemed the women he chose in his life either hadn't heard of the word or didn't pay much attention to it.

The voices played in his head, echoing down through the years. Only his achievements in the Guard kept them locked away.

John wasn't right in his assessment, though. Chase was a commander in the United States Coast Guard. He wore his uniforms and his designation proudly. It defined him. No woman would ever be able to compete with that or shake his confidence again.

No relationships. Ever. And he was fine with it, at last.

But damn. Now he felt guilty for avoiding his friends tonight. Why couldn't this be a practice night for the youth-league football team he coached? It would have given him the best excuse in the world.

Chase, you're an asshole.

Yeah, he probably was.

"Are you planning to stand there blocking the door all day?"

The words were hostile but the voice had a low, musical quality to it that for some reason teased at his nerve endings. He turned around and nearly smacked into the woman behind him. She took a step back and glared at him.

"Did you hear me?" she demanded.

A more fanciful man might call her an earth goddess. She was tall, the top of.her head coming just past his shoulder. Her long legs were emphasized by the short shorts she wore. Brown hair with streaks of light scattered through it was scraped back in a tight ponytail, the style accenting the hazel of her eyes, her high cheekbones, and her almost translucent skin.

Translucent skin?

What the fuck? Who was that stranger talking in his head? He'd been listening to his friends' wives and girlfriends too much.

"Well?" Her voice was impatient now. "You know standing where you are you're blocking the door, right? Some of us actually want to go inside and work out."

Chase shook himself.

"Sorry." He opened the door and stepped aside to let her enter, trying not to notice that she had a most excellent ass.

"Geez," she huffed. "Some people."

She flicked a glance at him over her shoulder as she moved into the building carrying her workout bag. Chase had to drag his eyes away from her. Tonight he was all about working out, not hooking up, not when his friend's engagement had dredged up yet again all the reasons why happy ever after wasn't for him.

Still, as though some evil elf were sitting on his shoulder, he tracked the woman's movements as she checked in at the reception desk and headed toward what he assumed were the locker rooms. The traces of whatever fragrance she wore still lingered, driving him crazy. As she walked, her ponytail bounced with the sway of her ass. He—

"May I help you?"

Chase rolled up his tongue and turned toward the front desk. Enough already.

"Uh, yeah, hi. I'd like to work out tonight. It's my first time here, so what kind of arrangements do I need to make?"

He tried to concentrate as the nice young lady behind the counter explained membership fees, guest passes, trial packages, and whatever else Pump It Up offered. But it was hard to concentrate when his brain seemed to have self-destructed. What the fuck?

"Yeah, I'll take that," he said, wondering exactly what he'd opted for.

"The thirty-day trial package?" The girl beamed at him. "That's a great way to start. Almost everyone who buys it ends up going for the full ride."

Thirty-day trial package? Had the snippy female mesmerized him so much he'd forgotten where he was? He'd only come here for one night. Oh, well, it would do him some good to take a step back from the group until they got over all the happy celebrating. He took the papers the girl pushed at him, filled them out, and handed her his credit card. Along with his receipt, she handed him a two-page brochure on the facility itself and a diagram showing where all the different machines and equipment were located.

He changed in the locker room, stowed his things in a locker, and hung the key bracelet on his wrist. His normal pattern was to start with either a treadmill or an elliptical, so he headed for the long double row of them facing the front wall of glass. The treadmills were first, but then he spotted Miss Ponytail at an elliptical so, perverse idiot that he was, he marched over and took the one beside her. After placing his water bottle in the tray and hanging his towel over the bar, he climbed aboard and set his program.

Why on earth was he doing this? He made it a firm habit to stay away from women with attitude like she'd displayed at the door. Women were problem enough without bothering with the hostile ones. Yet here he was, right in her space.

She glanced at him briefly, frowned, and went back to focusing on her routine and whatever she was listening to with her ear buds.

Chase did his one-minute warmup and then hit his stride. Occasionally he slid a glance at Miss Ponytail, working that elliptical like she had a grudge against it. He wasn't sure he'd ever seen a woman work it that hard. He didn't know if that was her usual pattern or if she was trying to prove something to him. As if he'd even care. She obviously had a chip on her shoulder bigger than his truck.

They finished at nearly the same time. Chase stepped away, doing his best to ignore her, and went to throw away his empty water bottle. Free weights were next, but when he went to that area, she was already there, adjusting her wristbands and checking the weights. Damn! Okay, he could ignore her and go ahead with his planned routine or he could walk to another area and work out on something else.

As he stood there, indecisive, she looked up at him, irritation stamped on her features.

"Are you following me?"

Chase was so stunned for a moment he couldn't answer her.

"Because if you are," she went on, "I'll have to report you to management. They'll revoke your membership."

He was dumbfounded. Who the hell was this person, and who did she think she was? "Excuse me?"

"They don't tolerate stalkers in here." She planted her hands on her hips. "And I've had enough shit from men to last me two lifetimes. Go find some other corner to play in."

Stalkers? For fuck's sake! He was irritated enough to force the issue, but it was his first night here, he'd signed up for the thirty-day trial (*Dumbass!*), and he didn't want to get kicked out because some snippy female thought he was following her. What was her problem, anyway?

He turned on his heel and walked to the farthest corner of the floor, not looking back. He located the strength and weight training machines he liked, found one he wanted to use, and set the program. Doing his best to clear his mind, he went into his routine. But a brunette with a bouncy ponytail, a sexy ass, and a well-toned body had lodged herself in his mind. The entire time he worked out, he couldn't get her out of there no matter what he did.

Fuck!

* * * *

Holly Funchess wanted to spit nickels. She was mad enough to spit quarters, but she wouldn't waste that much money on that asshole. She hadn't gotten much sleep the night before, thanks to a crappy date she never should have gone on. That had made her off her game today, putting her on the wrong side of her lieutenant at the firehouse. And somewhere along the way, she'd lost her lucky bracelet. Now this idiot jerk had to piss her off and make her already bad mood even worse. It was as if Life with a Capital L was giving her a big Fuck You finger.

Nice attitude, Holly.

Why had she been so bitchy to him, anyway? If she was truthful, he hadn't really done anything except stand in the entrance a few seconds too long. But by the time she'd finished what turned out to be an exhausting shift and gotten here tonight, almost any little thing would have set her off. Of course her ex, Brad, dipshit that he was, would say the shift had nothing to do with it. That she was just naturally a bitch.

She hadn't been able to help overhearing the guy sign up for the thirty-day trial membership. Overhearing was easy when you craned your head while trying to pretend you weren't paying attention. Was he even single? Damn it! She shouldn't care one way or the other. What was the matter with her? Hadn't she already learned her lesson about men like him? So he was hot and sexy. So what? He probably had an ego bigger than this building and an attitude to go with it.

She finished her reps on the machine she was using and reset the weights on it, deliberately ignoring the hot guy. Someone tapped her on the shoulder, and she nearly jumped a foot.

"Wow! I didn't mean to frighten you to death."

She looked up to see Adara Mann standing not six inches from her. Her college roommate had been a blessing when she moved to San Diego, even giving her a place to stay until she'd finished her fire science studies and been hired on. She'd been glad, however, to move into her own place, where she didn't have to listen to Adara lecture her all the time about her spotty social life. She was good with things the way they were. Fine. Excellent, even.

"I could have brained myself on this thing," Holly complained to the other woman. "What's up?"

Adara took a step closer. "Did you see the hot, hot guy who came in tonight? I mean, the really sexy one?"

Holly almost snorted. "Adara, you think every guy who walks in here is sexy."

"And you think every guy who walks in here or anywhere is an asshole," Adara shot back.

Holly shrugged. "He's just another run-of-the-mill jackass, as far as I'm concerned."

"No, no, no." Adara shook her head. "He's *really* sexy. Like sex on a stick. Poster boy sexy. Look. There he is working on the lat pulldown machine. No wonder he looks so fit. This must be his first time here, or I would have spotted him before."

Holly shook her head at her friend's instant focus on a guy. "That's the truth."

Adara seemed to look at every new male as a target in her hunt for the ideal hookup. Despite her determination to ignore the subject, she glanced over to where Adara was pointing.

She blinked. Of course. She should have known. The man she'd spouted off to on the way in.

Asshole.

Regardless, she found herself taking a closer look at him. *For Adara,* she told herself. *That's all.* She figured his height at just over six feet, and couldn't help but notice his well-toned body with its defined muscles and wide shoulders. His blond hair was cut military short, making her wonder if he was in the service.

Not that she cared, right? Of course not. She was checking him out for Adara. So what was with the unexpected, funny little feeling that zinged through her system when she looked at him? She didn't get zings these days. Not from him or anyone else. She'd promised herself she'd never get those zings again. Been there, done that. She'd declared a moratorium on zings. It had taken her too long to get past the pain of what had happened with Brad. She didn't need to deal with that kind of vulnerability again. She had a new life, a new career, and no time for some asshole to screw it up again.

"Well?" Adara nudged her. "What do you think?"

"Like I said, I think he's probably as much of an ass as every other man in here," Holly snapped, jerking back to reality. Alpha males made all her defenses pop up and lock in place.

"Well, geez, Holly." Adara blotted the perspiration on her forehead with the towel around her neck. "Are you ever gonna take that bug out of your ass? The longer you hold on to what happened, the harder it will be to let go. Stop giving that jerk so much power."

Holly shrugged, doing her best to wipe unpleasant memories from her mind. Adara was the only person outside her family who knew what had sent her hightailing it from North Carolina. She had arrived in San Diego a big hot mess, an emotional wreck, but determined to build a new life. The best thing to come out of it was her chance to pursue her dream of becoming a firefighter. A dream put on hold for so long, because…

Stop! Just stop!

"I hear you. But you know, they don't exactly wear signs that say Not a Jerk."

She was very comfortable behind her high wall of defense. She was finished being the one in a relationship who did all the giving and then got virtually smacked in return. She had control of her life now, and that's the way things were going to stay.

Out of nowhere Brad's words leaped to life in her brain.

"A firefighter? Come on, Holly. That's not a job for a woman. People will think I'm marrying a guy."

Even now the words still had the power to hurt. With ruthless determination, she shoved them away.

Adara squeezed her arm. "You know I'm here for you. Just don't smack me when I tell you you're wasting your life because of some shithead. You're more than that, Holly."

She was, and she knew it. She wasn't one to wallow in misery, either. But Brad's words had cut deeply, and she couldn't seem to wipe them out of her brain. She was too smart to give someone that kind of power over her, yet she couldn't seem to break the hold.

Get over it, Holly. And be nicer to guys. They aren't all assholes.

Maybe.

"I'm good." Holly's words were clipped, and she spit them out like bullets. "I'm doing just fine. In fact, I'm so fine I think I'll do some more core exercises before I finish for the night."

Adara threw up her hands. "Whatever. Maybe I'll make a move on Mr. Hot Guy myself."

Holly shrugged. "You do whatever you want. I've got other things to do."

"Hey! It's not as if I get to hang with gorgeous firefighters every day."

Holy tamped down her irritation. "First of all, I don't hang with them, I *work* with them. And second, to them I'm just one of the guys, and that's the way I want it. I keep telling you I'm not interested. Not in them or anyone else. Can we finally be done with this conversation?"

Adara cocked her head. "You need to stop being so snotty about it. The old Holly was a really nice person."

"Are you implying I'm not nice anymore?"

"No, just…" She flapped her hand. "Never mind.

But Holly knew the truth of that. Sometimes she missed the old Holly, the one who'd laughed spontaneously and thought life was an adventure. Then she'd discovered sometimes the adventure wasn't what you thought it would be. Sometimes it turned into a battle for control. Now she had all the control she wanted or needed, because she didn't let anyone in close enough to challenge her.

"Holly? Are you here with me?"

Adara was staring at her.

"Yeah. What did you say?"

"I think I'll go see for myself what's what with Mr. Hot Guy. If you don't want him, I'm going to check him out."

"You go ahead and do your usual thing." Holly grinned. "I'll watch the show from here."

She'd discovered her former roommate loved to explore uncharted waters. Not that she went swimming in all of them. Far from it. She was very selective. But she did love a challenge. She watched as Adara moved across the room to the machine next to the one "Mr. Hot Guy" was using. Well, okay, he *was* sexy. She couldn't lie about that. But sexy men, in her history, were untrustworthy, domineering, and a total pain in the ass. Brad McKeller had taught her that. He was—

Nope. She shut down that line of thinking. Not going there, not now, not ever again. She'd left him and all the bad memories that went with him back home in North Carolina.

"You think I want to come home and fuck someone dressed in turnout gear? Me or your butch job fetish, Holly. Make the wrong choice and we're done."

Yeah, they'd definitely been done. When she'd moved out of his place, she'd cried enough for the rest of her life. Then she'd packed up her things and left for the future she'd always dreamed of. Far away from her parents who thought she was crazy and Brad who thought she was... less than feminine.

Only her brother, Will, had supported her, even though he'd had reservations.

"Be sure you know what you want, kiddo," he'd urged her.

"I do," she'd insisted. "This is my dream, and I'm not letting anyone talk me out of it any longer."

"I just worry about you being out there away from everyone, starting all over. No support system."

"I have Adara," she'd pointed out. "I'll be fine." She'd squeezed his hands. "Just be there for me if I need you."

"Always," he'd promised, and kissed her forehead. "Just...be careful with yourself. Next time choose wisely."

She wanted to tell him there would never be a next time. She was done. Finished.

San Diego was a fresh new start for her, and she had no intention of letting some jerkoff ruin it. Someday, maybe, she'd find a man who wasn't threatened by her choice of careers. But not now. Not for a long time. It certainly wouldn't be some macho idiot like this one, an idiot who, objectively speaking, was indeed as hot as Adara said. Who set her misbehaving hormones to do a jitterbug if she was honest. Not that she was interested. Not one single bit.

Liar!

Still, she watched as Adara made her approach, waiting for the guy to finish his reps before trying her perfected, smooth intro on him. She was sure he'd—

Wait! What? That didn't look like any friendly intro-to-hookup conversation going on over there. The smile on Hot Guy's face was little more than polite, and Adara's entire posture screamed frustration. This was a first. Holly had yet to see anyone turn down her friend. Tall and lithe, with a tumbled mass of dark hair and curves in all the right places, she was usually fighting them off. Hmm. Didn't this guy like women?

In less than two minutes, Adara was back, frowning.

"Don't tell me Mr. Hot Guy was immune to your charms?" Holly teased. "Maybe you should give him another chance."

"In his dreams," Adara snarked. "I don't know what his problem is, but he was damn near rude to me."

Holly shrugged. "Maybe he's just antisocial."

"Like someone else I know."

"Har, har, har. Anyway, he's something, that's for sure. Come on. Let's finish our routines and get a pizza. I think we've earned some fat calories tonight."

"Okay. I can go for that. Food is a lot less complicated than men."

And wasn't that just the truth. Too bad it irritated the crap out of her that all through the rest of her workout, and even while they scarfed down their pizza, she couldn't get the image of Mr. Hot Guy out of her brain.

Meet the Author

Wife, mother and really young grandmother, **Mackenzie Crowne** shares her home with her high school sweetheart husband, a rambunctious Lab pound-puppy, and a blind cat. She calls Arizona home because the southwest feeds her soul. Her love of the romance genre has been a lifelong affair, both as a reader and a writer. A bout with breast cancer sharpened her resolve to see her stories shared with others. Today, she's an eight-year survivor, living the dream. Her friends call her Mac. She hopes you will too. Visit her website at mackenziecrowne.com, find her on Facebook, or follow her on Twitter at twitter.com/MacCrowne.